A Reunion to Die For

A JOSHUA THORNTON MYSTERY

A REUNION TO DIE FOR

LAUREN CARR

FIVE STAR
An imprint of Thomson Gale, a part of The Thomson Corporation

THOMSON

GALE

Detroit • New York • San Francisco • New Haven, Conn. • Waterville, Maine • London

LIBRARY OF CONGRESS CATALOGING-IN-PUBLICATION DATA

Carr, Lauren.
    A reunion to die for : a Joshua Thornton mystery / Lauren Carr. — 1st ed.
        p. cm.
    ISBN-13: 978-1-59414-548-3 (hardcover : alk. paper)
    ISBN-10: 1-59414-548-2 (hardcover : alk. paper)
    1. Chester (W. Va.)—Fiction. I. Title.
PS3603.A774255R48 2007
813'.6—dc22   2007008157

First Edition. First Printing: June 2007.

Published in 2007 in conjunction with Tekno Books and Ed Gorman.

Printed in the United States of America on permanent paper
10 9 8 7 6 5 4 3 2 1

To Mom with love. You believed in my talent the most, even when I didn't.

ACKNOWLEDGMENTS

Whoever said writing was a solitary art was wrong. Many people have made direct and indirect contributions to me, my career, and this book:

First and foremost, I owe a debt of gratitude to God and my family. Their love and encouragement has been invaluable, especially Jack, my husband, who knows first hand the meaning of "for better or for worse."

Beryl Carr, aka Mom, has been supportive in so many areas that there is no way to list it all. She started it all by reading Perry Mason to me at bedtime. She's willing to take either the credit or the blame.

I also want to thank my father-in-law, John "Grandpa" Zaleski, for his quiet support from the sidelines. Don't be scared, Grandpa. I only commit murder in my imagination.

Vice Principal Alice Ann Klakos and the rest of the staff at Oak Glen High School in Chester, West Virginia, gave me a tour of their high school and answered my numerous questions and requests to help bring this book together.

I would also like to thank the real Hancock County Prosecuting Attorney, James W. Davis, Junior. A few years ago, his staff was kind enough to give this struggling writer a tour of his corner office in the basement of a school building.

Lori Brindle, artist and designer of Divine Designs, is the creative genius who designed the cover for *A Small Case of Murder* and *A Reunion to Die For.* She has a lot of talent and a lot of class. She also lends her artistic talents as an independent beauty consultant for Mary Kay Cosmetics.

Another Mary Kay gal, independent beauty director Catherine Stewart graciously lent her beauty by "playing" my murder victim for the cover of this book. She put in many hours digging through her own high school memorabilia to bring this all together.

Lea Toland, business manager, for Spotlight Publicity has gone above and beyond the call of duty with her advice and friendship.

I know that I have forgotten someone. If you are that someone, thank you and please forgive me. I'm over forty and my memory is not what it used to be.

PROLOGUE

October 8, 1984

Dorothy Wheeler turned her Toyota into her dirt driveway and saw her rented cottage nestled between the twin maples in her front yard.

"Finally!"

It had been a long day.

First, Dorothy was late for work because the previous day she had forgotten to get gas on her way home from church. When she walked in three minutes late for her job as a bank clerk, she didn't overlook boss Susan Sweeney's evil eye.

Then, after being on her feet all day, Dorothy had to go to the store to buy groceries. Judging by the line at the checkout, everyone else in Chester, West Virginia, had the same idea.

She hoped her daughter, Tricia, had already started dinner. As Dorothy, the widow of a Vietnam soldier, drove across the creek to pull the car behind her house, she smiled and waved her fingers to greet her neighbors across the split-rail fence dividing their two properties.

Teenaged siblings Phyllis and Doug Barlow watched with little expression while her Toyota made its way up the driveway to rest under the first maple tree. Tricia and Doug were seniors in high school. Phyllis was a couple of years younger. The Barlows didn't return the greeting. They ran into their house and closed the door.

"I swear." Dorothy frowned. "Those kids are getting stranger every day."

She turned off the engine. With a groan, she lifted two of the three paper bags full of groceries out of the front passenger seat of the car.

She hoped things would be quiet that night.

"Tricia!" she called into the house when she dropped one of the bags in the driveway. "Can you come help me carry in the groceries?"

She didn't notice the eerie silence in response to her call. While clutching the bags and her purse, which dropped from her shoulder to hang by the strap at her elbow, she scurried to the back door to deposit the groceries inside the house before she dropped the rest of them.

"Trish, open the door," Dorothy yelled through the screen door. She waited.

Her daughter didn't answer.

Dorothy sighed and pried open the door with an index finger. "Help me unload the car!" Frustration crept into her voice. She forced her hand, then her shoulder, through the crack between the door and the door frame. "Get off the phone with Beth and help me!"

She dropped everything onto the table and went in search of her daughter, who, she assumed, was on the phone.

"Tricia, didn't you hear—?" Her tirade ended with a scream. She found her daughter laid out on the sofa as if practicing for her funeral viewing.

Tricia was dressed in the blue-and-gold cheerleading uniform she had worn that day for yearbook pictures. Blood oozing through the hole created by the bullet through her heart formed a red pool in the middle of the blue *O* trimmed in gold that stood for Oak Glen High School.

Thus ended Tricia Wheeler's young life.

CHAPTER ONE:
TWENTY-ONE YEARS LATER

"Dr. MacMillan, we have a shooting victim and a potential heart attack coming in. ETA three minutes," the nurse informed the emergency room doctor on duty that evening.

East Liverpool City Hospital was small compared to other hospitals, but it was as big as it needed to be. This Saturday night, the emergency room had only a doctor and resident on duty. Until now, the evening had been quiet. It was the first cold weekend of autumn, and most of the residents of the town nestled along the Ohio River, and its neighbor on the opposite end of the Chester Bridge, had stayed in their homes to keep warm.

As a matter of protocol, the nurse waited for her orders from the doctor in the green lab coat. She had known Dr. Tad Mac-Millan for so many years that she hadn't noticed the touch of gray that had crept into his brown hair and the smile lines that now framed his deep green eyes.

"How bad is the shooting victim?" he inquired.

"Conscious. In a lot of pain. Losing blood fast. BP is dropping."

"See if you can get Dr. Longstreet down here for the heart attack." He could hear the ambulance sirens in the parking lot.

"No go. He's in surgery."

The doors flew open and two attendants ran into the emergency room. The gurney between them was filled with the bulk of a man dressed in soiled work clothes. Reeking of booze

11

and sweat, he thrashed around so much that the attendants had to fight to keep him from falling off the gurney. His lower body was covered in blood.

Even though the doctor was unable to see the man's face under a nest of tangled hair that reminded him of the serpent locks on the head of a mythical monster he had read about in high school, Tad instantly recognized Rex Rollins. He was a regular visitor to the ER.

The attendants slowed down enough to hear the nurse's directions. "Examination room two." They ran off while the second gurney came in behind them.

A rail-thin man was curled up on the gurney with his hands over his ears. His face was covered with an oxygen mask. Tad couldn't make out the patient's mumbled words between the hysterical gasps for breath from under the mask.

Figures, he thought. *Rex must have been stirring up trouble at his wife's house again.* The second patient was the first's brother-in-law, Doug Barlow.

Tad directed the attendants to room one. He ordered the nurse, "Get an EKG on Barlow and his vitals. I'll take the shooting victim first."

The nurse took off after Doug before the doctor could finish his directions. He rushed after Rex with the rest of the emergency room staff behind him.

The attendants and orderlies already had Rex Rollins on the examination table when Tad got to his patient. The nurse assigned to assist him was setting up an IV to replace the lost blood.

Even though he was losing consciousness, the patient was still able to direct a string of obscenities at his wife. "That bitch tried to shoot my balls off! After all I did for her and she shoots me in the balls! She's crazy."

Tad examined the bullet wound in his upper thigh, which the

paramedics had exposed by cutting open his pant leg. He guessed from experience that the bullet was a small caliber handgun: little, but effective.

Luckily, Rex's wife missed her target by at least two inches.

The paramedics had tried to stop the bleeding with pressure above the injury at his hip. Even with the binding, blood spurted like a fountain from where he was shot.

While Tad pried into the leg to get at the bullet, the nurse appeared at his elbow to report on Doug Barlow's condition. His heart rate was elevated, as was his breathing, but the EKG was normal. She made the same diagnosis the doctor had guessed when he learned the identity of the patient.

Doug was having an anxiety attack.

She rushed off to administer the drugs Tad had ordered to sedate him.

"Son of a bitch! After all I did for that bitch and she hauls off and shoots me in the balls! Son of a bitch!" Rex muttered while slipping off into unconsciousness.

With a shake of his head, the doctor yanked the bullet from his thigh.

"It's so loud!" Doug complained when Tad stepped into the other examination room to see his next patient. Even though the medication had stopped the hyperventilating, his anxiety had not subsided.

The scene was ironic. The former town drunk was treating the genius, who was now an emotional cripple.

While he took his patient's pulse, Tad observed the scars on Doug's wrists, left there from a suicide attempt made a decade earlier. He had put three slashes on both wrists. "How are you doing, Doug?"

The patient took off his dirt-filmed eyeglasses and wiped his eyes. Without the magnification of the thick lenses, his eyes seemed to shrink to half their size. "It was so loud. I didn't know it would be so loud."

"What was loud?"

"The gun shot. I didn't mean to—"

"How is he, Doc?" Phyllis Rollins's question made Tad jump. He hadn't given permission for his patient to have any visitors yet.

Doug's sister had the attitude of a mother bear protecting her cub. The top she wore under her faded coat belonged to pajamas. Without bothering to run a brush through her long, ash-colored hair, she had pulled on a pair of jeans and thrown on her coat to follow the ambulance to the hospital after the police agreed to let her go for shooting her husband.

"We gave him a sedative. His heart rate has already come down. Once it returns to normal, he can go home." Tad referred to Doug's record of his previous visits to the emergency room and the list of medications he had been taking. "Is he still on antidepressants?"

"Yes," she responded briskly.

"Is he still seeing Dr. Dalton?"

"Yes." She watched her brother with her eyes narrowed to slits.

Tad could see that she was only interested in getting her brother home. "Well, after he goes home, I want you to be sure he sees his psychiatrist within two days." He signed the release form on his clipboard despite his concern at seeing Doug hugging his knees and rocking on the examination table. "Witnessing a shooting would be traumatic for anyone."

"He'll be okay." Her statement sounded more like an order directed at her brother.

"Still, he should see Dr. Dalton," Tad repeated on his way out of the room. He got to the door before he remembered Rex Rollins. "Oh, about Rex—"

"What?" She started at the reminder.

"Your husband is going to be okay."

"Thanks a lot." Phyllis's appreciation was sarcastic.

"Sorry," Tad responded.

Joshua Thornton's Monday was going badly.

The morning began with his ten-year-old son Donny remembering that he needed a science project for school—that day. The widowed father was able to recall how to make a cyclone out of two plastic liter bottles and tape, and spent his breakfast giving his son a science lesson.

After that fiasco, his two teenaged daughters, Tracy and Sarah, got into a fight over something that had to do with cosmetics. He stepped in before it turned violent. The girls did not speak to each other during breakfast. Sarah slammed the back door so hard when she left for school with Donny that the force knocked a flowerpot off the porch railing. Joshua was grateful that it was not him, but his twin sons, Joshua Junior (J.J.) and Murphy, who had to endure the drive to the high school with Tracy, who would surely present her side of the case.

The final straw came when he ran out of coffee before he got a full dosage of caffeine. The headache from the withdrawal had already settled behind his eyeballs when he left the house for his office down the river in New Cumberland.

Joshua pulled his black 1958 Corvette convertible into the space reserved for Hancock County's prosecuting attorney, got out, and had just slammed the door when the clouds split open and dumped all of their contents on the Ohio Valley. He was torn between digging out his keys to unlock the car door so that he could get back inside to escape the downpour or running twenty feet across the parking lot into the school building where his office took up one corner of the basement. He decided to run for it and got soaked.

He didn't even have time to take off his trench coat before Mary, his administrative assistant, announced that he had a visitor.

With rain dripping from his auburn hair and down his face, the tall, athletically slender lawyer stood in the center of the reception area. The pitter-patter of the rain in the parking lot above them drowned out the classic rock music he played in his office.

The visitor rose from the chair next to Mary's desk and extended her hand. "Hello," she greeted Joshua in a voice meant to warm up the rain soaking his clothes. "I'm Tori Brody. I just joined the public defender's office." Her brown eyes smiled at him.

The recognition was instant. "Tori," he mouthed.

One corner of her lips curled. She painted them a red that was a shade darker than was appropriate for a woman in what was still a man's business. Her honey-colored hair fell in one wave to her shoulders. She had darkened it since high school. It used to be the color of platinum and worn in permed curls down to the middle of her back. The darker shade was more becoming on her.

Aware that he was still holding her hand, Joshua released it and backed up. "Step into my office." He slipped his coat off and hung it up on the rack next to the door. When she passed him, he picked up the scent of her perfume.

"I guess you two know each other," Mary said. It was more an observation than a question.

"We went to school together."

"She doesn't look like your average public defender."

After he closed his office door, Joshua asked Tori, "Did I hear you say that you are with the public defender's office now?" He paused in front of the wall mirror by his door to wipe the rain

16

off his forehead and smooth his hair back with his hands. When he saw his reflection, he observed that her style wasn't the only one that had changed in the past twenty years. His hair used to fall to his collar and curl. Now, it was cut short and combed back off his forehead.

"Part time. I'm setting up my own legal practice here in town." Tori took the seat across from his desk. She crossed one leg over the other. The skirt of her gray suit was shorter than what would be appropriate in court.

While he made conversation, Joshua sat behind his desk and took out his notepad and pen. "Let me warn you, Ruth Majors is like a dog with a bone. She likes to keep all the good stuff for herself. You'll get a couple of cases—"

The warning didn't bother her. "As long as I get enough to be able to get a reputation."

He paused.

Tori Brody already had a reputation. Her looks made him doubt if time would ever erase the invisible scarlet A branded onto her chest from her youth.

"What case are you here to see me about?" he asked in a tone not unlike that of a school principal to a student.

"Saturday night Phyllis Rollins shot her husband. His name is Rex."

"I know the Rollinses. Rex is a regular visitor at the county jail. He has a tendency to get nasty when he drinks too much, which is all the time. Did Phyllis kill him?"

"No, she got him in the leg."

"Lucky guy."

"You're right there. She was aiming for his balls."

While she continued to present her defense, Joshua cringed at the thought of being shot in the testicles. It was a mistake for her to tell the prosecutor that her client was aiming to shoot her victim in the crotch. It showed criminal intent. If Phyllis wanted to claim that she shot her husband in self-defense, then her lawyer blew it.

"The husband is in the hospital and expected to recover," she finished.

"That's good for your client."

"He was violating a restraining order. He had kicked in the door and was in the bedroom. My client was on the phone with the sheriff, and the police were on their way there when she shot him."

Even though he was familiar with Rex's history, Joshua had not had a chance to read the police report on the shooting. "Your client and the victim are legally separated, but their divorce isn't final yet. Who owns the house?"

"My client. She put the house into her name when she took out a mortgage on it a few years ago."

His job was to decide what charges, if any, to bring against Phyllis Rollins. If he prosecuted a woman trying to defend herself against a husband with a history of violence, the newly elected county prosecuting attorney would be very unpopular. "I have to charge her with something. Otherwise, I'd be sending a message that it's okay for women to go around shooting off their husbands' balls."

"It was self-defense," she argued. "He has a record, and she had reason to fear for her safety."

"Was he armed?" He hoped Rex had made it easy for him by making a case of self-defense.

She shook her head. "But Phyllis didn't know that."

Joshua needed an out. "Let me read the police report and talk to the investigator to see what he's found out."

"Investigator?" she asked. "This is a simple case of self-defense."

"Unless Phyllis was actually trying to kill Rex," Joshua pointed out. "I don't know if Ruth told you. The sheriff's department has hired a chief of detectives. Actually . . ." He grinned. "He's the only detective. Seth Cavanaugh. Maybe you heard of him."

Tori shrugged while shaking her head.

"Maybe not," he conceded. "Seth Cavanaugh was the cop that solved the Quincy murders in Parkersburg last year."

"Has he investigated the Rollins shooting yet?"

Joshua thumbed through the reports on his desk and found none from over the weekend. "The best I can tell you is that based on what you tell me, we can charge Rex with breaking and entering, trespassing, and violating a restraining order and maybe make some sort of deal with your client that won't involve any jail time."

"Jail time? She was firing a gun in her own home in defense of herself against an abusive husband."

"Did she give him a warning?"

"Yes, the sheriff has it on the 911 tape."

"Then I think we can make a deal. Let me talk to Cavanaugh and the sheriff." Joshua noticed she let out a sigh of relief. "How long ago did you pass the bar?"

"It shows?"

He nodded.

Now that they were no longer talking business, her professional demeanor slipped away like a satin sheet. "I always knew you'd be gentle our first time together."

It was his turn to be nervous. Joshua sat forward in his seat and concentrated on a doodle on the corner of his notepad.

"I passed last year," she answered his question. "I went to law school in Morgantown."

"That's a good school. If you don't mind my asking—" He cocked his head and reconsidered asking her the question he had on his mind.

"What?"

"When we were in school," he reminded her, "I don't recall ever seeing any sign from you that you were interested in college, let alone going to law school."

"I don't recall you ever taking the time to find out what I was interested in." Tori prepared to leave.

Joshua stood up and leaned with his palms flat on his desk as a reminder of his position of authority. "It's hard to ask questions when someone is coming at you with a switchblade."

"That was not my fault," she fired back. "Let's not go there." She dug a business card from her portfolio and placed it in the center of his desk, inches from his fingertips. Bright white with blue print, it was crisp and new.

"Call me after you talk to your detective." She held out her hand to him to shake.

He took her hand.

She smiled. This one was pleasant and inviting. "It's good to see you again, Josh."

"You've come a long way, Tori," he said. "Congratulations." He extracted his hand from hers.

At the door, she struck a pose that mocked her own sexual reputation. "Call me some time."

"Jan Martin is on line one." Mary startled him out of his thoughts by calling from her desk into his office after the public defender had left.

Dreading the reason for his childhood friend's call, Joshua plopped down into his chair, groaned, and picked up the receiver. "Hey, Jan!" He forced himself to sound happy to hear from her. "How are you doing?"

"Splendid! I just signed the papers! The drugstore has been sold and I'm a free woman!"

The weak reception told him that she was on her cell phone. He guessed that she was on her way across the Ohio River to work at her new job as a journalist at *The Glendale Vindicator,* a local newspaper.

Jan Martin had spent her adult life running her mother's drugstore. Then, over the summer, Joan Martin had met a millionaire while on a bus tour. After a whirlwind romance, they married and moved to Branson, Missouri. She turned over the store to her daughter, who went about selling it to pursue a writing career. Jan was starting out as a reporter covering the courthouse.

"Did you get the invitation to the reunion?" She was referring to their twentieth high school reunion that she was coordinating. "Have you RSVP'd yet?"

"I have to check my schedule," Joshua lied.

She responded with a laugh. She knew he had no intention of going to their reunion. "What are you doing tonight?"

Quick, he told himself, *come up with something!*

They had grown up together. Joshua always sensed that Jan had a crush on him, but he ignored it. Then, after marrying someone else, having five children, and traveling around the world as a lawyer for the Judge Advocate General, he had returned to his hometown, on the cobblestoned streets of Chester, West Virginia, in the heart of the Ohio Valley.

It was upon his return that her crush turned to love.

Neither of them said anything about it—until the party celebrating his election in a special run-off election for prosecutor.

The Thorntons held an open house in their big stone house on Rock Springs Boulevard with its rolling front and backyards. The adults drank beer or margaritas, and sat on the porch to watch the younger hosts and guests play football.

After one too many margaritas, Jan confessed her love. While the encounter ended chastely, Joshua felt guilty for not handling it better.

That had been one month ago and neither of them had talked

about it since. It was as if the encounter had never happened. But it had happened, and thoughts about it lay beneath the surface.

"I want to celebrate my freedom," she told him. "I've got a lasagna put together. All I have to do is pop it in the oven. Tad is coming."

Relieved to realize that this was not a date, Joshua accepted the invitation and offered to let her bring the lasagna over to his place. His house had more room, and the kids would like to share in the celebration. The tension alleviated, he felt comfortable enough to ask, "Do you remember Tori Brody?"

"Yeah," she answered without enthusiasm. "What about her?"

"She's with the public defender's office now."

"Okay, now tell me for real. Sawyer found out that she was running a whorehouse and busted her, right?"

"No, really. She's a lawyer."

"You can dress a pig up in a tux and teach him how to dance, but that won't change what he is. He's still a hog. I'll see you tonight." Jan didn't wait for him to say good-bye before she hung up.

"After everything I've done for that bitch!"

In the ward reserved for patients without insurance who couldn't afford rooms, Tad was examining the hole in Rex Rollins's hand. The bullet had passed through the palm before it imbedded itself in his thigh. During the examination, Lieutenant Seth Cavanaugh broke the news to the patient that he was under arrest.

"You're shitting me!" Rex kept saying while the detective reminded him that he had violated the restraining order Phyllis had placed against him by forcing his way into her home.

Dressed in jeans and a sports jacket over his trim build, Lieutenant Seth Cavanaugh, with his blond hair and blue eyes, looked like a television version of a detective. Tad felt as if he was in a scene from a glitzy Hollywood cop show.

"I don't fucking believe this! Why aren't you arresting her?"

"She was defending herself. You broke the law. That's why you're being charged and she isn't." Seth went on to tell him that the deputy standing at his elbow was going to stay there. As soon as Rex was released from the hospital, he would be taken to the magistrate to have bail set, and then, if he could not afford bail, he would be taken to the jail to await his hearing.

"I got that house for her! You wouldn't believe what I did for her to get her that house!"

Tad was putting the finishing touches to the fresh bandage on his patient's hand, which resembled a giant white lobster claw.

Seth cut Rex off in his declaration. "The fact is you are under arrest." He gestured towards the deputy standing next to his bed like a sentry. "Darrel will stay here to make sure you don't decide to check out early and go elsewhere." The detective headed for the door.

"Do you believe this?" Rex asked his doctor to verify the irony of the circumstance.

"If I were you, I'd cross Phyllis off my list and move on," Tad said before instructing the nurse's aid at his elbow to pack up the bandages and disinfectants. Wanting to proceed with his rounds, he didn't care to hear any more rantings about how unfair life had been to his patient.

"I'd kill for that woman. Hell, I have!"

Things didn't improve during the course of the day. Even though the rain stopped, Joshua still had a cloud hanging over his head. The next storm hit an hour before going home.

The prosecutor massaged his temples while he studied a financial report for his office. The numbers swimming through his head made him dizzy. He slapped the folder shut and tried to clear his mind by tapping his pen against the edge of his desk.

The royal blue pen with gold trim felt good in his hand. The night that she proclaimed her love for him, Jan had presented to him the pen and holder with his name engraved on the base in honor of his election as Hancock County's prosecuting attorney. He felt guilty accepting it after telling her that he was unable to return her feelings, but she insisted, saying that she didn't know any other "Joshua Thornton, Hancock County Prosecuting Attorney" to give it to.

The pen had just the right weight and feel for him to use as a drumstick against his desk when he needed to take a break to clear his mind. He had fallen into the rhythm of a Credence Clearwater Revival tune playing on the radio when Mary called on the intercom.

"Josh, Gail Reynolds is here to see you."

He groaned.

"She doesn't have an appointment." She offered him an out to refuse to see the visitor.

Curiosity made him indecisive.

Gail Reynolds. What would she be doing here? The Gail Reynolds he knew from his past, the editor of the school newspaper, who went on to become a crime journalist, would not come back to Chester unless there was a reason. She never wasted her time on anything unless it meant something for her.

His interest was piqued. "Send her in."

He sucked in his breath and shoved his pen into its holder before going to the door, opening it, and preparing for yet another fight with his adversary.

In junior high school they were contenders for class president. After Joshua won, Gail led a revolt to have him impeached for not fighting the school board on its decision to keep the dress code.

In high school, when Joshua was student council president, Gail wrote editorials against him in the school paper claiming that, due to his Christian faith, he lacked objectivity. He led the football team in prayer before their games. This, she claimed, was an example of their leader's inability to separate church and state. Her view was moot when the praying quarterback led his team to the state championship two years in a row.

Gail was one Oak Glen alumnus Joshua had occasion to run into on a regular basis after he left Chester. Like him, she went on to the nation's capital to pursue her career.

By the time her classmate arrived in Washington to serve with the Navy in the Judge Advocate General corps, Gail had developed a reputation as a crime journalist. When Joshua was assigned to prosecute a naval admiral for murder, she was right there on the front lines, criticizing Lieutenant Commander Joshua Thornton every step of the way.

He didn't know why she was so critical. In youth, they traveled in the same circles. Yet there seemed to be nothing he could do that was not worthy of her criticism.

Joshua sucked in his breath, forced a grin on his face, and opened the office door.

Gail Reynolds was dressed in a blue pantsuit and gold jewelry that was hardly noticeable. Her makeup was understated and her short hair was combed back into place. Sexuality had no place in her life. She'd never had a serious relationship that Joshua was aware of.

She had a cocky grin on her face.

"Hello, Gail." He refrained from asking her what she was up to.

"Hello, Josh." She stepped into the small office and looked around before commenting with sarcasm, "I see you're moving up in the world." She was referring to the corner office on the top floor of the JAG office he'd had in San Francisco before he moved his family back to Chester. Now, he had a corner office in a basement.

Joshua closed the door and gave in to his inquisitiveness. "What's up?"

She took the chair across from his desk. "What do you mean?"

"What are you doing here? I would have thought you would be in California covering the Reinhold murders." In recent years, he had not known of one major murder case that she didn't investigate in order to write a book afterwards. Her first book had been about him.

She sighed dramatically. "I just so happened to be in the neighborhood."

"In New Cumberland? Doing what?"

"Taking a sabbatical."

"I don't believe you."

"Why not?" She pretended to be wounded. "I've been working hard my whole life. I've never had a vacation—"

"That I do believe." Gail was a classic workaholic.

"So, I decided to come back to Chester to take a rest." She turned her head to peer slyly at him out of the corner of her eyes. "And write another book."

Joshua cringed. He plopped down into the chair across from her. "Don't tell me that you intend to write about the Rawlings case."

The Rawlings case was a double murder in which he had been appointed special prosecutor when he returned back home. He had promised Jan an exclusive to write her first book about the case.

He dreaded what Jan would do if Gail wrote a book about the same case.

The two women had been rivals since they had ended up in

the same sandbox on the playground in Tomlinson Run Park. Joshua could imagine that Jan's sandcastle fell apart while Gail's sandy home went on to become a summer residence for a fairy princess and her royal spouse. Both girls would, every year, compete for the same editorial slots of the school paper, and Gail would always win.

In their senior year, it turned out that both competed for the same scholarship. Gail won. Jan ended up working in her mother's drugstore while her rival went out into the world to enjoy success and recognition.

Figures, he thought, *Gail would come home to write a book about the same subject as Jan's.*

Unaware of his dread, she elaborated on the subject of her next project. "I'm writing a book about Tricia."

Joshua started. It had been so long, that it took time for him to realize whom she was talking about. "Tricia?" As soon as the question slipped from his lips, he remembered: "Tricia Wheeler."

"Of course." Gail was pleased to see recognition in his eyes. "It's about time someone investigated it."

CHAPTER TWO

Nostalgia made Joshua rush home to find his high school yearbook. In one day, he had been assaulted by the past from all sides.

His master was in such a hurry to get his yearbook that Admiral, the family's huge mongrel, only had enough time to get his front legs down off the sofa before Joshua raced into the study and to the bookcase. When the dog realized that he was not going to be chastised for trespassing onto the furniture, he pulled himself back up and resumed his nap.

Donny and Sarah were up in their bedrooms doing their homework. Tracy and the twins wouldn't be home for another hour.

In no time, Joshua found the first section, which contained the student council's pictures. As president, his picture was at the top and center of the page. Beth Davis's picture was in the third row beneath his. Her title was secretary.

He cleared his throat when he recalled how pretty, with her strawberry blond hair and creamy complexion, the council secretary had been. She was the image of every boy's wholesome desire.

Beth had been his girlfriend. They had become engaged the night of the Valentine's Day formal in their senior year. The night of the prom, they almost eloped. Then they graduated and went out into the real world.

The newspaper staff was on the next page. Editor Gail Reynolds was front and center of the group photo. With her hair pulled back into a bun, she was dressed in gray slacks and a navy blue silk blouse with a plunging neckline. She looked like the serious news journalist.

Tucked in one step behind her, assistant editor Jan Martin was almost hidden. She struck an expressionless pose. She thought she looked stupid when she smiled. She had taken off her glasses for the picture. She only recently started wearing contact lenses on some occasions. She wore her straight hair loose. She was dressed in a blousy blue cotton suit with a long jacket. The suit's shoulder pads and wide skirt looked out of proportion on her small frame.

Joshua found Tori Brody's portrait shot several pages back. She had been a sophomore when they were seniors. The photograph displayed above her name bore only a slight resemblance to the lawyer he had met that morning. Even at fifteen, she had oozed sensuality. He sat behind his desk and stared at her picture.

In the decade following the era of sexual freedom, when it became acceptable for girls to let go of their virginity before marriage, the title of slut and whore was supposed to go the way of chastity belts. Not necessarily for girls like Tori Brody in Small Town, America.

She was from the wrong side of the tracks. She lived in a mobile home park by the river. Her father took off when she was a baby. Her mother was a barmaid with the reputation of having affairs with married men. Her older sister dropped out of school to get married. Without adult supervision, Tori was exploring sex when Joshua was still working up the nerve to ask girls to dance at the junior high social.

Tori Brody fell in with the type of people that Joshua and his friends avoided out of self-preservation. They were the first to smoke cigarettes and drink beer. By high school, they dressed in worn blue jeans and leather; rode in hot cars and motorcycles; dealt drugs; and thought nothing of inflicting injury on anyone unfortunate enough to cross their paths.

With bleached-blonde hair; eyes framed with lush lashes; slender hips; and breasts accentuated in daring styles that pushed the envelope of the school's dress code, Tori was hard not to notice when she entered Oak Glen High School. Within weeks, envious girls and lust-filled boys labeled her as not being the type of girl Joshua could take home to his grandmother. The most sensuous girl in the school, she was sought and won over by the leader of the school's roughest gang.

That was Max Bowman. Everyone knew he carried a switch-blade, though few saw it because switchblades were illegal. He cherished his girl like the trophy she was.

Joshua was indifferent to Tori and her friends. The gap between the two social classes in the world of high school was so wide that he would never even have met her if it weren't for a photography class that he took in the spring of his senior year.

As circumstance would have it, she was seated next to him. She managed to smile at him whenever possible. Within a matter of weeks, he laughed at her sexual innuendoes, which she could summon better than Mae West.

Eventually, his apprehension around the promiscuous girl gave way to a friendship—until one spring afternoon when Joshua stepped out of the boys locker room after softball practice into a mob led by Max Bowman, who announced that he was going to make an example of him.

It was Joshua's first fight for his life. Max was armed with his switchblade. Untrained in self-defense, other than the child-hood stuff he had learned from his grandfather, Joshua was uncertain about how he had been able to disarm the brute, but he had done so. Under the threat of having the weapon turned on him, Max and his friends ran away and never approached

Joshua again.

Tori claimed ignorance when confronted with the question of why her boyfriend had come after him. Joshua later heard that after finding out that her boyfriend had cheated on her, she started a rumor that she had slept with Oak Glen's star quarterback.

The snap of the fingers in his face brought Joshua back to the present.

Tad MacMillan peered at him with curiosity. After entering his cousin's home uninvited, he had raided his refrigerator to steal an apple. He was eating the stolen good while sitting on the corner of Joshua's desk.

"What are you in such deep thought about?"

"Nothing." Joshua held the yearbook on its end and slapped the front and back covers together to shut the book. When the album fell back onto his desk, the back cover flapped open to reveal the last page.

They observed the pretty face that peered up at them from the album. Her blue eyes were happy. Her golden hair was lush and full. Her smile was dazzling. She had her whole life before her and so far it had been a happy one.

Joshua ran his fingers across the face that lay before him. The words printed above her image read, "In memory of . . ." and below the picture "Tricia Wheeler" and beneath that: "1967–1984."

"I remember her." Tad took another bite of the apple and spoke around it. "That was awful. I would never have thought she would have killed herself."

"That's what everyone said." Joshua closed the book.

"Did you date her?"

"No, I dated Beth. Remember?"

"Did you sleep with her?" Tad knew that he could ask his cousin anything, no matter how personal it might be.

"No."

"Did you want to sleep with her?"

"She was my friend," Joshua responded firmly. He put the album back on the bookshelf from which he had taken it.

Tad's voice took on a naughty tone when he deduced, "She turned you down."

"I never asked." Joshua turned back toward him. "It was one of those situations where we liked each other, but one of us always seemed to be attached to someone else." He concluded somberly, "She died before the opportunity could present itself."

"Too bad." His sympathy was sincere. "Why the nostalgia?"

"Gail Reynolds is in town."

Tad chuckled.

"It's not funny. She's writing a book about Tricia's death and she's going to make me look like a fool. Why? Because she hates me and don't ask me why."

"She doesn't hate you."

"Then why has she made it her career to follow me around and criticize me on every case I get?"

"Sounds like someone has had a bad day." Tad pointed out, "Gail was not here when you were working on the Rawlings case. She wasn't here when you ran for office."

Joshua resumed as if he had not heard his argument. "She was there at the courthouse every day when I prosecuted Admiral Thompson."

Tad tossed the apple core into the trashcan. "When did you sleep with her?"

"What makes you think I slept with her?"

"Come on, Josh. I know you better than you know yourself. Gail isn't the first pushy woman to challenge you and she won't be the last. Why should you get so upset about her coming back to town?" He answered his own question. "You had a one-night stand with her and you feel guilty. When did it happen?"

"Right after that fight Beth and I had at your New Year's Eve party," Joshua confessed. "She told me that Beth sent her over to talk to me about making up. Grandmamma was out." He shook his head. "She ended up seducing me. I found out afterwards that Beth didn't send her."

"Some friend."

"That's what I thought. It just happened. Only once. I told her right afterwards that it was a mistake."

"Did she put a gun to your head?" Tad was unconvinced that Joshua was totally innocent.

"Okay, I went along because I was still mad at Beth for whatever it was we were fighting about. But then Gail tried to get me to continue seeing her; but I loved Beth. Within a few days, Beth and I were back together and a few weeks after that we got engaged. Gail and I never talked about it, ever, either of us. Beth never knew."

Tad gestured at the image of Tricia Wheeler now sealed in the album shelved in the bookcase. "Was she friends with Tricia?"

"Everyone was friends with Trish." Joshua rubbed an imaginary spot on the top of his desk. "I remember the day I found out she died. I was driving Beth to school in that red van I had back then and, when we got there, there were all these kids in the parking lot. The girls were all hugging and crying, and the guys were in shock. Cindy Patterson came running up and said that Tricia had killed herself."

He looked over at his cousin, whom he admired for his wisdom. Tad was only a few years older, but he had learned much in his youth while traveling down the path of alcoholism.

"It hit me like someone had dumped a bucket of ice water over my head. For the first time, I realized my mortality." Joshua cocked his head. "Does that sound insensitive? My friend was dead, and all I could think about was all the things that we had in common. We were the same age. Suddenly, out of the blue, she was dead. That meant that I could die, too."

"You were seventeen," Tad stated simply. "We all think we are immortal when we're seventeen. Her death was a shot of reality."

"Yeah. Reality sucks sometimes."

Joshua checked the time on his watch and realized that Tracy and his sons were late. "The kids must be gabbing with their friends and forgot about the time."

Tad told him, "I saw Hancock County's new star in action today."

"What new star?"

"Seth Cavanaugh."

"Oh, that new star," Joshua replied with no hint of emotion. "Sawyer wanted to promote one of his deputies from within the department, but the commissioner saw Cavanaugh on the news lapping up the media attention after the Quincy boys got convicted and went all gaga over him. She said that having a noted detective working in Hancock County would be good for our reputation." He confessed, "Between you, me, and the lamp post, my gut tells me that he's not as brilliant as the newspapers made him out to be. But that's just my gut talking."

Tad frowned. "My gut is telling me the same thing. He was there to question Rollins about the shooting. Funny thing is . . . I didn't hear him ask one question. He just nailed the guy. Isn't it the job of investigators to ask questions of everyone?"

Before Joshua could respond, the phone on his desk rang. While he reached across his desk to answer it, Tad's cell phone hitched onto his belt rang. The two men said "Hello" in unison.

They were speaking to two different callers about the same subject. While Tad was listening to the emotionless tone of the sheriff department's operator sending the medical examiner out on a call to conduct an on-scene examination of a murder victim, Joshua was listening to his eldest son report that one of their friends had been killed at the high school.

It was *déjà vu.*

As his Corvette rounded the corner of the high school into the parking lot, Joshua was struck by the similarity of the scene to what he saw that morning after Tricia Wheeler died. The girls were crying while the boys tried to decide how they should react to what had happened.

The more things change, the more they stay the same. The only difference between then and now was the clothes and hairstyles.

To collect their statements, the sheriff's deputies separated Joshua's three older children, as well as the other students who were there during the murder. Most of the teenagers wore athletic wear for football and other sport practice. Several girls were dressed in cheerleading uniforms.

Under the protective eye of J.J., Deputy Pete Hockenberry, an older officer, was questioning Tracy at the van while Murphy, dressed in shoulder pads under muddy sweats for football practice, spoke with another policeman several feet away.

J.J. and Murphy were their father's sons in every way. At seventeen years old, they equaled their father in their lanky builds. They'd also inherited his blue eyes and wavy hair, which J.J., the introspective twin, kept cut short.

Tracy looked and lived the role of the teenage girl with her silky auburn hair, creamy complexion and petite build. For her, it wasn't a matter of role-playing when she chose cooking and fashion for her interests. Unlike the other girls there, Tracy was dressed in her school clothes. The tryouts for cheerleading had been in the spring, before their move to Chester. She would have to wait until next year to exercise her dancing talent on the cheerleading squad as she had done ever since she was old enough to hold a pom-pom.

Yellow police tape was draped along the fence surrounding part of the practice field and across the walkway leading to the murder scene on the other side of the maintenance shed located at the end of the field.

While Tad took his medical examiner's bag and ducked under the tape to jog to the shed to check out the body of the murdered teenaged girl, Joshua crossed to the van where Tracy and Deputy Hockenberry leaned against the front fender. As soon as her father took her into his arms, she broke down and sobbed against his chest. Someone had given her a linen handkerchief in which to cry.

"It's okay," Joshua murmured into her hair.

On her other side, J.J. slipped his arm across her shoulders. "She's been putting up a brave front. I was wondering when it was going to hit her."

Deputy Hockenberry observed Seth, slipping evidence gloves on, cross the field toward the crime scene. "I see that our new investigator is here to show us how it is done." The deputy had put in for the job of chief detective. He had the experience and training, but none of the publicity Cavanaugh had acquired breaking the murder case in another part of the state. The deputy hitched his pants up over his potbelly, slipped his notepad into his pocket, and joined two other officers.

Seth was questioning the coach, who looked like he was going to be sick. The older man seemed unable not to stare at the shed at the far end of the field. The coach led the detective to where the girl had been killed.

Murphy had finished answering the deputy's questions and joined his family. "Can you believe this? In broad daylight with the whole team and cheerleading squad on the other side of the building? That guy had a lot of balls."

"What guy? What happened?" Joshua found it difficult to refrain from studying the forensics team searching for minute pieces of evidence. He yearned to be with them, working the case, instead of just being a concerned father consoling his children.

"The killer."

"Who was he?"

His children shrugged. "No one seemed to recognize him," J.J. said.

"Who was killed?" Joshua asked.

"Grace," Tracy sobbed.

"Grace?" Joshua felt as if he should know whom she was talking about.

"Grace Henderson," Murphy said. "She was one of the varsity cheerleaders."

"Remember?" Tracy added in a choked voice. "She came over a couple of weeks ago."

Joshua sighed and swallowed. "I remember her now." He strolled toward the practice field.

Murphy fell in beside him while his brother stayed to comfort Tracy, who didn't want to go near the scene where her friend had died. He sensed his father's nostalgia about when he used to lead his team toward field goals. History was repeating itself. Like his father before him, Murphy had made first-string quarterback in his junior year. So far, under his leadership, Oak Glen's Bears were undefeated.

"What happened?" Joshua asked again.

"We were finishing up practice. The cheerleaders were done and they were in the stands with Tracy and J.J. Suddenly we heard this shot from behind the shed, and I saw him running for the fence."

"Him?"

"I have no idea if it was a man or woman. They were wearing this big black trench coat—"

"Trench coat?" Joshua's thoughts raced to another high

school shooting that involved youths dressed in black trench coats.

"Yeah." Murphy added, "But I don't think it was anyone I know from here. It was way too big for him and he was no taller than Sarah. He wore this black bandanna and wrap-around sunglasses that, like, took up his whole face." He sucked in his breath and fought to keep the shudder out of his voice, "And he had the biggest gun I ever saw in my life."

"You saw the murder weapon?"

Murphy nodded and pointed out across the track field to the chain-link fence that marked off the school property. A deputy was taking a picture of something that had become stuck on the fence.

"I chased him across the field and over the fence and into the woods. When I was just about to tackle him, he turned around and pointed it right into my face."

"What were you thinking?" Joshua roared.

"That I could catch him."

"He had just killed someone, and you didn't think he'd do the same to you?"

Murphy stood at his full height. His shoulder pads made him appear bulkier than he truly was. "Dad, I did exactly what you would have done."

Joshua reminded him, "He had a gun. He killed Grace. Like he would think twice about shooting you? I thought you had better sense that that, Murphy."

"I do have sense!"

"Then use it!" Joshua sucked in his breath as if he were trying to pull back the words he had uttered. His son was right. He would have done exactly the same thing. How he sometimes hated the genes he had passed on to his children.

Murphy pressed his lips together while he watched his father grimace in what he concluded was anger at him for his foolish behavior.

"Was Grace going to meet anyone after school?" Joshua asked.

"I don't know. That's something that maybe one of the girls knew, or maybe not. She didn't really mix a lot. Her closest friend seemed to be Tracy, and she wasn't allowed to get that close to her."

Joshua recalled the Saturday afternoon he had spent having tea with Grace's mother, who had yet to learn of her daughter's death. They resumed the walk around the outside of the yellow-plastic-taped fence while Murphy reported what little he knew about the victim. "Grace was not allowed to date until she was eighteen. She had to fight tooth and nail to get her folks to allow her to be on the cheerleading squad. Her mother escorted her to every game and chaperoned her when we went out after the games. Most of the time Grace didn't go with us because she was so embarrassed about her mom tagging along."

"Bummer." Joshua didn't have the energy to keep such a tight rein on his children.

Sheriff Curt Sawyer had ducked under the tape and was coming down the steps to join them on the running track. His gold badge stood out against his black uniform on his broad chest. Not wanting to discuss the particulars of the murder in front of his son and a witness, Joshua suggested that Murphy wait for him at the van while he gathered the details from the sheriff.

Curt waited for the teenager to be out of earshot before he reported, "Doc says she's been dead for less than an hour, which we already knew."

They strolled along the fence in the direction of the shed. Curt handed Joshua a pair of evidence gloves, which he put on to prevent contaminating the scene.

"Single gunshot wound to the chest. Looks like a contact wound. No sign of a struggle." The sheriff speculated, "I think the killer caught her by surprise."

"Why are you telling me this? I'm just a guy whose kids happened to be on the scene."

Curt stopped and stuck his thumbs inside his thick belt and glanced in the direction of the shed. "I'd just like for you to take a look at the scene and tell me what you think."

"But—"

"Don't tell me you're not curious."

"Of course, I am. Why do you want me to look at it? My job is to prosecute the guy after your investigator catches him."

"If you were cooking a gourmet meal and Emeril happened to be around the corner, wouldn't you want him to take a taste and tell you what he thought?"

"Come on, Curt. You know that I can't cook." Joshua ducked under the yellow tape and around the corner of the shed to the open door. The deputies and forensics officers had gathered outside the building to confer with each other. He noticed several pairs of eyes following Seth, who was scribbling on his notepad.

"What do we have here?" Joshua tried to decipher the detective's notes from over his shoulder.

Seth flipped the notebook shut. "Looks like a jilted admirer decided to take out the object of his affection."

Joshua looked inside the darkened shed stocked with equipment used to maintain the school grounds. The teenaged girl was sprawled in a spread eagle position on the dirt floor.

While putting his equipment back into his medical examiners bag, Tad gestured for the attendants to wait for the county prosecutor to take a look before they removed her to the morgue across the river.

"Your son told one of the deputies that he touched the body," Seth told Joshua. There was a critical note in his tone.

Tad interjected, "J.J. said that he was checking to see if the victim was okay when he realized that she had been shot. It was dark in here, and he didn't see the blood until he had put his hand in it."

The investigator added, "He also mentioned that the victim's skirt was pulled up. He pulled it down because he didn't want everyone to see her that way. That indicates an attempt at sexual assault."

"Her fingernails are clean, no skin under them, no evidence of a struggle," Tad showed Joshua her hands covered in paper evidence bags sealed with rubber bands, as if he could see them through the paper. "There's no physical sign of sexual assault, bruising on the thighs or anywhere else. The skirt probably flew up when she hit the ground."

Seth's glare in the medical examiner's direction was interrupted when Joshua stepped between them to examine the girl on the ground. He knelt next to the body. Her dead eyes peered up at him. They were wide as if she still had something to fear.

Here was a girl he had met in life. Pretty. Sweet. The type of girl fathers imagined their sons taking to the prom. She was still dressed in her blue-and-gold cheerleading uniform that the squad had worn for their yearbook pictures that day. While the outfit had the same color and trim as when he was in school, it had been updated to be more form fitting and the skirt shortened for a sexier edge.

She could have been Tracy. He could only imagine the unbearable pain her parents were going to suffer when Sheriff Sawyer and the parish priest rang their doorbell to tell them that their daughter would not be coming home.

Joshua swallowed, closed his eyes, and transformed himself into the professional he was. When he turned his head away to regain his composure while distancing himself from the victim, he saw a blue athletic bag and purse set on the floor by the door. "Is that her gym bag?"

Curt picked up the purse and did a brief examination of the contents while Joshua studied her lifeless form. "What was she doing in here?" He peered around the shed used to house a lawn tractor, clippers, shovels, fertilizer, and other equipment.

"The cheerleaders were having practice right outside here," Seth answered. "After they finished, the rest of the girls went over to watch the football team. They thought she was with them until they heard the shot."

"So someone stopped her on her way to the practice field, or she met someone here," Tad observed.

"A loser who wanted to date a cheerleader," the detective theorized, "She said no and he couldn't take the rejection."

Joshua suggested, "Anyone could have lured her over here for a chat or whatever. A secluded building with no windows."

"Perfect place for a teenage girl and boy to have some fun," said Seth.

The prosecutor asked, "If they were having so much fun, why'd he shoot her?"

Curt removed a Polaroid picture from one of the pocket sections of the purse and held it out to Joshua, who stepped out of the shed to take it. He studied the blurry image. The photograph was of two girls, one blonde and one redhead. The blonde was Grace, but she did not look anything like the all-American cheerleader he knew. She was sexy. Her makeup was heavy. The hue of the other girl's hair was more orange than red. Both girls grinned broadly at the camera while hugging a bare-chested man, who had his arms around them. In the background was a bar with a portion of a sign that read: *Half-*.

"Does that girl look familiar to you?" Seth grabbed the purse from the sheriff to examine it.

"Nope." Joshua traded the picture for a driver's license the sheriff had removed from the wallet. At first, it looked like any other West Virginia driver's license. When he saw the lawman's knowing smile, Joshua took a second look. The sixteen-year-old victim's birth date had to be 1988, at the earliest. However, on this identification it stated that she was born in 1982, which made her over twenty-one, the legal age to drink alcohol and buy cigarettes.

"It's a good ID, too," Curt observed. "The average Joe wouldn't spot it."

Joshua handed the license back to him and strolled around the inside of the shed. "She was meeting someone. The gym bag was set down, not dropped or thrown. She came inside this shed to talk in private to her killer."

The sheriff reminded him, "The cheerleaders went over to the field to watch football practice. So she was alone with this guy."

"But the whole team and the squad were right on the other side of this building."

"They were alone long enough for her to get shot," Tad pointed out. "She didn't put up much of a fight, probably because she didn't have time. In this shed, if the killer used the element of surprise, he would have had the advantage."

Seth declared, "We're looking for a jilted boyfriend."

"She wasn't allowed to date," Joshua told them.

"Just because she wasn't allowed to date doesn't mean she didn't have a boyfriend," Tad said with a naughty grin.

CHAPTER THREE

The Glendale Vindicator wasn't *The Washington Post.* The small, privately owned newspaper operated on a shoestring and paid chicken feed, but Jan Martin didn't care. As soon as she finished writing about the valley's story of the decade, Joshua's solving of a double homicide in their own hometown, she was certain that her first book would be published and that she would be on her way to being a first-class author.

Jan had made a mistake by professing her love to Joshua at what she had thought was the opportune time, one year after the death of his wife. She'd been humiliated by his rejection, even if he was kind about it. At least he still wanted to be friends.

There was hope, she prayed.

Joshua and Tad returned to the Thornton home shortly before her arrival for dinner. She understood when Tracy begged out of dinner to rush to her room and sob. Murphy went upstairs to take a shower in the bathroom in his and J.J.'s attic bedroom. J.J. went to do his homework. He was working towards an academic scholarship and wasn't going to let dinner and murder stand in the way of his studies. This single-minded dedication, Jan noted, was something he had inherited from his father. Meanwhile, Joshua went to his study to make a couple of phone calls in regard to pending cases.

Sipping a glass of red wine, Jan prepared the Caesar salad and garlic toast for dinner while listening to Tad's account of the sixteen-year-old girl killed with a single gunshot wound to the chest in the maintenance shed, next to the practice field filled with the football team, the cheerleading squad, and assorted other witnesses.

She reminded Joshua when he came through the swinging kitchen door from the living room, "Tricia Wheeler was wearing her cheerleading uniform when she was found dead with a single shot to the chest."

"You must have been talking to Gail Reynolds." Preoccupied with his trauma-filled day, he did not stop to think about the reaction his words would have on her.

A silence fell over the kitchen.

She broke the silence. "Why would I be talking to Gail?"

Tad cringed.

"I have not had a good day." Joshua sighed. "Gail is in town."

"Whatever for?" she demanded to know.

Tad told them, "She's renting the old Marshall place out by the state line."

"Why would a big, famous network news journalist covering stories all over the world be here?" Jan asked Joshua, "Did she come here to interview you for a book about the Rawlings?"

"She wants to write a book about Tricia Wheeler," Joshua said.

Glaring at the mention of her childhood rival, Jan slapped Tad's fingers when he tried to sneak a tomato from her antipasto tray. "Why is she suddenly all interested in Tricia?"

Tad suggested, "Maybe because Tricia was a friend and she wants to find out what happened to make her kill herself."

"Gail had no friends, only connections," she said with a sneer. "That's how she got my scholarship."

"That was twenty years ago, Jan. Get over it already." Joshua poured himself a glass of wine. Between the murder, Tori, Gail, and Jan, he concluded that he had earned it.

Jan's tone continued to be accusing. "You never answered my

question. Why is she so interested in Tricia?"

He answered her with an exaggerated shrug. "I don't know. Tricia killed herself."

She scoffed. "Do you really think Tricia killed herself?"

Joshua started. He had thought of it in passing before, but never considered that Tricia Wheeler had indeed been murdered.

At dinner, Jan told of her adventure covering a case at the courthouse. The defendant led the police on a high-speed chase—on his lawn tractor. He was driving the tractor because his license had been revoked due to drunk driving.

Joshua and Tad found the case to be minor compared to the cases they had worked on, but Jan, who was in the middle of all the legal action at the courthouse, thought it was thrilling. The children, even if only out of kindness, confirmed that she was on the brink of an exciting career.

As Jan took in the country kitchen, she reminisced about when they were children. Grandmamma Thornton seemed to always be busy cooking something while Jan and Joshua would drink fresh milk from Tad's family's dairy farm and eat cookies still warm from the oven.

Built a century earlier by Joshua's great-grandfather for his bride, the three-story stone manor needed to be brought up to modern standards when Joshua moved his family back home. Since his renovations during that summer, the kitchen was chic with new appliances and furnishings. The wallpaper and wall hangings that Tracy had picked out cast a French country ambiance.

Jan concluded her memories of their childhood by laying her hand on top of Joshua's. Fearful of encouraging her feelings, he jerked his hand away.

Her cheeks flushed.

At the other end of the table, Tad lightened the awkward moment by suggesting they all take their dessert of ice-cream sundaes downstairs to the family room in the basement. This gave each one of the children permission to scatter throughout the house to pursue his or her interests.

The family room was cluttered with a hodgepodge of books, jackets and sweaters, and various childish paraphernalia. The adults ate their sundaes and made small talk about what the children were doing in school. As the evening wore on, Joshua suggested that they turn on the evening news to see what would be reported about Grace Henderson. Her murder made the news at the top of the hour, after a lead-in about a feature later in the hour on a local celebrity's return to the valley: Gail Reynolds.

"I don't believe it!" Jan sputtered.

"I want to see this," Tad announced.

"Are you kidding?" How dare he betray her by being interested in her rival?

"I want to see what all the excitement is about."

Gail and the reporter sat on the balcony of what appeared to be a restaurant overlooking the Pittsburgh skyline. "What now?" The interviewer questioned what had brought the local celebrity back to her hometown.

"Well," she demurred, "I'm a self-confessed workaholic. So a vacation is out of the question while I'm on sabbatical from the network. I'm researching my next book."

"What will that be about?"

"I'm investigating the murder of a very good friend of mine."

Jan scoffed, "You're kidding."

"Whose murder is that?" the reporter asked.

"Tricia Wheeler." Gail's voice held a hint of emotion. "She was one of my best friends in school. Her death, at such a young age, before she even had a chance to really live, was a defining moment in my life. Everyone knew that she would never commit suicide, but we were all so young, and when the sheriff declared it was suicide, like a bunch of sheep, my friends and I asked no questions. But now, things are different. I am no longer afraid to question authority. It is my right—no, my duty—as Tricia's friend to uncover the truth." Her face twisted in a show of emotion.

All was quiet on the screen, as if to punctuate the strength of her announcement.

"Good grief!" Tad muttered.

Gail was smiling with reserve at the camera as the show's jingle signaled the end of the program.

"How much do you want to bet that Gail has a publisher and she hasn't even written her book yet?" Jan asked.

"Jealousy doesn't look good on you," Joshua replied.

"Jealousy? What do you mean I'm jealous?"

"Come on! Gail is everything you've always wanted to be! She's a respected writer. She's traveled all over the world! The only thing she doesn't have is a husband and kids!"

"And I'm a nobody, huh?"

Tad sat quietly in his beanbag chair off in the corner of the room to watch the fight. *Dinner and a show!* he thought.

Accustomed to the noise of family arguments, Admiral rested under the coffee table while waiting for everyone to leave so he could climb back up on the sofa. After getting a treat of leftover lasagna sauce on his pellets, he thought the day was perfect.

"I didn't say you were a nobody," Joshua defended himself. "Admit it! Gail's coming back here with her feature on the local news when you can't find a publisher for your unfinished book is bugging you."

"Like you care!"

"I do care," he countered. "It just isn't the way you want me to care." He growled, "Why can't you grow up?"

"Why can't you stop being a chicken?"

Joshua looked to Tad for help. As confused as Joshua, Tad looked back at his cousin with no answer to his question. All the doctor could offer was a shrug of his shoulders.

"What do you mean I'm chicken?"

"You've never even given me a chance. You've slept with Beth. You married Valerie. But you've known me since we were taking baths together at two years old, and you refuse to give me a shot. Did it ever occur to you that it's because you were afraid of falling in love with me?"

Joshua told her in a soft voice, "I don't want to ruin our very good friendship by becoming lovers." He tried to stop her, but she was already running up the stairs.

She was backing her car out of the driveway when Tad grabbed the door handle and asked for a ride. Since he lived only two blocks away, Jan knew that he wanted to continue the conversation. After she responded to his request with a grunt, he jumped into the passenger seat for the ride down the hill to Church Alley, the back street that ran behind his doctor's office.

He waited for her to pull the car up to the steps leading to his apartment over his medical office before offering his advice with an observation. "Josh does care about you . . . so do I."

She coughed.

He continued in spite of her refusal to look at him. "Maybe he doesn't care about you the way you want him to, but he cares. You are lucky to have a friend like him. I know I am. If it weren't for him, I'd be dead."

She stared at the dashboard of her car to hold back the tears fighting their way to her eyes. She was damned if she was going to let him see her cry and report it to Joshua.

Tad knew the tears were on their way. "Listen, Jan, I have lived more than you ever will, and I have been around the block a dozen times more than you have ever been, and there is something that I learned that I think you should know."

"What?" she snapped.

"Bed partners come and go. Friends, good friends, are forever. You can't get a better friend than Josh Thornton." He added softly, "He is your friend, no matter what happens. Don't spoil it by trying to sleep with him."

Tad didn't wait for her argument. He got out of the car and went up to his apartment.

"What's wrong with this picture?" Dr. Tad MacMillan asked Joshua Thornton and Lieutenant Seth Cavanaugh.

The three men studied Grace Henderson's naked back. In death, the girl lay with no dignity on her stomach on the cold steel table in the morgue in East Liverpool City Hospital's basement. Every crevice and orifice of her body had been probed and studied in hopes of finding evidence to identify her killer.

There are no secrets in death.

Unable not to compare her to his own teenaged daughters, Joshua thought, *She shouldn't be here. She should be spending her father's paycheck at the mall.*

It was easy to see what Tad was talking about when he asked them what was wrong with her. Etched into the once pink flesh of the cheerleader who had been teased for the puritan boundaries set by her parents was an eagle with its wings spread out across her buttocks. The bird's head rose up above the top of the crack in her buttocks. Its body ran down along either side of her cheeks for the tail feathers to spread out where her legs parted.

The artwork took up her entire rear end.

"It's a tattoo," Tad told the speechless men. "I see a lot of them in my line of work. This is a good-quality one. It's quite expensive to get this type of artwork done."

Joshua noted what was obvious to him from his personal association with the victim. "This girl didn't even baby-sit.

Where'd she get the money for this?"

"Her folks?" Seth guessed.

"No," the prosecutor disagreed, "they would never have agreed to a tattoo, especially on the butt. A couple of weeks before she was killed, she came over to our house to see Tracy. Her mother and I had to chaperone. Our house, mid-afternoon on a Saturday to bake cookies with another girl. We are talking about a very strict family here." He took her earlobe into his hand. "She didn't even pierce her ears."

"Her parents can see her ears," Tad said. "What are the odds that they are going to be checking out her butt?"

"So we have a girl who's got a secret life," Joshua concluded.

"Oh, yeah." The medical examiner referred to the report he had pinned on a clipboard. "She was shot once through the heart. It was a contact wound. The gun was pressed against her chest when the shot was fired. She was killed instantly. The slug was a thirty-eight caliber. I sent it to the state lab for analysis. They'll call you with the results."

The detective nodded his approval.

"She had a blood alcohol level of point-zero-three. The forensics people found vodka in the water bottle in her gym bag."

"She drank?" Joshua was surprised by the revelations about the girl whom he considered to be one of his daughters' friends.

Tad covered her with a sterile white sheet to show only the back of her head. "From what I saw of her liver, she had been drinking regularly, recently, even heavily, but she had not been drinking over the course of the long term."

"What about drugs?" Seth wondered.

"None in her system at the time of her death, nor did she smoke. Her lungs were pink and healthy."

"What about sexual assault?" Seth reminded them, "She was found with her skirt up."

"Nope," was Tad's answer. "There is no evidence of sexual assault whatsoever, but she was pregnant."

"She was pregnant!" Joshua exclaimed.

"At least four weeks."

"She didn't even date."

"It isn't dating that gets you pregnant," Tad responded matter-of-factly.

"Maybe she was raped."

"She was no shrinking violet. She had consensual sex less than twenty-four hours before her death."

Seth concluded in a firm tone, "It's this girl's secret life that got her killed. She got herself a secret boyfriend, got herself pregnant, and the boyfriend decided to do away with her and the baby." He stepped towards the door to leave. "I'll start interrogating the football team."

Joshua shook his head.

Offended by the shake of his head, Seth snapped, "What's wrong with you? Whoever killed her got close enough to press a gun against her chest. That means it was someone she knew, someone she trusted—like trusted enough to let him get her pregnant."

"Don't waste your time on the football team. Murphy got closer to our killer than anyone. The perp was slightly built. That doesn't sound like a football player."

"It's my job to investigate this murder and catch the guy who did this," Seth reminded him. "It's your job to not screw up my collar and prosecute the son of a bitch!" He asked Tad, "What is he even doing here?"

"I invited him," the medical examiner answered. "If this guy was a football player, based on Murphy's description, he'd be mincemeat after fifteen minutes on the field."

Joshua told them, "According to everyone who knew the victim, Grace did not date anyone she went to school with."

"Did they know about this tattoo?" Seth lifted the blanket to reveal the eagle as if his memory needed to be refreshed. "Who is to say that she wasn't dating someone at the school? Our killer had to have access to the murder scene. You claim that she had no freedom to come and go. Who is she going to date and let get her pregnant except someone she had access to, and who does she have the best access to except a boy who goes to Oak Glen?"

Joshua argued, "I know teenagers. I have four. If a teenager wants freedom, she'll take it. Clearly, Grace managed to escape from her parents to create a secret life for herself. This life was so secret that she was drinking without anyone in her immediate circle of friends knowing." He chuckled. "We are talking about a very careful girl here."

"If she was so careful, how did she get pregnant and how did she get herself killed?" Seth cracked.

"She didn't reveal her other side to the girls on the squad because she was afraid one of them would rat her out. I don't think she dated anyone from school because her parents could find out. She kept that life outside of Oak Glen's environment because it was less likely for word to get back home." He shook his finger at him. "You're going to find this guy someplace other than her school."

Seth's flushed face warned them that his fury was rising.

Tad crossed to his desk and returned with a notepad on which he scribbled a name and phone number. "Start with the tattoo." He tore off a sheet of paper and handed it to the detective. "There's only one guy in the valley who does this type of work. Tell him I sent you."

Seth was right. Joshua's job was to prosecute the case after the detective brought the killer to him. Reminded of this, he told himself that he had to sit back and let Seth do his job. But, there was nothing that said that he couldn't talk to his kids' friends himself in his role as a parent.

Since his daughter Tracy was running for the cheerleader spot left vacant by Grace's death, the squad invited themselves to her home to teach her the cheers to help her win at the tryouts. The twins and their friends who got wind of the girls coming over gathered in the family room to play with their drums and guitars. Donny was playing games on his computer while Sarah loitered in the kitchen. The thirteen-year-old girl seemed to be searching for ways to annoy her sister.

Joshua had no idea how many people were at his home. The first batch of pizzas he ordered for the girls disappeared to the family room with Admiral in hot pursuit. There was not even one slice left, and he suspected that the dog was successful in begging more than one slice for himself based on the tomato sauce in his whiskers. Joshua had to order a second batch.

Grace's pregnancy was kept secret. Anyone who proved to have knowledge of that information would give himself away as knowing about her secret life. It was Tracy who unknowingly revealed that the dead girl might have known about her pregnancy. She was picking at the cheese on a pizza pie while stirring a pitcher of lemonade when she told her father about how annoyed the captain of the squad was with Grace. "She said she didn't want to be on the top of the pyramid anymore." Tracy fought the smile at the corner of her lips. "If I make the squad, Madison is going to put me at the top."

"Things are really working out for you, huh, Trace," Sarah noted with a wicked grin while taking a slice of pizza with everything on it. When a mushroom dropped off the pile of toppings to the floor, Admiral almost knocked her off her stool diving for the morsel. He snorted with disappointment when he discovered that it was not his favorite.

"That's not funny, Sarah," Joshua chastised her while pushing Admiral down from where he placed his front paws onto the counter to see if the boxes contained anything except mushrooms. His snout claimed that they did.

"People have killed for less."

Fear came to Tracy's eyes. "You don't think the police are going to suspect me if I get on the squad, do you?"

"Don't you have homework to do?" Joshua snapped at Sarah while he sorted the pizza boxes to divide up between the cheese, vegetable, and supreme.

"No." Sarah studied a slice of green pepper as if she were deciding if she should eat it or give it to Admiral whom she knew did not like peppers. "Everyone has been moving so quickly about replacing Grace. It's tacky, if you ask me." She held the piece of pepper up over her head and then dropped it into her mouth.

"No one is asking you. It's the sponsor who's rushing the tryouts to replace her." Tracy placed the pitchers of lemonade in the refrigerator. "Football season is really gearing up and the squad is short one cheerleader." She gestured towards Joshua. "I asked Dad if he thought it would be in poor taste for me to try out. He told me to go ahead."

The doorbell rang. Tracy rushed off to greet her friends. Sarah ducked out of the kitchen to her bedroom with another slice of pizza.

Joshua did not notice her thievery. He was thinking about Grace's request not to be at the top of the pyramid. If she was afraid of falling, then she didn't want to lose the baby, which told him that she knew she was pregnant and wanted to keep it. He helped himself to a glass of lemonade.

Tracy escorted the band of giggling girls into the kitchen. There were ten in all. Trying to be casual about casting her eyes about the room and out into the backyard, Madison, the captain of the squad, asked if Murphy was home. Before anyone could answer, the boys rushed in from downstairs. With shouts and squeals, the party began.

In a flash, Joshua recalled parties he had hosted in the same kitchen decades ago. He remembered one that was not so happy—the day he and his friends learned of another cheerleader's death. Somehow, he was not sure how, at the end of that day, everyone ended up at the home he shared with his grandmother. The house was quiet. They spoke in soft whispers, as if speaking in a normal tone would wake their dead friend.

Joshua was amazed by how unbroken these young people seemed to be about Grace's death. Twenty years earlier, the squad did not replace Tricia out of respect for her memory. Grace wasn't buried yet and they were already replacing her, most likely with his daughter.

After the pizza was consumed, the young people spilled out into the backyard for a football game with Murphy and J.J. as team captains. The game was well under way when Connie, a cheerleader who Murphy had noted was in his social studies class, took a break when Joshua and Donny came out onto the porch steps. The father and son were eating ice-cream sundaes.

Joshua had observed that Connie was different from the other girls on the squad. She was pretty without all the trappings of cosmetics. While her friends were diving for the pizza, she stood back to observe the goings on in the kitchen before taking her slice after the mob had cleared. Uncomfortably, Joshua noticed that often her eyes landed on him. He suspected that he was being sized up.

A few minutes into the football game, Connie took a break to sit on the steps to pet Admiral. It did not take her long to initiate a conversation about Grace's murder. The dog shook his head at her touch on his ears. She had interrupted his staring match with the ice cream.

Ignoring Admiral's order for a bite, Joshua responded coyly

to her question about the investigation's status. "We're still looking for suspects. Do you recall Grace having any disagreements with anyone?"

"There was that fight she got into in the locker room with Heather Connor last week."

Madison came up onto the porch to help herself to another glass of lemonade. "Oh, yes. That's right. I forgot about that." She was gently patting her sweaty face with a hand towel so as not to smear her mascara.

"One of your friends gets blown away, and you forgot about the fight she got into the week before?" Joshua asked.

The rest of the girls came up to get refreshments. The boys had taken over the backyard. J.J. proved to be a bigger match in leading his team than Murphy's players had thought.

"It was not an actual fight," Madison said. "It was more of a shoving match. It was nothing serious."

"I'd say having Heather Connor gunning for me would be serious," Tracy muttered.

"Connor," he asked. "Is that Connor as in the Connor Estate, as in the same neighborhood where the killer had escaped after the shooting?"

"The very same," Connie answered before asking her friends, "What was the fight about anyway?"

"I have no idea." Madison told Joshua, "It was over as soon as it started. It was so minor that the coach didn't even write it up. She told Heather that she would give her detention if she caused any more trouble with anyone on the squad."

"Who is this Heather?" he wanted to know.

His daughter answered, "Her mother's big in real estate. She builds and sells all these housing developments. She's real rich."

The kids had taken over the family room after the football game. Joshua had put Admiral on a leash and had dragged him away from the chips and dips and salsa spilled around the basement to walk down Rock Springs Boulevard to Church Alley to knock on Tad's door. He wanted to ask his cousin about Heather Connor.

The blue Mustang outside could have belonged to one of the other residents whose homes backed up to the alley. It was only after Tad, dressed in his bathrobe, invited them inside and put the kettle on the stove that Joshua discovered he had company.

"Oh, geez, I'm late!" he heard a shriek from the back of the one-bedroom apartment.

A woman with her red hair cut in a pixie-type style rushed into the kitchen doorway. She was stuffing her panty hose into her purse with one hand while slipping her black pumps onto her feet at the end of her legs that seemed to go on forever. She was gorgeous.

"Tad MacMillan, you are awful! Why is it that every time I come over here you make me forget about the time?"

He chuckled at her while he reached for mugs from the cupboard in which to pour the tea.

Playfully, she slapped his arm. When he turned to her, she pecked him on the lips. He retaliated by pulling her close and kissing her full on the mouth.

"Until next time, darling," she whispered. "You know my number."

She was not flustered when she noticed that someone was in the room to witness the farewell to what had to be an intimate encounter shortly before. Her blouse was still untucked when she waved good-bye to them on her way out the door.

"If you had told me you had a date—" Joshua sat at the kitchen table. Admiral plopped down in the middle of the floor with an eye on the door in preparation to leave if Tad's dog appeared. Though Dog was a fraction of his size, the young canine exhausted him.

"She was a friend who just stopped in to say hello," Tad explained.

"A friend? What kind of friend?"

"A very good friend." His naughty grin matched Joshua's.

While waiting for the water in the kettle to boil, Joshua told him, "None of the kids know about Grace's pregnancy."

"Maybe she didn't know." Tad placed a mug in front of his guest. "She was no more than six weeks along." The kettle's whistle called him back to the stove to fill their mugs.

"No, she knew. Tracy said that she requested to be taken off the top of the human pyramid."

"She didn't want to fall and lose the baby." Tad pushed his tea bag down into the cup and squeezed the herbs inside together. "I wonder if her boyfriend drove a white Pontiac Firebird."

"A white Firebird?"

"Or it could have been tan. Or it could have been a Camaro." Tad smiled. "Deputy Hockenberry told me that on a house-to-house search of the development behind the school, he found a girl who saw someone in a black trench coat take off in a white or tan Firebird or Camaro. Cavanaugh took credit for finding the witness. What a jerk."

"But she doesn't know if it was white or tan or a Camaro or a Firebird," Joshua said. "That witness doesn't sound credible enough to use in court."

"No, she doesn't." Tad shook his head sadly. "It's such a shame about Grace. Sweet kid like that. Who would want to kill her?"

"Who is Heather Connor?"

"Second generation of trouble, that's who."

"Who?"

"She's Margo Connor's daughter and every bit as arrogant as her mother."

"Who's Margo Connor?"

"You know Margo Connor."

"Remind me." Joshua was getting perturbed by his teasing.

"I'm sure you'll remember her by her maiden name."

"Which is—?"

"Sweeney."

"Damn!"

CHAPTER FOUR

Jan had spent the morning hanging around the courthouse hoping to catch Joshua so she could suggest that they have lunch together. Her intention was two-fold. While spending time with him, she might be able to get information about Grace Henderson's murder that a journalist less intimate with the county prosecuting attorney would be unable to discover. She also hoped to make him forget about their argument.

She failed. He was having a luncheon meeting at his desk with one of his part-time prosecutors. So, she decided to try for the man on the front line, Lieutenant Seth Cavanaugh.

"What do you want?" was his greeting when Jan popped her head around the partition marking off his cubicle that was to serve as his office.

"I'm working on the Henderson case for *The Glendale Vindicator.* Do you know—?"

He snorted. "A jilted boyfriend. Who else?"

"But I heard that she didn't date."

"Clearly she did."

Deciding it would be harder for him to dismiss her if she sat down next to his desk, Jan pulled up a chair. "Can you tell me who your suspects are?"

Seth looked both ways before answering in a whisper, "She had a split personality. By day, she was the virginal cheerleader, by night, she was—"

"Josh, did we have a one o'clock meeting?" Curt Sawyer's

voice boomed from the other side of the partition.

Joshua did not see Jan when he went into the sheriff's office. "Curt, you have a calendar. Why don't you use it?" He shut the door.

Seth rose from his seat. "I don't have time for you right now." He ushered her out of his cubicle.

Jan gave up and drove through a burger place on her way back to the newspaper. Her failure felt complete when she sat down at her desk outside owner/editor Ernie Gaston's office and saw Gail Reynolds meeting with her boss. They were laughing while she recounted a story from her life as a globe-trotting journalist.

Jan forced herself to turn away from the scene and laid out her burger, fries, and milkshake in preparation to begin writing about a pre-trial motion in magistrate court for Rex Rollins, who was charged with violating a restraining order and trespassing. It wasn't a big story, but it was enough to get her name on a byline in the paper. She had written the lead to her story when Ernie's office door opened and he led Gail to her desk.

"Jan, look at who has come in for a visit." Ernie gestured with a wave of his hand in Gail's direction. "Jan Martin covers the Hancock County courthouse . . . Jan, you know Gail. It's like old times. Remember back at Oak Glen when I was the editor of the paper and you two were my top reporters?" The year after he graduated from high school, his protégé had beaten out Jan to take over his position as editor.

"Yes, I remember." Jan squinted and flexed her cheek muscles to force her face into a smile.

Ignoring the tension that filled the air between the two women, Ernie continued, "Gail is researching the death of a local girl who died twenty years ago."

"Tricia Wheeler," Jan said to him. "I know. She was shot. The sheriff ruled it a suicide."

"I told Gail that we would do everything we can to help. Can you take her to the morgue to get her what we have on Wheeler?"

Jan fought to conceal her displeasure by forcing herself to sound cheerful. "Sure." It sounded like a squeak. Grabbing her milkshake, she ushered Gail toward the stairs leading to the basement of *The Glendale Vindicator*, where they stored their old issues of the paper.

Gail said, "I heard you sold the drugstore."

"That's right. I'm writing full time now. I cover the court-house, Josh's beat."

"I remember my first reporting job, at this little television station in Pennsylvania while I was going to school." She sighed. "I look back and realize that things were so much easier and less stressful then. People expect less of you when no one notices your work."

Jan stopped, her hand on the doorknob leading into the dusty file room. She told herself not to say anything.

"You are really lucky, Jan. Staying here in this small town with no one depending on you to be the best all the time."

"I know why you're doing this." Jan whirled around. "I know why you're here."

Gail smiled. "Everyone knows why I'm here. I've made it no secret."

"It's also no secret that the network didn't renew your contract."

Her smile dropped.

Aware that she finally had the upper hand, Jan continued, "I saw you on the news, playing all emotional and suddenly having to come here to uncover the truth about your good friend's murder. But I know the truth. I was there."

An edge of fear crept into Gail's tone. "What do you mean?"

"Come on! You and Tricia may have taken a few classes together, but you were not friends!"

"We were friends."

"No!" Jan elaborated, "She hung out with the cheerleaders and the jocks. She and her friends were at the top of the social hierarchy. The student government and the school paper were below them. That was where you and I belonged. We were one step above the science geeks. The student government and school paper committee interacted with the jocks, but we were never really in that circle." She concluded, "You weren't friends with Trish."

Gail's lack of a reaction told Jan that she was on the right track. "Of course, for you to come to town and say that you were investigating the death of someone you didn't give a damn about wouldn't make for very good press, and without that, you can't get another network job. Now, why, I wonder, can't you get another network job without publishing another book? Did I read something on some Web site about a hospital visit? Could it have something to do with drugs?"

"Tricia Wheeler was murdered."

"I don't doubt that. And I believe her case does need to be reopened. But I don't like you using her murder for your own ambitions. That's the difference between you and me."

Gail's eyes narrowed. "If you don't open that door and get me everything this paper has on Tricia, I am going to go tell your boss some very unpleasant things about you and you're going to be looking for a new job."

"Mary, have you seen my pen?" Joshua called out of his office to his administrative assistant.

She glanced around her desk and responded with a no.

He once again rummaged through the drawers of his desk in his search of the blue-and-gold pen that Jan had given him. Unable to find it, he slammed the last drawer shut and looked at the empty holder at the front of the desk.

With a hand on her hip, Mary questioned him from the doorway of his office, "When was the last time you saw it?" Her voice held a tone that reminded him of his grandmother when he asked her to help him find things. Grandmamma Thornton would consent to aid in the search, but not without a lecture about putting his things away.

"A couple of days ago," he answered.

Mary proceeded to remove folders from his IN box to see if the pen had slipped under the files.

"I know I didn't take it home. I've been keeping it here in the office in the holder where it belongs." He groaned when the ringing phone interrupted the search. "This is Joshua Thornton."

Without any greeting, Seth Cavanaugh launched into the reason for his call, "We got a break in the Henderson murder. The lab got a match on the slug that the medical examiner took out of the girl."

"The gun was used in a previous crime?" He sat back in his seat to let Mary reach in front of him to open the center top drawer of his desk to search for the pen.

"Yeah," Seth answered. "It was a four-year-old murder case in Weirton. The victim was Matthew Landers, an eighteen-year-old college kid, killed execution-style. He walked in on his father's house being robbed. There was a string of break-ins in the area at the time."

"But the burglaries stopped." Joshua shook his head when she held up an old blue pen to ask if that was it.

"After the thieves broke into the wrong house. The owner blew one of the guys away with a shotgun. Justifiable homicide. The guy who got blown away was Bobby Unger. They didn't find the murder weapon of the Landers boy so they could never officially connect the burglaries to his murder, but all the circumstantial stuff was there. Now, the guy who shot Unger says there were two of them and the second one got away. He said it was a boy, but he was unable to identify him because it was dark. Unger had a little brother named Billy. He was fourteen at the time."

Joshua added four years to fourteen to arrive at Billy's current age. He leaned back in his chair. "Just the right age to get a sixteen-year-old girl pregnant. Do you have any way of connecting Billy Unger to Grace?"

"Nope."

"That gun could have been in a hundred different hands since that kid was killed. Has Unger been in any trouble since then?"

"He turned eighteen this past summer. So his record is officially clean. However, my sources in Steubenville tell me that he has a juvie record as long as your arm."

Joshua ordered, "Get Heather Connor in here as soon as possible. The kids say that she's a party girl and, from what I have learned, Steubenville is the place to party. Maybe she can connect Billy to Grace."

With a shake of her head and a shrug of her shoulders, Mary left the office, defeated in her search for the pen.

Joshua had sat up in his chair and was about to hang up the phone when the investigator added in a by-the-way tone, "Interesting thing that Connor's name has come up in this case."

"Why?" Joshua leaned back again in his chair.

"You know Rollins was arraigned in the magistrate's court today on those charges of violating the restraining order?"

"Yes. Foster is working that case." Joshua would hand off his smaller cases in the magistrate's court to one of his two part-time lawyers, who, like Tori Brody, were just getting started.

"Did Foster tell you that when Rollins came into court he had a Pittsburgh lawyer there to defend him? Christine Watson.

She's supposed to be big."

"I know her. She doesn't usually defend clients of his . . . uh . . ." Joshua looked for the right word. ". . . caliber?"

"She's pleading him innocent and requested a jury trial. He's out on bail."

"A jury trial?" Joshua did not expect Rex Rollins to put up such a defense. He was certain he would plead no contest. "Watson doesn't come cheap. What rich relative did he kill off?"

"That's why I said this was so interesting," Seth chuckled. "The deputy who was keeping an eye on Rollins after we arrested him says that he called Margo Connor from the hospital the night before he was released. Watson was waiting for him at the jail. I did a little digging this afternoon and guess what former employer has Watson on retainer?"

"Margo Connor. Maiden name Sweeney."

"What have you got on the Grace Henderson murder?"

Jan bristled. Gail was poring over all the clippings on Tricia Wheeler that the reporter had printed from the microfiche in the file room. She had perused the clippings herself while she printed them. Now, when Jan thought that she had spent as much time with her as she could take, Gail once again intruded into her territory.

"Sorry," she responded politely, but firmly, "that's my story." She assumed that the seasoned professional would understand that reporters, as a rule, did not give away their stories.

"Wasn't she a cheerleader?"

Jan laughed. "Those murders are not connected."

"They were both Oak Glen cheerleaders, shot once through the chest, after school, in their uniforms."

"Twenty years apart?"

Again, Gail was condescending. "That's the difference between you and me, Jan. I know a story when I see it. That is why I am here." She indicated her perfect ensemble. "And you are there." She wiped a smudge of dust from her colleague's cheap blouse.

Jan emptied the melted remnants of her milkshake onto Gail's silk blouse.

When a sweet thing like Grace Henderson gets killed in a quiet small town, the public gets nervous.

The father of a teenaged daughter away at her first year of college, Tad was so sickened to have to conduct an autopsy on Grace that he felt compelled to find out who killed the girl who had no reason for being on his examination table. That was why he had changed from his doctor's robes and dressed down into jeans and a polo shirt to go to Steubenville to seek out the orange-haired girl posing with Grace for the picture found in her purse. Steubenville, Ohio, was out of his jurisdiction. Murder investigations were not in his job description, but Tad believed that rules were made to be broken.

It was at the third bar frequented by young people that he spotted her. He guessed that he was on the right trail when he saw the name and logo of the establishment: Half-Moon. They matched the partial name and logo in the picture. He recognized the bartender as the bare-chested man hugging the two girls. In the late afternoon, the piece of beefcake was working his regular job of tending bar.

Since it was a school day, most of the regular patrons were home living their public lives. That didn't seem to have any significance for the girl with orange hair, who sat alone with her vodka and orange juice at the bar.

"Hello." Tad took a spot on the stool next to her. He gestured to the bartender for a root beer.

The girl looked over the attractive older man and decided

that he might be worth her while. "I've never seen you here before."

"First time."

"Ah, so you're a virgin?" she quipped.

"Not exactly."

As she took another sip of her drink, he observed a ring she wore on her right hand. The stone that resembled a ruby surrounded by rhinestones looked oversized. *Has to be a fake,* he thought, *like the orange hair.*

He sipped his soda. "I'm from Chester."

"Really?"

"I think we might both know someone."

"I don't know anyone from Chester."

"How about the late Grace Henderson?" He waited for her reaction.

It was slow to come. She asked defiantly, "Who are you?"

"Medical examiner." He showed her his badge. "Did you know that your friend was dead?" When she tried to slide off her stool away from him, he grabbed her arm and pulled her back.

"You have no authority here," she objected.

"One phone call to your police and I can have you taken into custody. Citizen's arrest."

"For what?"

Tad tapped her glass. "Underage drinking. You can talk to me here, or in the police station while we're waiting for your parents."

"Her ID says she's twenty-one, man," the bartender interjected.

Tad stood up. His attitude was sufficient to intimidate the man behind the bar.

"It's okay, Mitch." She turned to the doctor and scoffed at his threat of arrest. "My parents don't care. They're home getting drunk themselves."

"Then you can sit in a cell until they sober up enough to come pick you up." He pulled her alongside him toward the exit.

She yanked him back before jumping back up onto the stool. "What do you want to know?"

"Your name for one."

"Nicki. Nicki Samuels."

"How long had you known Grace?"

"I met her this summer. We met at the swimming pool at the resort in Newell. Her parents never let her do anything. So I invited her to come along with me to the clubs. She sneaked out after her parents were asleep, and I'd pick her up."

"And do what?"

"Hit the clubs. Play with the guys. Her parents didn't even let her date. We had a good time until she decided to go get herself pregnant."

"She got herself pregnant? Did anybody ever tell you girls that it takes two to get pregnant?"

"The dummy thought that Billy would marry her if she got knocked up."

"Billy who?"

"Billy Unger."

"How did Billy take the news that he was going to be a daddy?"

Nicki giggled. "He went ballistic, of course. He wanted her to get rid of it, but she wasn't about to do that."

"And so someone got rid of both her and the baby," Tad pointed out.

"He didn't kill her."

"What makes you so certain?"

"He was going to run away. He told me Saturday night. He's been working on something that is going to have a big payoff, and then he'll have enough money to take off where no one will ever find him."

"Did you tell Grace that her boyfriend was going to leave her high and dry?"

"It was none of my business. The little idiot thought the two of them were going to elope." Her sneer told him that she really didn't give a damn about the predicament the girl she had led into the nightlife was going to be left in.

"Who else would want to kill your friend?" Tad used the term "friend" loosely.

Nicki shrugged, and then took another gulp of her drink.

"She said I was a bitch." Heather Connor was explaining the reason for her fight with Grace to county prosecutor Joshua Thornton. She was the millennium version of her mother.

The former Margo Sweeney had graduated from high school with him.

The daughter of the bank vice president and a county commissioner, who were both active in the PTA, Margo managed to get herself onto the varsity cheerleading squad. Whereas the stereotype of cheerleaders used to be perky, pretty girls who aspire to make their high school experience the best it can be before studying husbandry in college, Margo's major field of study was causing trouble.

She was not as athletic or as pretty as the rest of the girls on the squad. She wore heavy cosmetics and dyed her hair bright red. To be kind, her figure was voluptuous. She dressed to accentuate her large breasts that she let fly during her cheers, much to the amusement of the adolescent boys.

Joshua disliked her cruel sense of humor. The butts of her jokes were those less fortunate than she. When he intervened, she would turn on him to make him the object of her ridicule. By their senior year, Margo split his inner circle into two camps:

his, who believed in being kind to their fellow students; and hers, who got their kicks by cutting down those they considered beneath them.

Joshua looked across the conference table in the courthouse interview room at Margo Sweeney, now Connor. With her polished, metropolitan lawyer perched at her side to defend her daughter, she smirked at him.

Her figure had ballooned to fat. Her breasts, which seemed to grow along with the rest of her figure, were encased in a bright dress with a plunging neckline. She still dyed her hair red and wore a hat like something you would see on the Queen of England.

Her real estate and development business was one of the biggest employers in the valley. For her daughter's interview with the county prosecuting attorney, Margo displayed her wealth like a king showing a rival country his weaponry. She wore jewels on every body part upon which they could be displayed.

In contrast to her client's brilliant appearance, her lawyer, Christine Watson, dressed in a black suit and was devoid of jeweled ornaments. She wore her short black hair slicked back.

Joshua had come up against Christine before in the short time he had been county prosecutor. She was a humorless professional who considered any show of femininity a revelation of weakness to be penetrated by the male enemy. He didn't know if Watson was married. She lacked so many of the qualities associated with feminine behavior that he found himself wondering if she was a lesbian.

Joshua studied Heather after she explained away her beef with Grace by claiming she had been upset to learn that the blue-eyed blonde had said an unkind word about her. "So you burst into the girls' locker room and tried to beat her up for telling someone that she thought you were a bitch?"

She wiggled her head from side to side. It was a gesture her peers adopted to use as a sign of strength, much in the way dogs let the hair on their back stand up on end right before a fight. "I wanted to talk to her about it. There's no law against talking."

Heather had her mother's cocky smile. She also used the same hair coloring. She wore her thick hair down to her waist in loose waves. Like Margo in high school, Heather wore heavy makeup and showed off her large breasts. She also displayed tattoos on each arm and one around her neck that resembled barbed wire.

Like mother, like daughter.

"There is a law against murder," he reminded the girl.

Sneering, she turned to her lawyer to return fire at their enemy.

"Josh," Christine said, "it was nothing more than a catfight. No one was hurt. The coach didn't even write it up."

"She started a fight because she heard from someone—" He turned to Heather and asked, "Who told you that Grace said you were a bitch?"

She answered with an exaggerated shrug, "I don't remember."

"It was upsetting enough to you that you got into a fight with Grace for having said it, but you don't remember the name of the person who told you she had said it?"

"If she had called me a bitch to my face I would have respected her for it."

He doubted it.

"Are we done here?" Heather asked her mother. It was an order for them to go. "There are other things I'd rather be doing."

"Yes, we are." After ordering her lawyer to end the interview, Margo stood up.

"No, we're not," Joshua objected.

"Yes, we are." She ushered her daughter to the door.

"Are you charging my client with anything?" Christine slapped her notepad shut and stood up. She tucked her pen in the inside breast pocket of her suit jacket.

"Obstruction of justice if she doesn't tell me where she was when Grace Henderson was killed."

Heather paused at the door. She rolled her eyes when she answered, "Let's see. Where was I Monday between four-thirty and five o'clock? Oh, yeah, I remember. I was fucking my boyfriend."

Without giving Joshua a name or place or phone number, Heather went out the door. Even with the sophistication he had developed in his travels around the world with all types of people, he was still shocked by her mother's lack of shock at her teenage daughter's announcement that she was having sex while one of her schoolmates was being killed.

"I guess that means Heather has an alibi and you have nothing." Margo snickered on her way out the door.

"Nice seeing you, Josh," Christine quipped while she moved toward the door to follow her clients.

"Wait a minute."

At the door, she turned to him. "Margo is right. You don't have anything against her daughter."

"Not yet." He draped a leg across the corner of the conference table. "My question is why are you defending Rex Rollins?"

"What's it to you?"

"Your clients are usually of a higher caliber than he is. He's been in court almost as much as I have and he always gets a public defender because he's broke, and right now he's unemployed."

"But he still has the right to the best defense possible."

"The best defense he can afford. Who's paying his bill?"

"That's none of your business."

CHAPTER FIVE

The next day, Joshua groaned when he and Seth Cavanaugh arrived at the Henderson home to find Gail Reynolds's sports car parked in the driveway. The detective and county prosecutor had arrived to search once again Grace's bedroom to look for evidence that would further connect her to Billy Unger and tell them where they might find their suspect.

The artist to whom Tad led the investigator had put the eagle on Grace's rear end and confirmed Nicki's statement about Billy and Grace's relationship. According to the tattooist, Billy brought her in and paid cash for the artwork. The artist thought her fake driver's license was real. Otherwise, he swore, he would never have broken the law by giving a minor a tattoo.

With two witnesses to claim Billy was her boyfriend, the authorities could assume he was the baby's father, and that made him their prime suspect. Joshua obtained a warrant to bring him in for questioning.

The problem was that no one knew where to find him, and time was running out. Sheriff Sawyer had heard a rumor from an informant on the street that Billy had something—most likely illegal—going down, after which he was planning to leave the area.

"Nice wheels." Seth Cavanaugh paused to admire the red sports car in the Henderson driveway.

Joshua pressed the doorbell on the front door. Martha Henderson was wiping her eyes with a tissue when she opened it.

He took a deep breath and expressed sympathy for her loss before asking if they could speak to her. As he stepped inside, he gestured for Seth to leave the driveway where he was studying the leather interior of Gail's car.

The living room looked like something out of a home decorator's magazine. The fireplace mantel was loaded with photographs of their daughter.

Gail sat in the chair across from the middle-aged couple who had lost their only child. Holding out a micro cassette recorder to capture every word that was uttered, she contorted her face into an expression of sympathy.

Sam Henderson told the prosecutor and detective, "She says that Grace's murder has the same MO as this other cheerleader, and that her murderer might be a serial killer. Is that true?"

"Excuse me." Joshua whirled around and ordered Seth to take over the interview. He then grabbed Gail by the arm and yanked her across the room and outside. "What the hell do you think you are doing?" He demanded to know when they were out of earshot.

"Your job, as always," was her answer.

"No. My job is to prosecute Grace's murderer. All you're doing is sensationalizing her murder for one of your books and upsetting these people with some wild theory."

"It's not a wild theory! Did you know that Tricia and Grace were related?" She elaborated, "Their mothers are cousins. That makes our victims second cousins."

He was incensed. "Gail! This is a small town. If you look far enough into anyone's genealogy you are going to find that we are all related in some way or another. Hell! A genetics expert could probably make a case for this valley being inbred. Now go home!"

"Josh, look at the MO! Both of them were cheerleaders. They were both wearing their uniforms when they were killed. They were both shot in the chest."

"You forgot that they were both blondes!" he added with a laugh. "Get a grip!" He ticked off on his fingers. "Two different guns. Tricia was killed at home. Grace was killed at the school. The gun was left at Tricia's crime scene. The gun was not left at Grace's."

"You said Tricia's crime scene. Are you admitting that she was murdered?"

"When I have time, I will look over the case file. I'm not saying I will reopen the case, but I will look."

"Want to make a bet on who solves the case first?"

"I don't consider murder to be a game."

"It's just an innocent bet between friends," she added, "or lovers."

"Go home and stay out of this investigation!" He opened her car door and ordered her inside.

She refused to move. "You can't tell me what to do, Joshua Thornton."

"Let me remind you that I am the prosecutor, and if you interfere any further with this investigation, then I will have you arrested for obstruction of justice."

With a scoff, she climbed into the car and turned on the engine. She raced at least ten miles over the speed limit down the street, rolled through the stop sign, and then turned left to make her way to Route 8.

"Damn fool is going to get herself killed," Joshua muttered to himself before he became aware that he was being watched. He scanned the windows of the houses around him until he spotted the two faces peering out at him from the second-story double window on the opposite side of the Hendersons' driveway.

The one face belonged to a woman with dark hair cut to her bare shoulders. She did not appear to be wearing anything more than a black brassiere over her overly endowed breasts. He could only guess at what she was wearing below the window frame. The man appeared bald. His fleshy chest was bare. Aware that they had been spied, he pulled the woman back from the window and closed the blinds.

Before he dismissed the incident, Joshua paused to take in the van in the driveway next door. It was a red van with the gold lettering "Tender Lawn" scrawled on the side.

"Hmm," he hummed.

"What is all this that I'm hearing about you reopening that case of that other cheerleader who died a while back?" Seth wrote the name in his notebook to hunt down the case file and evidence that Joshua had requested he send to the prosecutor's office. "And why is Gail Reynolds so interested in her? I doubt if any of the physical evidence is still around. The case was closed as a suicide. After so long, the department cleans house and gets rid of the evidence from closed cases."

"But there has to be something in our files," Joshua replied.

Unlike the watering holes Joshua used to frequent with his colleagues in the big cities before his return to home, Dora's was not furnished in oak and trimmed with antique brass. The locally owned establishment featured down-home comfort with tables in need of polishing and wood floors that needed another coat of varnish. The patrons would yell greetings across the lounge to each other, and the favorite drink was cold beer or Jim Beam, rather than martinis and cognac.

In Washington, the clientele, accustomed to diligent service, would have abandoned Dora's years before. Joshua was unsure why the place remained the hangout for New Cumberland's courthouse crowd, what with the uncivil attitude of the head waitress, Wanda, a bleached blonde in her twenties.

The two men had taken a corner booth from which they could observe the comings and goings of their colleagues.

"What do you want?" Wanda stood before them with a hand on her wide hip. Her expression was not unlike that of a mother who caught her children making a mess after she had cleaned the house.

"Draft," Seth said.

Joshua ordered a beer while he studied the menu of appetizers scrawled on a chalkboard hanging over the bar. "Can I have the chips with guacamole instead of salsa?"

Her hand flew from where it was perched to point a finger between his eyes. "No, you can't." Before he could find the words to argue, she was on her way back to the kitchen to get the beer and tortilla chips with salsa, not guacamole.

After she delivered their order, Joshua recalled his youth, something that had become a daily occurrence. "Tricia was supposed to graduate with me."

"She was a blonde cheerleader and was wearing her uniform at the time she was killed." Seth raised his eyebrows. "Interesting," he muttered when the same theory that Gail submitted to the Hendersons crossed his mind.

"Chuck Delaney was the sheriff at the time. He wasn't exactly on the straight and narrow." Joshua sighed. "I never thought of it before now. The police said it was suicide, so I figured they knew something I didn't. That's why I want to see the case file."

"There had to be some grounds to rule it a suicide."

"Because Tricia and her boyfriend broke up the day she died." Joshua shook his head. "Knowing what I know now, I don't think so."

"You mean because of Grace Henderson?" Seth scoffed. "Nah! Reynolds is off her rocker. Unger blew Henderson away because he didn't want to deal with a kid."

Joshua swallowed and chewed his lip. He was not comfortable with how quickly Seth had concluded the case against Billy Unger before speaking to the suspect. "There's no connection between these two girls and their deaths. In the matter of Tricia committing suicide, statistically, women commit suicide with pills—"

"Not a hundred percent."

"Tricia looked good and she knew it. If she were to kill herself, she wouldn't do it by putting a big hole in her chest." Joshua sat forward while he thought of more arguments. "Plus, she displayed no suicidal tendencies, especially the day she died. I was there when she broke it off with her boyfriend—"

Joshua took a sip of his beer while he recalled that last time he saw Tricia Wheeler.

It was the beginning of his last year of high school. Joshua and his friends had gathered together in an auditorium called "the little theater" located around the corner from the cafeteria to socialize during their lunch hour. The students took up two camps in the seats with the center aisle acting as the dividing line between them. Those who were not socially elite would sit on his side of the auditorium where they were safe from Margo and her friends on the other side of the aisle.

The final split of the class of 1985's upper crust resulted from a civil war waged on the varsity cheerleading squad.

Cheerleading captain Tricia Wheeler and football team captain Randy Fine had been dating since the junior prom. With their good looks and popularity, they became one of the royal couples, second only to Joshua and Beth.

With the start of the new school year, Randy began cheating on his steady girlfriend with Margo Sweeney. When Margo declared her intention to break the couple up, the cheerleading squad split down the middle.

The battle spilled onto the football field during the game between Oak Glen and Weirton. Quarterback Joshua Thornton was so wrapped up in trying to pull the team from where it lagged behind by three points that he didn't notice the mutiny on the cheerleading squad along the sidelines.

Captain Tricia would call a cheer and start to lead her squad, only to have her rival call another and lead her cohorts in it. The result was one half of the varsity cheerleaders performing one cheer, while the other half would be chanting another.

Their coach, the pep squad, and the fans in the stands watched the battle in confusion. The sponsor was furious. Before the first quarter of the game was over, the cheerleaders were ordered off the field and replaced with the junior varsity and freshman squads. Suspended for the fiasco, they were ordered to sit in their uniforms on the sidelines while the junior varsity and freshman cheerleaders led the pep club for the next game, which was scheduled for the next week.

Tricia Wheeler died four days before that game took place.

The last time he saw her, Joshua was the only male sitting with girlfriend Beth and her friend in the back of the little theater in the midst of girlish talk and laughter.

They were chatting away about the goings on at a party that the three of them had gone to on Saturday night. An unspoken element of that night was that Randy had begged out. He claimed that something had come up. As had become her custom, Tricia went to the party with Joshua and Beth. Not one of them had the nerve to voice it, but they all knew that Randy had gone out with Margo.

When there was a break in the conversation as the three friends ate their lunches, Joshua became aware of Margo's voice across the aisle. ". . . Randy and I were groping around in the dark looking for my panties. We were laughing so hard that I thought I was going to bust my gut."

The hurt in Tricia's eyes was unmistakable.

He raised his voice an octave to drown Margo out. "Hey, Tad is giving a party this Friday. How about if the three of us go after the game?"

Margo answered, "Randy's parents are going away. We're going to spend the whole weekend together."

"Shut up!" Beth whirled around in her seat to order the girl seated across the aisle from them to cease her taunting. Joshua motioned for her to be quiet, but Margo had already picked up the gauntlet.

"Make me."

Tricia challenged her for the first time since the war was declared. "Just because you're a slut, doesn't mean you have to advertise it. Some of us have higher standards."

"Keep saying it, and maybe you'll convince yourself that it was your choice to give Randy up, instead of the other way around."

Tricia turned her back to her.

Margo resumed picking away. "He told me that it is like making a choice between a diamond and a lump of coal."

Tricia's jaws worked while she ground her teeth.

Encouraged by her allies, Margo continued, "You do know the difference between a diamond and coal, don't you? A diamond is exciting while all coal does is lie there."

"Margo, eat your lunch!" Joshua ordered.

"Eat shit!" she snapped back. "You guys act like you're so high and mighty. Then, you get your noses out of joint because the rest of us are having fun with each other." She stepped up to the aisle but didn't cross it. To do so would be to go into enemy territory.

Tricia faced Joshua, who sat with an arm around her shoulders. She kept her eyes focused to the wall behind him.

"That's why Randy has been spending so much time with me," Margo taunted her. "I'm woman enough to know how to have fun, and you don't even know how to play the game, let alone where the bases are."

He stood up to his full height. "Margo, go back to your side of the theater before I put you there."

She ignored the warning. "Randy and I have both gone around all the bases. As a matter of fact, he's hit a home run every single time." She giggled. "You're still in the little league, while I'm playing the majors."

"As the whole team will testify," Tricia shot over her shoulder.

"At least I'm not alone on the bench. That is where you'll remain for the whole season with all the rest of the old maids."

Tricia whirled around and delivered a slap across Margo's face with the speed and intensity of a whip. She retaliated with a slap that only clipped the tip of her rival's nose before Tricia pulled her to the floor by her hair. Before Joshua could jump in to stop them, the two girls were screaming and writhing like cats tearing at each other with their claws.

Randy Fine, the center of the triangle, appeared from where Joshua did not know.

Tricia was on top of Margo when Joshua picked her up by the waist and yanked her back to their side of the auditorium. Randy lifted Margo up off the floor with both arms around her waist. Her breasts looked like two water balloons spilling over his arms while he held her back. Both girls strained and kicked to grab at her opponent.

Randy attempted to alleviate the tension with laughter. "What's going on here?"

Tricia snarled at him. "Oh, Randy, please! Like you don't know." She freed herself from Joshua's hold and smoothed her cheerleading uniform that she had worn for yearbook pictures that day—the same one she would die in.

"Ladies, please! There's enough of me to go around!"

Margo expressed amusement along with him. She had scored a big success by making the reserved Tricia lose it in front of all their friends.

"Go to hell, Randy!"

There was silence within the room.

Joshua had never heard Tricia curse before. The words didn't sound right coming out of her mouth.

Randy was the most speechless of all. "What?" he finally gasped out.

Her voice was low and steady as she stepped up to him and yanked the blue class ring that hung on a gold chain from around his neck. "Go to hell." Tricia tore off his ring that she wore on a chain around her neck and tossed it into the air. Too shocked to move, Randy didn't make the catch.

The ring landed on the floor with a thump.

"Whoa!" Joshua heard breathed from more than one of the witnesses.

There was only silence in the auditorium when Tricia turned around and gently pushed Joshua out of her way to leave. The last time he saw her she was walking tall and proud out of the little theater's doors.

He saw Doug Barlow attempt to speak to her when she passed him while he held the door open for her, but she kept on going without saying a word to anyone. Before following her, Doug glanced at the students who could not miss the brush-off.

All cockiness gone, Randy took in his peers who were looking at him with a mixture of satisfaction that he got what he had coming, and pity for Tricia's public rejection of him. He gave a nervous laugh, which he had hoped to come off as self-confident, before snatching his ring from the floor and running after her.

Margo was smoothing her cheerleading uniform. She declared herself the victor of the war. "I guess that's over."

"In more ways than one," Joshua heard.

He realized it was Gail Reynolds's voice. She had been sitting in her usual seat towards the front of the theater with members of the student government and the newspaper staff. Jan sat with this group.

"It's like watching Diana dumping Prince Charles," he heard Gail announce.

Jan disagreed. "More like Jackie Kennedy dumping John after catching him with one bimbo too many."

Twenty hours later, Joshua was told that Tricia had committed suicide by firing a bullet through her heart.

"Who is that?" Seth Cavanaugh asked.

Joshua was startled to see Tori Brody at the bar. The eyes of every man in the lounge took in her figure encased in a bright blue sweater dress. Even though the dress had a high collar that came up around her neck and the skirt fell down to her knees, she was still seductive.

Her feminine colleagues eyed the addition to their crowd with scorn at her open sensuality, which they deemed as an affront in their battle to be accepted as unisex equals in a man's world.

Joshua answered his question. "She's a part-time lawyer with Ruth Majors."

"She's a lawyer?"

Wanda came out from behind the bar to deliver a beer mug filled to the brim to their booth. Some of the brew splashed on the table when she plopped it in front of Joshua. "Here. It's from her." She tossed her head with displeasure in Tori's direction.

The defense attorney raised her glass of wine in a toast to the prosecutor. Joshua's face reddened when he felt every eye in the joint now turn to him. He picked up the beer mug, raised it in a halfhearted toast to her, and then took a sip. She sashayed across the bar to join them.

"What were you talking so seriously about?" She took a seat

in the booth next to him.

"Murder." Joshua was aware of the warmth of her thigh against his. "Tori, have you met Seth Cavanaugh? He's the chief of detectives with the sheriff's department."

The investigator welcomed her. "I guess we're going to be on opposite sides."

"I guess so."

Seth's cell phone rang. He snatched it from the case on his hip. "Cavanaugh here."

Joshua tried not to look at her, which was difficult. He felt the heat of her body pressed against his side in the booth.

"What murder were you talking about?" she asked in a low voice so as not to disturb Seth during his call. "That high school girl?"

"Tricia Wheeler's."

"Tricia?" she responded. "Ah, I heard that Gail Reynolds was back in town digging that up. I thought she killed herself."

"Maybe. Maybe not."

Seth hung up and got up from the table. "I have to go."

Joshua could tell by his manner that it was urgent. Before he could dismiss the detective from their meeting, Seth was out the door in a dead run.

"I can't stay long." He realized as soon as the words were out of his mouth that his tone was abrupt. He sounded rude.

Tori didn't seem to notice. "Who killed her?"

"We don't know. I have the authority to reopen the case. With Gail in town going around asking questions, I have to, or it will look like I'm covering something up." He eyed her. Now that the conversation had turned to murder, he felt more comfortable to be with her. "Did you know her?"

She shook her head with amusement. "Tricia and I did not run with the same crowd. I wasn't even there to see that famous last fight between her and that bitch cheerleader—What was her name?"

"Margo Sweeney. It's now Connor."

"Everyone called me a slut, but she slept around, too."

"Your mother wasn't vice president at the bank and your father was not a commissioner."

"I heard she screwed every player on the football team. Did you hump her? You were the quarterback."

"No." He returned to the topic of their conversation. "Do you have any idea who could have killed Tricia?"

Tori responded with a question, "Why do you care so much about finding Tricia Wheeler's killer?"

Joshua started. "Because she was my friend and she did not deserve to die so young."

"Was she your girlfriend?"

"I was dating someone else." He turned in his seat to observe her profile. He saw a spark of jealousy in her eye. "Why do you ask?"

"I had the impression that she was more than just your friend."

"You were wrong."

"Pity—for her." She purred, "Before you go looking for Tricia Wheeler's murderer, want to come take a look at my place?" Her hand was on his thigh. She placed it close to his crotch.

Joshua took her hand into his and placed it on top of the table. "Thanks for the offer, but I have to get home and help my son with his algebra." He gestured for her to get up and let him out of the booth.

"Where is J.J.?"

"He went to the Mountaineer Inn to put in his application." Tracy turned off the oven.

"Application for what?" Joshua opened the oven door and

picked at a piece of crispy skin hanging at the edge of a chicken breast before returning to the table to watch Donny work the math problem he had ordered him to attempt on his own.

"He got wind of a job opening up for a personal trainer at their spa," Tracy answered. "They pay really good, too."

"How's that?" Donny shoved the notebook over to show his father.

Before Joshua could examine his work, the phone rang. It was Sheriff Curt Sawyer telling him that he needed to return to New Cumberland.

"We got Billy Unger and he's screaming for a lawyer," the sheriff said. "Ruth is sending Tori Brody out here to defend him."

The news was enough to interrupt Joshua's check on his son's algebra homework. "Tori is kind of green to be defending a murder suspect, don't you think?"

"Ruth took the bigger fish. She's handling Walt Manners. My boys got him and his whole gang, seven in all including Unger, for attempted robbery, resisting arrest, and attempted abduction. They tried to rob an armored car at the Mountaineer Inn. Deputy Hockenberry picked up a lead about the robbery going down from one of his sources in Steubenville."

"You nailed Manners." Joshua was pleased. "Cool!"

Walt Manners was bad news. It was easy for Joshua to assume that he was the brains of the holdup. Not yet thirty years old, he had been arrested and convicted twice for armed robbery and burglary. This arrest would be his third strike, which was why the public defender herself was already on hand for his defense. A conviction would mean mandatory life in prison.

Curt was equally proud. "I wish I could say it went down without a hitch."

"What happened?"

"Manners took a hostage. A young woman. There was a

standoff and he tried to get away in a white van that was parked near the hotel's entrance."

Joshua groaned at the thought of the media response to an attempted arrest by the county sheriff's department that ended in a hostage situation. "Was anyone hurt?"

"Manners got a broken wrist. The kid who was driving the van he tried to steal saw what was going down and hid in the back with a tire iron. When Manners climbed in, he swatted him good. Manners dropped the gun and his hostage made a run for it. My men swooped in and picked him up."

"Sounds like a smart young man who took Manners down with a tire iron."

"Like father, like son," Sheriff Sawyer laughed. "It was Joshua Thornton, Jr."

Joshua Thornton, Senior was not so amused.

"Billy was carrying a thirty-eight when we caught him," Seth Cavanaugh announced when Joshua came through the doors at the sheriff's office. "We've got him red-handed for armed robbery and resisting arrest." He fell in step with the prosecutor.

Joshua jogged up the stairs towards the interrogation room. "Is the lab checking the gun to see if it's the murder weapon?"

"As we speak." Seth trotted up the stairs behind him. "Not only did we catch him with the gun, but guess what he was wearing?" Before the prosecutor could answer, he responded to his own question. "A black bandanna, dark wrap-around glasses, and a trench coat with a tear in it. I sent the coat to the lab to see if they can get a match to the hunk of material we took off the fence at the Henderson murder."

"Good!"

"We also picked up six other guys. One is Walt Manners," Seth added with a chuckle. "Guess I earned my paycheck tonight."

Joshua stopped at the top of the stairs.

He had told himself on the way back to New Cumberland that he would not get into a fight with Seth about letting the ambush of the gang of robbers get so out of hand that Walt Manners was able to take a hostage and put his son in equal danger. When Joshua reached him on his cell phone, J.J. swore that he had been in no danger. That was little comfort to him. His son would never have admitted it if he was.

The detective's cockiness made him change his mind.

Joshua turned around on the steps. "How was it that my seventeen-year-old son apprehended a sociopath like Manners in a parking lot filled with deputies under your supervision?"

Seth's smile dropped. "Your kid was lucky he didn't get his head blown off. He stepped in where he did not belong."

"He was minding his own business filling out a job application in our van when Manners took that woman hostage! It was your job to make sure no innocent bystanders were in the area while making this arrest."

Seth shouted, "I had everything under control."

Before Joshua could respond, deep laughter erupted up the stairs from behind him. He whirled around to find Deputy Pete Hockenberry chortling so hard that his beer belly shook. "Sure! You had everything under control!" He directed his sarcasm at the lieutenant from over Joshua's shoulder.

Seth's face filled with rage.

"He froze," Pete announced.

"I did not!"

"I had Manners in my sights after he nabbed the lady. I could have taken him out, but Cavanaugh refused to give the order. I asked—"

"You could have hit a bystander!" Seth tried to reach around Joshua to grab at the deputy, who was delighting in his failure.

"You were going to let him get away! That woman would not

have lived through the night if J.J.—a kid!—hadn't have nailed him!"

Seth charged.

Joshua stumbled on the stairs before regaining his balance and shoving Seth up against the wall in the stairwell. "Why didn't you clear the parking lot when you went in for the bust?"

"I ordered him to clear the area." The detective pointed at his subordinate.

"You did not," Pete said.

Joshua blocked Seth's attempt to punch the officer.

Still laughing at the detective's blunder, Deputy Pete Hockenberry continued on his way down the stairs and out the door.

"You blew it," Joshua said when he released the detective. "You put innocent citizens, including my own son, in danger."

"It wasn't my fault! Those rent-a-cops that Sawyer has working in this department were supposed to clear the area!"

"You were in charge, Cavanaugh! That makes it your fault!"

"Hey, I got Manners!"

"Wrong! J.J. got him!"

Tori Brody and Billy Unger were in deep discussion when the prosecutor and detective came into the interrogation room. Since it was the defense attorney doing the talking, Joshua ran the interrogation.

Billy was the youngest of Walt Manners's gang of hoodlums. His sandy-colored, waist-length hair was tied back in a ponytail. He unbuttoned his wrinkled, black shirt down to his navel to display an assortment of gold chains that hung around his neck. In doing so, he advertised his association with Grace Henderson. The eagle tattoo that took up his muscular chest was a duplicate of the one he had paid to have etched on her buttocks.

Joshua was impressed with how Tori was able to shift her

demeanor when it came to business. Everything changed about her. Even the way she held her body took on a professional attitude.

"So, Billy," the prosecutor greeted the suspect when he came into the room. "I heard that you went to pick up a bank deposit tonight that didn't belong to you."

"My client was riding along with some friends, who decided to commit this robbery," Tori countered. "He had no idea what was going down." When the detective scoffed, she asked, "Did you see him actually participate in this robbery?"

"He had a gun aimed at the driver of the armored car," Seth responded.

"His friends coerced him into it."

"Why don't we talk about Grace Henderson?" Joshua suggested.

"Never met her," Billy said.

"Then why did you buy her a tattoo?"

"I didn't."

"The tattoo artist picked your picture out of a photo lineup. Another witness says you went ballistic when she told you that she was pregnant with your baby. Why would you go ballistic over a stranger getting pregnant?"

Billy looked at Tori, who defended him, "That doesn't mean he killed her."

"She was killed with a thirty-eight, which was what he had on him when he was picked up tonight." Joshua added, "A witness says the killer was wearing a black trench coat, black bandanna, and wrap-around sunglasses. The same outfit he had on tonight."

"So did the rest of my friends," Billy retorted.

"But they didn't get her pregnant."

"Are you sure? Grace slept with a lot of guys."

"Give us some of your DNA and prove that you didn't get

her pregnant."

There was a knock on the door. Seth stepped outside and left the prosecutor to continue the interview.

"I didn't kill her," Billy sneered.

"What were you doing at the time Grace was killed?" Joshua asked him.

"When was that?" Tori wanted to know.

"Approximately five o'clock on Monday, the twenty-seventh."

Seth opened the door and gestured for Joshua to join him in the hall. He could see that the detective's bubble had been burst.

"It's not the gun," Seth told him once they were alone in the corridor.

"What?" Joshua hoped that he had misunderstood.

"The thirty-eight Unger had on him was not the murder weapon."

"So unless Murphy can identify him, we can't place him at the scene when Grace was killed."

Neither of the men was optimistic about Murphy's ability to pick Billy out of a lineup. "Every one of those guys looked alike in those trench coats, sunglasses, and bandannas," Seth told him.

"What else have you got?"

"We have a witness who says they were seeing each other. The tattooist says Unger brought her in and paid for the tattoo on her butt. We might be able to get something on that tear in the trench coat, but that will take some time."

"If his DNA proves that he's the father of her baby, then we can prove motive. In the meantime, let's get him in a lineup and see what Murphy says when he sees him."

"We still have him on armed robbery," Seth said.

The prosecutor agreed with a nod of his head. "That's enough to hold him until we can make a case for murder."

Joshua put on his poker face and stepped back into the interrogation room. "How are we doing?" he asked Tori.

She grinned up at him from where she sat next to her client. "My client has an alibi."

"What is it?"

"He was with his other girlfriend. Heather Connor."

It was the middle of the night that felt more like winter than fall and Joshua was absorbed with the theory of how one act, one touch, one word could change the path of fate for those around you. He had parked his Corvette in the garage in the corner of the backyard and was making his way up the cobblestone path to his house when he heard movement in the shadows.

Braced to defend himself, he stopped and listened.

"Josh," he heard his name whispered.

"Jan?" He squinted at the form by the hedges.

"Were you expecting Jan?" Gail stepped out into the light from the yard lamp. She was dressed in a black trench coat and wore a black fedora on her head: the stereotypical image of a woman of intrigue.

Joshua stepped backwards. "What are you doing here? It's after one."

"Yes, it is. What were you doing out so late?"

He started to tell her that he was at the sheriff's office, when the question flashed through his mind, "Why are you asking?"

"Because I care about you, Josh. It's a dangerous world out there." She was gazing up at the full moon over their heads. "Middle of the night, anything can happen. In the dark, you can't even tell who your friends are."

He cocked his head at her. He couldn't see her face, but he could tell that she was in a solemn state. "Gail, are you all right?"

"I am now that I'm here with you." She reached out and

brushed her hand across his cheek. "You're a father, Josh."

He smelled the wine on her breath. "You're drunk." He brushed her hand away.

"Still the Puritan." She smiled. "That's one of those things that I both hate and love about you." She staggered. "You have such high morals."

He caught her by the arm to keep her from falling to the ground. "I'm taking you home."

Gail almost fell into the passenger seat of the Corvette. Her black hat fell off her head and landed in her lap. Joshua was aware of her eyes on him during the drive out toward the state line. He recalled that Tad had told him that she'd rented the Marshall house. He had to lift her out of the car and hold her on her feet to guide her inside the house through the front door that he found unlocked.

"Where's the bedroom?" he asked her.

Gail giggled and pointed down the hall.

With his arms around her, Joshua took her to the room at the end of the hallway. In the dark, he was unable to determine if the house was neatly kept or not. He pushed the door open with his hip and tossed her onto the bed. He threw her fedora into a corner of the darkened room.

Gail grabbed him by his jacket when she fell back onto the bed. In her drunken state, she was unable to keep her grasp and fumbled for something with which to pull him down with her. She scraped her fingernails across his neck.

With a yelp, Joshua pulled back. He felt a trickle of blood from the wound she had left.

"Oh, Josh, can't you stay with me just for a little bit?" She clutched his hand and held it against her breast.

"I have to go home." He pulled away.

"But, Josh—"

He rushed from the room.

She was calling to him when he collided with the coffee table in the living room in the dark. He heard and felt papers swoosh to the floor. A glass clinked against a bottle.

Cursing, he rubbed his bruised shins. When his foot kicked something cylindrically shaped, he felt it roll away from him toward the sofa. In the dark, he gathered the papers together and stacked them back on the table. A three-ring binder lay upside down on the floor. He turned it over. His fingertips brushed across the rough texture of newspaper glued to the pages. He concluded that it was her portfolio.

The thud of footsteps in the hallway frightened Joshua with the thought that she had gotten up to come after him. He dropped the binder on top of the stack of folders and papers and rushed to the door. Pausing only long enough to turn the button on the doorknob to lock the door, he rushed from Gail's house and home to his own bed.

It was two o'clock in the morning before the pretty young barmaid locked up the State Line Lounge. Rita was ready to go home. She hated closing the bar. She was always conscious of anyone who might be lurking around to rape her before shooting her brains out as she had seen numerous times in recent movies at the mall. Hugging her purse under her arm with her hand on the handgun her father had given her for protection, she slammed the back door shut and locked it.

Rita saw the old beat-up truck sitting alone by the garbage bin at the corner of the parking lot. It looked like there was a man inside.

She took out her gun and hurriedly got into her car. After her doors were locked, she studied the truck and its occupant.

He made no move for her.

Why was he sitting there at two in the morning? Maybe he was in trouble. He seemed to be passed out. It was not uncommon in the bar business for a drunken patron to fall asleep in his car.

It was hard to tell because the windows were dirty. From where she sat, it looked like mud splattered across the windshield.

Rita remained in the safety of her car and took a look inside the truck on her way out of the parking lot.

She could see that the side window was shattered. That did not concern her. Her customers' vehicles were often beaten up.

The reddish-brown splatters across the windshield caught her curiosity. She had thought it was mud, but it was too red to be mud.

Clutching her gun, Rita opened her door and stood, with one foot in her car, to peer through the window into the cab.

It took her a minute to ascertain if she was seeing what she thought she was looking at. Her mouth opened in horror, but the shock constricted her throat so that the scream could not escape. When it managed to work its way past her beating heart and the lump in her throat, she could be heard at the service station on the other side of the Pennsylvania border.

CHAPTER SIX

Dr. Tad MacMillan took off his motorcycle helmet, ran his fingers through his hair, and yawned. He climbed off his Harley-Davidson and took his medical examiner's bag from the travel compartment. Suppressing a second yawn, he put on a pair of evidence gloves from the bag.

State forensics officers and county sheriff's deputies had already descended onto the State Line Lounge parking lot and roped it off. Lights had been erected to aid in seeing the crime scene. Police were labeling and photographing the smallest evidence. The morgue attendants were waiting for Tad to do his thing so that they could take the body to the morgue.

He was the last one to arrive.

Lieutenant Seth Cavanaugh stepped away from his car where he was talking to one of the deputies and crossed over to the medical examiner, who was checking to make sure he had film in his camera. "Sorry to interrupt your date." His tone was sarcastic.

"Where's the body?" Tad hung the camera around his neck.

Seth led him over to the truck and gestured for him to take a look inside.

"Who is it?" The doctor set his medical bag down.

"Rex Rollins."

Tad sucked in his breath and looked through the shattered window.

The top of Rex's head was splattered across the back of the

passenger seat and side and front window. His mouth hung open. What was left of his head rested against the headrest and was tilted towards his right shoulder. His unseeing eyes looked up to the roof of the truck as if he were looking to the heavens for help.

Tad snapped picture after picture while he reported what he saw. "Looks like two shots." He glanced at the shattered window. "Came through the driver's side window. Hit him square between the eyes. That one took off the top of his head and exited out. Betcha you'll find the slug in here somewhere. Big caliber. A forty-five at least." He turned the head to examine what was left of the back. "Second shot was in the mouth. He was already dead. We have overkill here."

He noticed the gun on the floor of the truck where it had landed between Rex's feet. "Did you see the gun here?"

Seth followed the invisible line from the end of Tad's finger to the floor of the truck where the revolver rested. It was concealed under the cover of darkness. "Yeah, I saw it," he lied.

Tad felt the body with his palm flat on the bloody corpse. It was cooling down fast in the chilly night air. "Been dead approximately two hours. Bar had to be open when it happened."

"Yeah. The barmaid who found him said the music was up and people talking. You know how bars are on weekends."

"No one saw or heard anything." Tad spied a pretty blonde-haired woman sitting in the backseat of a patrol car. She was sipping coffee from a convenience store across the street. "Is she the one who found the body?"

"Yep," Seth chuckled. "Scared the hell out of her."

The medical examiner gestured to the attendants waiting nearby. "He's ready to go."

"When will I get the report?"

"After I'm done with the autopsy." Tad put his camera back in the case and zipped it shut.

"This time around make it only one copy for the sheriff's department. Thornton doesn't need to be in on this until I'm ready to make the arrest."

"Give it a rest, Cavanaugh." He ducked under the yellow police tape more to end the conversation than to greet the woman in the back of the patrol car. "Hi, Rita."

Startled, the barmaid splashed her coffee on her white button-down shirt. Tad apologized and handed her a tissue from inside his medical bag. "I didn't know you were working here at the State Line."

"Not anymore." She stepped out of the back of the car. "I'm quitting. It was bad enough serving drinks to a bunch of drunks always looking down my blouse and telling wild lies, but this—" She pointed at the truck a few feet away and shuddered.

Tad held her coffee cup in order to free her hands to mop the spill on her bosom. "Can't say your mother didn't warn you. She didn't want you working in places like this. That's why she broke her back to get money to send you to school."

"I know." Rita sighed. "Mom is always right."

"What happened?"

"What does it look like? Someone blew away a drunk." She dug through her purse.

"Was Rex one of your customers tonight?" he asked.

"Yeah, he was already smashed when he came in."

"What time was that?"

"About midnight." She took a pack of cigarettes with a lighter tucked inside the wrapper from her purse. "I've seen him since I first started working here. He was always shooting his mouth off about how important he was. Then, Margo Connor fired him and he didn't show up as much. Some of her crew hangs out here and I guess he was embarrassed. I don't know." With trembling fingers, she stuck the tip of a cigarette between her lips.

"But he came back tonight." Tad lit her cigarette. "Did he talk to anyone?"

"Just me." She took a drag from the cigarette and blew the smoke out of the corner of her mouth. "Lucky me. Nut."

"Why do you say he was a nut?"

She shook her head with a laugh. "He said that he had just finished writing a book—like I didn't know that he was a loser. Everyone in Chester knows Rex Rollins. If brains were dynamite, he didn't have enough powder to blow his nose, and he's telling me loud enough for everyone to hear that he was the next Ernest Hemingway." She scoffed. "Give me a break. He didn't even leave me a tip."

"I guess everyone had a good laugh when he said that he had written a book," Tad smiled.

"Yeah." She flicked the ashes from her cigarette to the ground and pawed at them with the toe of her athletic shoe.

"Did he tell you what his book was about?"

"He said it was about the wicked witch of Chester."

Tad squinted. "The wicked witch of Chester? Did he say if it was fiction or—"

"He said it was a true story about this wicked witch who got away with murder. Then he laughed and said that he was the only one who knew her secret."

"How did the customers in the bar react when he said that?"

"Everyone laughed at him."

Tad felt sympathy for the dead man who spent most of his life being the butt of jokes. "Who all was in the bar tonight while he was there?"

"Only the guys who worked construction for Margo Connor. They were all playing pool when Rex came in and started talking about how famous he was going to be. You should have heard him." Rita paused to visualize the inside of the bar while sucking on the end of her cigarette. She flicked another ash to the gravel in the parking lot and pawed it into the gravel. "Herb Duncan was sitting at the end of the bar. He isn't one of Margo's crew, but he's a regular. He came in right after Rex did. I remember because I served him a Coors Light after I waited on Rex. He paid for it with a twenty-dollar bill and gave me a five-dollar tip. He usually has me put his drinks on his tab, which he paid up tonight. By the way, Rex was three months behind on his tab. I guess the boss is going to have to eat that, which will put him in a foul mood."

"Did Herb hear about Rex's book?"

"Everyone who was there tonight heard about it. Rex was not exactly keeping it a secret. Herb had himself a good laugh right along with everyone else. He said that Rex was going to get himself killed." She quickly explained, "Because he was so drunk." She dropped the last of her cigarette to the ground and stubbed it out with her toe. "Can I go home now?"

Tad looked around for a deputy to inquire if they needed any more information from her. "Did anyone leave the bar right after Rex?"

She shrugged. "I don't know. I was in the back getting a case of Miller when he left."

The attendants were carrying Rex's body, encased in a black body bag, to the van for transport to Tad's lab.

At the sight of the body bag, Rita grasped his forearm and shuddered. "Do you have any idea who did this?"

"No, but from what you tell me, I guess the first suspect we need to question is the wicked witch of Chester."

"Haven't you read the newspapers or seen the news?" Sheriff Raymond Stains did not try to contain his disgust with the call made to his home in Parkersburg, West Virginia, on a Saturday morning. He was still in his bathrobe and had not yet finished his first cup of coffee. If Joshua had called fifteen minutes earlier he would have roused him out of bed. "The Quincy murder was the biggest crime that Parkersburg has suffered since I've been sheriff. Seth Cavanaugh had the intuition and know-how to find the evidence to nail the killers."

"I know about the Quincy case. What did Cavanaugh do before that? How good was he before he appeared on Larry King?" Joshua heard silence from the other end of the phone.

"Why do you want to know?" the sheriff finally asked.

"You didn't even know who he was until that case came along."

Sheriff Stains responded with a lecture about how he could not possibly take the time to get to know every one of his deputies. Seth Cavanaugh had to be exceptional or he never would have had the know-how to put together how the Quincy brothers had killed their parents for their inheritance and hidden the evidence. This was the mark of a superior detective.

Joshua hung up the phone, sat back in the chair behind his desk in his study, and examined the detective's resume. Nothing stood out. It was the resume of an average cop. He had been to the state police academy but graduated with an average class ranking. His only exceptional talent was a ninety-eight percentile in marksmanship.

He laid the resume on his desk. Someone had to know what Seth's pedigree really was.

If it weren't for the media attention for solving the Quincy murders and the county commissioner's insistence that he be hired for the position of chief of detectives, Sheriff Sawyer would have promoted Deputy Pete Hockenberry.

Joshua reviewed the list of references on Seth's application. Sheriff Stains was at the top of the list. Judging by their jobs, he guessed the rest were friends. He also noted that his partner was not on the list. He dug through the personnel folder until he found the name and phone number of Deputy Kenneth Hanson.

The phone rang several times before the deputy sheriff from Parkersburg answered. Joshua introduced himself and explained that he was doing a background check on his former partner. "How would you rate him as an investigator?"

Deputy Ken Hanson responded with a sarcastic laugh. "Did you notice that he did not list me as a reference? That was for a reason."

"The news reported that he broke the Quincy case."

"If it weren't for me, he would have gotten himself shot when he tripped over those shotguns."

"But—"

"The only reason Seth got all the press he did about his role—if that is even what you want to call it—in solving the Quincy murders was because a local television reporter he was sleeping with bought every story he would spin about his investigative genius." Kenneth added, "Between her creativity and his pretty blue eyes, he became a star."

Joshua asked, "Are you saying that you would not recommend him as a detective?"

"Let's just say he's not my problem anymore. Now he's yours. Good luck."

Perplexed by Hanson's referral, or lack thereof, Joshua sat back in his desk chair and swiveled in the direction of the window to gaze out at the lawn. The leaves on the hedge were turning brown and falling to reveal the red of a sports car on the other side.

Gail's car.

He had noticed it parked in the alley behind the house when he woke up that morning. He recognized it from the Henderson home. He checked the time and concluded that it was late enough to call her. When she did not answer, he left her a voice mail.

"Gail. Josh. How are you feeling? Listen, your car is parked behind my place and I can't find your keys. I assume you have them. Give me a call if you need me to give you a ride to pick it up. My cell number is 304-555-4684."

"Take your time," Joshua advised his son.

He almost hoped Murphy wouldn't recognize Billy in the lineup. Then, he wouldn't have to put him on the stand during Billy's trial. Even inexperienced defense attorneys were brutal against eyewitnesses. Tori could have Murphy doubting his own assessment of the weather on the day of the murder by the time she was through.

Murphy studied the group of men on the opposite side of a two-way mirror. They all looked the same to him. Each of the six men was dressed in a black trench coat and wore a black bandanna down over his forehead.

Billy's glare dared him to pick him out. His gaze gave him away as their chief suspect.

Joshua watched Murphy's eyes while the teenager studied each of the men lined up on the other side of the mirror. He saw his eyes pause when they hit Billy. "Do you see him?"

"Easy, Mr. Thornton," Tori chastised the prosecutor from the corner behind them. "You told him to take his time."

Murphy sucked in a nervous breath. "He was wearing sunglasses."

Joshua nodded to Deputy Darrel Carter, who was waiting on the other side of their witness. The officer spoke into a mike next to the two-way mirror. "Put on your sunglasses."

Each of the men put on sunglasses to hide his eyes.

Murphy groaned. Now, they *really* all looked the same. They could have been a rock group that called themselves "The

Trench Coats."

"Maybe number three," he finally said.

Joshua's heart leapt and dropped at once. He had picked out Billy Unger.

Deputy Carter ordered Billy to step forward so the witness could take a closer look at him.

Murphy held his breath. "Maybe not," he mumbled. "The guy I saw was shorter."

Tori stepped up behind him. "That doesn't sound like a positive ID to me."

Murphy glanced from the defense attorney to his father. "I'm sorry. I could be wrong."

"You have to be positive," Joshua told him. "If you think this suspect is too tall, then we can't charge him for Grace's murder."

"We're through here," Tori said. "I'm taking my client home."

"No, you're not." The prosecutor chuckled. "We still have him on armed robbery and accessory to attempted abduction. Both charges are felonies, and he's an adult."

"But you don't have him on murder. Your witness can't positively identify him."

He told her more for Murphy's sake than hers, "That's no big deal. You tell your client not to plan on seeing the light of day in the near future."

She turned around and walked out with a sense of success. She had saved her first client from a murder rap.

The deputy said into the mike, "Okay, men. We're through here." They filed out. Another deputy escorted Billy back to his cell. It was not standard procedure, but Joshua draped his arm around Murphy's shoulder and gave him a hug.

"I'm sorry, Dad."

"You have nothing to be sorry for. It's a *positive* ID. It would have been wrong for you to ID him when you weren't sure. You did the right thing by telling us that you weren't."

"They all looked alike."

"I know." Joshua led him from the room. "I don't think I could have picked him out either. The only reason you picked him was because he had the attitude. He was daring you to pick him."

"He's the one who killed Grace, isn't he? And I let him get away."

"Murphy, we have him on armed robbery and attempted kidnapping. He's not going anywhere, and eventually we're going to get him for murder."

"Eventually. Maybe. If I had been sure—"

"Murph—" He wondered if he should tell him the truth. "Son, he has an alibi."

"He's lying."

"Is he?" Joshua could have been talking to a colleague, not his son. "His alibi is positive that they were together at the time of the murder. You aren't positive about him being at the school. Which one should I believe?"

Joshua returned home to switch from the Corvette to the van and retrieve the rest of his children to go to brunch.

On an impulse, he stopped on the way to the restaurant to invite Tad to join them. While he ran up the steps to his cousin's apartment, the kids stayed in the van to argue over what music to listen to on the CD player.

After letting himself in with his own key, Joshua called to Tad while he made his way through the living room cluttered with patient files and other things.

Dog ran in from the bedroom and jumped up on the visitor to beg for a petting. "Where's your master?" he asked the dog as if he could answer.

The mutt had no interest in responding. He continued to

paw at Joshua until he gave him a treat from the kitchen cupboard.

Joshua found Tad sprawled out on his bed in his underwear. His arms were crossed over his chest, and his eyes were shut. He was the picture of tranquility.

"Hey, cuz, what are you doing? I've come to take you to brunch."

"You paying?" Tad asked with his eyes shut. If he was determined enough, he could continue the conversation in his sleep.

"If you insist."

He opened one eye and raised an eyebrow. "That was easy."

"I'm too tired to fight with you. I was up half the night."

"So was I." Tad shut his eye again.

"Anyone I know?"

"I wish. I was working."

Joshua slapped one of his feet. "Are you coming?"

"Yeah, give me a minute." Tad sat up with the effort of an old man and staggered into the bathroom.

"You must have had some night." Joshua observed the messy bedroom.

Tad didn't live this way due to lack of money. Simple was his lifestyle. He didn't think that he needed more than the one-bedroom apartment over his medical office and a motorcycle. Even when he had spent all his money on booze and pot and cocaine, he hadn't lusted for material possessions.

He called out of the bathroom over running water, "I did an on-scene examination on Rex Rollins early this morning."

"Rex? Phyllis's husband?"

"Late husband. Someone blew him away at the State Line last night." Tad stepped into the bathroom doorway with a loaded toothbrush in his hand. He caught Joshua holding up a pair of red lace women's panties. "They're a friend's."

"What's she wearing now?" He dropped them onto the top of his dresser. "How did Rollins get himself blown away?"

"Have you talked to Gail about her book?" Tad went back into the bathroom to brush his teeth.

Joshua didn't mention the writer's late-night visit. Tad would make some sort of joke in reference to his one-night stand with her. "Yeah, we got into a fight about it. I caught her over at the Henderson place making a case for Grace's and Tricia's murders being connected. She got them all upset." From the bathroom doorway, he watched Tad brush his teeth. "I'm reopening the Wheeler case."

"Why am I not surprised?" Tad rinsed his mouth by sticking his head under the faucet and spitting out the water after letting it flow into his open mouth.

"I owe it to Tricia to find out what really happened."

Tad tossed his toothbrush into the cabinet. "That all happened a long time ago." He stepped around Joshua to return to the bedroom. "Even if you can find out what happened, it's going to be near impossible to find enough evidence to get a conviction." Noticing the scratch above the collar of his shirt, he paused. "What happened to your neck?"

"What?" Forgetting about the wound Gail had inflicted on him, Joshua rubbed his neck. When his fingers touched the scratch, he shrugged. "It's nothing."

"Looks like it drew blood." The doctor examined it. "Did you disinfect it?"

"Yes, Daddy. Will you get dressed? I'm hungry, and I want to know what Rollins got himself into that got him killed."

Tad picked up two pairs of jeans in search of the cleaner pair. He made his determination by sniffing them to see which one smelled less offensive. "The bartender at the State Line told me that Rollins was bragging to everyone last night that he had written a book about a woman he called the wicked witch and her getting away with murder."

Joshua couldn't help but smile. "Don't you have to be able to read before you can write?"

"I didn't say it was a good book. Think about it. Rex was soon to be the former Phyllis Barlow's ex-husband. He was really mad when she shot him a couple of weeks ago. She lived next door to the Wheelers when Tricia died." He slipped on a pair of jeans with faded knees.

"Come on, Tad! This is Rex we're talking about. I hate to speak ill of the dead, but the man was a drunken blowhard. He was always bragging about something or other. He heard that Gail was writing a book about solving a real murder and saw a way to make a quick buck."

"Just because a man is a drunk doesn't mean that he is incapable of knowing anything. Some of my best information comes from drunks and addicts. When you're in a bar with a friend and you see a drunk next to you, do you lower your voice, or do you pretend he's not there?" He answered his own question. "You tell yourself that it's just some drunk. You'd be surprised what people say in front of them."

"Why would Phyllis kill Trish? They didn't exactly run with the same crowd, but they weren't enemies, either."

Tad slipped a gray long-sleeved sweatshirt on over his head. "You know, Rex did a lot of work for Margo throughout the years."

"And her lawyer was representing him on violating that restraining order," Joshua mused.

"Why would Margo's lawyer defend him?" Tad saw a suspicious look cross his cousin's face. "Didn't Margo and Trish have a feud?"

Joshua shook his head at the notion of Rex Rollins having any knowledge of Margo committing Tricia's murder. "Margo is miles out of his league. What could he possibly know about the murder if she did it?"

Unable to give him an answer, Tad shrugged. "I don't know. I just know that Rex Rollins was in the State Line bragging about writing a book about a killing and shortly afterwards two bullets went through his head."

Tad's words stuck in Joshua's craw until he couldn't go on without knowing everything. At brunch at Elby's in Calcutta, located on the other side of East Liverpool, he called Seth on his cell phone during the children's claim-to-be-the-last-trip to the buffet during a feeding frenzy.

"You'll get my report when people stop killing each other long enough for me to write it," the detective said in response to his question about Rex Rollins's murder.

"Can you give me the highlights?"

"Come to Grant and Second in Newell and I'll give them to you."

In Newell, Joshua found the fire department cleaning up their equipment from putting out the fire that destroyed the top floor and roof of the boardinghouse in which the late Rex Rollins had lived. "What happened?" he asked Seth when he found him sitting in his cruiser.

The detective answered without humor, "I believe they call it a fire." He reported, "Rollins lived on the top floor of this rooming house. Fire started shortly after one o'clock. The doc said he was killed between midnight and one. Guess where it started?"

"His room. Anyone hurt?"

"Nah, landlady smelled the smoke and got everyone out. The top floor and attic were destroyed. The bottom floors only got smoke and water damage."

"Anybody see or hear anything?"

"Can you let me do my job and send you the report when I'm done?"

"From what I'm seeing, the effectiveness of your job performance leaves a lot to be desired."

Seth made a remark in reference to the previous night, which now seemed like an incident in the distant past to both men. "If I didn't have kids playing Clint Eastwood, I'd be more effective."

The fire marshal came from inside the house and told the detective that he could investigate the remains of Rex Rollins's room.

Joshua was turning to leave when the marshal, assuming that he was there to survey the crime scene, offered him a hard hat. Not wanting to argue any further with Seth, he hesitated, and then decided that he wanted to see what was inside.

An elderly woman dressed in a tattered bathrobe held together by multicolored patches darted out of the crowd of spectators. She grabbed the detective by the arm with a boney claw. "When can I get my stuff?"

"As soon as they say it is safe to go inside."

She squinted at Joshua with suspicion. "Then why is he going inside?"

Seth answered in a tone devoid of respect, "This is Joshua Thornton, the county prosecutor." He gestured with his head toward the old woman. "This is Bella Polk, the owner of the boardinghouse."

"I'm sorry about your home." The lawyer's most charming grin had no effect on her.

"I knew something like this was going to happen," she said in a raspy voice.

Joshua did not doubt that the detective investigating the case heard her statement. Yet, Seth dismissed her and went inside the house without any comment.

The prosecutor treated her remark as a clue. "Why?"

Bella explained, "There was trouble brewing ever since my husband started renting out rooms here. That good-for-nothing didn't want to get a regular job like a real man, and the other tramps who lived here were no better. He always said that they were down on their luck and that letting them flop here was Christian charity. Christian charity, my ass! Tramps, perverts, and degenerates!" She looked around to see if anyone was listening. "I even caught some queers a few times." She giggled. "There was a couple that swore they were straight, but I knew better. Why would two grown men share a room if they weren't fairies? One night, I waited until it was late and I sneaked—"

"What about Rex Rollins?" Joshua reminded her of the reason he was there. "Was he having trouble with anyone before the fire last night?"

Bella frowned that he had interrupted what she considered a great story. "Rex was the worst: always drunk; never had a job; never paid his rent. I heard that he got himself killed. How did it happen?"

"I'm afraid we can't discuss the particulars of the case."

"Do you know who did it?"

"We're working on that. Did he ever have any guests visiting him here at the boardinghouse? Phone calls?"

"No," she answered quickly. "Do you know why he got himself killed?"

"Once we know that, we'll know who killed him." He offered her another question, "What did he do most of the time?"

"He spent all of his time up in his room working on that damn computer he got."

"Rex had a computer?"

"Yeah, he brought it home a little more than a week ago." Bella snorted. "He was typing away on it day and night ever since he got out of the hospital. I'll bet he was surfing around on those porno Web sites they talk about. I was about to call the sheriff to have him come bust him for pornography but I guess now it doesn't matter." Her lips wrinkled together to resemble a bird's beak.

"Well," Joshua said while backing up toward the house, "thank you for all your information, Mrs. Polk."

"Is there a reward for catching his murderer?" she asked.

"Not that I'm aware of."

"Suppose someone gave you something that could help you catch 'em?"

He stopped his backward retreat. "Like what?"

"What are you looking for?" she squinted at him. "What are you going in my house to find?"

"Evidence to find out who killed Rex and torched your house."

"Like what?"

"I don't know. We'll know it when we see it. Do you have any suggestions of what we should look for, Mrs. Polk?"

"No," she responded quickly. "Who is going to pay for fixing my house?"

"Well, your insurance—" he started to answer, but she interrupted him.

"Bunch of crooks." She launched into a speech about the unscrupulous nature of insurance companies. She had canceled the homeowners insurance thirty years earlier after they refused to pay for damage to her roof after a storm.

As Bella advanced during her speech, Joshua backed away until he was able to escape inside the smoky building.

The would-be author's room was a black hole. It was still smoldering and hissing from the meeting of fire and water. Rex did not have much in the way of possessions for them to observe, and what he did have was destroyed.

The detective was searching through the closet of torched

clothes when Joshua found him.

"Tad talked to a barmaid last night who said that Rex Rollins was bragging to everyone that he wrote a tell-all book about a woman getting away with murder," Joshua told him.

Seth scoffed, "Give me a break. She told me that he was inebriated when he came in and inebriated when he left. I'm putting my money on a second drunk with a hot temper who Rollins owed money to."

"I can see where you would come to that conclusion." The lawyer poked through what was left of a table that had served as Rex's computer desk. "Except that the landlady told me that he had come home with a computer a week ago and has been working on it ever since." He bent over and rested his hands on his knees. It was a cheap table that had enough room for the computer and not much else.

"If that drunk wrote a book," Seth continued, "then anyone who knew him would know that the odds of him ever getting it published were equal to winning the lottery." He peered over the lawyer's shoulder at the table that had collapsed under the weight of the melted monitor resting on top.

Joshua poked with his pen through the things on the desk.

"Come on, Thornton. If he had walked into your office and told you he knew something about a killing, would you take him seriously?"

After stabbing through the charred equipment, he responded, "Tell me, Cavanaugh, since you became a cop have you ever had a saint for a witness?"

Seth admitted he hadn't.

"It's a fact that ninety percent of the time witnesses are from the dregs of society. They aren't necessarily credible, and they do have something to hide. That's why lawyers like to destroy their credibility in front of the jury—because they can. Everyone has something he or she wants to hide, whether it be an illicit affair or cheating on taxes. When a defense attorney digs up dirt on my witnesses, I ask the jury to consider what sins they have committed for lawyers to use as stones to throw at them if they ever become a witness. When jurors think about that, they usually get back on track."

"What are you looking for?" Seth gestured towards the desk.

Joshua stood up. "What is wrong with this picture?"

The melted monitor had slipped over onto its side. The keyboard swung off the desk by its cord. The printer was barely recognizable where it rested on the floor. Cords with nothing to connect to hung from the monitor and the power outlet.

"Where's his hard drive?" Joshua asked the detective.

CHAPTER SEVEN

"What could your client possibly have to offer us in exchange for a lesser sentence?" Joshua asked Tori Brody.

"Matt Landers's killer."

He sat up straight in his seat at the table in the conference room on the fourth floor of the courthouse. The courtrooms were two floors below them. A brick wall separated them from the prisoners housed on the same floor.

It was Monday morning and Billy Unger was scheduled to be arraigned for attempted armed robbery at ten o'clock.

On Sunday, Tori had called Joshua at home and asked that they meet with her client at nine o'clock to work out a deal. Billy offering up Matthew Landers's killer was not what he expected.

Matthew was the college boy killed with the same gun used to kill Grace. The police withheld the information that the gun was used in both killings. Now it seemed that secret would pay off since Billy was offering himself as a witness to Landers's murder to protect his own butt. By doing so, he was connecting the dots between the two murders: himself.

"My client witnessed the murder," Tori told Joshua. "He'll testify against Landers's killer in exchange for immunity on the burglary."

"You are aware that he'll be admitting that he had a part in the murder?"

"He was a juvenile at the time."

"So now, according to precedent, he can be tried as an adult for murder, which took place during a felony. How could he have witnessed the murder if he wasn't taking part in the burglary?"

"But you can't get Landers's killer without my client. If you could, you would have before now."

"Do you really think I'm going to let him walk away from all of this?"

"Listen to what he has to say." Tori turned in her seat to her client.

"Walt killed him," Billy announced.

Joshua showed no reaction. He waited for him to go on.

When her client didn't offer any more information, Tori prodded him, "You have to give him all the details."

Billy sighed, rolled his eyes, and sat forward to tell his story. "Walt and my brother, Bobby, knew each other since they were little kids. Well, Walt comes up with this bright idea that they break in these big old houses in Weirton, and they told me to be their lookout. That was all I did." He paused for a sign from Joshua that he believed that he had had nothing else to do with the break-ins.

He offered Billy none. "Go on. I'm listening."

"So one night, they were cleaning out this house up on top of the hill, and I see this truck pull into the driveway. So's I get on my radio and I tell them to get out. That was what they were supposed to do."

"But they didn't."

"It turns out there was like four computers in this place and all this really bitchin' stuff, and Walt didn't want to walk away from it. We didn't even know that he had a piece on him. He waits for the kid to come in and he wastes him."

"How did he waste him?"

Billy hesitated.

"Weren't you there?" Joshua asked. "Then I can't offer you any deal. For all we know you're lying, and it was you who killed him."

That was enough to make him respond. "I went inside when they hadn't come out." He laughed. "The kid was scared shitless."

Joshua contained his distaste over Billy's amusement at the boy's terror in the face of death.

"Walt was knocking him around. He told him he wanted his watch. The kid gave it to him and said that he wouldn't say anything if we took what we wanted and left. Then, Walt tried to grab this gold cross that the kid was wearing around his neck, and he tried to stop him. Walt punched him in the face and blood squirted out everywhere. Then, he made the kid get down on his knees. He was crying like a baby. He was saying this prayer, and Walt put the gun to the back of his head and blew him away."

The room was silent while the defense attorney and her client waited for his verdict.

After pushing away the image of one of his own children experiencing Matt Landers's fear when he felt the barrel of the gun pressed against the back of his head before it was discharged, Joshua broke the silence. "What happened to the gun?"

"Walt got rid of it."

"Did he give it to Bobby?"

Billy shook his head. "Bobby got himself blown away about a month after that."

"During another burglary," Joshua noted. "You have to tell me what happened to the gun, Billy."

Tori prodded him. "You have to tell him."

"I don't know," the young man insisted.

Joshua shook his head at his denial. "One of the factors that we take into consideration when making a deal is the honesty of the defendant."

"I'm telling you the truth. I don't know."

"No, you're not. Where is it now?"

Billy shrugged. "Ask Walt."

Joshua stood up. "Okay."

"Have we got a deal?" Tori asked.

"No."

"He gave you Manners."

"He told me a story with no proof to back it up. I'll go ask Walt, and I can tell you right now what he'll say. Your client did it. Then he'll want a deal in exchange for his testimony. It will be your client's word against his. Now, you tell me, Counselor, who should I give the deal to?"

"What more do you want?"

"The murder weapon."

She turned to Billy, who glared at her. "Give us a minute."

Joshua welcomed the excuse to leave the room. During the statement, Deputy Hockenberry, who was watching through the two-way glass, went to retrieve the case file for the Landers murder so they could compare his statement to the facts.

Hockenberry was studying it when the prosecutor stepped through the door. "That kid was there." He went on to report, "It was never released to the public that four computers were stolen from the Landers'. A watch and gold cross his dead mother had given him were taken. The victim was beaten up and had a broken nose. That was never released to the public, either."

"So he was there. But did Unger witness or commit the murder?" While referring to the autopsy report in the file, Joshua studied Billy, who was in discussion with his lawyer on the other side of the two-way mirror. "The victim was six feet tall and weighed a hundred and ninety pounds."

At eighteen, Billy had a build that lacked the bulk that comes with adulthood. He was still physically developing into a man. His flat stomach, which he displayed by wearing his orange overalls unzipped to his navel to show off his eagle tattoo, had muscle definition that the lawyer had given up on achieving in his own physical training.

"I wonder if at fourteen—his age at the time of the murder—if Billy could have taken on Matthew Landers."

Walt Manners was a brute. Over six feet tall, with two hundred and forty pounds of muscle that he used to intimidate anyone who challenged him, the criminal could easily have terrorized and killed the victim the way Billy described.

Joshua rubbed his tired eyes. "But we need more than the testimony of a juvenile delinquent turned adult offender—and possible killer—to make a murder charge against Manners stick. We also need that gun to connect Billy to Grace's murder."

Deputy Hockenberry agreed. "That's why he won't cough it up."

Joshua stepped back into the conference room. He could tell that Tori, who had yet to develop a poker face, had something to offer. "Has your client remembered what happened to the murder weapon?"

"Walt got rid of the gun," she told him. "But my client does have proof that he killed the Landers boy."

"What?"

She turned fully to her client. She placed her arm across the back of his chair and gestured for him to tell the prosecutor his proof.

"Walt wears a gold cross around his neck." Billy chuckled. "He ain't no Jesus freak. He says it's a souvenir. Ask him what it's a souvenir of."

His information checked out. Two members of the gang, who were up on the same charges, admitted that Walt Manners had bragged to them about killing Matthew Landers and that he had taken the cross off the victim before shooting him in the back of the head. They were willing to testify against their leader in exchange for a deal.

Joshua Thornton postponed the arraignment in order to adjust his charges.

"Number one," Phyllis Rollins shook her index finger at her visitors, "it's laughable that Rex thought he could write a book. Number two, if I knew he was writing a book about me, I could not possibly care less."

Tad looked at Joshua, who, he was surprised to notice, was not paying attention to their suspect, but observing the beams in the cathedral ceiling of the Rollins's log-cabin home.

Phyllis was dry-eyed during the interview about her husband's murder.

Doug, who sat on the sofa next to his sister, gazed at Tad with wide eyes. The doctor wondered if he understood the meaning of the news that they had delivered.

"Then you don't know what Rex was talking about when he said he wrote a book about the wicked witch of Chester?" Tad asked.

She scoffed. "I have no doubt that he was talking about me. Big whoop. Like I care if he wrote a book about me?"

"This is a nice house," Joshua interjected.

Tad started. It was not like his cousin to change the subject during an interview with a suspect. Joshua was like a dog with a bone when it came to murder. Maybe exhaustion had caught up with him.

"How many square feet is it?"

She answered, "Twenty-eight hundred. Double that if you count the finished basement."

"You must do better business at the café than I thought."

Phyllis Rollins was the owner and cook at the Rollins Corner

Café, a diner, gas station, and market located on the country crossroad one hill before the Pennsylvania state line. Doug waited tables and cleaned up. The restaurant, which was frequented by truck drivers and other blue-collar workers in search of hot meals, was busy the first half of the day. After lunch, business would slow down to a crawl until she locked the door at eight o'clock.

Rollins also made a lot of business from the bean grinder Phyllis bought from a coffee house going out of business. After deciding that Chester's residents weren't the type to read deep literature over café lattes, she nixed the idea of turning her business into a coffee house. But she kept the grinder. Rollins Corner Café was the only local place to buy fresh ground coffee in assorted flavors.

Joshua lowered his eyes from the beams and returned to the reason for their visit. "Where were you Friday night?"

"Here with Doug."

Joshua regarded her brother.

To look at the two men, it was hard to believe they had graduated the same year. Doug Barlow was a wisp of a man. Worry lines etched deep into his face made him appear years older than his former classmate.

While Joshua studied the man whom he had expected to become a scientist or scholar, Doug's unfocused eyes, hidden behind thick glasses, were drawn to his face.

"How are you doing, Doug?" Joshua's question was sincere.

He responded with a nervous smile. "Okay."

"I heard that you work at the diner with your sister?"

"Yeah, I wait on the customers and grind the coffee, and she even lets me cook sometimes."

"That's good. I guess that's one of the perks of—"

"Any other questions?" Phyllis inquired sharply.

"No." Joshua stood up and gestured to Tad for them to leave.

"Thank you very much."

The Corvette raced around the curves of the country road through Birch Hollow while Tad voiced his confusion over Joshua's lack of conviction while interviewing the victim's widow. "What was that all about? You gave up back there."

Joshua gestured towards the home back in the hollow they had just left. "Unless we can find a viable motive, Phyllis didn't kill Rex. If she wanted to kill him, she could have done it and gotten away with it weeks ago when he broke into her house and violated the restraining order."

"She tried to shoot his balls off, but missed her target by two inches."

"That was a simple domestic dispute," Joshua said. "Whoever killed Rex went to the boardinghouse to get his book to make sure no one read it. What murder could Phyllis have committed that he would have known about?"

"Come on, Josh! The Barlows lived right next door to Tricia Wheeler."

"Why would Phyllis kill Tricia?" Joshua offered another theory. "Margo Sweeney Connor bailed Rex out of jail. She isn't known for her charitable nature. Now I want to know why Margo would send her lawyer to defend and bail out an employee she had fired."

He continued, "We can't make assumptions about which murder Rex was writing about. He spent most of his life on the wrong side of the tracks. There are a lot of murders, solved and unsolved, that he could have happened onto."

"Then we need to find that book," Tad said, "which our chief of detectives swears doesn't even exist."

"That's because he's an idiot," Joshua muttered. "Cavanaugh has already chalked up Rollins's murder to a drunken brawl over an unpaid loan. Do you think Rex was smart enough to back up his book onto a disk? Maybe we can find that."

With a shake of his head, Tad declared that Rex wasn't that smart.

Jan was waiting at Joshua's office to invite him out for a cocktail at Dora's.

His solemn expression when he plopped down in the chair behind his desk contrasted with hers.

"What's wrong?" She slipped onto the corner of his desk.

"Tad and I went over to the Rollins place to talk to Phyllis. Doug was there—"

"Of course," she said, noting that the siblings were constant companions.

Joshua shook his head. "I think of what he used to be and I see what he is now, and it just breaks my heart. The guy was a certified genius. He never had to study. He knew everything." He looked up at her. "What happened?"

Jan shrugged. "Tad says that it is clinical depression. Doug has been on antidepressants ever since his only semester of college. He went nuts one night and broke all the windows in his dorm. They had to take him away in a straightjacket. His family didn't have the money to send him to school, so after he lost the scholarship, he had to make do the best he could."

"I remember him crying all the time, out of the blue, for nothing, during our senior year."

"That's the first time I ever noticed anything not quite right with him," Jan recalled. "He's tried to kill himself, I don't know how many times. I think it was over a woman."

Joshua chuckled, "Why is it that every time someone gets messed up you blame it on a failed romance?"

"Doug was pretty fragile to begin with. He meets a woman who shows him the ways of the world. She ups and leaves him high and dry, and he can't handle the pain of a broken love affair. It won't be the first time someone's life was ruined because of unrequited love."

"Are you blaming me for Gaston firing you and ruining your life?"

Jan glared. "Tad told you."

"No, there was another journalist from *The Vindicator* at the courthouse to cover Manners's arraignment—"

"And the detective who screwed up a stakeout that almost got a hostage killed until the first-born son of our county prosecutor single-handedly captured the county's baddest bad guy."

"It's in the genes," Joshua said proudly.

"It's an irresistible story. Can I have an exclusive interview with J.J. that will let me write a story that will get me my job back?"

"Ask him." He patted her knee. "Don't let it get you down, Jan. I've gotten fired myself. When God closes one door, He always opens another. You just have to find that open door."

"Did you get fired for throwing a milkshake in someone's face?"

"No." Joshua tried not to look surprised. When Tad had told him that Jan got fired he mentioned nothing about an assault with a milkshake.

"I guess I need to apologize to Gail."

"I should say so," he told her in a paternal tone.

Jan slipped down off his desk. "I guess I better do it now." She went to the door.

He muttered for her to hear, "Don't take any loaded milkshakes with you."

Of course, Gail's house would be more beautiful than Jan's own two-bedroom cottage in which she had lived since birth. Even though her rival was renting, Jan felt a pang of jealousy when she pulled up the drive to the redbrick ranch house that was sprawled out across the lot tucked back into woods next to the Pennsylvania state line.

It was secluded. The way a writer's retreat should be.

Jan gulped down her envy. She remained in her car to work up the nerve for another encounter with Gail. Now she had to humble herself and apologize. She walked up the brick sidewalk to the front stoop and rang the doorbell. The glass-paned storm door was shut. The inside door was ajar, which allowed her to see through the great room to the patio doors on the other side of the house.

Anticipating her hostess's arrival to let her in, Jan waited. "Gail!" She rang the doorbell a second time.

All was silent.

She stepped inside.

"Gail," she announced herself when she went into the great room. "It's Jan. Are you here? I came to apologize."

She listened to the silence.

A lunch counter separated the great room from the U-shaped kitchen with a pantry behind it. The bedrooms and bath were in a wing to the left. The contemporary furniture was cheap. Jan wondered if it came with the lease on the house. It wasn't the type of furniture that a successful journalist would have.

A sickening sweet scent met her nostrils. She sneezed and rubbed her nose. "She needs to take out her garbage more often."

A folder lay open on the coffee table. An empty bottle of wine and wineglass were sprawled on the floor next to the sofa. A blue ink pen rested between them.

Recognizing the writing instrument, she picked it up. Joshua Thornton's name was engraved along the side. Her eyes narrowed with jealousy.

When she threw the pen down onto the coffee table, she

noticed the label on the file's tab. It was the research folder on Tricia Wheeler. Jan glanced around. Seeing no one, she opened the folder to study the pages inside.

An Associated Press news article downloaded from the Internet lay on top. Not touching it so that she could make a quick get away if Gail walked in and caught her snooping, she read the first paragraph from where she stood above it: "Bingingham.com vice president, Randall Fine, was charged with two counts of sexual assault. The charges came as a result of a complaint filed by his administrative assistant . . ."

Randall Fine? Jan repeated the name while trying to recall who Randall Fine was and what connection he would have to Tricia Wheeler. *She put it together. Randy! Randy was Tricia's boyfriend and now he is up on two rape charges.*

Intrigued, Jan picked up the folder.

Then, she saw the photo album underneath the folder. Curious still, she flipped open the cover of the book. Pasted inside was another article. This was a yellowed newspaper clipping. The headline read, "Bears Undefeated—14 to 0." The sub-headline read, "Thornton leads the Bears to State Semi-finals." A picture of Joshua in his football uniform was under the headlines.

She turned the page. At first, she squinted to make out what was glued to the cardboard. When she did, she flushed. It was a used condom.

She turned the page to the next article. They were all clipped from newspapers. Then, there was the front-page article about Joshua being accepted to the Naval Academy.

The album had many pages filled with articles. She flipped to the next page to find even more articles from *The Vindicator* reporting his achievements after Joshua left Chester. There were snapshot pictures of him. None were of him with his family. Jan concluded when she saw by his expression and the candid nature of the poses that he didn't seem to be aware that his picture was being taken. Mingled with the pictures were other articles about court cases that made the news as his career flourished.

Swoosh!

She found that she was so immersed in the album that she forgot she was holding the folder and had dropped all the contents. She dropped to the floor to pick up the papers and stuff them back into the file.

While she was on the floor, she saw the framed picture on a table up against the wall. That one was also of Joshua. He was with a woman in this picture.

Jan put the album and folder back where she had found them and scurried over to study the picture. Joshua was several years younger. He held the woman from behind as they stood sideways for the camera. In profile, she showed off her pregnant stomach. They were both smiling at the camera.

Jan had never met Valerie, Joshua's late wife, but she had seen many pictures of the woman whose image was displayed in the Thornton home.

This woman was not Valerie Thornton. It was Gail Reynolds.

Suddenly afraid of what Gail would do if she caught her snooping through her things, Jan dropped the picture back on the table. Her hands shook as she tried to make sure it was in the same position she had found it.

Then, her heart pounding, she ran out the door, got in her car, and raced back into town.

I'm getting old, Tad concluded, as he plopped down into the chair behind his desk, closed his eyes, and laid his head back against the headrest to enjoy the sound of silence.

His last patient of the day was an obese woman who wanted him to prescribe diet pills for her to lose weight. She was unhappy when he suggested that she try exercising and dieting first. When she left his office, he suspected that she was on her way to see a doctor he had heard a rumor was selling amphetamines.

"Tad, I need you! Quick!" Jan threw open his door and ran in. She was so excited that she was out of breath.

He started out of his nap. "What?"

She tried to pull him up out of his chair. "Gail's stalking Josh."

"You've got to be kidding."

"No, it's true." She tugged on his arm. "She's been stalking him for years."

He pulled away from her. "Come on, Jan! Gail is a respected journalist!"

"Then what's she doing here?"

"Investigating the death of an old friend."

She stomped a foot. "I wish people would stop believing that crap Gail dished out on television."

"So she came back to write a book for fame and fortune."

"No, she came here to stalk Josh! She has a photo album filled with clippings and pictures of him."

"So? She's a fan of his investigative talents."

"She also has a picture, in a frame, of Josh and her and she's pregnant!" Jan interjected.

Tad hesitated to comprehend what she was saying. "What? Gail was pregnant? I didn't know that she had a kid."

"Neither did I," she told him. "But there they were. Josh was hugging her and they looked like they loved each other."

He smiled. "Did it ever occur to you that maybe she did have a baby? Josh is her friend. They ran into each other while she was pregnant and had their picture taken together."

"And she put it in a frame and has it displayed in her living room?" she finished in a suspicious tone.

"You yourself said that Gail has no friends. Maybe Josh is the closest thing to a friend that she has."

She was shaking her head. "You have to see this for yourself."

"Are you asking me to break into her house and go through her things?"

Jan almost said yes, but then realized the foolishness of breaking into Gail's house to pry into her private business. "Can't you go talk to her and see for yourself? You know about this stuff."

Tad paused. He didn't want to admit that she had his interest. After all, Joshua had confessed that Gail did seduce him. "I can't just drop in on her. I only knew her casually when Josh was in school and I haven't seen her since then. She probably doesn't even remember me."

She agreed. "I did go over to apologize, but I didn't see her. How about if I go back and you go with me? Then you can see what you think . . . and then you'll agree that she is stalking Josh and he's the reason she came back here."

Nighttime was one of the worst times for widower Joshua Thornton.

The house in which he grew up with his grandmother, even with five children, was too quiet when he went to bed. Fourteen months after her death, he still longed for Valerie and would spend his evenings reading books that forced him to concentrate on something other than the emptiness on the other side of his bed.

Tonight, he was reading *The Case for the Creator* by Lee Strobel. Tad had lent Joshua the book written by a former atheist, who was saved when he went on a fact-finding mission to prove that God did not exist, only to find conclusive evidence that He did.

When the phone rang at ten o'clock, Joshua assumed it was

someone calling for one of his kids. Since he was the only family member with a phone in his room, he answered it in a sharp tone to deter the caller from dialing their number so late in the future.

"I love a man with a forceful voice," Tori Brody purred from across the phone lines.

"I'm sorry," he explained. "When you have teenagers in your house you have to do what you can to maintain control. Otherwise, the phone will be ringing at all hours."

"I feel sorry for you." It was not pity he heard in her tone.

"I'm not asking for sympathy." Joshua asked, "Why are you calling me?"

"You owe me. I got you Walt Manners. I should get something for that."

"I'm letting your client walk away from a burglary and murder charge. What more do you want?"

"Okay, I owe you. I have an unopened bottle of cognac here. Why don't you come over and get it?"

"I don't think so. Thanks anyway."

"You certainly know how to hold a grudge, don't you, Josh?"

"It's not a grudge. I'm just wise enough to avoid trouble when at all possible."

"I'm not involved with anyone, and I had nothing to do with Max trying to slice up your face with that blade."

"You told me that twenty years ago."

"Don't you believe me?"

"Frankly, my dear, I don't." Joshua hung up the phone and returned to his book.

Jan's eyes followed Tad's while he took in the woods surrounding Gail's home.

"I always wanted to live in a secluded place like this," she said wistfully.

"You'll get yours, Jan."

"How can you be so sure?"

"Good things come to those who wait." He knocked on the door since they received no response to the doorbell.

"Her car isn't here," Jan observed. "It wasn't here earlier, either."

Tad turned to leave. "Looks like she's not here."

She grabbed him by the arm. "Don't you want to see? Gail is stalking Josh."

He shook his head with a smile. "Jan, I've been stalked. I know what stalking is. She may be infatuated with him. She may even love him, but she's not stalking him."

"Maybe she's not stalking him," she relented, "but her elevator clearly isn't going all the way to the top." After making certain that no one was around to see them, Jan yanked open the door and pulled Tad into the house behind her.

It was dark. She turned on the light in the front foyer with the wall switch.

"We are now breaking and entering," he told her.

"We didn't break anything. The door was open already."

"But we weren't invited to enter."

She dared him, "Call Josh and turn yourself in." She led the way to the photograph on the end table. "See."

He took the picture and studied the image. "I've seen this before."

"When?"

He turned on the table light and held the photograph under the bulb. "At Josh's house in Washington. It was a long time ago." He squinted at it. "Only Gail was not the woman he was holding. It was Valerie. This picture was taken the first Christmas they were married when she was pregnant with the twins."

Jan felt vindicated. "I told you she was sick."

"We need to get out of here." As Tad replaced the picture on the end table, he smelled a familiar odor. He sniffed in order to confirm the scent and shuddered. When he saw the door open as they had found it, he asked, "Was the front door open when you came here earlier?"

"That's how I got in." She was flipping through the pages of the scrapbook. "Look at this album. She has to have cut out everything she has ever seen in print that has Josh's name in it."

"It's kind of late in the year to leave the front door open at night." He covered his nose with his hand and he headed toward the bedrooms.

"Where are you going?" Jan grabbed his hand.

"I want to see what is down this hallway."

"It's the bedroom." She clutched his forearm.

He reached for the knob to the door between them and the bedroom. The scent was stronger. He hesitated.

"Jan," he extracted his arm from her grasp, "wait for me in the car."

"Why? What are you going to do?"

"I want you to wait for me outside."

"No."

He could see that she was not going to leave his side. "Suit yourself."

When Tad opened the door the sweet putrid scent hit them in the face. Jan gasped and covered her mouth when she felt her stomach lurch. "What is that?"

He had switched on the light with the wall switch and was removing the pillow that covered the head of the figure on the bed. His examination of Gail's body triggered the release of gases forming in the decomposing figure.

"Death." Tad coughed and covered his nose and mouth with his hand. "That is the smell of death."

CHAPTER EIGHT

"Who called you?" Seth challenged Joshua when he saw him climb out of his Corvette. He had to park at the corner of Gail Reynolds's yard. The police and emergency vehicles filled the driveway.

"The medical examiner." Joshua did not slow his pace to go inside to escape the drizzle that had started. "Gail was a friend."

"How good of a friend?"

Joshua found the living room packed with the forensics team scouring the scene for evidence. He halted. Seth stepped in behind him.

Jan dashed away from the kitchen where Deputy Pete Hockenberry was questioning her and threw her arms around his neck. "Oh, Josh, I'm so glad you're here! It's awful."

"Where is she?"

She gestured toward the bedroom at the end of the hallway.

Seth blocked his path. "First, I need for you to answer a couple of questions, Counselor."

"What questions?"

"How close were you and the victim?"

"I told you. We were friends."

"Are you sure that's all you were?" The detective chuckled at him.

"What are you talking about?"

Seth stepped aside and laid his hand on the photograph on the table. He grinned when he saw confusion cross Joshua's face when he saw the image of the pregnant Gail with his arms around her.

Jan blurted out, "She was stalking Josh."

"Yeah. Right," Seth replied.

When Joshua turned to go down the hall, Seth grabbed his arm to stop him. He slapped the detective's hand away before shoving him back against the wall.

"Back off, Cavanaugh!"

His on-scene examination complete, Tad was packing up his instruments into his medical case when his cousin came into the room.

"What happened to her?" Joshua looked down at the body.

In the weekend since he had last seen her, death had transformed Gail's body so that she bore only a slight resemblance to the woman he had known. She was wearing the same black trench coat she had worn when she had stepped out of the shadows in his backyard a few days before. The hat was still on the floor where he had discarded it.

"I'll know for certain after I open her up," Tad replied to his question, "but bruising on the inside of her lips and fibers in her nostrils suggests that someone smothered her with the pillow."

Joshua gazed at the pillow that Tad had suggested was the murder weapon. In the room that was brightly lit in order to reveal any clues, he could make out a faint brown outline on the case that resembled a hand. Reluctant to touch the coarse material for fear of disturbing evidence, he bent to look at the shape. "Her killer had dirty hands."

"I'd say so. The lab should be able to come up with a chemical breakdown of that dirt to trace it back to our guy."

"When did this happen?"

"She's been dead for at least three days, based on decomposition and the stages of larvae in the corpse."

Joshua repeated the words, "Three days." He subtracted the days of the week. "Friday."

"Friday night, Saturday morning, early hours." Tad proceeded to fold her hands, encased in paper bags sealed with rubber bands, across her chest as if to make her comfortable for the trip to the morgue.

"I saw her Friday night," Joshua muttered a single octave above a whisper.

Pete Hockenberry, who had followed him into the room, started upon hearing the announcement.

Tad turned away from the bed to face his cousin. "You saw her Friday night?"

Three days seemed to be eons in the past. Joshua searched his memory for clues to her death in his last meeting with her in the darkness of the night. "She came by the house. It was after midnight and she was drunk, so I drove her home."

"You were here?" Tad asked. "In this room?"

"Yes. I helped her inside, I put her on the bed, and then I left."

"You put her to bed," Seth chuckled from behind his back.

"She was drunk," Joshua said.

"Won't be the first time an old friend decided to take advantage of a drunken woman," the investigator said before asking Tad, "Any sign of hanky-panky?"

The medical examiner glared. "None."

"Of course, you'd say that."

"If you want Johnstone to do the autopsy, fine," Tad said. "I'd rather go home and go to bed anyway."

"Why would I want to kill Gail?" Joshua challenged the detective's suggestion.

"You tell me. You were the last one to see her alive."

"But you have yet to ask me one question about that meeting. Instead you have been making obscene insinuations since I walked in the door."

Seth asked Tad, "Why did you call Thornton here tonight?"

"Because he knows what he's doing and you don't."

Impressed by his cutting remark, the deputies in the room and hallway, who had gathered with the promise of an interesting scene to witness, let out a whoop.

Seth's face reddened. "Where did you get that scratch, Thornton?"

Joshua's hand flew up to the mark on his neck. In an instant, he recalled Gail groping for him while he pushed her down onto the bed. Now, his skin was under her fingernails to be found during the autopsy.

Seth smiled broadly at his hesitation. "I'll be seeing you, Counselor."

Deputy Medical Examiner Gary Johnstone was called to meet Gail's body at the morgue.

Tad went home with Joshua to find out what had happened the night of her death.

While the children, in various stages of preparation for school, ate their breakfasts, Joshua sat at the head of the table and stared into his coffee mug. They could see that he had been awake the whole night.

The kitchen was filled with the scent of an egg scramble that contained a mixture of ground beef, onions, and cheese. The meal was accompanied by home fries topped with country gravy and thick slices of toast. Tad had prepared the feast more for himself and Joshua than the kids after he realized at four o'clock that he had not eaten since lunch the day before.

Admiral, who usually waited next to his master during meals in hopes of getting a morsel of food, chose to move to the other end of the table where Tad, easy pickings for handouts, distracted the children from their father's distress by recounting stories from their youth.

After they had left for school and Admiral had wolfed down a bowl filled to the rim with the leftovers for his breakfast, Joshua let down his guard to pace the kitchen.

"How is it that you never had any idea that her feelings for you were other than friendship?" Tad asked while wiping down the stovetop. "You were the one who told me that she came over and seduced you right under this roof."

"This roof was replaced fifteen years ago," Joshua reminded him. "It was under the old, leaky roof that she seduced me."

Tad grinned at his cousin's attempt at humor and dumped the coffee into the sink to make a fresh pot.

Joshua rinsed out the sponge that Tad had put away to clean up a gravy spill he had missed on the kitchen table. "We were hormonal teenagers back then. She came across like the sophisticated feminist who considered love and family beneath her. I bought it. I honestly thought that whole seduction thing back then was a one-night stand and nothing more."

"Clearly it was on your part."

"She seduced me," he reiterated.

"You did sleep with her."

"Not Friday night!" He threw the sponge into the sink. It bounced off the rim and landed on the floor.

"Hey!" Tad picked it up. "I'm on your side. What about all that stuff she had of yours—and that picture?"

"That was Valerie in that picture. I was looking for it when we were packing up to move back here and couldn't find it."

"Gail must have taken it and morphed her head onto the body."

"Why would someone do that?" Joshua asked in a steady tone. "What else did she have of mine?"

"I don't know. All I saw was the picture and the scrapbook."

"Cavanaugh is going to try to hang this on me. He's too

stupid to look anywhere else."

"Am I correct in assuming that your skin will be found under her fingernails?"

"She was drunk," Joshua fingered his wound. "She scratched me while I was helping her into bed."

"Or she scratched you while fighting you off when you tried to take advantage of her drunken state. What we need to find is another suspect. What time did you take her home?"

"One o'clock Saturday morning."

Tad sat up on the kitchen counter. "That's about when Rex Rollins was killed. He was killed around midnight and the fire in the boardinghouse was set around one."

Joshua leaned against the edge of the counter next to where Tad sat. "And Rex wrote a book about a wicked witch who got away with murder and Gail was writing a book about Trish's death. We have two victims writing books about murder here in Chester and both of them are now dead."

"Maybe Rex wasn't as stupid as everyone thought."

"If he was so smart, why is he dead?"

The e-mails were flying.

At this point in Jan's career, if anyone had asked her, she would have said that she didn't have much in the way of sources.

She was wrong. After spending her whole adult life running the pharmacy, she knew almost everyone in town.

Jan went home and sent out a mass e-mail to every addressee in her address book to announce the murder of Gail Reynolds and to ask about her life before her return to Chester, West Virginia.

It did not take long for her phone to ring. The call came from Liz Yates, a young woman who had recently moved to Chester from Charleston and went to Jan's church. Her new husband was a teacher at the elementary school. A realtor, Liz began working for Margo Connor.

"Is it true that Gail Reynolds is dead?"

Jan confirmed that the news was true.

"When did it happen?"

"Tad says that it had to have happened Friday night sometime."

Liz gasped. "I may have been one of the last ones to see her before she was killed!"

"Where?"

"At Antonelli's. I went to dinner with Margo Connor to talk about my job with Connor Realty and Gail Reynolds showed up. I recognized her from television." Liz laughed nervously. "They got into such an awful fight that I thought it was a joke."

"Of course!" Jan responded to the news. "Gail was writing a book about Tricia Wheeler's murder. Margo and Trish had an awful fight right before she was killed. She had to be one of Gail's prime suspects."

"That's what the two of them were fighting about," Liz confirmed. "I was never so embarrassed in my life!"

"What time was this?"

"I met Margo at five o'clock. She was eating her spaghetti when Gail showed up and launched right into asking her about this dead girl."

"I'll bet Margo was furious." Jan envisioned her former classmate's reaction to the journalist tracking her down and interrogating her about Tricia Wheeler's murder in public.

"At first, Margo told her to talk to her lawyer."

"Then what?"

"Then Gail Reynolds told her that she and this other girl got into a lot of fights. Margo said that it was because they didn't like each other."

"They didn't," Jan said. "Margo hated Tricia. Did she threaten Gail?"

"Yes," Liz answered quickly. "I was trying to get out of there as fast as possible. They were screaming at each other and everyone was looking at us. I couldn't believe it was really happening and here I was in the midst of all of it. I tell you, Jan, I don't care if Connor Realty is the biggest realtor in the valley, I don't need that type of grief."

"I don't blame you." Jan steered her back to the details of the fight. "What did Margo threaten to do to her? Do you remember Margo's exact words?"

Liz paused to remember the details of the fight as it happened.

On the other end of the phone line, Jan waited.

"First," she said slowly, "Margo said that this Tricia committed suicide. Then Gail said that she had seen the fight they had the day she died and that Tricia had no reason to kill herself. Then Margo said that she killed herself because she had stolen some guy—I don't remember his name—"

"Randy."

"Yeah, Randy. That was it. Margo stole him from this dead girl." Liz paused before she continued, "The next thing that Gail said did not make any sense. It sounded like she was then saying that Margo didn't kill her, but that this boyfriend did because something happened between him and the dead girl and he needed to keep her quiet."

"What?" Jan gasped. This was not what she was expecting. "What did Margo say to that?"

"She then told Gail that if she wrote her book, it was going to be over her own dead body."

Liz wasn't able to give Jan any more details about the fight. She had run out of the restaurant without looking back after the threats of murder started flying between the two women.

After encouraging Liz to call the police to tell them what she had witnessed, Jan hung up the phone and proceeded to do a

Google search under the name Gail Reynolds. Her search produced thousands of results, some of whom were the Gail Reynolds she knew, but most were not. Jan cursed the dead woman for having such a common name. Several pages into the list, she discovered an article dated four months earlier from a small newspaper in Connecticut:

"Journalist Gail Reynolds did not appear in New London County Municipal Court today to answer charges of stalking . . ."

Stalking!

". . . Adam O'Neal (19) attended the hearing with his parents, Glen and Sylvia O'Neal. The O'Neal family's request for a restraining order was approved . . ."

Adam O'Neal was nineteen years old. Jan smiled. Gail liked them young.

She sent the article to PRINT. While she waited for the hard copy, she scrolled to find any proof that the Gail Reynolds mentioned in the article was the same one whose body she and Tad had found the night before.

The defendant in the stalking case sent letters and gifts, made phone calls, and followed Adam O'Neal from high school to college. He was afraid to move away from home to campus because of her. The stalking climaxed when Gail appeared in his bedroom with a knife one night and threatened to kill him and then herself. He managed to disarm her. She was arrested and taken away to a psychiatric ward where she spent three days before she was released.

Jan's computer dinged to signal an instant message. It was from Angie, a source Jan had acquired years before when she was writing for the lifestyle section of *The Review, The Vindicator's* chief competitor. Angie had moved to Philadelphia where she worked as an administrative assistant for a television station that happened to be an affiliate for Gail's network.

"I didn't know Gail came from Chester," Angie replied to the news. "What a small world. Were you friends?"

"Acquaintances," was Jan's answer. She was tempted to put the word in bold type, but chose not to. "Did Gail ever live in Connecticut?"

"No, Gail was not the Connecticut type. She was a cosmopolitan girl through and through."

"Why didn't the network renew her contract?"

Angie responded, "I heard rumors of a nervous breakdown."

Tad was writing as fast as his hand could move on the yellow notepad he had found in the center of Joshua's desk in the study. Dr. Johnstone was a friend as well as a colleague. He couldn't send him a copy of the report that he had yet to write out for Seth Cavanaugh, but he could gossip about his findings. While Tad scribbled out cryptic notes in single misspelled words, Joshua strained to put together conclusions based on his "ah-hah's" and "uh-huh's."

"Well?" Joshua whirled the tablet around to read his notes as soon as his cousin had hung up the phone.

"Gail died of asphyxiation," Tad announced. "No big surprise there. Her blood alcohol level was .16." Hearing the sound of a truck in the quiet town, he parted the blinds of the window behind him and peered outside.

"I told you she was drunk when she showed up here." Joshua tried to decipher one of the words his cousin had scribbled out. It started with an "e."

"Johnstone found cotton fibers caught up in the hairs of her nostrils. While she was possibly passed out, someone held a pillow over her face until she suffocated." Tad peered through the shrubs that bordered the backyard and the alley behind the home. He could make out the tilted-flatbed of a tow truck. "Someone is being towed."

Joshua handed him the notepad and took a turn to look out the window at the truck on the other side of the hedges. "What's that word?" He pointed to the word beginning with an "e."

He recognized the uniform of a Hancock County deputy sheriff. Through the bushes, he could not tell which deputy it was. "They found Gail's car."

Tad dropped the tablet and joined him in watching as the sports car was hoisted up onto the flatbed. "What's her car doing behind your house?"

Joshua hung his head. "She was too drunk to drive back home when she showed up here, so I drove her. I left her a message the next day to tell her where it was and to come get it."

"But someone killed her before she could do that, and Cavanaugh got the message."

"Yep." Joshua turned from the window. "Was there any evidence of sexual assault?"

Tad shook his head with a chuckle. "Nope, she was as clean as a whistle."

"What do you mean by that?" Joshua had heard the term "clean as a whistle," but he had never heard it used in connection with a medical exam on a murder victim, except when it meant that she had been sterilized by the killer to remove all evidence.

"Her genital membrane was intact." The corners of Tad's mouth curled with amusement.

Once again, Joshua heard himself asking what the doctor was talking about.

"When a woman or girl is penetrated, the genital membrane is broken—"

"Also referred to in slang as breaking a girl's cherry." Joshua frowned as he repeated, "Her genital membrane was intact."

Tad nodded his head.

Joshua shook his. "But Gail was not a virgin. We had sex together right upstairs in what used to be my room—"

"Twenty years ago. With no sexual activity over a long period of time, and I'm talking years, the membrane can grow back. You know," he said, putting his hands on his hips, "there is a theory that every seven years we end up with a totally different body as a result of cells dying and then replacing each other."

Joshua interrupted him, "Therefore, Gail didn't have a lover for a very long time."

"We also know that she had a baby." Tad pointed to the word on the yellow pad. "Episiotomy. She had an episiotomy scar."

"She had a baby."

Tad shrugged. "An episiotomy scar does not necessarily mean that a woman had a baby. There can be other reasons for the scar. But, yes, Johnstone did also find a distended uterus to indicate childbirth at some point."

"What point?" Joshua swallowed.

"Not recently."

Jan was proud of herself. She may not have had the experience of a hard-hitting journalist, but she was developing the mind of one. If she could not get anyone at Gail's network willing to talk about her and what had occurred in Connecticut, then she would call the O'Neals. Considering that they were driven into getting a restraining order against the journalist, they should be willing to talk about what drove them there.

She found Sylvia O'Neal's phone number on the Internet. She was not sure if the woman knew or cared who she was talking to. As soon as Jan mentioned Gail Reynolds, the story poured out over the phone line faster than she could type on her laptop.

"They told us that those records were sealed. There should

be laws to protect decent people like us. We invested our heart and soul into that boy. He was a part of us, even if he didn't come from us. And then, nineteen years later, that woman goes digging through the records and turns our world upside down. Poor Adam has had to start seeing a shrink because of her."

Sylvia was talking so fast that the words were swimming in Jan's head while she tried to put them together to comprehend the meaning behind them while she wrote her story. "Wait a minute," she sputtered while typing out that Adam had to see a therapist after his experience with Gail Reynolds. "She found you. Why was she looking for you?"

"Because she suddenly started feeling all maternal," Sylvia spat out. "He might have come out of her womb—"

"Gail was his *birth* mother?"

"—but I'm still his mother. You can't give your child over to another woman to raise and then pop back up in his life with this insane idea that you can take this boy—who's now in college—home to live with you and his daddy and be some big happy family! That woman is insane!"

Joshua didn't intend to fall asleep. He was resting his eyes when the *dongs* of the doorbell echoed through his head. He sat up at attention in his desk chair so abruptly that he pulled a muscle in his neck. His knees banged against the underside of his desk, and he let out a yelp.

Admiral must have been asleep, too. Uttering a bark, he jumped into a sitting position from where he was stretched out in the middle of the study floor. He looked at his master for an order about what to do next.

Rubbing his knees, Joshua went to answer the door.

Tori waited for him on his threshold. Her seductive style of dress had been transformed in a casual ensemble of blue jeans, a sweater, and boots. She held a bouquet of flowers and a carton of McDonald's food and drinks. "I thought you could use some company." She offered the flowers to him.

He refused to touch them. "Now's not a good time."

"Why will you not even accept a token of friendship? Do you hate me that much?"

"I don't hate you." With a sigh that she interpreted as defeat, Joshua took the flowers and stepped back to permit her into the foyer.

She tried not to gape at the interior of the three-story stone home at the end of Rock Springs Boulevard. In her youth, she could only imagine being invited inside the home that had been in the Thornton family for five generations. It was several times bigger and homier than the trailer in which she had grown up.

Joshua led the way to the kitchen to set the table with paper plates and plastic utensils. Admiral followed the scent of the burgers.

"I'm a gourmet cook. Did you know that?" Tori chatted away while she set up the fast food with the elegance of a three-course meal. "I went to Europe for a couple of weeks with this guy. I tried authentic European cooking. It's nothing like anything that you get here. But, I have to tell you, when I got back, I was dying for a big ole greasy burger." She held out the sandwich to him.

As he slid into his chair at the head of the table, Joshua stared at the hamburger that she offered to him. Admiral was also staring at the ground beef that was four inches from his nose. He licked his chops. If his master was not going to take it, he would.

Joshua accepted the burger, much to the dog's disappointment. "Tori, why did you come here?"

She took a bite of her hamburger and chewed. She watched him gazing at the burger on his plate. "I did not have anything to do with Max coming after you."

His eyes were tired. "That is ancient history."

"If you really believe that, then why can't we be friends?"

"You seem to have this warped idea that friends should engage in casual sex with each other and I don't. I'll be your friend, but I'm not going to sleep with you." Joshua took a bite of his burger, but didn't taste it.

"Why do you assume that I sleep with every man who I'm friends with? Is it because I'm a whore?"

He was exhausted with the topic of their discussion. "I've said no thank you. Why do we have to keep talking about it?"

"I want to sleep with you because I have always been attracted to you, and I know you are attracted to me."

"This conversation at this time is inappropriate." Joshua reminded her of his friend who was found dead.

"I'm sorry." She balled up the wrapper from her burger. "I did not come here to pick you up." She stood up. Her voice rose an octave. "Yes, I like sex. I make no apologies for that. If that makes me a whore, then I guess that's what I am."

She had gathered up her purse and tossed the bag from McDonald's into the trash as she added the closing line of her statement. "The problem with people from your side of the tracks, Joshua Thornton, is that you won't look beyond the label that you stick on people to see what lies underneath."

She left him alone in the kitchen with the bouquet of flowers sitting in the middle of the table without a vase to stand in.

Admiral ate his hamburger in one gulp.

Joshua had resumed his nap on the sofa in his study when the sound of the doorbell brought him back to the foyer. Assuming that it was Tori returning, either to argue for the affair she was wanting or to apologize, he swung open the door. "Can't you see that now is not a good time?" He started at seeing Seth Cavanaugh on the other side of the door.

"Now is as good a time as any, Counselor." He pushed open

the door and stepped in without invitation. "We have to talk."

Joshua folded his arms across his chest. "If you want to interview me about Gail, I suggest we make an appointment to do it downtown in Sheriff Sawyer's office."

Seth took in his tired eyes and disheveled appearance. "You look like hell."

"Lack of sleep."

"Guilt does that."

"One," Joshua replied, "I did not kill Gail. Two, what evidence do you have to suggest that I did?"

"Opportunity. You were on the murder scene. We have witnesses who heard you admit to that." The detective pointed out to the driveway. "And I just saw your motive leaving. Were you going over your stories for the police?"

"Damn it, Cavanaugh!" He gritted his teeth. "Tori Brody is a colleague. She came over here to offer condolences on the death of a classmate. If you had bothered asking me, instead of jumping to conclusions—"

"Why bother asking? You would have told me the same lie you are telling me now."

"Well, I do bother asking, and then I take the time to go after the truth. You just jump on the train and ride it until you railroad your case into court!"

"Is this railroading?" Seth held up a plastic evidence bag containing a blue pen with gold engraving on the side.

Joshua uttered a gasp at the sight of his lost pen.

"Aren't you even going to ask where I found it? Or do you already know?"

"I lost that pen weeks ago."

"And I found it . . . in Reynolds's living room. How did you lose it? Did it fall out of your pocket while you were unzipping your pants? Then she found out that she wasn't the only woman you were dipping your pen into—"

"Have you spoken to the medical examiner?"

Seth snorted.

Joshua opened the door and gestured for him to leave. "Talk to Dr. Johnstone and then, after that, we'll talk in Sawyer's office."

"We will talk again, Thornton." He could feel the frost of Seth's breath in his face. "You should be more careful about whose past you go around checking out."

"So that's what this is about. What are you afraid of my finding out?"

"Nothing now." Seth predicted, "By the time I'm through with you, no one will believe a thing you say."

Joshua closed the door behind him and then went to the window to watch Seth pull out of the driveway and down Fifth Street to town. Then, he picked up the phone and hit a speed dial number.

Tad picked up on the first ring.

"Cavanaugh was just here."

"And?"

"I think I need to lawyer up."

CHAPTER NINE

"Gail did not have any baby," Carey Hoffman stated.

The writer's sister worked as a clerk for an automotive service in New Cumberland. She glanced around to make sure that none of the three customers waiting for their cars were listening to her conversation with Jan Martin, who countered her version with proof of the lie.

"That's not what the autopsy said. They did find evidence of childbirth."

With a combination of a sigh and a snort, Carey asked, "Why can't you leave well enough alone?"

"We have to check out all possibilities." Jan pressed her lips together. "Had you seen Gail since she came back home?"

"We were not that close."

"I noticed. I recall back when we were all kids that you two didn't exactly hang out with the same crowd."

Carey rationalized the lack of friendship. "I was three years younger than Gail. That's a big difference when you're kids."

"But you're not kids anymore."

"When Mom was sick, Gail started planning for her death and had the legal connections to get everything of value. All I got were the photo albums and the chipped family china. There were hard feelings about that."

"Then why are you so set on protecting her name now?"

"I have a daughter who wants to be a journalist just like her Aunt Gail. I don't want her name dragged through the mud,"

Carey told her. "That's what they do every time someone famous dies. Dig up all the dirt on them. They don't think about the person, and all the pain and hurt she might have suffered."

Seeing a light in the tunnel that pointed in the direction she was seeking, Jan offered, "Why don't you try telling me about the pain and hurt she went through?"

"Gail did not want to put the baby up for adoption. My parents insisted that she give it up. Either that, or they weren't going to pay for her to go away to college."

"Do you know who the baby's father was?"

Carey shrugged.

"Gail didn't tell you?"

She responded with a hollow laugh. "Gail was not a well person. Of course, when I mentioned that to Mom and Dad, they practically disowned me."

"How was she not well?" Jan didn't want to confess to knowing about the nervous breakdown.

"Gail fantasized. She told me that Joshua Thornton was the baby's father. But I was there at the Valentine's Day dance when he and Beth Davis announced their engagement. He was with her that whole evening. There was no—"

"Could—?"

"That was the night that Gail got pregnant. I know. I found her in the backseat of our car afterwards."

"I guess you are wondering why I've been in the twilight zone."

Joshua sucked in a deep breath and observed the faces sitting before him around the kitchen table. He tried to think of the most diplomatic words to express the sin he committed in his youth that threatened to come back now to bite him in the butt. It would mean risking the loss of his children's respect.

"It's hard losing a friend." Tracy reminded him of Grace's

murder with a nod of her head.

Joshua shook his head. "Gail was a friend. I've lost friends before, but—"

"Did you two have an affair?" Sarah asked.

He asserted, "We were friends, nothing more."

"Mom said that she was trying to get you."

Joshua cocked his head at his younger daughter. He had realized that he and his wife would fight after Gail came to visit. He wasn't aware that the children had noticed it as well. He had thought that his late wife didn't like Gail because she was a hardcore feminist. There was another reason. Valerie sensed her attraction to him.

Jan rushed in through the kitchen back door. "Josh! We have to talk!"

He groaned.

"I think you are going to want to hear what I found out." Her tone told him that she was bursting with news.

With the effort of an emotionally and physically exhausted man, Joshua raised himself up from the table and led the way into his study. He was aware of five pairs of eyes on his back.

Jan plunged ahead. "Were you aware that the network let Gail go from her contract and paid her off? In other words, she was fired." She explained the termination of Gail's contract. "There is a family in Connecticut that had a restraining order against her for stalking their son, whom she'd hunted down after giving him up for adoption. She ended up spending some time in a psych ward."

"Are you aware that there is a possibility that that boy is my son?"

She squawked. "Is that why Ernie is nosing around to find out if you were sleeping with Gail?"

"How did Gaston find out about all this so fast?"

"I don't know. He called me wanting to know about your

love life. I told him that it was none of his business." Jan asked, "Exactly what was going on with you and Gail?"

"It was a one-night stand back in high school! We were kids!" He forced her back on track. "What did you find out about this kid in Connecticut?"

She responded to his question with a question. "When did you sleep with Gail?"

"Jan!"

"It's for the math. I have the boy's birth date. He was conceived in February. When did you and Gail do the deed?"

"First week of January." He sighed with relief. "He can't be mine."

"She wanted him to be yours. She wanted it so much, she convinced herself that he was."

"But who is the father?"

"Gail was not exactly a hot date back then. Her sister is convinced that the baby was conceived Valentine's Day night at the school dance. Gail got drunk and went out to the parking lot. She was drinking with a bunch of the jocks. Carey kept trying to get her to come back inside, but she refused. After the dance, she found Gail passed out in the backseat of their car. Her panties were missing. She told Carey that you sneaked out of the dance to make love to her."

"That's not true! I was with Beth. We got engaged that night!"

"Gail had some big issues, but she was so good at coming across like she had it together that no one saw it."

The phone rang on his desk. "Now what?" He snatched up the phone. "What?" He barked into the receiver. After Tad, who was on the other end of the line, reminded him of his manners, he apologized.

While Jan watched him plop down behind his desk with the phone at his ear, her mind reeled. She had done it. She had helped Joshua in the case Seth was racing to put together against him.

But once again, Gail had one-upped her. Not only did she live the life Jan had dreamed of having, but her rival also had the pleasure of having Joshua make love to her, even if it was only once. Jan imagined the feel of his body touching hers.

With a curse, he hung up the phone.

"What?" she snapped out of her thoughts to ask him.

"The housekeeper at the motor lodge just found Bella Polk's body. She had been beaten to death."

"Who is Bella Polk?"

"She was Rex Rollins's landlady," Joshua told her. "You know, she was very inquisitive about if there was any reward for information leading to the arrest of Rex's killer. I wonder—"

"If maybe she knew who killed him."

Joshua squinted while asking himself more than her, "You don't think Rex's landlady was foolish enough to have gotten hold of his manuscript and tried to blackmail his killer with it?"

Excited by the prospect of getting the jump on one of Ernie's reporters, Jan raced out to get the story of yet another murder in Chester.

Joshua sat in silence. He stared out the window at the backyard without seeing anything but the swift second hand making its way around the clock while Seth Cavanaugh put together his case against him.

"Did you read the newspaper?" Sheriff Curt Sawyer tossed *The Glendale Vindicator,* its front page displayed, on the center of his desk as a gesture for Seth to read the subject of their meeting, which had been called before the detective had a chance to finish his first cup of coffee.

Seth frowned deeply in order to conceal the smile that crept to the corners of his lips.

Somehow, somewhere, the owner and editor of *The Glendale Vindicator* had found a picture of a teenage Joshua Thornton and Gail Reynolds, her sitting in his lap, to print on the front page of the newspaper with the headline, "All the Women Thornton Has Loved."

After suggesting that Joshua and Gail had had a secret love affair for years, Ernie Gaston then led into the collection of mementoes she had. He insinuated that the prosecutor was currently having an affair with lawyer Tori Brody, whom he had been seen sharing drinks with at Dora's.

When asked about her relationship with Hancock County's prosecuting attorney, Tori stated that she was unable to comment. "After all, a sexual relationship between a defense attorney and prosecutor could be construed as a conflict of interest in some criminal cases." The newspaper journalist then noted that Joshua Thornton had struck deals for two of Tori's clients, including a murder suspect.

The editor went on to list the women in Joshua's life who were now deceased: Beth Davis, his late wife, Gail Reynolds, and finally Tricia Wheeler. The last name was complemented by a picture: Tricia, the deceased topic of Gail's book, held in the arms of the valley's favorite son.

The chronology ended with an unasked question about his innocence. What was his connection with Tricia Wheeler? Was there something in their relationship that he feared Gail would discover during her investigation? An unnamed source had told *The Glendale Vindicator* that he was the last person to see the journalist alive. Gaston left much up to the readers' imaginations—which was more damaging than drawing a conclusion.

"Who is the unnamed source in the Hancock County Sheriff Department that told Gaston about Josh's stuff being at the murder scene?" Sheriff Sawyer flipped the newspaper to show a second article about Grace Henderson's murder. "Is it the same idiot who leaked that Grace Henderson was pregnant?"

"That source could have been any of those rent-a-cops you have working for you."

Curt was almost half a foot shorter than his chief of detectives, but his solid muscles, which bulged when he crossed his arms across his chest, were enough to make Seth flinch. "You mess with Thornton and you mess with everyone in this valley."

Before Seth could respond, Joshua came through the glass door to the sheriff's office. He held the newspaper with the article in his hand. "You son of a bitch!"

"Hey!" Seth held up his hands. "Don't blame me if your womanizing has finally caught up to you! All of the women I have slept with are still alive!"

Joshua grabbed him by the front of his suit jacket and threw him up against the wall. "My children read this over breakfast before I woke up!"

The doorway to the sheriff's office was filled with deputies hoping to see their chief of detectives brought down to size by the county prosecutor.

In spite of the pair of fists threatening to damage his pretty face, Seth Cavanaugh was smug. "Looks like the great Thornton has a temper."

Ashamed of his display of anger, Joshua released him.

Seth smoothed his hair with both of his hands. "You were at the scene of the crime and that is your skin under her fingernails."

"I did not kill her. We weren't having any affair. My love life is no one's business."

"But murder is everyone's business." Seth suggested to the sheriff, "Considering Thornton's involvement with the victim—"

"You don't have to do that," Joshua interjected. "I called the attorney general yesterday—before this article came out. A special investigator will be here today to take over the Reynolds case. I'm out of it."

"Do you have everything you need?"

Tad could see the answer to his question in Hallie Shearer's face. The widow-to-be lied when she said that she had all she needed. There was no health insurance for her dying husband, nor was there any life insurance that would help with the financial burden she was doomed to encounter after his death. Bankruptcy was the only thing that kept the family from losing their home along the rural stretch of Route 30 on the Pennsylvania side of the state line. It was because of the desire to spend his last days with his family as much as to conserve money that Bert Shearer refused to stay in the hospital.

Tad was willing to make time to come to their home to check on his progress instead of forcing Hallie to go through the ordeal of transporting him to the doctor's office to be told that the cancer was spreading through her husband's body with the speed of a pop culture fad. On this last visit, he was barely aware that they were in the room.

"How much more time does he have left?" Hallie wanted Tad to tell her that he would soon be dead. It was exhausting to care for her husband, work full-time, and at all times appear optimistic in front of their children.

Tad took the medical bag he had asked her to help him to carry to his motorcycle and slipped it into the carrying compartment. "Jesus was the one who said that no one knows the day or the hour."

"But it's close." She lowered her eyes to her feet. "It will all be over soon."

"Soon." He clasped the compartment shut.

Tad took her hand. Hallie grasped his fingers and palm to take in the comfort of his touch. Instead, she felt paper against her palm. She tore her eyes from his sympathetic expression to study her open palm. He had slipped a wad of twenty-dollar bills into her hand.

"Doc—"

He couldn't hear her objection over the roar of his cycle as it sped out onto Route 30. He didn't stop until he got to Rollins Corner Café to have lunch before going to the hospital for his afternoon rounds.

"Hey, Doug," the doctor greeted yet another one of his patients when he stepped up to the counter to order a bag of cinnamon coffee and an egg sandwich. He unzipped his coat and set his helmet on the stool next to him.

Doug rushed back to the kitchen.

Tad swung around on the stool to take in the handful of customers during the mid-morning lull. Two farmers were eating a late breakfast. Their table was filled with an assortment of food that made up a major feeding. In the corner booth behind Tad's seat, a deliveryman was enjoying a slice of pumpkin pie and a mug of coffee.

"Hey, aren't you Doc MacMillan?"

Tad didn't recognize the deliveryman, whose bushy hair was collected into a ponytail that extended to his mid-back. His clothes were worn and his face was unshaven. Phyllis was sitting in the same booth across from him in what appeared to be a break for the café owner.

"That's what they call me." Tad scanned the menu that consisted of a single typewritten sheet of paper encased in a plastic cover. Its torn edges were sealed with yellowed tape.

"You're the one whose cousin killed that reporter he was screwing around with," the man in the booth chuckled after Phyllis returned to the kitchen.

Even with the distance between them, Tad could smell the stench of cigarettes and beer on the deliveryman.

Before he could respond to the comment, Phyllis escorted

Doug from the kitchen. She held up the coffeepot as if in a toast to offer Tad a cup, which he accepted. With shaking hands, her brother grabbed the cup and saucer to place before him.

"What was he afraid of? Her finding out about him and that cheerleader?" the bushy-haired man asked. "Or did she know that he was screwing around with both of them at the same time and was afraid that she was going to ruin his goody-two-shoes image?"

"Want some more coffee, Lou?" Phyllis blurted out the question.

"Nah, I had enough."

She went back into the kitchen. On her way, she stopped to give Doug a silent order.

Lou continued, "You know, it isn't like I give a shit about who killed that stuck-up bitch or shot some cheerleader back before the beginning of time." He rose and put on his ball cap with "Dell Appliance" embroidered in the front. "What irks me is that just because some guy has a pretty face, he's going to get off for murder while if it was some working stiff like me, I'd be strapped to a table with a needle in my arm."

"Josh didn't kill anyone." Tad slapped the newspaper on the counter with his open palm. "Before this is over, Gaston is going to print a full retraction with the truth in it."

"Whose truth?"

"The whole truth. People can't get away with murder that easily anymore. Science has come too far. Whoever killed Gail was in her house. They left physical evidence of their presence there and I will find it. When I do, I'll find them, and Josh's name will be cleared, and idiots like you will be sorry for what you are assuming based on jealous innuendoes made up by a eunuch like Gaston."

He realized as the words were coming out of his mouth that he was wasting his breath. Lou's response proved it when he strutted out the door. With a sigh, Tad turned back to the counter. Seeing the picture on the front page of Joshua and Gail, the cause of the encounter with the deliveryman, he shoved the paper aside.

Doug placed the egg sandwich on a white saucer in front of Tad and a brown bag containing the freshly ground coffee with the top folded down and secured with a twisty next to it. Anxious to get out of the restaurant, Tad took a big bite from the sandwich.

He was chewing as fast as he could when Phyllis rushed out of the kitchen with a paper bag in her hand. Without taking the time to put on her coat, she ran out the door to the parking lot.

"She had no right coming here to write that book."

Tad was so startled by Doug's statement that he had to ask him to repeat what he had said in order to decipher the words and their connection to the argument with Lou.

"She didn't even know Trish, not the way I did."

"Did Gail ask you about her?"

"Yeah, but Phyllis said we didn't know anything."

"When was this?"

"The other night. She was here with Trish's mom, looking through some picture books."

"What other night?" Tad wondered if Rollins Corner Café was the last place Gail went before she was killed.

"That night. She started asking Phyllis about Trish and she told Gail that we did not want any part of her book."

Tad wiped his mouth with a paper napkin. "Doug, do you know anything that you want to tell me?"

Doug grinned. "Trish didn't want anyone to know."

The slam of the door signaled his sister's return. "Let Doc eat in peace!" She grabbed Doug by the arm and led him back into the kitchen.

"I was just telling him—"

"Shhhh!"

Normally, Tad would not notice who was behind him when he was on his motorcycle. But after he had left Rollins Corner Café, when he hit the crest of the hill on Route 30 that led to the bridge across the Ohio River, a delivery truck flew over the top and came up behind him so quickly that he thought it was going to ram him and his motorcycle across the road, over the guardrail, and down the steep slope into what had once been Rock Springs Park.

Better watch this guy, Tad told himself. He had been riding motorcycles since getting his driver's license and was aware that some drivers used motorcyclists as targets for whatever rage they might be harboring.

With the straight stretch of the bridge across the river, the truck bore down on the back of the Harley-Davidson.

If Tad had not been watching the truck in his rearview mirror, he would not have been able to make the lane switch that sent it whizzing past him. Wondering who could want to run him over, he looked over at the driver.

His bushy ponytail blew out the open window.

It was Lou from Rollins Corner Café.

Lou threw the steering wheel to the left to send his truck sideways in an attempt to crush the motorcycle and its rider against the guardrail acting as a lane divider.

Tad dropped back.

The truck hit the guardrail to send sparks flying when speeding metal hit metal.

The motorcycle whipped around the careening truck, off the bridge, and down Route 11 in search of the exit for the hospital.

Tad's hope that Lou had worked out his aggression on the guardrail was in vain when he checked out his rearview mirror and saw the truck with a crumbled fender bearing down on him again.

"Damn!"

He whirled his bike around onto the exit before the hospital and hit the access road leading up the river toward Midland, Pennsylvania. After crossing under the bridge, the freeway narrowed to two lanes. It had turnoffs going up the steep hill into the East End of East Liverpool. Some roads, blocked with cement barricades, had been closed since the freeway and bridge were built.

By the time Tad crossed under the bridge with the truck a hair's breath from seizing its prey, he knew where he was going to lead him and what he was going to do.

Now well aware of his mortality, Tad had not pulled a hazardous stunt in the decade since he had stopped drinking. He knew he could do it. Hey, isn't drinking supposed to dull your reaction time?

He led his pursuer halfway through East End to a service road that ran under Route 39. While making sure the truck did not clip his rear wheel and send him flying, he tried to recall where the road he could use to end the chase was located.

It was the second entrance. Or was it the third entrance?

Mentally, he flipped a coin and said a prayer. He chose the second because it was closer. He leaned over the handlebars and raced under Route 39 with the truck close behind him.

If it was to work, he needed the truck right on his tail. If not, then Lou had time to slow down, go around the obstacle, and continue the pursuit.

Tad came up onto the barricade and looked for the ramp he and his buddies had made out of dirt dumped by the road crew from which to launch. If his memory served him correctly, and if kids were indeed the same today as they were back in his youth, it would still be used, if not improved, to jump ATVs.

The cyclist found the jump as soon as the barricade came into sight, and he was indeed born lucky. It was not wide enough for a truck, nor was there room on either side of the hurdle for it to get around.

Tad rose up on his haunches and hit the gas with all he had.

While sailing through the air, he experienced all the exhilaration of his youth. He wondered why he ever stopped doing stunts like this. Then, the sobering reality hit him, and he recalled why he had stopped doing foolish things.

Fear.

There is something to be said for lack of anxiety. It leaves you free to concentrate on what to do and not on what could go wrong. One of the things that can go off beam is that the state road crew can dump a pile of dirt on your landing strip.

Tad hit the fresh soil as if he were doing a belly flop into a pool of water. Upon impact, dirt flew up to create a mushroom cloud.

His chest hit the handlebars; he toppled over the front of the bike and somersaulted down the hill until he landed spread eagled on his back. The air knocked out of him, he lay while he waited for his head and the world around him to stop spinning.

He heard a roar in his ears that he assumed came from the pain and injuries he had inflicted on himself. When he regained his senses, he realized that the noise was from outside his body.

In his shock at making the jump almost perfectly (except for the landing) and in his amazement at the fact that he had survived, Tad had forgotten about the man trying to kill him. Too shaken to stand, he crawled on his hands and knees around the dirt pile.

Lou had followed the cycle up the ramp.

He tried the jump—and failed.

The delivery truck was too big for such feats. It toppled forward onto its front, shattering the windshield, before somersaulting onto its back. Propelled by its speed, it then whirled around on its back not unlike an overturned turtle. Gasoline spilled from the tank. When the sparks from the spinning metal on the cement road caught the fuel spilt from its ruptured tank, it caught fire.

The truck was engulfed in flames with Lou from Rollins Corner Café trapped inside.

CHAPTER TEN

"What were you thinking?" Joshua scooped a spoonful of vanilla ice cream into his mouth and devoured it, but not before a drop of hot fudge fell to his chin. "What was going through your mind?"

"That I'd pull it off." Tad reached from where he lay on the chaise next to the swing on the Thorntons' back porch to hand Joshua the napkin in his lap. He gestured towards his chin.

"You could have been killed!" Joshua wiped his chin and resumed swinging while eating his sundae. "You're lucky that all you did was get your shirt dirty."

Tad stopped petting Admiral to wipe the brown powder from his chest. "That's not dirt, it's coffee. I bought a bag at Rollins and it broke open." He continued his defense of the motorcycle jump. "I couldn't let that maniac chase me through town and kill someone. I was going to double back and go to the police. There was only one hitch. Some idiot had dumped a pile of dirt on my landing strip since the last time I made that jump."

"Which was when?"

"Maybe fifteen years ago," Tad mumbled into the dog's ear.

Admiral did not enjoy the ear scratching as much as he would have enjoyed the ice cream his master was eating a couple of feet away from his mouth. He didn't dare go for it. The Great Dane–Irish Wolfhound mongrel had already made the mistake of letting Tad coax him up to lie next to him on the chaise for a petting. Deciding to take what he could get, he pressed his head against Tad's chest and uttered a moan of pleasure.

Joshua had been called to the hospital after Tad was taken there by ambulance. The driver of the truck was taken away by Columbiana County's medical examiner's wagon. Judging by what was left on the bloody windshield, he had been killed on impact. He wasn't wearing a seat belt.

Since the attempt on Tad's life took place in Ohio, outside of the Hancock County prosecutor's jurisdiction, Joshua had no authority in the case. The uniformed officer from the East Liverpool Police Department who answered the call looked young enough to be either one of their sons.

The name of the trucker turned out to be Lou Alcott.

At first, Tad claimed that he had never seen nor heard of his assailant before that morning. Then he remembered that he had a patient whose name was Judy Alcott. She was Lou's wife, now widow.

Even though Tad insisted that he had no relationship with Lou Alcott's wife beyond that of doctor, the police officer concluded that Lou Alcott was trying to kill the man he believed to be his wife's lover.

Tad said that it was a simple case of road rage.

After taking his cousin home from the hospital, Joshua made himself a sundae while Tad took two aspirin for the body aches seeping in from his bike jump. Joshua found Tad stretched out on the chaise with their dog beside him. Admiral took in his petting like a tired man enjoying a massage after a hard day's work.

It was mid-afternoon and Joshua felt like the day had dragged on three days too long. He could imagine the conversation his children were having with their friends after seeing his imagined love life featured on the front page of the newspaper.

"Herb Duncan got a new truck," Tad announced abruptly.

Joshua followed Tad's eyes to where a truck, its red paint

shining in the sun, cruised the alley at the back of the property in the direction of Fifth Street. Through the hedges, they could make out the profile of a young couple in the cab. They looked like a couple of kids out joyriding in their daddy's new big pickup truck.

Joshua recalled the one time he had met Herb Duncan's wife Blanche. She had come to the courthouse to bail her husband out of jail with money she had borrowed from her mother when he was arraigned on misdemeanor charges of selling stolen goods.

At the time, Joshua thought Blanche Duncan, with her pimply face and underdeveloped figure, did not appear old enough to be married. She stood out in the magistrate's court in her spiky black hair with bronzed tips. Her clumsy attempt to look older with cosmetics and hair coloring made her look clownish.

Likewise, Herb's lack of maturity led him to associate with men in the local bars who boasted of friends who knew of ways to make a quick buck.

In court, the prosecutor detected a sense of desperation in the young couple to achieve the American dream overnight. At least, that was the explanation Herb Duncan's public defender offered for how his client ended up trying to sell stolen auto parts.

"Nice truck," Joshua said before explaining what Tad already knew. "Blanche visits her mother every day." She lived in a house at the end of the alley.

"Has to cost at least thirty thousand dollars."

"Maybe." Joshua was more concerned with getting the last drop of hot fudge at the bottom of the bowl that refused to slide onto his spoon.

"Where does a man who has never had a full-time permanent job get the money to buy a thirty-thousand-dollar truck?"

"They call it a car loan. You can get them either at a bank or the dealership."

"But you have to show an ability to pay. He doesn't have that. Blanche doesn't work. He's afraid that if she gets a job, she'll meet someone else and run off."

Joshua offered as explanation, "Maybe he inherited it."

"None of his people have money and they are all still alive."

"Why do you want to know?"

"Curiosity. I can't help it. It's in the gene pool. I hate not knowing something."

"There's a fine line between curiosity and nosiness." Joshua gestured towards the truck that was now out of sight. "That is nosiness."

"Rita told me that Herb was at the State Line the night Rex was shot. She said that he paid up on his bar tab, plus gave her a big tip."

"Isn't paying off your bar tab a good thing?"

"Depends on where and how you got the money to do it." Tad asked himself more than his friend, "I wonder what Herb has gotten himself into now."

"Why do you assume that he got the money illegally?"

"If it looks like a duck—"

"Just like how everyone assumes when they see you talking to a woman that you have, are, or will soon be sleeping with her."

Tad disagreed. "They don't assume that about me now. They assume that about you."

Before Joshua Thornton had been elected Hancock County's prosecuting attorney, he had his own law office in the heart of Chester. Located within walking distance of his home, it was more convenient than the office in New Cumberland. Since he owned the building, he kept it to work in when he didn't need to be down the river.

His part-time secretary, Debbie, was on her cell phone when

he walked through the door. "As a matter of fact, she called just today." When she saw her boss, she flipped the instrument shut without any farewell and dropped it into her purse. "Mr. Thornton, Mrs. Wheeler is here to see you." Then she added, "Tori Brody called."

Pretending not to notice her suggestive tone, he took the message sheet without a word and slipped it into his pocket.

Joshua would not have recognized Dorothy Wheeler if Debbie had not introduced her. While she had the same good looks her daughter did, he recalled that when he had met her in his youth that she always looked tired.

Since her child's death, Dorothy, he could see, had moved on and beyond her grief to get on with her life. She was dressed in a soft, fuchsia-colored sweater and black slacks under a leather coat with a matching purse. She shook his hand and greeted him in a strong voice. "I understand that you are now the county's prosecuting attorney."

"That I am, Mrs. Wheeler. I'm not sure if you remember me—"

"Oh, I remember you, Josh." She smiled. "Trish talked about you a lot. I've come to see you because I don't want her killer to get away this time."

He gestured to his office at the top of the stairs at the back of the reception area. "Then step into my office, Mrs. Wheeler. I think we should talk."

Taking up her purse and a white paper bag that appeared to come from a dress shop, she climbed the stairs. He paused to tell Debbie that he did not want their meeting to be interrupted before going to his office, where he slipped off his jacket and sat next to Tricia's mother on his sofa.

"I was meaning to call you," he began their discussion. "Going through Gail's effects they found that she had called you a couple of times. I assume to discuss Tricia."

She assured him that his assumption was correct. "A few weeks ago, she came to Canfield to interview me. That's where I live now. I didn't see her again until we met at Rollins's diner right before she died."

"Rollins Corner Café?" he asked.

She nodded her head.

"What time was that?"

"We met for dinner about six-thirty. We spent the whole time talking about Tricia's murder. She had a couple of questions. I answered them as best I could. Then she left a little after seven-thirty." She sighed. "How was Gail killed?"

"She was smothered." Joshua didn't tell her any more details. Nor did he mention that he seemed to be the last person to see her alive. "Did she tell you what she had found out?"

"I thought her main suspect was Margo Sweeney. She was always mine," she said. "I assumed when the case was closed so fast that Commissioner Ross Sweeney had something to do with it. If Trish's death had been ruled a murder, his princess Margo would be the prime suspect and we couldn't have that, could we?"

Joshua nodded in agreement that Dorothy's suspicions made sense. "Was that the route Gail was taking in her investigation?"

"She said she had another suspect."

"Who?"

"She didn't say. She said that she remembered something that happened and wanted to check it out before going public with it."

He grinned at the suggestion of a lead in finding Gail's killer. "Did she tell you what it was?"

She shook her head sadly. "I wish she had."

"Do you remember who else was at the diner when you met Gail there that night? Maybe her killer was following her."

"I don't know anyone who lives here in Chester anymore,"

she claimed. "There were a couple of guys in work clothes at the counter. They were staring at us, but I assumed it was because Gail was a public figure and they recognized her. Phyllis chewed them out for staring and they ate their dinners and left. They were the only people there, except for Doug and Phyllis."

"Can you think of anything else that happened that night?" he urged her. "Anything. No matter how minor or insignificant you think it is."

"Just . . ." her voice trailed off.

"What?"

"Phyllis practically ordered us to leave because she did not want us discussing Tricia in front of Doug."

Joshua sat up straight with this information. He tried to make sense of Phyllis Rollins's reaction to Gail and Dorothy meeting at her café to work on her book about Tricia Wheeler.

She explained, "I guess it was my fault. I've known Phyllis since she was a little girl. She's exactly like her mother, who I thought, pardon me, was a very cold fish. But that night, since we were discussing Tricia, and Phyllis happened to be at our table refilling my coffee cup, I asked her if she could remember anything about what happened the day that Tricia died." She added, "A few weeks ago, after Gail told me that she was going through with writing the book, I called Phyllis and she practically hung up on me."

He understood why Dorothy would have called Phyllis and Doug. Their parents were the Wheelers' landlords and they lived next door.

"Doug and Phyllis were right outside when I came home that day and found Trish," she recalled. "But she always swore that they didn't see or hear anything. I guess she got sick of my asking."

"Why did meeting at the diner to talk about the book upset

173

Doug?" Joshua asked.

"He had an awful crush on Tricia. He was devastated when she was killed. That night at the café, he was so upset that he dumped a whole bag of coffee on the floor. Phyllis ground another bag for Gail and practically threw it at her when she told us to go."

Joshua nodded. "Doug is emotionally fragile. As a matter of fact, he's been declared mentally incompetent."

"So I heard."

"Did you see or speak to Trish at all that day that she died?"

She responded with a shake of her head. "The last time I saw her alive was when she left for school." She rubbed an imaginary spot on her purse with her index finger.

Even though Dorothy spoke with a strong voice, Joshua could see she was still wounded. As a parent, he couldn't see how anyone could get over losing a child.

He swallowed. "Did Gail tell you that it will be difficult to prove Tricia's death was murder when it was originally ruled a suicide, especially after all this time? The sheriff's department is looking for the original case file. I doubt if there will be much there."

"I told Sheriff Delaney that Trish didn't kill herself. He told me she did. He said she did it because Randy dumped her. After the shock had worn off, I went to see him with a list of questions about what he found in his investigation. That man walked away from me while I was talking to him. I had questions that to this day have never been answered."

"Ask me," he pleaded. "If I don't know the answers, then maybe this mess will get cleared up when I get them."

Dorothy forgot about the spot on her purse and set it aside. She sat up straight when she asked, "Where did the gun come from?"

For his answer, he looked back at her. He had assumed that

the gun had belonged to the Wheelers. Her late husband died in Vietnam. He was in the military. Most families in the rural valley owned guns because of their centuries-old feeling that they needed to be responsible for protecting themselves. Her question was one of the first ones a lawman asks in a crime involving a gun, even a suicide. Where did the gun come from?

Joshua frowned. "The sheriff didn't ask you that?"

"I asked him. We didn't have any guns in that house, not since the day those men came and told me that my husband was dead. Tricia didn't know the first thing about how to use a gun. As far as I know, she had never even seen one other than on television. Tricia didn't shoot herself."

"Can you prove it?" he asked. "If you can prove it, then that will give me ammunition when we catch her killer. Otherwise, the defense attorney will say she committed suicide, and that will create a reasonable doubt for the jury, because that was the original ruling."

With a grin, Dorothy picked up the white paper bag and stuck her hand inside. "I was waiting for you to ask me that." She whipped a dress out of the bag. A slip of paper was pinned to the top of the dress. She handed them to the prosecutor. "This proves that Tricia did not kill herself."

He unfolded the dress. It still had the tags on it. It was a pink sleeveless dress. The skirt was full with a petticoat underneath the silky material. Nowadays, it would be considered out of style, but it would have been in style for a semi-formal affair like, he recalled, the homecoming dance scheduled for less than two weeks after Tricia died. This dress was something she could have worn to the formal.

The price tag indicated that it came from a dress shop out at the mall. He knew without checking that the shop was still there. Tracy bought her dress for an upcoming formal at the same shop.

He examined the receipt pinned to the dress. It was one hundred forty-two dollars plus tax, paid for with cash. That was a lot of money for a girl who babysat for her spending money. Tricia would have worked months to save the money to buy this dress.

Dorothy was reporting what she knew about the dress while Joshua studied it and the receipt. "I found it on her bed after the police left. It was still in this same bag. She didn't even have a chance to hang it up."

The date and time on the receipt confirmed what Tricia's mother knew in her heart. The dress was bought at 3:22 p.m. on October 8, 1984—one hour before Tricia Wheeler supposedly took her own life.

Everyone in the Thornton household went to bed early that night. If they didn't go to sleep, they each went to their rooms to be alone with their thoughts about the cloud of suspicion that loomed over their family.

Unable to sleep, Joshua surfed the Internet on his laptop in bed for information about Gail Reynolds and cases she had worked on. Possibly, someone with a grudge from one of her previous cases followed her to Chester in order to extract revenge. He wondered what Gail could have recalled that caused her to eliminate Margo as her prime suspect. He found himself replaying his senior year of high school over and over in his mind in search of what he might have missed.

He was discouraged with his progress when the phone rang.

"Everyone now assumes that we are sleeping together," Tori purred across the line. "I guess we might as well do it."

"The way I feel about you right now, I don't think it would be humanly possible for me."

The purr decreased in volume. "Gaston called me. I did not call him. Someone saw us together at Dora's. Once again, you are blaming me for something that is not my fault."

"You are not a stupid woman, Tori. You purposely suggested that there is more between us than there really is, or ever will be."

The laptop *dinged*. The message balloon announced that he had an instant message from Hank, a friend in his contact list. He felt as if the smile that came to his lips was the first one he had all day.

"I've got to go." Without waiting for a farewell or curse from Tori, he hung up the phone and opened up his Windows Messenger.

"Did you miss me?" the note read.

He typed, "I haven't heard from you in four months. Where have you been?" He punched the SEND button and waited. A moment later, the messenger indicated that Hank was typing out a response.

"You know the Navy nowadays. I can tell you where I've been, but then I'd have to come kill you. What's new?"

His fingers flew across the keyboard.

"Moved the kids back to Chester. Was elected prosecutor. Gail Reynolds came back home and got murdered. Boob detective trying to railroad me into jail. You still at Pearl? How's the wedding plans?"

He sent his response and waited.

"I'll see you in the morning."

He was still typing out his objection when the next note popped up, "Where's Chester?"

CHAPTER ELEVEN

"Remember," Tad warned Joshua before folding back the sheet to reveal Bella Polk's body, "if Cavanaugh finds out that I discussed this case with you, he'll have my hide."

"Cavanaugh is either incompetent or crooked. I haven't decided which." The lawyer studied the landlady's body. "While I'm trying to find that out, we have a killer or killers out there who have to be stopped before anyone else dies." He picked up the old woman's hand. Her hands and arms were covered with scratches and bruises. Tad had clipped her nails down to the quick and scraped out the skin and blood for evidence to identify her killer.

"She didn't go with a whimper, but with a bang," the medical examiner told him. "She put up a good fight. There was skin and blood under her fingernails and in her mouth, too." He pulled back her lips to show her broken teeth. "He broke three of her teeth. When he punched her in the mouth, she bit him. I got his DNA."

"But we need someone to compare it to." Joshua concluded, "If she bit him, then that means we are looking for someone with a human bite on his hand."

Tad held up a plaster cast he had sitting on his desk. "If the perp's bite mark matches this impression, we got the guy with his hand in her mouth."

"You are good."

"And you look good." Tad noted that Joshua had a fresh

haircut and was dressed in pressed slacks, a gray herringbone sports coat, and tie. "Have you got a date?"

"What makes you think I have a date?"

"You're wearing aftershave."

"I wear aftershave."

"Not since Val died."

Joshua and Jan figured that if anyone had incriminating information about Margo Connor and wanted to share, it would be her ex-husband.

After he graduated from Oak Glen High School, Karl Connor went to West Virginia University in Morgantown on a partial football scholarship. Large and muscular, Karl was a good linebacker, but a lousy student. He was baffled to discover that the university expected him to study.

After flunking out of college, he returned home, married the recently widowed Margo Sweeney Boyd, failed at real estate, and was fired by his wife, who divorced him. He eventually became a fire fighter, a profession that let him use his muscles.

Joshua did his homework before visiting his old friend. He learned from Karl's divorce lawyer that, even though his ex-wife was a millionaire, Karl ended up paying her child support for their daughter. While Margo lived in the mansion they had bought during their marriage, he was forced by his financial situation to live with his parents in Newell.

"Do you want me to say that she killed her first husband?" Karl volunteered, "Yeah, she told me that. What details do you need me to say?"

Joshua looked at Jan, who fought to keep from smiling at his offer.

The three former classmates were sitting on the Connor family sun porch, which looked out onto the street where a group of children were playing kickball. Karl was drinking what could not possibly be his first beer of the day while they sipped iced teas.

Joshua replied, "Margo killed who?"

"Her first husband." he answered. "Isn't that what you're here about?"

Jan's ears perked up. She recalled that Margo's first husband was killed in his dental office while working late one night. "I thought she had an alibi for his murder." She turned to the prosecutor for the answer to her question.

Joshua was surprised not only by the news that Margo had been married before she married Karl, but that her first husband had been murdered.

"She was married for only a couple of years," Jan explained. "That was after you had gone to Annapolis. She got a job working as a receptionist for his dental office and—"

"Stole him from his wife and kid," Karl finished.

She added, "He was, like, fifteen years older than her. It was a classic Margo scandal."

"And he was murdered?" The thought of another unsolved murder was daunting to the prosecutor.

Karl answered, "Yeah, he was stabbed while she was giving a big dinner party for her real estate friends. I can say that she told me while we were having sex that she paid someone to do it. Who do you want me to say she hired?"

"Karl, I do not work that way. I want to know the truth."

"Truth is a foreign object to Margo."

"Gail Reynolds was investigating Tricia Wheeler's death," Jan told him.

"That cheerleader who killed herself?"

"She didn't kill herself," Joshua announced. "Do you remember that she and Margo got into this big fight at lunch the same day Trish was shot? Now I seem to recall that you and Margo had a thing going back in school."

"Hey, it was just sex, man. That was the one thing we were good at."

"Did she ever tell you anything about Tricia?"

"She told me she was a bitch," Karl said. "I didn't think so. Trish was nice and had a hot body. Margo hated that. She was so jealous of her that she couldn't see straight."

"Do you remember when Trish died?" Joshua asked. "It was after school on a Monday."

" 'Course I remember that. Everyone does."

"Do you know where Margo was?"

"You want to know the truth, huh?" Karl frowned. "She was with me, damn it. We went out to Adam's apple orchard and was doing it in the back of my car. We were there until dark. But I can say that she wasn't. It'd be her word against mine."

Joshua looked at Jan with regret. Margo didn't kill Tricia.

"When was the last time you saw Tricia?" she asked.

"Same time as Margo. When we were leaving school. Phyllis Barlow was harping on Trish about something."

"Phyllis Barlow?" Joshua repeated the name.

"She was always harping on someone about something. Well, that day she was chasing after Trish, picking at her like some damn vulture."

"What about?"

Karl's answer was a shrug with raised eyebrows. He then suggested, "Cindy Patterson might know. They left together. I think Phyllis was still bitchin' when they drove off in Cindy's car. I remember it real good because it was the last time I ever saw Trish."

"Yeah, I'll check with Cindy to see what that was about." Joshua was thinking of others who might be able to tell him what Phyllis was fighting with her about.

"What about Gail?" Karl interrupted his thoughts. "You want me to say Margo killed her?"

"Karl, all I want from you is the truth," he asserted.

Jan shifted the topic. "Do you recall the Valentine's Day dance following Tricia's murder?"

Karl laughed. "No."

Joshua prompted him with a reminder. "It was the Valentine's Day dance in our senior year. Beth Davis and I got engaged that night."

He responded with sarcasm, "Yeah, I remember the night the king and queen got engaged. Then, the king dumped his queen the second he got out of the kingdom."

"My only crime was growing up."

Jan gestured towards his beer mug. "I seem to recall seeing a bunch of jocks out in the parking lot drinking beer and shots."

Karl scoffed. "So what if a bunch of us was drinking in the parking lot? There was always a bunch of us out there drinking during the dances."

"I have a very good memory," she stated. "So does Gail's sister. She says that Gail was drinking with the football team. You were one of them."

Joshua saw fear in Karl's expression. "Was Gail with you guys?"

"What if she was?" Karl answered too firmly.

"She got drunk," Jan told him, "and someone took advantage of her."

"So?"

"She got pregnant."

"I heard that was Josh's baby."

Joshua told him, "I was with Beth all that night."

"Are you sure you didn't leave her for a little while to go out to your van and relieve yourself?"

Joshua drained his glass of iced tea before asking casually, "When was the last time you saw Heather?"

"A couple of months ago. You'd never know we lived less

than twenty minutes from each other. Would you believe I pay child support for a kid I never get to see? Margo turned her against me. She spends more time in Steubenville with her friends than she does with me."

"What friends?"

"Don't know. Never met them. Once, I saw her at the mall with this girl—didn't even introduce me—acted like she didn't know me."

"What did the girl look like?"

"She had orange hair." Karl looked at Joshua. "Why are you asking me all these questions? You don't think Heather killed Gail, do you?"

"She is the alibi for our chief suspect in Grace Henderson's murder."

"If Heather says she was with this guy, she was." He stood up to his full height. "You got that, Thornton?"

"Yes." Joshua stood up and looked him in the eye. His expression betrayed no fear. "But if she is lying, I will find that out."

Jan stepped between the two men. "It was good seeing you again, Karl."

He kept his glare on the prosecutor and the reporter while they climbed into his Corvette to go on to New Cumberland.

The Corvette came to a halt at the red light at the edge of Newell. Jan observed Joshua's sports coat and tie. The scent of his aftershave excited her senses. "You look good today."

"Thank you. I thought I always looked good." He shot a grin in her direction. When the light turned green, he hit the gas and they raced along the river toward New Cumberland.

"You look especially good today. Court appearance?"

"No."

She frowned. "Date with Tori Brody?"

"I'm not going out with Tori. Jan, I don't believe you."

"I didn't think that you had anything going on with Gail and I turned out to be wrong."

"One time!" Joshua held up his index finger to make his point. "One time, twenty years ago! We were kids and why am I telling you this? I don't owe you any explanation for my behavior!"

Miserably, Jan stared out the passenger window of the car. They were racing along the river. She widened her eyes in an attempt not to let him see the tears forming.

"I'm sorry," he apologized. "I am so sorry."

She sniffed. "I took the liberty of looking into the history of that guy who tried to run Tad down," she said more brightly than she wanted to sound. "Lou Alcott and his wife have been married for three years, and both have been cheating on each other left and right since day one."

"Tad swears he did not sleep with Judy Alcott. The police in East Liverpool think Lou thought he was and that was why he tried to run him down. Tad says it was road rage."

"I may have another motive," Jan said. "Lou drove a delivery truck for Dell Appliance, an appliance distributor in East Liverpool. Judy works as a clerk in a real estate office. Guess whose."

"Margo's?"

"Yep."

"Do you think she hired her clerk's husband to run the county medical examiner down so he wouldn't find any incriminating evidence for us to use against her?"

"Or her daughter," she suggested.

"Margo has to be smart enough to know that if Tad died, the county would get another medical examiner. Besides, we just found out that she couldn't have killed Trish because she has an alibi for the time of her murder. She was having sex with Karl."

"And her daughter was having sex with Billy when her rival was killed."

Joshua discovered the similarities in Tricia's and Grace's murders. "Like mother, like daughter."

"You insulted me." Tori had slipped into Joshua's office after Mary left to deliver a warrant to the sheriff. She was waiting for him in the chair across from his desk when he returned from his interview with Karl Connor.

"I have a lot of work to do. If you don't have any business to discuss, then I would like you to leave." Joshua hung up his sports coat and sat behind his desk.

Tori shifted tactics. "Do you intend to keep our agreement for the Rollins case?"

"What agreement?" He had forgotten about the deal he made with Tori in regard to Phyllis shooting her husband.

"That if Phyllis testified against Rex then you would not charge her for shooting him."

"Now that Rex is dead, she doesn't have to testify, does she? She doesn't have to be afraid of him anymore."

"She isn't a suspect in her husband's killing, is she?"

"There's a reason the spouse of the victim is usually the prime suspect." With a cock of his head, he told her, "He never changed the beneficiary on his life insurance. She just came into a cool one hundred and fifty thousand dollars."

Tori sat up straight at this news. "My client did not kill anyone."

"What about Tricia Wheeler?"

"*The Glendale Vindicator* says that you killed her."

"I never had any disagreement with Tricia about anything," he told her. "But I have a witness who saw your client arguing with her only hours before she was killed."

"Do you now suspect her of killing Tricia Wheeler, too?" Tori scoffed.

"Maybe. Rex was telling people that he wrote a book about

the wicked witch who got away with murder. He was married to
Phyllis. He had a beef with her. She lived next door to Tricia."

"If you had any real evidence, my client would be at the
police station."

"That may come later."

"You have a real problem, Josh," she replied angrily. "Back in
school you blamed me for my boyfriend attacking you, and now
you are blaming me for a newspaper slamming you—all because
of my reputation. Now, you are accusing Phyllis Rollins of two
murders based on what? Because she called a stuck-up bitch a
few names twenty years ago? How much do you want to bet
that if she was lucky enough to get to sit in your lap back then
that you would not be so fast to put her on your suspect list?"
She concluded, "And if I didn't grow up in a trailer park down
by the race track that you would be more accepting of me?"

"You are out of your mind." Joshua gritted his teeth. He
hated saying what he was about to say, "Ms. Brody, I am sick
and tired of you harassing me. Yes, I said harassing. I have
rejected your offer for us to have a sexual relationship and you
have done nothing to change my mind. On the contrary, I am
less interested than I was the first time you came into my office.
In the future, I will only see you to discuss your clients' cases
when you have an appointment. If you don't leave me alone,
I'm going to report you to the public defender. Have I made
myself clear?"

"You son of a bitch!" she hissed.

"It is best if you leave now."

She made it to the door before she stopped, picked up the
silver water pitcher in which he kept fresh water on a tray on
the end table, and hurled it across the room at him. While the
pitcher missed him, the water did not. It spilled across his desk,
his papers, and him.

"Damn!"

She ran out.

Cursing women in general, he found a roll of paper towels in the outer office to mop up the water that had dripped onto the floor.

"Now that's a sight worth flying halfway across the world to see: Commander Joshua Thornton on his knees at my feet."

The lilt of her New England accent caused him to stop mopping. "Hank?" He sat back on his haunches and looked back over his shoulder at her.

Hank, a nickname she credited to Joshua shortly after she was assigned to him as his assistant in San Francisco, was slender from a life born to the outdoors. Her jeans hung low on her hips. Her white T-shirt was short enough to reveal a hint of her flat stomach. Her old Navy blue pea coat hung open. Hank was at an age when most women would have switched to less formfitting clothes, but her build and lifestyle let her put that off a while longer. A New England Patriots ball cap covered her shaggy reddish-brown hair, which was cut in short curly layers so that she didn't have to spend much time taking care of it. Her purse consisted of a backpack that she had slung over her shoulders.

"What happened here?" She observed the flood.

"Women." He climbed to his feet.

"They're still chasing you, I see."

"Don't ask me why, because I don't know." He gazed at her as if for reassurance that he was not imagining her presence in his office. "I can't believe you're here."

Hank slipped the backpack off her shoulders and propped it against the wall. She then took off the coat and draped it over the backpack. "From your message, I gathered you needed a lawyer. Being railroaded by a boob for murdering Gail Reynolds. That's serious stuff, and a lawyer who defends himself has a fool for a client." She held out her arms. "So here I am."

He took her into his arms. When her body made contact with his, he felt a wave of warmth flow through him that he had not felt for a long time. He tightened his arms around her and brushed his cheek against her ball cap. "I'm glad you came. It's good to see you again."

She smiled up at him. "It's good to hear you say that."

Joshua offered her the chair that Tori had vacated moments before. "There's a lot we have to go over if you are going to be defending me."

She sat down. "Civilian life hasn't changed you one bit. Still work now; play later."

He handed her a yellow notepad. "Valerie used to say that she hoped that you could loosen me up a little."

"I miss Val." She reached for the pen he offered her. "How are the kids?"

"Good." When he realized that their fingers were touching, he released the pen with the quickness of an electric shock.

"And you? How are you doing?"

"Everyone thinks I'm a lady killer—figurative and literal." He swallowed the frustration that he felt creeping into his tone. "How do you think I'm doing?"

"Anyone who knows you knows that you would never do that." She lowered her eyes to the notepad. "Tell me about Gail. What was she doing here?"

Joshua tried to be brief while still giving as many details as possible of the series of murders that had occurred since Gail arrived in town, until her death, which revealed her obsession with him.

"Well," Hank mused, "that explains why she kept showing up every time we were assigned to a major case. I suspected that she had the hots for you. This proves it." She tapped the pen against the notepad. "Do you think Gail's murder is connected to that cheerleader you went to school with?"

"A murder made to look like a suicide. The killer gets away with it. Then, twenty years later, a journalist decides to write a book—"

"And a second cheerleader is killed."

He interrupted her. "Grace Henderson's murder has nothing to do with this."

"A cheerleader is murdered then and a cheerleader is murdered now. You can't ignore that."

"I have one or two suspects for the Henderson murder. All I need is to break an alibi, which will probably happen as soon as a romance is broken up."

"What do you have on the Wheeler murder?"

"Nothing. There is no physical evidence whatsoever."

She laughed. "Stop kidding me. What about the murder weapon?"

He shook his head. "I wish we had it. Every ten years the county cleans house. They throw out everything they don't need, including the physical evidence on closed cases. Since her case was closed as a suicide, her evidence box was disposed of—including the gun used to kill her."

"Don't you have anything?"

He held up a folder. "The case file and that's it. Tad is still hunting—"

"Who is Tad?" She snatched the case file out of his hand. It contained nothing but a simple form, typed up on a typewriter, a narrative by the former sheriff, copies of internal memos and a couple letters.

"My cousin," Joshua answered her. "He knows everyone and everything. He's also the county medical examiner. He thinks that he might be able to find the former medical examiner's file with the pictures of the crime scene. I'm hoping that that old pack rat kept more detailed records that would be of help. That's one advantage to pack rats. They don't clean house." He checked his watch and put on his sports coat.

She looked up from where she was studying the narrative of Tricia Wheeler's death. "Where are you going?"

"I have an appointment. I guess since we are working together again, you're coming with me." He was surprised to hear himself say, "Then we can go have dinner."

"Who is the appointment with?" Hank noted that she was not dressed for any legal hearings.

He picked up the scent of the outdoors in her hair when he reached behind her to pick up her backpack. "Tricia's best friend."

Tricia's best friend, Cindy Patterson, was now Cindy Rodgers. Shortly after high school, she quit her job as a grocery store clerk to marry an older boy she had met at a Catholic youth retreat. The Rodgers family owned a plant nursery outside the park on Tomlinson Run Road. The greenhouse rested along a creek at the end of a steep dirt road behind their home, which was in a constant state of renovation.

Cindy fell close to a foot shorter than Joshua. Weighing just over a hundred pounds, she was the one on top of the pyramid when she was cheerleader. He recalled that no party was complete without the jocks picking her up and tossing her around. She had put on a few pounds, but she didn't seem to notice or care.

Despite the oncoming winter season, Cindy was dressed in a short-sleeved T-shirt and dirt-encrusted blue jeans to sort a shipment of bulbs in the conservatory.

"Come on back." She waved to her visitors.

In an attempt to get air to his body in the building's humidity, Joshua discarded his sports coat while he walked the length of the building to where Cindy sat on a stool at a workbench. Hank took off her jacket and shook out the front of her shirt.

Cindy teased him, "Are you here to RSVP for the reunion in person?"

"I'm here for some information." He loosened his tie.

"Aren't all you lawyers after that?" Seemingly unaware that his companion was also in the profession, Cindy winked at Hank.

"It's about Tricia," he said with a somber tone.

Her cheery mood disappeared. "Does this also have to do with Gail?"

Hank asked, "Did you know that she was writing about Tricia?"

Cindy wiped her hands on a rag. "Gail interviewed me for her book before she announced it on that TV show."

"When did she interview you exactly?" Joshua wanted to know.

"About three weeks before she died, right after she found out about the dress."

"I saw the dress." He told Hank, "Trish had picked up her homecoming gown from out of layaway just one hour before she was killed. Why would a girl pay off a gown for a dance that she didn't intend to be alive to go to?"

"That proves it wasn't suicide," she concluded.

He asked Cindy, "Did you take her to the mall to get it that day?"

"Of course. She didn't have a car. We left right from school the same day she—" Her eyes said what day it had been.

He paused to allow for her to regain her composure before he asked his next question. "Was she planning to wear the dress to the homecoming?"

Cindy said that she was, and then added that Tricia was going to the dance with Randy Fine.

"But she dumped him," Joshua argued. "We all saw it. Why would she go with him after the way he treated her?"

"I know what you are thinking," Cindy stated. "That she had her heart set on going with Randy, and he cheated on her, and so she killed herself. But that wasn't the way it was." She went on to explain, "After she dumped Randy in front of everyone, he begged her to give him another chance. Well, Trish had had it. She had no intention of going steady with him anymore. But she had that dress on layaway. She had to buy the dress or lose all the money she'd already paid for it. So she figured she'd keep the date with him and, if he dropped her for Margo before the dance, then she'd go alone. But if he kept the date, she'd have a date for the dance and then dump him afterwards anyway." She asserted at the end of her explanation, "Trish knew that she was too good for him. She had no reason to kill herself."

He remembered how he found out about her suicide. "You were the one who told Beth and me that Trish shot herself."

Her gaze dropped to her dirty hands, which she had folded in her lap. "Because that was what her mother told me. Mrs. Wheeler called the night it happened and told me. I believed it because that was what I was told. Then, after the shock wore off, I realized that it couldn't be true."

"It isn't. Someone had to have killed her." Joshua requested, "Tell me about the fight with Phyllis Barlow."

Cindy's mouth opened, but no words came from it. She gazed at him with big eyes. "I forgot all about that!"

"I was told that they argued a lot."

Cindy answered while giving thought to a memory long forgotten. "Yes, they did fight a lot, but I can't believe Phyllis would kill Trish." She giggled when she recalled, "It was stupid. Not worth killing over."

"What did they argue about?" Hank repeated Joshua's question.

Cindy said, "She was mad at Trish about Doug."

"Her brother?" Joshua asked.

"Yeah, the brain," Cindy explained to his companion. "Everyone called him the brain because he was a genius. I mean he really was certified as a genius."

Joshua wanted to know, "Why was Phyllis mad about him?"

"Tricia blew him off for Randy." She laughed in spite of the serious matter. "My, Josh! When you went to school, you kept your mind focused on scholastics and sports, and nothing else."

Hank explained, "Josh never did get into dramas."

"And now he is paying for it." Cindy said to her before turning back to Joshua. "If you knew all the soap operas going on, you wouldn't be here now." The levity putting her more at ease, she returned to sorting the bulbs. "Doug was in love with Trish. That's why he went nuts."

"I heard that he had a crush on her," Joshua said. "Was Phyllis upset just because Trish rejected her brother?" He considered the motive for her anger.

Hank wondered out loud, "Or did she lead Doug on?"

"Trish never led Doug on. That's what Phyllis says, but that isn't what happened. Trish was polite, but she never let him think there was any possibility of a relationship beyond friendship." Cindy held up her finger when she recalled another fact long forgotten. "Of course, there was that matter of the necklace."

"What necklace?" Joshua and Hank asked in unison.

"Doug gave her a necklace. It was two gold interlocking hearts with a real diamond where they met. He had to have paid a lot of money for it. Well, she accepted it. I told her that was a mistake and so did her mother. I remember we were both there in her kitchen telling her that she never should have taken it, and she was telling us that he insisted and she didn't want to hurt his feelings. Well, we knew how bad he had it for her and told her that it was leading him on. She ended up giving it back to him."

"Was that when Phyllis got mad?" he asked.

"No, that trouble started with the junior prom." Cindy told them with displeasure, "Randy asked Trish to go with him two weeks before the dance."

"You don't think too highly of Randy, do you?" Hank noted Cindy's tone when she said his name.

"Never did," she confessed before she apologized to Joshua. "I know he's your friend, but personally I think Randy was, and is, a jerk. That crap he pulled on Trish proved I was right." She grinned. "He's coming to the reunion. Are you coming?"

Joshua hoped to duck the subject, but now that Randy Fine was going, it was an opportunity to question a key witness, or suspect. He couldn't ignore the fact that Tricia's boyfriend—or ex-boyfriend—was an important piece of this puzzle.

While he planned his interrogation, Cindy pitched her case. "You can't not come now that you are living here. All of the old gang will be there."

"Except Gail, Beth, and Trish." He cocked his head at her and changed the tone of his reminder. "Randy is coming all the way from Columbus?"

She nodded her head. "When he called me to RSVP he went on and on about how he was meeting his wife, the vice president of some public relations firm, at the country club for a cocktail party. I never understood how you two became friends."

"Randy could be a bit much but he had his good points."

"So you'll come?"

"Yeah, I think so."

She made a note of his RSVP on a notepad next to her stacks of bulbs.

He returned to the subject at hand. "What happened at the prom that got Phyllis mad at Trish?"

"Trish had told Doug that she would go to the junior prom with him." Cindy smiled at Doug Barlow's eagerness. "He had asked her back in November."

Hank was confused. "If he had asked her to the prom in November, six months before the formal, then how did she end up going with a boy who asked her two weeks before? Did she break her date with him to go with Randy?"

Cindy crossed one leg over the other and rested her elbows on her knees to explain the episode. "When Doug asked her she said yes. Even if he was a nerd, she would have gone with him, and she was strong enough that she could have handled the ribbing. But, when he asked her, he didn't know if he could go."

"Didn't know if he could go?" Joshua couldn't imagine not being allowed to go to your junior prom.

Not quite understanding either, Cindy shrugged. "He said that he needed his mother's permission to go. I guess their parents were domineering that way. Anyway, Trish kept asking him if he could go, and he kept saying he didn't know. Meanwhile, time kept passing. So then, Randy asked her to go with him, and she said yes. She did feel bad about it."

"And that started the trouble with Phyllis." He knew that would be enough to start a feud with Doug's sister.

"Trish meant to tell Doug as soon as she got home from school, but Phyllis told him first and he went ballistic. I didn't see it, but Trish's mom did. He was devastated."

Joshua pointed out, "But Tricia was killed six months later. I was told that Phyllis was yelling at Trish in the school parking lot on the day that she was killed. It couldn't have been the prom still."

Cindy gave the prosecutor a shrug and made a mocking face of helplessness. "Trish was running to the car because she had to be home by five o'clock and it was almost three. We had to get to the mall, get the dress out of layaway, and get her home.

Meanwhile, Phyllis was chasing after us going on and on about how Trish couldn't get away with treating people like dirt . . ." Her voice trailed off. "Come to think of it, I can't even say for certain it was Doug she was talking about. I told Trish to hurry up. She jumped in the car, and we took off. I asked what that was about, and she just said that Phyllis was having another one of her fits. That was all she ever said about it."

She watched him digest that information. Then, she added, "I can't believe Phyllis would kill anyone."

Joshua announced, "She shot her husband in the leg a few weeks ago and now he's dead."

Cindy's composure dropped a shade. "He probably deserved it." She slid off the stool and stretched her legs by bending over to touch her toes while she said, "Now there is a marriage I never understood. It never looked to me as though she even liked him. Then, suddenly, she just up and dropped out of school in the eleventh grade, and ran off and married him. She wasn't pregnant, so it wasn't like she had to get married. They had to live with her folks. She went to work out at the gas station because he never could hold a job. Go figure." She dismissed any further analysis about the Rollins marriage with a shrug.

They finished the interview with pleasantries. After kissing Cindy on the cheek, Joshua followed Hank back through the greenhouse while putting their coats back on in preparation for stepping into the chilly weather and going to dinner.

"What do you think? Do you think Phyllis killed her?" Hank asked while watching the waiter fill their glasses of wine.

Joshua had taken her to the Ponderosa Golf Club, a restaurant overlooking a golf course, for dinner. He started off the meal, which had romantic overtones, with a bottle of Shiraz. Over the wine, Hank watched a flock of black swans through the picture window. When he looked at her, his thoughts turned to another woman from long ago, a friend whom he wanted to know better. He failed to hear her question about Phyllis.

She seemed to read his thoughts when she suddenly said, "We all have regrets."

Joshua blinked out of his stare. "Regrets?" He sipped the red wine.

"Regrets over questions not asked, lost opportunities, or relationships not pursued."

"What relationship are you talking about?"

"Were you in love with Tricia Wheeler?"

They broke their conversation to allow the waiter to serve their appetizer of Oysters Rockefeller. After he was out of earshot, Joshua told her, "Tricia was the girl I was afraid to ask out."

Hank dove into the oysters. "What scared you about her?"

"She was beautiful, smart, sweet—"

"And naïve," she added. "Otherwise, how did she end up with the likes of Randy Fine?"

"She thought everyone was as sweet as she was."

"Then she wasn't perfect," she concluded. "How about this other girl? Grace. You said her boyfriend is the perp in that murder."

"Except that he has an alibi." He added, "His other girlfriend."

"What real evidence do you have against him?"

"We have a witness who is very anxious to testify that he gave him the gun that was used to kill her. Billy made the mistake of striking a deal in exchange for testifying against him. Now Walt Manners can't wait to get into court to get even."

"That should be enough—"

Joshua shook his head. "He gave it to him four years ago. It could have been passed on a hundred times since then. But we also found threads at the crime scene that appear to come from his coat. I'm still waiting for the lab report on that. If they are a match, I could put together a case against him in spite of his girlfriend, who is not credible."

"Threaten to try her as an accessory," Hank advised with a wave of her oyster fork. "There's nothing like the threat of jail time to take the dew off romance."

"Not Heather Connor. She's headstrong. She won't break. But I may do that anyway and not just as a ploy to break her. Knowing her genetics, I wouldn't be surprised if it wasn't all her idea to kill Grace to get her out of the way."

Hank washed the last oyster down with a sip of wine and wiped her mouth with the napkin. "Have you considered that maybe girlfriend number two was the perp herself, and not the boyfriend? When she became his alibi, he became hers."

He disagreed. "There were over a dozen witnesses. Heather has a head full of bushy hair down to her waist. The perp was wearing a bandana covering his head. There's no way she could have covered up all that hair. She definitely didn't pull the trigger." Joshua watched Hank scrape the remnants of the breading from the oyster shells with her fork.

"You're not going to get a conviction until you break that alibi. It plants the seed of reasonable doubt."

They broke their conversation while the waiter served their dinners. She had ordered a prime rib while Joshua ordered the veal Parmesan with spaghetti.

While slicing through the beef, Hank returned to her observation. "Believe me, Tricia was not so perfect. She was a teenaged girl."

"And I was a teenaged boy, with all the insecurities that go along with it."

"Is it really so far-fetched to think that she led this Doug on? She did take that necklace."

"She gave the necklace back when her mother pointed out that it was wrong to accept it," Joshua argued. "She made a mistake in taking it. She made a mistake in telling Doug that she would go to the prom with him when he was not sure if he would be allowed to go and then accepting the date with Randy. She did not purposely hurt him. Trish would not do that."

Hank paused in devouring the meat on her plate to have another sip of her wine. "Wasn't it you who told me that no one knows what someone is truly like behind closed doors? I seem to recall you saying that it is our job to find out those secrets because usually it is the things we fight to keep hidden that lead to murder. Isn't that what got Grace killed?"

"Billy and Heather got her killed."

"Which would not have happened if she had stayed in her room after curfew like her parents told her to."

"Trish wasn't like Grace."

"You really had it bad for her, didn't you? How objective are you in this case?"

"I did not sleep with her."

"But that article said otherwise."

"It also said that I was sleeping with Gail."

Hank laughed. Having had more than one encounter with the late journalist, she knew that Joshua would never be attracted to Gail Reynolds. She picked up her knife and fork as if to resume eating her prime rib, but instead looked at him across the table.

Aware of her gaze on him, Joshua looked up from his plate and noticed the fingers of her left hand holding the fork. "You're not wearing your engagement ring."

"It is customary for the woman to give the ring back when she breaks off the engagement."

"Why did you do that?"

"Because I didn't want to marry Mark."

"Why not?"

"I didn't love him." She stabbed the beef with her fork and sliced through it with the steak knife while she told him, "Mark was the man that any mother would want her daughter to marry. A real Boy Scout—"

He pretended to be wounded. "Hey, I was a Boy Scout."

"Sorry. Mark was handsome, virile, successful, and he loved me."

His thoughts turned to Jan and her proclamation of love for him. "But you couldn't return his love."

"Nope."

"You tried. On paper, the relationship made total sense," he explained. "You probably even questioned your own sanity for not being able to love him."

"You're talking like someone who has been there."

"Yeah."

"Have you started dating yet?"

The setting had all the trappings for romance, something that was not present in the past at the dinners he and Hank had shared after working late. Joshua had chosen the Ponderosa for their dinner that night. The diners in town were open, and even closer, but without thinking, he had taken her to the golf course and ordered a bottle of wine for them to share. "I don't know."

"We need to be careful." She looked around the room. More than one pair of eyes were on them. "I haven't read that article about you and your list of loves, but it is apparent that you are developing a reputation."

"So I see."

A couple across the room turned away when he returned their probing stare.

"You having dinner with an old friend will be yet another sexual conquest by morning," Hank predicted. "If I go back to your place, even if I sleep in the guest room, tongues will be wagging."

"I guess that means you're going to have to stay elsewhere while you're here. I have a good friend who would love to put you up."

"Is it someone you can trust?"

"I've known Jan my whole life. She'd do anything for me."

CHAPTER TWELVE

"Figures Josh would have a woman lawyer."

Tad stopped typing on his laptop with his fingers poised to resume as soon as he dismissed Jan and her jealousy of the woman who was now her houseguest. "Now you sound like everyone else. Need I remind you that Josh pulled you out from under a lawsuit not too long ago?"

Tad was disgusted, not just with Jan for barging in on his lunch of a sub and chips in his office while he was trying to complete overdue hospital reports, but also with his cousin. He had predicted this scene the previous night when Joshua told him about putting Hank up at Jan's house. Joshua was one of the smartest men he knew, but when it came to women, he was one of the dumbest.

Giving up on eating any more of his lunch since her barging in, Tad threw the remaining three-fourths of his sub into the trashcan.

Jan rationalized her jealousy. "Cindy Rodgers told me that he made reservations for two for the reunion. He's taking Hank. I don't mind him having a woman lawyer as much as she has to be a pretty woman lawyer." She blinked back the tears she felt coming to her eyes. "I never got asked to any of the formals or proms. I know Josh told me that he'd never feel for me the way I feel for him, but I hoped that maybe since he was back and the reunion was coming up—"

"That you two could go as friends." Tad's heart ached for

her. "Josh is trying very hard not to send you mixed messages or give you any false hope." He shrugged. "I honestly don't know how he feels about this woman."

"He looked at her the same way he used to look at Beth and Tricia."

"Speaking of Tricia," Tad opened up his valise and removed a folder yellowed with age. "I've got Doc Wilson's autopsy report on her right here. Complete with pictures of her at the crime scene and in the morgue."

She observed the folder. "Where did you find it?"

"I simply dug through all his old records until I found it."

"What does it say?"

"Nothing we didn't already know. It was a contact wound. The gun was pressed up against her chest when it was fired and the bullet went right through her heart."

"Just like Grace's murder. What kind of gun was it?"

"Forty-five caliber Colt revolver. It was left at the scene." Tad removed color pictures from the envelope and held them up for her to see. He pointed to the picture of Tricia lying on the sofa where her mother had found her. The gun was visible in the picture at the opposite end of the sofa from where her head rested on a throw pillow. "Here's something interesting."

"She looks like she's sleeping." Jan tried not to betray the shudder that ran through her body at the sight of her late classmate.

"Doesn't she?" he said. "Someone laid her out like that. Her hands are placed across her chest. If she shot herself she wouldn't have fallen back onto the sofa in such a perfect position."

"What if she was lying down like that and then pulled the trigger?"

"The gun is all the way at the other end of the couch." Tad pointed at the revolver on the floor. "No, Tricia Wheeler's death was no suicide, and these crime-scene pictures are all we need to have her death reclassified as a homicide."

In his prosecutor's office, Joshua was flipping through a stack of DVDs in search of a volume of law books for Hank when Tad arrived with three folders tucked under his arm. "Where have you been?"

"Treating my patients. I do have a full-time job, you know."

Never failing to notice a pretty woman, Tad took in Hank, who was sitting on the edge of the desk.

Joshua apologized and plopped down behind his desk. "I just got off the phone with yet another reporter asking about my love life and my connection to the victims in this murder spree."

Tad handed him two of the folders. "I finally got a copy of the report from the forensics lab on Rex Rollins's and Bella Polk's crime scenes."

"And?" Joshua opened the top folder.

The doctor shook his head. "Nada. The gun used to kill Rollins traced back to some guy in East Liverpool, who had reported his gun stolen one week before. He's legit. His house was broken into and some other stuff was stolen along with the gun."

Joshua sat back in his chair to study the ceiling.

"What are you thinking about so hard?" Hank thumbed through the folders.

"I was thinking about Margo Sweeney Connor, the common denominator of Tricia Wheeler, Gail Reynolds, Rex Rollins, and Bella Polk."

"Is there any real connection between the old woman killed in the motel and this Margo?" she wondered.

"Haven't you ever played the 'Six Degrees of Kevin Bacon'?" Tad asked her.

"What's that?"

Joshua answered, "It's a bar game."

"I don't hang out in bars," she told them.

"And you call yourself a sailor." The prosecutor explained, "Name any actor and within a matter of six steps, or less, you can connect him to the actor Kevin Bacon. The object of the game is to use as few steps as possible. Now, let's go back to the connection of Margo and Bella. If Rex's landlady stole a copy of his book, which she had to have known about—"

"We have no proof that she knew about the book," his cousin pointed out. "According to the motel and phone company, Bella only made local calls, all untraceable."

"If she phoned Margo, the call would have been local and untraceable," Joshua argued. "Even if we can't prove Bella Polk knew about the book, we have the connection that she was Rex's landlady and he worked for Margo."

"Used to work for Margo," Tad corrected him. "Past tense."

Joshua continued, "Suppose Bella stole the book and tried to blackmail the antagonist, who turned out to be Margo. We've got the fatal connection between Margo and Bella."

Tad shook his head. "Didn't you tell me that Karl Connor was doing it with her in the apple orchards when Tricia was killed? That means Margo didn't kill Trish, which means she has no motive for killing Gail for writing about the Wheeler murder. If anything, knowing Margo the way you and I do, she would have wanted her to write the book so that she could sue her."

"Isn't it ironic that both Margo and her daughter were having sex with someone at the time of their rivals' murders?"

Hank interjected, "The nut never falls very far from the tree."

"Do you seriously think Margo and Heather hired someone to do it for them, in both cases?" Tad squinted at Joshua. "What about her motive for killing Tricia? Not over Randy. How long did Margo and Randy last after she died? Was that love triangle important enough to warrant murder?"

"Some women, like men, just plain hate losing," she suggested. "Maybe the motive for this murder was not so much love as pride."

Joshua recalled, "I was there when Margo picked a fight with Tricia at noon, less than five hours before she was killed. On Friday, Margo and Gail get into a shouting match at a restaurant in which a witness hears her state that Gail was going to write that book over her dead body. Before the next sunrise, Gail is dead. That same night, Rex Rollins, who used to work for Margo, ends up with two bullets going through his head right after telling a barmaid that he wrote a book about the wicked witch of Chester."

"But what about Bella?" Tad asked.

"Did you know her?" Joshua replied with a question. "What two words would you use to describe her?"

"Nosy and greedy."

"Rex told anyone who would listen that he wrote a book that was going to make him rich and famous. Hearing him say that, how long do you think she waited after he left the rooming house that night before checking it out?"

Agreeing with a wide grin, Hank finished the theory, "And when her house was torched, she knew who did it when she found out that Rex was dead. Instead of using the book for justice, she used it for blackmail."

Joshua concluded, "I'm willing to bet money that Bella's copy of the book is long gone."

Tad reminded them once more, "But Margo has an alibi for Tricia's murder."

"That's why I want to take a closer look at the death of Dan Boyd."

"Who is Dan Boyd?" Hank was having difficulty keeping track of all the players she had already heard about without adding another name to the mix.

Tad answered, "Margo's first husband. He was killed while working late at his dental office."

"If she didn't kill Tricia, then what murder could Rex have been writing about?" Joshua laughed out loud. "I just remembered something. When I first mentioned murder to Karl, he said that Margo had her first husband killed."

Tad said, "Margo had an airtight alibi for that murder, too. She was hosting a dinner party for about a dozen people. Her husband was killed by a junkie looking for drugs."

"From a dentist? What were they looking for? Nitrous oxide?"

Mary threw open the door and ran in. Her expression was one of horror.

"Mary—" was all Joshua got out before Seth Cavanaugh strutted into the office.

"Counselor, I have a warrant here to bring you in for questioning by the special prosecutor in the murder of Gail Reynolds." He waved a folded sheet of paper with blue backing. Deputies Carter and Hockenberry, who were with him, did not appear as cocky.

"You didn't need to get a warrant." Hank yanked the paper out of his hand and read it quickly. "Seth Cavanaugh, I presume."

He observed her feminine figure. "And you are—?"

"Alana O'Henry. Mr. Thornton's lawyer."

Seth smiled at a victory. "Lawyered up, huh? I haven't missed the fact that she's a woman. Another one of your conquests? How long does she have before you kill her?"

While passing the warrant on to Joshua, Hank stepped between the two men. "You're out of line, Cavanaugh. I suggest you leave."

"Not without Thornton." Seth ordered Carter, "Take him into custody."

"You touch him and you're going to find yourself wearing a

cast on your arm and egg on your face."

Joshua held up the warrant. "Did you bother reading this, Cavanaugh?" He explained, "It's not a warrant to take me into custody. It's to come in for questioning before the special prosecutor—which was completely unnecessary."

"All you had to do was ask and say please," Hank told the investigator. "The warrant says to be at the courthouse in Weirton at ten o'clock tomorrow morning. We'll be there. If not, then you can put on your show of bringing in your man."

Joshua sat down behind his desk. "Now, I am going to ask you to leave my office before I am forced to have my lawyer break both your legs."

Seth turned to the deputies. "You heard that. He threatened me with bodily harm."

Deputy Hockenberry responded, "I didn't hear a thing. Did you, Carter?"

"Nope."

The children's first reaction to the news of the warrant was to be at the courthouse with their father. Joshua insisted that they would not be permitted in the courtroom during the questioning. Only Hank, the special prosecutor, his or her assistant, Joshua, and any prosecution witnesses would be permitted inside.

Joshua was grateful for the break in the tension during dinner when Tad knocked on the back door. He was accompanied by Sheriff Curt Sawyer. "They got a witness," Tad whispered before leading them to the study.

Curt waited for Hank to close the study door before he announced, "A witness has come forward to say that she saw you and Gail together. Sally Powell. She lives next door to the Hendersons and claims that she saw the two of you arguing in the driveway."

"Cavanaugh was there," Joshua argued.

"Was he there the whole time you were with her in the driveway?" Hank asked.

"No. Gail was upsetting the Hendersons with this wild theory about a serial killer targeting cheerleaders. I took her outside and ordered him to stay inside to calm them down."

"And after having a fight, you kissed and made up," Curt finished.

"We didn't kiss."

"This witness says you did and it wasn't a kiss between friends. She claims that it was a full-fledge lip-lock. She says you even patted Gail on the butt before she got in the car."

"I guess this witness can also say what the argument was about," Hank said.

"She says she overheard Josh threaten Gail if she did not stay away from his family, which backs up Cavanaugh's theory that it was a secret relationship."

She asked, "Where was this witness when she overheard this fight?"

Curt answered, "Inside the house. Upstairs bedroom. The window was open, which is how she says she could hear them."

In his mind, Joshua replayed the scene with Gail in the driveway. He tried to visualize the woman claiming that she witnessed a lovers' spat. The upstairs window. The van in the driveway. The bald man behind her. "Is there one witness or two?"

"Isn't one bad enough?" Hank asked.

"Why aren't there two witnesses?"

Tad told them, "Josh is asking why Sally Powell's lover hasn't come forward to back up her statement. To answer his question, it is because he's married, too."

"Does he work for Tender Lawn?" Joshua asked.

Tad nodded. "His van is parked in the Powell driveway

Monday through Friday from eleven-thirty to one-thirty. Either the Powells have a serious problem with crabgrass or your witness is having an affair."

Hank grinned. "That is very interesting."

After Curt and Tad left, together Joshua and his lawyer went over the list of possible questions and rehearsed his answers.

"Why would Sally Powell lie?" Exhausted, he lay down on the sofa with his arm draped over his eyes to block out the light from the lamp. He hoped it would ease the headache he'd had since Seth served his warrant that afternoon.

"Do you know her?" Hank perched herself next to his feet, which had spilled up onto the arm of the sofa.

"Never met her."

"Maybe she misunderstood." She picked at a thread on his sock. "You said that you warned Gail to stay away from the Hendersons. That is what she heard, but then, when she read Gaston's article, she filled in the blanks to understand that you warned her to stay away from your children when she tried to expose your affair."

He laid his arm back to rest behind his head. "You know that I would never cheat on Valerie."

She went to the desk. "I know that very well."

Hank picked up the folder Sheriff Curt Sawyer had given them during his visit that evening. It consisted of everything pertaining to Gail Reynolds's murder that he got from Seth Cavanaugh. She sorted through the information.

"There was a folder on Randy Fine in Gail's research. Did you know that he had two sexual assault charges filed against him? They are still pending." Hank turned around to face him. "Do you know what else was found in her papers?" She held up a single sheet of paper for him to see.

"What?"

"A letter from a Clarence Bostwick, attorney at law." She clarified, "He's Fine's lawyer. He was responding to a letter that Gail had sent to Randy asking for an interview saying that if she so much as mentioned his name in her book, that he would sue her."

"If Randy did nothing wrong," Joshua wondered, "why did he lawyer up so quickly? He will be more forthcoming if he thinks that we are just another couple of old friends chewing the fat at that reunion."

"I thought you didn't do reunions."

He didn't do reunions. She knew him so well. "I need to question a lot of people from back then about Gail and Tricia. They will be looser with their lips if I'm one of the gang there to show how much weight I did not gain since I graduated." He saw that she had returned to leafing through the files on his desk. The light from his desk lamp brought out the red in her hair.

"Plus, you still have all your hair."

Joshua had crossed the room in time to catch her by the arms when she turned around to fire off her next question.

"What?" She did not object when he stepped up close to her.

"Why did you come here?"

"Because you needed me."

"Is that all?"

She reached up to his cheek. "What else could there be?" She kissed his lips tenderly. "Maybe just enough of something else to make it interesting."

CHAPTER THIRTEEN

The evidence collected from crime scenes was stored away in the state lab in Weirton.

Since the lab was along the way to Joshua Thornton's hearing, Tad decided to stop in and check on the status of the DNA analysis of the tissue he had collected from Bella Polk's body.

Such test results could take weeks to get, but not so much for Tad MacMillan, who had become an expert at using his charisma to get his requests brought to the front of the line. The blonde with her hair scrunched into curls working the day shift in the lab had a particular fondness for the handsome doctor. When he walked through the door, he thought this was his lucky day—until he saw that she was with Seth Cavanaugh.

"Hey, Sharon!" Tad said with forced enthusiasm.

"Tad! What a pleasant surprise!" While crossing the room where he waited at her desk she fluffed her hair to make it fuller. "I wasn't expecting to see you today. I thought you would be at the hearing."

"I'm on my way there now. I wanted to stop by to see if you got the results from the DNA testing I requested from the Polk murder." He glanced over her shoulder at Seth who was taking a clear plastic evidence bag from a brown manila envelope.

Sharon tried to hold Tad's eyes with her own. She didn't seem to know or care that there was anyone else in the room.

Seth folded up the plastic bag with his fingers.

"Cavanaugh, I expected you to be at the courthouse already."

Tad stepped away from the technician to where he was in the process of slipping the evidence bag into his pocket.

"He's got a theory for the Henderson murder," Sharon said to Tad. "He's re-examining the evidence."

Tad grabbed the bag from Seth's pocket. "Where were you taking it to re-examine it?"

"I wasn't taking it anywhere," the detective said.

"What's the theory you are working on?"

"You'll find out when everyone else does." Seth handed the manila envelope to the technician and stepped toward the door.

"Cavanaugh!" Tad said sharply.

Forcibly, Seth turned to him.

"You forgot to sign out." Tad held up the material encased in the bag. "We don't want to break the train of evidence, do we?"

Seth snatched the envelope from him, scribbled his name on the sign-out sheet, and slammed the door on his way out.

"What was that all about?" Sharon asked Tad, who was studying the evidence envelope to answer that question himself.

The copy of the report attached to the evidence bag identified it as the material from a trench coat caught on the fence over which Grace Henderson's killer escaped. Witnesses saw the killer climb over the fence before running into the woods separating the high school from the housing development.

On a separate sheet stapled to the report, Tad read that the lab found that a trench coat belonging to William Unger taken into evidence was tested to prove that the material found at Grace Henderson's crime scene was from his coat. The torn edges of the coat perfectly matched the edges of the material found on the fence.

"Did you send this report to the county prosecuting attorney?" Tad asked her.

"We sent it to the investigating officer. You know that is our standard operating procedure."

"So Seth already knew that this—" He held up the plastic envelope containing the scrap of cloth. "—came from Billy Unger's coat."

"He should." She took the report and pointed to a date noted at the bottom. "See? This says that the report was sent to him a week ago."

"Then what is he waiting for?"

"Let me do the talking," Hank instructed Joshua as they stepped through the door into the lobby of the courthouse.

"Why are you telling me this? I've been in court before."

"Haven't you ever heard that doctors make the worst patients? It is the same for—" Her observation was cut short when Joshua whirled around, grabbed her by both arms, and pushed her down a short hallway. "What—?"

He peered across the lobby.

She strained to see what excited him.

"It's Margo Connor," Joshua said. "And look at who she is talking to."

Hank recognized Seth.

"What's she doing talking to him?" Hank asked. "From what little I know about her, she wouldn't let herself get within a mile of a detective investigating her for murder without her lawyer being present."

Seth tugged at the collar of his shirt while he looked around.

"Why does he look so scared?" Joshua wondered.

"I recognized Mr. Thornton from television," Sally Powell said in a soft voice from her seat on the witness stand. She mopped her face and neck with a tissue.

Sheriff Curt Sawyer and Tad were seated in the last row of the gallery. Tad wasted no time in reporting to the sheriff and

Joshua about Seth's attempt to remove the evidence against Billy Unger from the lab. After learning about his detective's meeting with Margo Connor in the lobby and his lack of action against Billy Unger after receiving the lab report, Curt wondered exactly how crooked his lieutenant was. He called Deputy Pete Hockenberry to do some checking.

In the meantime, since he had an official role in the investigation, Seth Cavanaugh was permitted to remain seated next to the special prosecutor, Stan Lewis, a plain-looking man in bifocals. When Stan came in, he greeted Joshua with a shake of his hand and no smile. "Nothing personal, Thornton. Wish things could be different."

"No offense taken," Joshua responded, but Stan didn't hear him because he was already on his way to his seat to organize the prosecutor's table for the hearing.

The hearing began with the judge ordering the prosecution's chief witness to take the stand.

Sally Powell was dressed up in a fashionable women's suit for her day in court. Joshua guessed her weight to be close to two hundred pounds, which did not fit well on her short frame. She compensated for her weight by using heavy cosmetics.

"Well . . ." Sally licked her lips. "I was upstairs. Eddie . . . my husband . . . was at work. I'm home alone during the day." She gasped when her eyes met Joshua's at the defense table. She turned away.

"Continue, please," Stan stated in a monotone.

"I heard voices and they were getting louder. It was a man and woman. They were arguing. I looked out the bedroom window and saw him," she gestured in the direction of the defense table, "and a woman. She was a reporter. I had seen her on TV a few times. Gail Reynolds."

"Did you hear what they were saying?"

"Parts."

"What did they say?"

"He told her to stay away from his family. His exact words were, 'If you come near my children again, I will kill you.' "

"And her car was found behind his house," Stan noted for the judge. To Sally, he instructed, "Go on. What did she say?"

She paused before answering his question, "She said that if he didn't tell them that she would. Then, he grabbed her by the throat and shoved her up against the car and said something, but his voice was so low that I couldn't hear."

"He shoved her," Stan repeated.

"He scared me watching him," she threw in. "He was really mad." She started when her eyes met Joshua's. She turned her head to look at Stan.

"In your statement, you say that they parted on friendly terms."

"She was really scared and he had his hand on her throat. Then he kind of smiled—He looked like he was crazy—and started stroking her neck and then he kissed her real hard on the mouth. And they made up. Then, he opened the car door and she got in. He slapped her on the butt when she turned around. Then she got into her car and drove off."

She signaled the end of her story with a shrug.

Hank rose from her seat to cross-examine the witness. "Mrs. Powell, that is a very interesting story that you have told this court. Now, could you please tell us the truth?"

"Your honor—!" Stan shouted.

Hank raised her voice an octave to speak over the prosecutor's objection. "How much were you paid to make a false statement implicating Mr. Thornton in Gail Reynolds's murder?"

"I wasn't paid anything!" Sally insisted.

"Are you sure?"

"Yes!"

"Are you aware of the penalty for perjury, Mrs. Powell?"

"I'm telling the truth. I didn't want to get Mr. Thornton into trouble, but my husband said that it was my duty."

"So you aren't here because someone paid you to be here?"

"No!"

"Then where did you get the five thousand dollars in cash that you deposited at the Hancock County Savings and Loan this morning?"

Sally's shriek could be heard outside the courtroom.

The defense lawyer didn't let up. "Isn't it true that this morning you opened up a new savings account for yourself, without your husband's name on it? The clerk remembers you, Mrs. Powell. It isn't every day that you see five thousand dollars in hundred-dollar bills. Where did that money come from?"

"Your honor, I'm sure—" Stan did not have time to finish his plea for a chance to get a reasonable explanation before his star witness fell apart along with his case.

It started with the tremble of Sally's hands that went up her arms to her double chin, which quaked up to her lips. Her body shook as the tears spilled from her eyes.

"Ms. Powell." The judge handed her a box of tissues. "Would you like a minute to collect yourself?"

Unable to speak, she shook her head.

"Ms. Powell," Stan Lewis asked, "have you accepted a bribe in exchange for making a false statement against Mr. Thornton?"

She blubbered, "I got an e-mail . . . I don't know who sent it. They said that if I did not call the sheriff and say that I saw Mr. Thornton and Ms. Reynolds fighting outside my house—they even told me what to say—they would tell—I—I have a boyfriend, and they would tell my husband about him! My boyfriend—he said that if that happened he would leave me so I couldn't let them tell!"

The judge interjected, "Ms. Powell, are you saying that

everything you told us today is a fabrication to protect your extramarital affair?"

"After I went to the sheriff I found an envelope in my car with five thousand dollars in it. The note said thanks for all my help!"

"Do you still have that e-mail and the envelope that you received the payoff in?" Hank wanted to know.

Sally rolled her eyes. "I deleted the e-mail and burned the envelope. I didn't want my husband to see it. He doesn't even know about the money. I opened the account to hide it. If he knew, he'd want to know where I got it and what it was for!"

"We are going to have to find out who sent you that e-mail and gave you that money," Stan told her.

Joshua directed his gaze to Seth to find a sign that he knew or was in some way connected to the bribery and extortion. He recalled that the detective had been with him the day of his encounter with Gail outside the Henderson home.

Curt left the courtroom in search of the source of the e-mail sent to Sally.

After excusing the witness with an order to the special prosecutor to investigate and possibly file charges against her for making a false statement, the judge asked Stan if he had any other evidence to question Joshua about.

Sally Powell fled the courtroom in tears while Stan Lewis answered, "Your honor, prosecution has reason to believe that Joshua Thornton once had an affair with Gail Reynolds and fathered her child out of wedlock. His reputation is built on his moral character. If this affair became public, then his political career would be ruined. The investigator tried to question him at the scene of the crime—"

"Which Mr. Thornton came to of his own free will because of his friendship with Ms. Reynolds and where he readily admitted to the investigator in front of witnesses that he had seen the victim on the night of the murder—without being asked. If he had not, your detective never would have known that he was there," Hank interrupted to tell Stan.

"Her car was behind his house," Stan said. "Once it was found there, then he had to give it up."

"Her body was not found until three days after she died. If my client killed her, then he had more than ample time to move the car to a place that would not have incriminated him."

"He didn't have the keys," the detective said.

"He was in her home with her purse and her keys." Hank laughed at the silliness of Seth's argument.

"What about his fingerprints and the other assorted evidence that connected him to the victim?" Stan asked the judge. "His fingerprints were found on the scene. That proves their relationship."

"Where were the fingerprints found?" Hank asked them.

The judge tapped the top of his desk with the tip of his pen while they waited for the prosecutor to dig the crime scene report from a stack on the table.

Stan read out loud to the court: "Coffee table in the living room. A wineglass and bottle—"

Hank interposed, "One wineglass? Not two?"

Seth theorized, "He cleaned his fingerprints off his glass and put it away."

"He wiped his fingerprints off a glass but left them everywhere else?" Hank cocked her head at Joshua and smiled. She then turned to Stan. "Were his fingerprints in the bathroom? Or how about the kitchen?"

Stan paused to put together the purpose behind the question.

"If Mr. Thornton and Ms. Reynolds were the red-hot lovers you and the media have been describing—if they had an intimate, sexual relationship—why would he not use her bathroom? If he was over there doing the deed, wouldn't he go into the bathroom if only to comb his hair, if not for other things?"

Seth blurted out, "He cleaned them up before he left after killing her!"

"But he left a wine bottle and one glass with his fingerprints on them?"

Stan's expression darkened. "Then their relationship was not current, but in the past."

"Past long enough for her to become a virgin again."

Stan almost broke his neck turning his head to face her.

"A little fact that you have kept from the media. Gail Reynolds had not had a sexually intimate relationship for a very long time." Hank told the judge as she stepped forward and handed the autopsy report to him, "It is right in the medical examiner's report. But Mr. Lewis is saying nothing while the media is ripping my client's reputation apart."

In response to the judge's displeased expression, Stan argued, "That report is not meant to be made public." He asked her, "Where did you get it?"

"We won't make this report public unless we have to. Ms. Reynolds was a friend of Mr. Thornton. He wants her killer caught. But he will defend himself and his reputation with whatever means necessary."

The judge told the prosecutor, "I believe the autopsy report alone throws your motive for Mr. Thornton killing Ms. Reynolds out the window."

"But Ms. Reynolds did have a baby several years ago. She had told more than one witness over the years that Joshua Thornton was the child's father."

Hank handed the prosecutor and the judge each a copy of another report. "Mr. Thornton's medical records, which include his blood type. Again, if you had simply asked, he would have volunteered it to you. A simple comparison of his blood type to the child's, and you would have found that there is no way possible that he could have been the father."

Stan blurted out, "The victim thought he was and was going to tell the world!"

"At which time he would have proven that he wasn't."

"Why would she have thought that he was the father if they had not had sex?" Seth asked.

Hank answered his question by telling the judge, "Ms. Reynolds's contract with the network was not renewed because she had exhibited signs of unbalanced behavior and had been committed to a mental hospital shortly before her return to Chester. She imagined that she and Mr. Thornton had a relationship that never happened. The things that were found in her home had been stolen from Mr. Thornton in her obsession."

Seth said, "There was a used condom in her scrapbook."

"Can you prove that was his?"

Aware of the ability to gather DNA from the most minute and ancient material, Joshua held his breath.

"Josh, what are you doing?" Hank demanded when Joshua pulled away from her after they stepped out of the courtroom into the blinding lights of the media. "They want a statement."

"Then give it to them," he called to her while racing to catch the elevator at the end of the hall before Stan closed the doors. "You told me to let you do all the talking."

Seth Cavanaugh had ducked out the back door of the courtroom to escape the public embarrassment of his failure to discredit the county prosecutor.

"What do you want, Thornton?" Stan asked when the doors closed to capture him and Joshua alone together on the elevator going to the offices on the top floor. "You heard the judge. You are cleared as a suspect, and my office is to release a statement to the media saying so. I will announce it myself tomorrow morning."

"That's not what I want to talk to you about."

The prosecutor observed the confines of the elevator. "You want a piece of me? Listen, I don't blame you for being mad—"

"Stan, all you had to do was call me and I would have co-operated in finding out who killed Gail. Didn't the attorney general tell you? I was the one who called him to ask for a special prosecutor. I knew that once the media found out that I was on the scene the night she was killed, there would be the appearance of impropriety no matter who was arrested."

"My investigator said that you refused to cooperate and threatened him."

Joshua gestured angrily. "Seth Cavanaugh never once asked me to come in for questioning. He only threatened to bring me in in handcuffs. I don't deserve that, and I didn't deserve any of this." He took a deep breath. "But that isn't what I got on this elevator to tell you."

The elevator stopped its ascent. Stan waited for the doors to open. "What do you want then?"

"Gail was my friend. I knew that she loved me, but I wasn't aware of the unbalanced nature of it. I didn't know that she had a baby until the autopsy report."

The doors opened.

"Which your cousin got for you." Stan stepped into the corridor.

Joshua followed him. "It pays to have friends."

Stan stepped to a picture window at the end of the hall. The top floor window looked out across the city of Weirton and the Ohio River. A barge filled with coal was traveling down the river.

Stan asked, "Do you know who the father of her baby could have been?"

"No, but I can find out."

"I'd hate for you to waste your time on a dead end. She had that baby a long time ago."

Joshua suggested, "Has your investigation even started down the avenue of the motive for her murder being her book on Tricia Wheeler? She had dinner with the victim's mother the night she was killed. She told Dorothy Wheeler that she remembered something that she thought could be a link to Tricia Wheeler's killer. Did you find anything about that in her research?"

"She had some research on a Randall Fine, but he lives in Columbus and was no where near the crime scene at the time of Gail's murder."

Joshua told him, "I heard that he's got a couple of rape charges pending against him—"

"At the present time. The only reason he's never been convicted for past allegations was because he's got friends in high places."

"He's coming to our high school reunion."

"Really?" A smile fought its way to Stan's lips.

"You said you wanted to help." Special prosecutor Stan Lewis had met with Joshua in the study of the Thornton home. It was the first opportunity Joshua had to examine all the evidence collected on Gail's murder.

Curt had only been able to supply him with the evidence Seth Cavanaugh had given to him. In light of the detective's suspicious behavior, they wondered if he had concealed or dismissed any evidence that could lead them to her murderer.

Joshua studied the forensics report from Gail Reynolds's crime scene. "The killer smothered her with a pillow. Of course, there are no fingerprints on the pillow case, but there was epidermal matter." He ran his finger along a line on the report. "Dark powder. Found to be finely ground coffee."

"She drank the stuff all day long according to a lot of sources." Stan referred to her intoxicated condition. "She should have stuck to the caffeine. Then she would have been alert enough to defend herself."

"Tad had coffee all over the front of his shirt after Lou Alcott tried to kill him."

"What?"

"He had just gotten a bag from the Rollins Corner Café when Alcott tried to kill him, and Gail had dinner there the same night that she was killed."

"Who is this Alcott guy?"

"He drove a delivery truck for an appliance store."

"His name hasn't come up in our investigation. Why would he want to kill her?"

"I have no idea. We can't come up with a viable motive for him trying to kill Tad, either." Joshua set the forensics report aside. "Gail's murder has to be connected to Tricia's. She comes to town and announces that she is investigating her death. Why else would someone from Chester kill her?"

"In theory, start with the boyfriend," Stan directed him. "Tricia dumped him that day. From what Reynolds says in her research file, Randy Fine had a big ego and a babe like Wheeler dumping him in public had to be a bruiser."

"But you said that he was in Columbus when Gail was killed." Joshua referred to her autopsy report. "Randy liked to be in control," he recalled. "I don't know the circumstances behind the assaults, but my guess is that he is a power rapist." He sighed with regret. "I never would have guessed back in high school that he was like that. Now, looking back, all the bragging about the girls he was with, some he didn't even know their last names—He would tell us about how they started out saying no and then he convinced them—I can see it now."

Joshua dug through the folders on his desk until he found the yellowed folder that Tad had given him. It was Tricia Wheeler's autopsy report. He flipped through the pages. "There was no sign of sexual assault in Tricia's death, either," he told Stan, who was reading the report for the first time over his shoulder. "I don't think Randy killed her."

"Are you concluding that as an objective investigator or as Fine's old friend?"

"Gail's murder doesn't fit his profile, and he wasn't here when she was killed."

"Fine may not have committed the murder, but he could have been connected." Stan removed a copy of a phone bill from his report. "Karl Connor was in town. He and Fine were good buddies."

"I remember. They hung out together."

"Randy's lawyer threatened to sue Gail if she so much as mentioned him in her book. Right now, he is under indictment for two rapes. The last thing he needed was a book coming out insinuating that he was involved in a murder."

Joshua placed the copy of the letter from Randy's lawyer that Stan handed him on top of his pile of papers.

The special prosecutor continued, "Reynolds had contacted Fine to request an interview. That letter was not all she got. She had caller-ID on her phone. We traced all the numbers in the log and found that she got phone calls from Karl Connor."

"Karl is Margo's ex-husband. I'm sure that Gail used him as a source to get information against her."

"Connor was also calling Fine. These phone calls did not start until after Reynolds came to town. Before that, they hadn't spoken in years." Stan smiled. "He recently deposited five thousand dollars in his account and became current on his truck payments. They were about ready to repossess it—until Reynolds died."

With this information, Joshua dreaded the thought of appearing at the reunion. "If Randy didn't kill Trish, why would he care about the book?" He gestured at her autopsy report. "He would have raped Trish if he was going to kill her, but no one touched her."

"I guess this was for the book." Joshua took a color photograph of a young man from Gail's research file. It looked like his old friend from long ago until he noticed that the style of his shirt was too modern and his hair was shorter than he recalled. "Who is this?"

Stan told him, "That's Gail's baby. All grown up. Nice looking young man."

Joshua's eyebrows met in the center of his forehead. The teenager had dark hair and eyes, and a perfect profile. He was a handsome boy. "I know this guy."

A knock on the study door interrupted their conversation. Stan stood up from where he had rested against the corner of Joshua's desk.

Tracy smiled with anticipation. "Dad, your date is ready."

Reminded of his first date since his wife's death, Joshua's hands went to his head to smooth his hair. He stood and buttoned his suit coat.

Hank O'Henry stepped into the doorway.

Stan let out his breath and said, "Now I see why you hired her for your lawyer."

Hank had not planned on a semi-formal evening when she threw her things into her backpack to rush across an ocean and a country to be at Joshua's side. With only a couple of days notice that she was to be his working date at the reunion for the class of 1985, Hank had needed to enlist the aid of his daughter, who was a skilled seamstress and had a keen eye for fashion.

Honored to be asked for her assistance, Tracy had refashioned a sapphire-colored, sequined gown her mother had worn to the Navy ball with her father years before. She cut a slit up the side to show off Hank's legs, and removed the shoulders and their pads to make it a halter dress. With a couple of inches taken in at the waist and reshaping the skirt to hug her flat stomach, Hank looked more sensuous than Joshua had ever imagined his assistant being.

"She can go over my briefs any day," Stan cracked.

CHAPTER FOURTEEN

The before-dinner cocktail party for Oak Glen's Class of 1985 appeared to be gearing up when Joshua Thornton and his date Alana O'Henry arrived at the Mountaineer Resort in Newell. The banquet room on the top floor of the casino had a balcony with a view of the river. The center of the room contained a dance floor for those who chose to dance to a selection of rock tunes from their youth.

Cindy Rodgers was manning the reception table set up next to the entrance when Joshua held one of the double doors open for Hank to step inside. Cindy was dressed in a two-piece evening dress with a paper nametag stuck to her left breast. It had a copy of her senior picture with her maiden name printed beneath it.

"Well, hello there, Joshua Thornton—and his date, I presume!" she announced loud enough for those nearby to hear. Heads turned in their direction. A few of the guests called out to him while others waved.

Joshua could see that Karl Connor had taken up residence on a stool at the end of the bar. After signing in and picking up his nametag, Joshua guided Hank with a hand on her waist in Karl's direction.

"Hey, Josh, you're looking good. You haven't changed a bit." A blond-haired man with a receding hairline and glasses took his hand and pumped it before Joshua had a chance to move in on his suspect.

Joshua checked out the man's nametag to recall who he was. In an instant, he remembered Tom Jarvis. Tom had participated in all the sports, and, while he had made varsity, he had never stood out. Joshua did recall that he sat next to him in French class, was head of the Latin club, and was exceptional in both subjects. He also remembered that he dated Tricia Wheeler until she broke up with him after making the varsity cheerleading squad in her junior year.

After Joshua introduced him to Hank, Tom told them that he and his family lived in Beaver, Pennsylvania. He worked for a pharmaceutical company near Pittsburgh.

Joshua's close working relationship with his date made it possible for him to communicate wordlessly. While he sipped the beer the bartender had delivered to him, he told her with nothing more than his eyes that Tom was a witness from whom he could gather information. She slipped onto the seat of the bar stool between Tom and Karl.

Joshua put his hand on Hank's bare shoulder. Her flesh felt warm on his palm.

"You haven't changed a bit, Thornton," said Karl. He made no attempt at discretion when he checked out Hank's feminine features.

"Watch it, Karl," Joshua warned. "Hank trained as a Navy SEAL before she switched to the JAG Corps."

"What does that mean?" Karl's speech slurred.

"It means that she is licensed to kill," Tom interpreted.

Karl looked confused.

Hank smiled demurely in Karl's direction.

"I bet you couldn't hurt a fly," he said as if he were speaking to a child.

"How much do you want to bet?" she asked.

Joshua wanted Hank to put Karl in his place, but he didn't want her to turn him against the two of them. "Hey, Karl," he said in a tone that he realized, as soon as the words came out of his mouth, was too abrupt, "what is Randy doing now?"

"He's a big executive with some computer company in Columbus. He's married to a rich bitch with important friends. They're stopping in here on their way back from a health resort."

"I guess you two have kept in touch."

Karl paused before he responded. "Some of us remembered our old friends from the past."

"Friends or debts?"

"What does that mean?"

"You had to make passing grades in order to remain on the football team. Before making the team, you were failing almost every course, but then suddenly you were passing. The question crossed my mind more than once if you were cheating. If so, you needed someone to help you do it. You certainly weren't smart enough to get away with it on your own."

Karl floated past the insult about his not being smart enough to cheat on his own. "Randy Fine was my real friend."

"Did he help you cheat your way through high school? Is that why you flunked so miserably in college? Because you never learned the basics?"

The former linebacker rose from his bar stool. "Do you want to take this outside, Thornton?"

"No." Joshua turned away.

Karl threw a punch.

Before his fist could make contact with Joshua's skull, his leg collided with Hank's. Thrown off balance by the interception, he fell forward. His collapse to the floor was assisted by her elbow to the back of his neck.

Oak Glen's Class of 1985's star linebacker fell flat on his face.

"I wish you hadn't done that," Joshua told Hank in a low voice while Tom helped the fallen athlete to his feet.

Humiliated, Karl shoved Tom away and returned to his bar stool to brood while he started on his next beer.

"I saved you from a punch alongside your head," she muttered.

"Go to the ladies' restroom and freshen up. I need to question Tom, and you are a distraction."

Hank took her glass of wine and pretended to go in search of the powder room.

Joshua stepped up to the stool on the other side of Tom, down from where Karl was perched at the end of the bar. Tom started the conversation. "I heard that you were a widower. How long were you married?"

With a pang of guilt about being on a date with someone other than Valerie, Joshua answered, "Seventeen years. We had five children."

"Everyone thought you were going to marry Beth Davis."

"I loved Beth, but us being married would never have worked."

"I know what you mean. I've been married for eighteen years and I love my wife, but I still think about Tricia every day. I never really got over her, you know."

"That's right." Joshua pretended to be surprised by the mention of her name. "You two were going steady at one point."

They were surprised to discover that Karl had been listening to them from his seat three stools away. "Yeah, she dumped him after she made varsity."

Tom claimed, "But I never held it against her or anything like that. I mean, she got all taken in by that high school social stuff."

Joshua responded, "Which she never got to outgrow because someone killed her."

"Even if she hadn't died, Tom, she never would have come back to you," Karl said, "because she dumped you because you weren't good enough for her."

Tom responded with a nervous chuckle. "Is that what this reunion is all about? How I ended up like everyone figured? A working stiff." He turned on Joshua. "And so did you, Mr. Most Likely to Succeed. A hero—overseas and at home. Me? No one knows who I am. Admit it. You didn't even remember who I was until you looked at my nametag and class picture. What is my claim to fame? Dating the class beauty until she dumped me after she discovered she could do better."

"It could be worse." Karl scoffed. "You could have married her."

Joshua apologized, "I was only making conversation. I didn't mean anything."

"Yeah, you did," Karl shot at him before telling Tom, "Didn't you hear? Josh is the county prosecutor. Gail Reynolds's book was about Tricia's murder, and he's trying to find out who killed the two of them."

Tom's eyes widened. He looked at the lawyer searching for the killer of his high school sweetheart. "Do you think I killed Trish?"

Karl answered, "And Gail."

Joshua wanted to put a cork in the drunken linebacker's mouth, and he had precisely the right one to shut him up. "Who said Gail got herself killed because of her book?"

"What?" Karl gestured for yet another beer.

"Tricia's murder was a long time ago."

"There's no statute of limitations on murder," Tom reminded them.

"But up until now, everyone assumed that it was suicide," Joshua said. "What are the odds that Gail showing up here and asking questions would dig up anything incriminating against anyone? Without evidence to prove that Tricia was murdered, Gail's book would have been mostly speculation. It is more likely that there was another motive for Gail's murder."

Sensing that he was going to witness one of the most interesting scenes in his boring life, Tom edged up closer to the prosecutor so as not to miss a word directed at Karl. "Like what?"

Joshua explained, "Gail grew up around here. She was the editor of the paper and she made a lot of friends and enemies. She pulled no punches about anything."

Karl growled, "Who cares?"

"This is a small town," Joshua reminded him. "In small towns, reputations, once you get one, last forever, unless something happens to change it." He added in a low voice, "Like an accusation."

"What kind of accusation?" the edge in Karl's voice held a warning.

"Did you know that she had a baby?"

Tom's gasp was audible. "Gail Reynolds had a baby?"

"He was born in mid-November of 1985, which means he was conceived in February 1985. Now what happened in February?"

Karl paused with his beer mug perched at his lips.

The prosecutor prodded him, "Do you recall anything significant about that time period, Karl?"

Karl took a gulp of the beer before he quipped, "I guess she loosened up."

"I remember," Tom interjected. "I remember because it was so unlike her. I was coming into that dance, on Valentine's Day with my date. Judy, I think . . . Anyway, it was so weird, I saw a bunch of guys smoking pot over by the practice field and I saw Gail with them. She was laughing real loud. I never saw her like that."

"What guys?" Joshua asked.

Tom opened his mouth, and then, seeing Karl's glare, closed it. "It was so long ago, Josh. Besides, what does it matter now?

Why would anyone kill her because she had a baby out of wedlock twenty years ago?"

"That's my thought exactly," Joshua said. "I mean, the baby was adopted and has grown up. He doesn't care about his birth parents. Child support is no issue. So what does it matter?"

"Yeah," Karl grunted.

"She found this baby she had put up for adoption. She had made assumptions about who the father was. But then, I think, when she found him, now, as a young man, she realized who the father was and started to recall events that his birth father would not want to be made public."

"What the hell are you talking about?" Karl growled.

"Gail recently had a nervous breakdown. She was hospitalized. She told someone that she remembered something that happened and was investigating it for her book. Her sister found Gail after the Valentine's Day dance and her panties were missing. I suspect that what she remembered during her hospitalization was what happened to her panties."

"So what? Isn't there a thing called statute of limitations?"

"But for people who have reputations to protect, it's not too long to do any damage. Nowadays, it would not be called taking advantage of an opportunity, but rape, especially if the one who took advantage of her gave her the booze and pot to get her in a condition in which she couldn't say no."

"Go to hell, Thornton." Karl took his beer and left.

"So, I'm not one of your suspects, huh?" Tom asked as soon as Karl was out of earshot.

"Should you be?" Joshua didn't want to say he wasn't a suspect.

Tom said, "Of course, you wouldn't think me capable of something so brazen as killing the head cheerleader?" He seemed to be asking the prosecutor to suspect him. "Could I be so clever as to kill the beauty queen and not even be suspected of it? I, Tom Jarvis? Oak Glen's invisible man."

"Why would Oak Glen's invisible man want to kill the beauty queen?" Joshua didn't know if he should take him seriously.

"Because she was a stuck-up bitch." Tom had drained his beer and waved to the bartender for another one.

Once again, there was a social event in Chester that Jan Martin had organized, but did not attend due to the lack of a date. She was able to bear such humiliation in her youth. Back then, she knew that it was only a pipe dream that the man she loved would invite her. This time, she had a glimmer of hope, only to have it dashed with the appearance of Hank O'Henry.

That was more than she could stomach.

Since Jan did not drink heavily, she was unable to drown her sorrows with alcohol. Therefore, she decided to spend the night of the reunion consoling herself with a carton of broasted chicken, mashed potatoes, and gravy from a little place called Hot Shots, located down the street from what had once been her drugstore. She broke into the comfort feast while deep conditioning her hair and waiting for the mud mask on her face to set. She was on her fourth piece of chicken, and had downed half of the quart of mashed potatoes when the doorbell rang.

Wiping her greasy fingers on the front of her rattiest bathrobe, which she always wore when she needed coddling, Jan glanced out the window to see Tad waiting on her porch. Instead of his usual faded jeans and baggy sweatshirt, he was dressed in a sports coat and slacks.

"What do you want?" she asked when she opened the door.

Her eyes widened when he pulled a bouquet of red roses from behind his back. "I thought maybe you would like some cheering up."

"I don't make a very good mercy date."

He turned away. "Then forget it. I'll go find another girl to take to the club." She made a noise that he took as a request to stop. With a sly grin, he turned back to her.

She took the roses and quickly counted them. There were a dozen, and they were long-stemmed, too. No man had ever given her a dozen long-stemmed roses. "Why would you want to take me to the club?"

"I like you, Jan."

"Tad MacMillan," she said with a hand on her hip, "there's not a woman on God's green earth that you don't like."

"Oh, I've met one or two that I have not been very fond of," he laughed. "But I am very fond of you. I know I tease you, but I only tease people I like."

"Then you must really love me, considering some of the things you have said to me."

His smile held a hint of shyness. He said in a soft tone, "I don't like to see you hurt. I was hoping that maybe we could go out tonight and have a good time since you didn't go to the reunion."

She hesitated. A date with Tad MacMillan would certainly add a new dimension to her reputation, which at this point was non-existent. When she looked down to admire the roses in her arms, she saw the old chocolate stain on the lapel of her bathrobe. Her hand flew to her face, which was crusty with dried mud. Her hair was twisted in a discolored orange towel.

"Hey, Doc! How you doing?" Fred and Patty Sinclair slowed down as they strolled around the corner during their evening walk to wave at them.

With a shriek, Jan ran back inside her house and slammed the door.

"That's never happened to me before," Tad muttered to himself.

Margo Sweeney Boyd Connor had made her entrance. Everyone

in the banquet room at the reunion paused to take in the woman who had to be the most financially successful member of the class of 1985.

She made sure that was apparent to one and all.

The businesswoman was dressed in a mink coat that she whipped off to reveal a scarlet-sequined gown with a plunging neckline that showed off her ample breasts and fleshy back. She did not stop at the mink and sequins. She further flaunted her success with jewels sparkling off every part of her body that could be adorned.

She waved to her former classmates like a starlet welcoming her fans. Some of them returned her greeting. Those who resented her arrogance turned their backs.

Joshua slipped off his stool and crossed the room to where Margo was holding court with a couple of women who, in their youth, had been her cohorts in the mutiny against Tricia. He noticed that all three women had gained significant weight since high school.

His biggest surprise was Judy Tudor. As a young woman, she was both beautiful and vain. Judy had matured into a grossly overweight mother of four now on her third marriage. Each marriage was worse than the previous. He recalled that she had worn heavy makeup and the latest fashions. Her hair color had changed with regularity. Tonight, it was midnight black and fell to her chin in a blunt cut with bangs reminiscent of the hottest hairstyle from a popular movie.

In school, Veronica Bain had been one of Margo's closest friends. She found fault in everyone and everything. She tried out for nothing because nothing was good enough for her. Joshua suspected that she encouraged, if not instigated, cheerleaders Margo and Judy to rebel against Tricia.

Unattractive, Veronica lacked the femininity and social skills that Tricia Wheeler, Cindy Patterson, and Beth Davis possessed, which made them popular. Joshua could still visualize her sitting in the same corner seat she sat at every day in the little theater during the lunch hour, critiquing whatever took place within her sight. She only left to go smoke in the bathroom.

Now, Veronica, like her two friends, was divorced with children. She had been working at the china plant since she graduated from school. She didn't bother dressing up for the reunion, except to put on black slacks and a sweater faded with age. The scowl that never seemed to leave her face had etched itself into deep lines around her mouth that made her look like a comic character. The smell of cigarette smoke that grew stronger as he approached the group told Joshua that she had not stopped smoking.

"Hello, ladies," he greeted the three of them.

Judy made no pretense; she gave Joshua the once-over and liked what she saw. She held out her hand like she expected him to kiss it. "I heard you were back in town, and single again."

Margo and Veronica greeted him with growls deep in their throats.

"Turn it off, Judy. He's a lawyer," Veronica stated as if she were announcing that he had a highly contagious disease.

"Some of my best friends are lawyers," Margo said. "Go ask Karl." She gestured over Joshua's shoulder at her ex-husband, who was downing another beer at the bar.

"I don't do divorces," Joshua told them.

"No, you try hanging murder raps on innocent people." Margo revealed to her cohorts, "First, he accuses my daughter of killing that cheerleader. Then, he says I killed Gail because she was writing that idiotic book saying that I killed Tricia."

"Well, your daughter is no longer a suspect in Grace's murder. We have a warrant out for her boyfriend." Joshua guessed her reaction to his next question, but asked anyway. "I don't suppose Heather knows where Billy is. He seems to have disappeared."

"Even if she knew, she wouldn't tell you."

"If she knows and doesn't tell the police, she will be guilty of harboring a fugitive."

"I said *if* she knew." Margo smirked. "She doesn't, and you can't prove that she does."

Joshua chuckled, "Okay then, let's talk about your favorite subject, Margo. You. You were seen arguing with Gail just hours before she was killed. I was told that you were upset about questions she was asking about Tricia."

"Why would she have killed Tricia?" Veronica asked. "If anyone was going to kill anyone, it would have been the other way around. Randy was leaving Tricia for Margo."

"Yeah," Margo agreed.

"Besides, Tricia killed herself. Sheriff Delaney said so." Veronica gave him a glare. "And if you try to prove otherwise, then you can go to hell because the three of us were together when she died, and we'll testify to that in court."

Joshua was thankful when the debate ended with Randy Fine's entrance.

The high school charmer threw open both doors and stepped inside the room. With his arms outspread, he announced, "Oak Glen class of '85! Randy Fine has arrived! Let the party begin!"

The guests greeted him with a cheer.

Margo rushed to throw her arms around Randy's neck and kiss him on the mouth.

Joshua guessed that the woman on his arm was his wife. Her flawless face was expressionless, not unlike the faces of models when they strut down the runway. She was a slender woman, who dressed the role of success in a tastefully expensive gown. Her hair was swept up into a twist with a rhinestone comb. She stood erect and looked down her nose at her husband's friends who gathered to welcome him.

The former Lothario dressed to impress. He wore a tailored suit that had all the touches of a *Gentleman's Quarterly* cover. Even with the extra thirty pounds hanging over his belt, he still looked good.

Joshua was struck to see that the dark wavy locks Randy had always kept perfectly combed were reduced to barely enough to cover his head above his ears and around to the back with nothing on top except for a few complimentary strands.

While Joshua tried not to stare at the change, he sensed, rather than saw, Hank emerge at his side. She took his hand. "I assume this was the class prom king," she murmured into his ear while they watched Randy shaking hands and giving high fives like a presidential candidate.

Joshua turned to her when he was taken into a bear hug by a mountain of a man.

"Remember me?" the hulk asked. "Hoss!" he answered before Joshua had a chance to check out his nametag.

The name was all Joshua needed to remember Randy's right-hand man. Hoss, nicknamed for his size and strength, followed his best friend around like a golden retriever. "Man! You haven't changed a bit! You get a hold of some age-defying stuff or what?" He then yelled across the room, "Hey, Rand! Look who's here! It's Josh!"

Randy and his entourage made a turn in their path to cross to them. Margo held on to one of his arms as if they were still lovers. On his other side stood the woman Joshua assumed to be his wife. He wondered if she was as cold as she appeared.

Randy grabbed him by the hand and shook it. "Where have you been? How long has it been?" He then seemed to notice Hank for the first time. He gave a cat-like noise from deep in his throat. "Is this Valerie?"

"No, Valerie passed away. This is Hank." Now aware that Randy was a sexual predator, Joshua could see his eyes taking in the prey. He slipped his arm around her waist and held her close to him. It was a protective move.

"Way to go, Josh. Still only the best when it comes to women." Randy then introduced his wife, who gave him a firm, businesslike handshake. "This is Mabel." He went on to give a progress report on his life, which sounded not unlike a well-written press release.

After graduating in the top ten percent of his class from Ohio State University, Randy had managed to land on the ground floor of the computer technology business and had done well with it.

He was so successful that he was able to help out his best friend Hoss when he was down on his luck during a recession by hiring him as his assistant. Randy's sidekick was still taking orders from him after all these years.

As a result of his ingenuity, Randy and his wife, who was the vice president at one of the largest public relations firms in the state of Ohio, lived in a mansion, belonged to an exclusive country club, and were ranked high on the list of Columbus's movers and shakers.

Joshua envied Mabel Barkely-Fine, who was able to disappear into the crowd while her husband reported the success of his life. Even Margo slipped away to find someone to whom she could boast about her own achievements. He did not have that luxury if he was to steer the conversation toward Tricia and Gail. Therefore, he had to endure Randy's bragging about his life on the fast track.

"Tell me the truth, Tad," Jan asked in a tone begging for his confidence, "were you the least bit surprised to find out that Gail Reynolds was obsessed with Josh? I know I was."

Sensing the reason behind the dismay that caused her to slam the door in his face, Tad had waited to allow Jan the opportunity to clean up for their evening out.

With a sense of abandon for what he had assured her would be an elegant evening, Jan dressed in the gown she had bought in hopes of wearing to the reunion with Joshua. It was a soft rose color and fell just the right way across her slender frame to reveal her boyish figure. Her hair shone and her cheeks were flushed. She had to admit even to herself that she looked lovely.

Tad had taken her to the Ponderosa Golf Club where he had reserved a table for two in the corner next to the picture windows with a view of the course and the black swans. He had even ordered a half a carafe of wine for her to accompany his iced water with lemon.

In the soft light and music, Jan found herself looking at a man she had considered a lifelong friend, and sometimes tormentor, in a different light.

Tad chuckled while he buttered his roll. "Isn't every woman obsessed with Josh?"

She flushed with embarrassment.

"It isn't the man, it's the image," he observed.

"Do you mean because he's a lawyer?"

"I mean because he is Joshua Thornton, Oak Glen's most likely to succeed. Star athlete." He smiled broadly. "That was twenty years ago. I still can't believe how people can pick a specific moment in time and never realize how much everything and everyone around them has evolved since then."

She swallowed. "Who are you talking about?"

"Josh is not Oak Glen's star quarterback anymore. He's no longer prom king. He's not the prized catch he used to be."

She tried to keep the moment light by giggling. "Is that jealousy I hear?"

"No, it is the truth. Even Josh is having trouble understanding why you and Gail and Tori Brody keep chasing him. He's a single father with five children who hasn't got a clue." Tad reached across the table for her hand. "This isn't high school, Jan, and you aren't the Plain Jane you used to be. Winning Josh is not going to prove anything to those who treated you like a geek twenty years ago."

"I'm not trying to prove anything to anyone."

"I don't think you are in love with Josh. I think you are in love with the idea of playing Cinderella to his Prince Charming. The homely nerd suddenly blossoms into the beautiful princess to be escorted to the prom by the handsome prince." He finished in a gentle tone, "It's too late, Jan. Prince Charming has grown up and left the castle and you are too old to play Cinderella."

She blinked. "I thought you promised me a good time tonight."

"Look around. We are in the real world now, and this is a much better place to be in."

Jan was too surprised to react when he pulled her hand across the table to kiss the inside of her palm. The warmth from his lips traveled up her arm and to her heart. She felt its beat quicken.

"Your hand tastes like . . . chicken?"

She blushed.

"Why don't you ever kiss me that way?" a woman sitting at the next table hissed at her husband.

Unperturbed, the man continued eating his salad. "Because you don't taste like chicken."

Joshua had ducked into the bathroom for the solitude necessary to suck in a second wind. Randy had agreed to meet them downstairs in the lounge for a drink after the reunion, which was winding down. When he stepped out of the stall, he found Tom Jarvis waiting for him.

"Hey, Tom." He patted him on the back before crossing to

the sink to wash his hands and splash water on his face.

"You may have everyone else fooled, Josh, but not me."

Joshua froze and waited for his wrath, over what, he was not sure.

"You want everyone to think that you are a shallow politician with no scruples. I know differently. I knew you for twelve years of school. You're obsessed with truth and justice, and can't bear anything less than that. You won't be able to live with yourself until you personally throw Tricia and Gail's killer in jail. You can't help it. You're just that type of guy."

Joshua observed Tom's reflection in the mirror while Tom continued, "That's why you're here."

"What did Karl do to Gail?" Joshua turned to face him. "You saw something that night of the dance."

"It was a joke. Most everyone knew about it except you. That made it even better."

"Made what better?"

"Randy, Hoss, and Karl got Gail wasted. She was all upset about you getting engaged to Beth. Then, they put her in the back of your van and told her that they were going to go get you and that you would sneak out to do it with her without Beth knowing. She was drunk out of her mind. They took turns with her and she was so high that she thought it was you."

Joshua felt sickened by the cruel joke. "They raped her."

"They thought it was funny," Tom said with distaste. "Randy bragged about it, of course."

"He didn't brag about it to me."

"Because he knew that you would kick his ass if you found out."

"He was right."

"Calm down," Hank warned him.

They went for a walk around the parking lot to allow Joshua

time to cool off after finding out that his friends had taken turns raping a classmate in the back of his van. When they got to his Corvette, he stopped to lean against the fender. He admired how the moon reflected on Hank's hair.

"I'm glad you stayed in town long enough to come with me tonight. I'll probably need you to keep me from knocking Randy into next week."

"I guess I'm destined to always be your Girl Friday."

He wrapped his arms around her waist and held her close to him. He could smell her perfume. It was soft and delicate. Her eyes had a slant to them that made them more exotic looking than Valerie's had been. In anticipation, she closed her eyes and brought her lips to his.

He kissed her.

While Valerie had been affectionate, she limited public displays to kisses and hugs. Hank had no such inhibition. In the parking lot with people coming and going around them, she took in his kiss and reached for more.

It was like trying a different flavor of ice cream after having the same type for years. When he stroked her cheeks with his hands, she reached for them and directed them to her bare back.

He kissed her ear and breathed, "Oh, Va—" He stopped when he realized that she was not Valerie.

Hank pulled away.

"I-I'm sorry," he stammered.

"We better go back inside."

Ashamed of his blunder, he caught his breath and led her back to the entrance of the resort.

All was silent in the elevator as Joshua pushed the scene out of his mind and transformed himself into the Oak Glen High School valedictorian who had fulfilled the promise in his senior year of being most likely to succeed.

With his hand on the small of her back, he stepped into the lounge on the second floor like a dealmaker with his trophy on his arm. Randy was sitting in an armchair next to the roaring fireplace. Hoss and Karl were playing a game of blackjack at a game table. The three men had started on a bottle of scotch.

"Josh! I was beginning to think you wimped out on us!" Randy rolled a cigar between his fingertips.

"I never walk out when I'm winning." Joshua escorted Hank to the loveseat across from Randy. He observed the game of blackjack. They were playing for money, and Karl was losing.

"And you never lose." Randy pointed out with a hint of envy while he poured a glass for his classmate and handed it to him.

"No one wins all the time." Joshua pulled over a footstool to prop his foot on. He wanted to be close so he could observe Randy. "If you win all the time, then you don't know what it is like to lose; and if you don't know what it is like to lose, then there is no fun in winning."

"When have you ever lost anything?"

"You had Tricia."

"Tricia wasn't that great."

"I guess that's why you cheated on her with Margo."

"Who is now a fat cow."

"I'm talking about back then."

"That's history."

"Isn't that why we're here?" Joshua gestured towards the room above them, which was in the process of cleanup after the party. "To recall the days back when we were free of responsibility. Sex and drugs and rock and roll!"

"You didn't do drugs," Karl reminded him from the game table. He cursed when, once again, he lost a hand.

Joshua could see that Hoss was cheating with a selection of choice cards under his thigh. Karl was too drunk to see it. "Let's go back to Tricia," he said.

Randy chuckled, "I thought you were here to find out who killed Gail, and I read in the papers that that was you. You two have been tearing up the sheets for the last twenty years behind your wife's back."

"My lawyer cleared me of that."

Randy made a low sound in his throat when Joshua indicated that Hank was his lawyer. "Some guys have all the luck."

Uncomfortable with his gaze, Hank covered her legs with the skirt of her gown.

When Joshua asked him about Gail, Randy answered, "I was in Columbus."

"But Karl was here."

The sound of his name caused him to look up from his cards.

Randy suggested to the prosecutor, "Then talk to Karl."

"I hadn't seen her since we were kids," Karl blurted out.

"Then why were you calling her?" Joshua asked him.

"I was giving her dirt on Margo. She thought Margo killed Trish."

"But she didn't. You were her alibi. So—" He turned to Randy. "Someone else had to kill Trish."

"Trish killed herself. She wasn't wrapped too tight. When she lost me, she lost it."

"The evidence says otherwise. It says that she was murdered." Joshua also added, "I was there. She dumped you and you went chasing after her."

"And I got her back."

"Come on. This is Josh you're talking to. She dumped you!"

Randy said in a threatening voice, "No one ever dumped me."

"Rand, I was in the little theater when she ended it. So were all our friends. Everyone heard her say that you weren't worth the hassle."

"Trish loved me, and I loved her. I would never have hurt her."

"If you loved her so damn much, then why were you doing it with Margo? Don't tell me because of her winning personality."

"Because Margo would do it with anyone. Hell! She married Karl, of all people!" Randy added with a chuckle, "Josh, you were the only member of the football team she didn't sleep with."

"There's another achievement I can put on my resume," Joshua said. "Why did you fool around with Margo when you had Tricia?"

Randy rolled his eyes. "Because Trish refused to give it up."

"So you wanted them to fight over you. You were dating a bitch like Margo to get Trish jealous so that she would sleep with you to keep you." Joshua let his disapproval slip out. "That's the oldest trick in the book."

"It's the oldest trick for a reason. It works."

"Only it didn't work that time."

"What makes you think it didn't?"

"Because Tricia dumped you, and don't tell me she didn't."

"That scene in the little theater was what you saw. What you didn't see was what happened afterwards."

This was what Joshua was waiting for. What happened after they left the little theater? He concealed his anticipation behind a façade of disbelief. "Are you going to tell me that you two kissed and made up?"

"Yeah. Sure, she said I wasn't worth the trouble and went outside, but she was still in love with me. I gave her a little sweet talk and promised my devotion and before you knew it—" His smile was cocky. "I have no doubt that if she had lived, homecoming would have been the night. I was getting a room at the Econo Lodge for the occasion."

Even though Cindy had told him that Tricia had led Randy

to believe that they had made up by agreeing to go to the homecoming, the prosecutor pretended he didn't believe him. "Judging by the way she dropped you, I think that was all in your mind."

"Screw you, Josh!"

"Hey," he put up his hands in defeat. "I'm just telling you the way it looked to me."

"Who gives a shit how it looked to you?"

"A jury."

The two words told Randy the reason for his presence at the reunion. For their old friend, it was not a social gathering. It was an impromptu interrogation. Joshua warned him, "You should care how I perceive things."

"Should I call my lawyer?"

"Are you talking about the one defending you against two rape indictments?"

The gloves were off.

The hatred that had grown out of envy during the years that Randy pretended to be friends with a boy who was always one step ahead of him in life boiled to the surface.

"Gail's book could not have come at a worse time," Joshua said. "If she told the world what happened that night of the Valentine's Day dance, then it might reach the ears of the jury and you would be a dead man."

"My lawyer was handling it. We were going to sue her."

"You put her in my van."

"She was drunk out of her gourd!"

"You convinced her that it was me!"

"If she was so convinced it was you, what was she doing writing that it was me?"

"Because she found the son she had put up for adoption and saw you!" Joshua said. "That's right, Randy! You're a Daddy, and your son is the spittin' image of you! Gail saw him and started remembering what happened that night. It drove her into having a nervous breakdown. She was going to tell the world what you did to her, which would have revealed to everyone that you are nothing more than a common rapist, and that scared the hell out of you!"

"My lawyer was not going to let that happen."

"There is no way your lawyer could have stopped her from writing the truth about what happened to her. She told Tricia's mother that she had a theory she was working on about Tricia's murder. Gail's research shows that she was investigating you and the host of sexual assault charges that have been filed against you throughout the years. You were her chief suspect, not Margo."

"I did not kill either of them!"

"Where were you when Trish died?"

Randy shook his head. "I was with Hoss!"

A blank look crossed Hoss's face before he nodded in agreement. "Yeah, we were together at his place, playing pool."

"And we were both in Columbus when Gail was killed and you can't prove otherwise."

Joshua said with sarcasm, "And you had nothing to do with her murder."

"That's right."

"Then why did you pay Karl five thousand dollars?"

Randy snorted. "It was a loan to an old friend."

"Who happened to be at Gail's house the night she was killed," Joshua said. It was a bluff in order to study their reaction.

"I was not there." Karl suddenly forgot about the card game he was playing.

"Suppose I said that evidence suggests otherwise?"

Karl was breathing hard. "You were the one who killed her! I saw you. I saw you take her in and I saw you leave and when I went in she was dead!"

Stunned by his admission that he'd been at Gail's house, Joshua forgot about the suspect he had come to the reunion to question and turned to face Karl, who was pointing a finger of accusation in his direction.

Randy grinned. "Looks like you're on the wrong side of this interrogation now, Thornton."

Joshua asked Karl, "How did you get into her house? I locked the door on the way out."

"The patio doors were open." He went on, "I just wanted to talk to her about her book. She said that she remembered what we did to her in your van and she was going to write about it and say that we killed Trish because she was going to accuse Randy of raping her—which was a lie! I'd be kicked off the fire squad if she said that. Margo would use it to take my visitation away from Heather."

Hoss quipped, "It isn't like you get to see her now."

Joshua stepped towards Karl. "You went inside after I left. You found her passed out. So you took the pillow and you smothered her."

Karl backed out of his seat to get away from him. "No, she was dead already when I found her. I tried waking her up and she wouldn't. So I turned on the light and that was when I saw that she was dead." He repeated, "She was already dead and the only one I saw go in and come out was you." Once again, he pointed a finger, trembling with anxiety, at his former friend. "You killed her!"

Randy told Joshua, "Looks like we have a standoff. Both you and Karl were there that night. One of you killed Gail. Since you've been cleared, then I guess Karl is it."

"It's not a standoff," Joshua insisted.

Karl snatched a knife used to slice limes from the bar and grabbed Hank. He held the blade up against her throat.

"Don't anybody move or I'll slit her throat!"
Joshua told Randy, "Now this is what you call a standoff."

CHAPTER FIFTEEN

"Put down the knife, Karl."

Karl shook his head at Joshua. "No way. I'm not going to sit here and let you put me away for something you did!" He had his arm wrapped around Hank's shoulders while pressing the blade of the paring knife to her throat.

She waited for a sign from Joshua to make her move.

As soon as Joshua was distracted by Karl's desperate act of taking Hank hostage, Randy and Hoss ran down the stairs and out into the parking lot where Stan and his team of investigators took them into custody for questioning about the murders of Gail Reynolds and Tricia Wheeler.

"I didn't kill Gail," Joshua said.

"Well, I certainly didn't!" Karl yelled as if by raising his voice to the highest volume he could convince everyone within hearing distance that he was telling the truth.

"Karl, listen to me," Joshua said in a gentle tone while reaching under his coat for the gun he concealed in a belt holster behind his back. "We can talk about this."

"Like anybody is going to believe me over you! Randy is going to tell them that I told him I killed her!"

"Why did you tell him that you did it if you didn't?" Hank asked in order to take his attention and eyes from Joshua.

"For the money." Karl guided her in the direction of the door. "He was the one with everything to lose if that book came out. He told me to scare her into not writing it. When I found her dead, I figured that if I told him that I killed her for him that he would help me out."

"And keep you quiet," she concluded.

Joshua had his gun in his grip. In hopes of not having to use it, he kept it tucked behind his back. "While you were outside waiting for me to leave, did you see or hear anything?"

"No!" Karl judged the distance between them and the door. "You were the only one there."

Joshua stepped closer to them. "And you went in through the back door?"

"Because the front door was locked."

"I locked it. When you left, what door did you go out?"

"The same way I came in. The patio door." Karl pressed the blade against her neck. "Get away from me, man!"

Hank's eyes told Joshua they were running out of time.

"Karl, don't make us have to stop you. I'm telling you to put the knife down."

Karl snarled, "I'll put it down. I'll put it down right—"

Before Karl could finish his threat she lifted her leg and dug her high heel into his shin and brought it down to his foot. At the same time, she pulled his arm away from her throat while plunging her elbow into his ribs.

Before he could recover to go after her with the knife, she dove for the gun in her handbag on the loveseat.

"Bitch! Damn bitch!" Seeing that his hostage was gone, Karl lunged for Joshua but came face to face with the barrel of his Berretta.

"Don't make me use this, Karl."

"I guess we can file this case as closed," Stan announced the conclusion of the Gail Reynolds murder case.

"I'm not so sure about that," Joshua countered.

He and Hank had given their statements to the state police,

who took over Karl's hostage situation, which was determined to be part of their investigation.

"Why not?" Hank asked. "You saw what happened here. Karl killed Gail to stop her from writing about the gang rape that was going to ruin all of their lives and reputations. Then he got Randy, who had the most to lose, to pay him for his silence."

"Karl said he didn't do it."

Stan scoffed. "Of course. He's not going to confess to the county prosecutor."

Joshua shook his head in hopes of shaking everything into place. "He said that he left her house through the open patio doors because I locked the front door."

"So?" she asked.

"When Jan Martin came by three days later, the front door was unlocked and open. Who unlocked it and left it open?"

"Karl Connor," Stan answered. "That's what I'm telling the jury." He turned away to go home and back to bed, but stopped when he remembered something. "Oh, we got a trace on that e-mail that Sally Powell got that threatened to tell her husband about her affair."

"Who sent it?"

"Margo Connor."

"Karl's ex-wife," Hank observed.

Stan acknowledged the family connection between the source behind framing Joshua and the man he had arrested for murder. "She claims she didn't send it. Her lawyer says that anyone in her office who had access to her computer could have sent it from her e-mail account while she was away from her desk."

Hank suggested, "Maybe she doesn't want her daughter to suffer the humiliation of having her father arrested for murder. Frame Joshua to keep suspicion off Karl."

"And get the man prosecuting her daughter off the case," Joshua surmised.

Mabel Barkely-Fine was on her way back to Columbus, Ohio, to hire a lawyer, but not the kind her husband needed. Fed up with the controversy he had brought to their lives, she was looking for the best divorce lawyer money could buy.

Seeing the end of life as he knew it, Randy was angry by the time Joshua stepped into the Hancock County jail's conference room to finish the discussion they had started in the lounge at Mountaineer Resort. His suit jacket and tie were gone. With the few strands of his thin hair messed up, and his stomach hanging over the waistband of his pants, he held little resemblance to the high school Romeo Joshua had known long ago.

"Get out, Josh!" he ordered him. "My lawyer is going to move to have you taken off this case. You're prejudiced against me."

"If you mean that I have a personal dislike for rapists, yes." He sat down across from him.

"I never raped Trish."

"But you raped Gail."

"She wanted it. She couldn't get enough of me."

"She wanted me, not you—"

"The story of my life," Randy muttered.

"What are you talking about?"

"Do you know what it is like to make love to a woman and have her call you by someone else's name?"

Joshua caught his breath while recalling the night before. He found himself wondering once again if Hank heard him whisper Valerie's name into her ear.

Randy's voice interrupted his thoughts. "All you had to do was give Trish the sign and I would have been history." He scoffed, "You had no idea, did you? She was in love with you."

Joshua felt a hole in the pit of his stomach. "Is that why you killed her?"

"I told you already. I did not kill her. Gail was off her rocker, saying that I killed Trish because she was going to accuse me of raping her."

"Maybe that wasn't your reason for killing her," Joshua agreed with him. "Maybe you killed her because she had the gall to dump you in front of all your friends for cheating on her."

"She took me back! You saw me chase after her. I followed her out of the theater and out the side door, and begged her forgiveness, and she took me back."

"I don't believe you."

"Josh! We used to be friends. You have to believe me."

Joshua leaned across to challenge him. "Make me believe you."

Randy thought, and then smiled. "Ask Doug Barlow. He saw the whole thing."

"Doug Barlow?"

"He followed Trish outside, too. He was going on and on to her about how much he loved her. I told him to get lost. He tried to be gallant and told me that she didn't want to talk to me. Then, the little twerp threw a punch at me. So I decked him. Then she told him to leave us alone because we had to talk. But he wouldn't leave. He went over to the door and listened in on the whole thing. After we made up, he started crying like a girl and ran off."

Finished with his tale, Randy sighed. "Ask Hoss if you don't believe me."

"Hoss will say anything to protect you."

"Check the school records. Hoss was pissed after that because Doug was his chemistry partner. You remember how lousy his grades were. They had a lab test that afternoon, and the twerp wasn't there to help him. Doug didn't show up for the next two days. The attendance records will confirm that. Hoss was as mad as hell. Don't you remember? He almost got tossed off the team because he flunked that test. *You* ended up tutoring him."

Joshua wasn't listening while Randy went on asserting that if he checked the school records he would find that Doug Barlow had left school that afternoon after seeing him make up with Tricia. As much as he did not want to believe Randy, he could not deny recalling Doug following her out of the little theater. If he had been in love with Tricia, then it was possible that he chose that time to proclaim it.

"So, Mr. Prosecutor," Randy concluded with a sneer. "Do you believe me or am I under arrest?"

"I believe you," Joshua muttered, "and you are under arrest."

"For what? You can't arrest me for raping Gail. The statute on that ran out a long time ago."

It was the prosecutor's turn to scoff. "Karl told you that he killed Gail and you did nothing but cut him a check. That is accessory after the fact. You're under arrest, Randy."

"You look like you're going somewhere." Joshua observed the backpack in Hank's car. She was waiting for him on the front porch when he and his children got home from the Sunday church service. Nineteen hours earlier, she was dressed in a stunning gown when he escorted her to the reunion.

The one piece of information Joshua considered lucky to have gathered from the reunion was that Doug Barlow had witnessed Tricia and Randy making up. Joshua doubted if Doug would be able to give them more details about that day. However, he did think Phyllis, if she chose to be cooperative, might be able to enlighten him about what her brother had told her about Randy and Tricia's discussion after the fight.

"I have to get back to Pearl," Hank explained when he asked

about her backpack in the back of the rental car. "I think you can handle yourself from here on out."

"I thought you would maybe hang around for a few more days. You said you had vacation time to use or lose."

She kissed him on the cheek. "I have work that won't wait." She descended the steps to the driveway. "It was great seeing you again. Love you." She got into the car and drove off.

Aware of the five pairs of eyes watching him from various windows in the house, Joshua stood up straight, swallowed, and scratched his head.

As her car disappeared down the hill on Fifth Street, he heard the roar of Tad's Harley. It came into sight as Hank's rental faded from view. The motorcycle turned onto Rock Springs Boulevard and pulled into the cobblestone drive.

Joshua was surprised to see that it was Jan who rode on the back of Tad's bike with her arms wrapped around his waist.

Hopeful for a ride on the motorcycle, Donny, still dressed in his church clothes, came running out onto the porch with the pretence of saying hello.

"Where was Hank going?" Tad asked after cutting off the engine.

"Back to Hawaii. She couldn't stay any longer. She has cases that won't wait." Even coming from his own mouth, Joshua thought the excuse was not the whole truth.

When Tad started to dismount from his bike, Donny jogged down the steps to greet him with a hopeful grin.

"Do you want to go for a ride?"

After his father consented, the boy put on the helmet Jan had been wearing and went off down the road with his cousin.

Shaking out her hair that had been matted from the helmet, Jan followed Joshua to his study. "How was the reunion?"

"You didn't miss much."

"I didn't think so," she replied. "Tad took me to the Ponderosa for dinner."

Joshua was startled to hear this. He turned to see that her cheeks were glowing. "I guess you had a good time."

Her grin said that she did. "Did Randy kill Trish?"

He answered with a shrug and a shake of his head at the same time. "His profile doesn't fit with the murder." He plopped down in the chair behind his desk.

"Who did kill her?"

The slam of the front door relieved Joshua of the burden of answering. Tad found him sitting behind his desk with his head in his hands studying Tricia's case file.

"What have you got there?" Tad pulled the top sheet from the folder. He let Jan read it over his shoulder.

It was a copy of a letter from the former county prosecutor, dated fifteen years ago, to Dorothy Wheeler in regard to a missing class ring. It stated that the county was not responsible for the theft. However, to settle the matter, they would reimburse her the cost of the ring in the amount of one hundred and fifty dollars. The letter noted that a check was enclosed.

"I've heard of cops and ambulance people who would take stuff off dead people," Jan said.

"Didn't we all see Trish take back her class ring from Randy that day?" Joshua recalled.

The original letter stapled to the copy signed by the prosecutor was from Dorothy. The letter read that it had come to her attention that her daughter had taken her class ring back from her ex-boyfriend on the day of her death, but she did not find it among any of her effects. If it was taken into evidence with her clothes and other items, she wanted it back for sentimental reasons. When she had checked with the sheriff, she was told that no class ring was found, nor was it logged in. Suspecting that it had been stolen, she wanted to be paid for the cost of it, or she was going to go to the media.

"Josh, have you looked at the crime scene pictures yet?" Tad asked.

Jan said, "Tad and I decided that someone moved her body after she had died."

Joshua braced himself to look at the photographs of Tricia. The father could imagine the horror Dorothy had experienced when she came home to find her only child dead.

Tricia looked like she was taking a nap; that position should have told the previous sheriff that she had not committed suicide. Dressed in her cheerleading uniform with her blue-and-gold pleated skirt and turtleneck sweater with a gold trim "OG" on her chest, she was laid out in state. Her head rested on a pillow and her feet were up off the floor. Her hands were folded across her chest.

It was a picture of peace.

According to the medical examiner's report, death was instantaneous.

Joshua took out his magnifying glass to study the bullet hole through the *O* on her chest.

"What are you looking at?" Jan bent over the desk to see what he was examining.

When the phone rang, she knocked it off the hook.

"Here." Joshua handed them the picture and the magnifying glass with one hand while he answered the phone with the other. "Hello, Mrs. Wheeler. How are you today?"

"I'll be fantastic if you can tell me who killed my daughter," she said with a pleasant, yet serious, tone in her voice.

"I'm making headway." He turned around in his chair and directed his attention to the woman on the other end of the phone. "I don't have any or enough evidence to make an arrest, but I am closer than Sheriff Delaney was, that's for sure." He took out his notepad. "Tell me about the ring."

"What ring?" As soon as she asked, Dorothy remembered.

"Oh, her class ring. Yes. Trish had given it to Randy Fine when they started going steady. When she died, I thought he had it. Then, years later, I ran into Cindy Patterson, now Rodgers. She told me that Trish took her ring back on the day she died. So I figured the police had it and, since they weren't doing anything with it, I wanted it back. But they couldn't find it. One of the deputies confided to me that a couple of years after Trish died, one of the hospital attendants who worked in the morgue had been caught stealing and was fired, and he was working at the time she was brought in. So I got them to pay me for it."

While it sounded like a good explanation of what happened to her ring, Joshua made a mental note not to forget about it. He couldn't dismiss that the killer might have taken it as a souvenir.

After assuring Dorothy Wheeler once again that he was making headway in finding her daughter's killer, he hung up the phone with a sigh of physical and emotional exhaustion.

Seeing that they had no other information to exchange, Jan announced that she had a lot of work to do. She hesitated for Tad to follow or offer to give her a ride down the street to her house only to have him plop down in the chair. Concluding that they had man-talk to discuss, she went home.

"How was your date with Hank?" Tad asked once he heard Jan shut the door in the front foyer.

"I'm not meant to date women."

Tad shot him a wicked grin. "Who are you meant to date?"

Joshua was not amused by his humor.

"Want to talk about it?"

Joshua shook his head. "I need some time off, away from all this." He indicated the stacks of files on his desk. "I came back home so the kids and I could have a more stable life. But the minute I get elected county prosecutor, my love life is called into question and we have a killing spree with an idiot for a detective. Sarah is barely passing English. I haven't been to one scout meeting with Donny. Murphy is taking him. I missed the last parent-teacher conference. I forgot about it. I don't do things like that." He concluded by announcing, "I wish I had never run for this job."

"And then Hank went back to Hawaii. What is that all about?"

"I screwed up royally." Joshua shook his head in his hands. "She comes flying out here like a knight on a white horse. I didn't ask her to come. Did you hear me ask her to come?"

"I didn't even know about her."

"She comes out here and tells me that she broke it off with her fiancé. We decide—I thought we decided—to give it a shot, and then the next thing I know I called her Valerie while in the middle of a kiss. She couldn't get back to Pearl fast enough after that."

"You called her Valerie?" Tad whistled. "That was a big mistake."

"Her name just came out of my mouth. I thought I stopped in time—"

"Did she say anything about the ring?"

Joshua started. "What ring?"

"Maybe the wedding ring turned her off, too?" Tad's eyes were on the ring on Joshua's left hand.

Joshua looked down at his fingers.

The gold band fit as perfectly as the day Valerie had slipped it onto his finger. Over the years it had become scratched and the shine had faded. He saw his late bride's image forever captured on her wedding day in the crystal frame beyond his hand on the corner of his desk.

"You know, Josh," Tad explained while scratching the side of his head, "the whole one-year-of-mourning thing is custom. It's not a rule. The period of mourning isn't the same for everyone. I remember when Dad died. Mom had been married to him for twenty-one years. She loved that man. But, four months later, she was out there dating and she hasn't stopped since. I have to beat them away from her with a stick."

Comparing his beautiful, socially active aunt enjoying a life of retirement in Florida to her amorous son, Joshua noted, "Like mother like son, huh?"

"But then, I have a patient in her fifties. Her husband died twenty-seven years ago. They were married for four years. She has never been out with anyone else. She still wears her wedding ring. She is still in mourning." He concluded, "Everyone is different. There's nothing wrong with you if you aren't ready to move on to someone else."

The two men sat in silence.

When it appeared as if his cousin had become lost in his thoughts, Tad rose. "I guess I should be going home."

Joshua fingered the gold band. "That patient you were telling me about? The one who is still mourning her husband after twenty-seven years? Is she happy?"

Tad paused to think about the woman, who lived a life of solitude. Her home had not changed one iota since the day her husband died. "In her own way. She's alone and she likes it that way."

"I don't want to be alone."

"That's good. I'd think it'd be impossible to be alone with five kids."

After Tad left, Joshua, determined to push Hank and Valerie from his mind, picked up the phone and dialed Doug Barlow's phone number. As he expected, Phyllis answered the phone.

"What do you want to talk to him about?" she startled him by asking when he asked to speak to her brother.

"We are investigating Tricia Wheeler's death and believe he might have some information about it."

"He doesn't," she snapped back.

He grimaced. Phyllis Barlow Rollins did have a way of making the simplest things difficult. "Can I ask him that?"

"No, you can ask our lawyer. Her name is Tori Brody."

He cringed. Tori was the last woman he wanted to talk to.

He advised her in the polite tone of a well-informed friend, "Phyllis, I have to tell you that when somebody 'lawyers up,' as we call it in my line of work, that makes them look guilty of something. Right now, I only want to ask Doug a couple of questions about what he might have seen the day Tricia died."

Her tone was terse. "That was a long time ago. My brother is not well. If you try to interrogate him, there is no telling what damage it would do. Besides, we told Sheriff Delaney all we knew about Tricia back when she shot herself, which is nothing."

"Then let Doug tell me himself he knows nothing."

"Call our lawyer."

Joshua took off his gloves. "Phyllis, I'm going to talk to your brother, whether I have to go through your lawyer or not."

"Over my dead body."

"We can get a court order to have your brother brought in against his, and your, will, and interrogated before a judge, if need be. Now, if you are really worried about his well-being, how do you think that will affect him?" He expected her to respond to his threat by making an appointment to bring Doug in to see him.

"Go to hell, Josh."

Click!

CHAPTER SIXTEEN

"You've been avoiding me."

Joshua kept his back to Tori, who had appeared in the file room where he was looking for a folder that Mary had forgotten to retrieve for him before she left for lunch.

"Do you have an appointment, Ms. Brody?" He closed the drawer and opened another.

"I came to apologize for the water pitcher incident, but it wasn't all my fault."

"That is what I call a backhanded apology." He gave up his search and turned around. "I will accept your apology. Do you have anything else to discuss?"

"Phyllis Rollins called me this morning. What do you want to talk to Doug about?"

"I believe that he may have some information that could be useful in the Wheeler case."

"Is he a suspect?"

"Everyone is a suspect."

"Is Phyllis still a suspect in Rex's murder?"

"Until I get a better suspect, she's not off my list. So far, she's gained the most from his death. What does she have planned for the check she's expecting from his life insurance?"

"They won't pay until his murder is solved. When are you going to scratch her off your list?"

"When we find Rex's book."

"Do you seriously believe that Rex wrote a book?" She

laughed. "He was a blowhard. There's no book."

"They had a bitter divorce. He wrote about a woman who got away with murder. Phyllis lived next door to Tricia Wheeler who was murdered, she was seen arguing with her the day she was killed, and she refuses to let me question her brother, a possible witness."

"Screw you, Josh! If you believed all that you would have gotten an indictment before now."

"Give me a reason and I'll get it. I have enough circumstantial evidence to have your client indicted for Tricia's and Rex's murders, and maybe even Gail's."

"But you haven't."

"I wouldn't be so anxious if I were you." He gently pushed her out of his way in order to return to his office. "Where's Billy Unger?"

"I told the sheriff already. I don't know. Why do you have it out for him, anyway? He's simply a kid who got mixed up with the wrong people."

"This kid committed murder," Joshua told her. "Walt Manners is chomping at the bit to get in front of a jury to tell them that he gave Billy the gun used to kill Grace Henderson. Between his testimony and the material from the trench coat left at the crime scene of her murder, your boy is going down." He added, "Plus, I'm re-filing charges against him for the attempted armed robbery at the Mountaineer and I'm also charging him with the Landers murder, too."

Tori hissed, "We had a deal!"

"Any deals we've made are now null and void, since he skipped the second we got a warrant for his arrest in the Henderson murder."

"It's not my fault that he disappeared," she said with a roll of her eyes. "I told Billy that you would throw the book at him."

Joshua asked, "When did you tell him that?"

She paused. "When we made the deal. Why do you ask?"

"How could you have warned him about my throwing the book at him if you didn't know that he intended to run away?"

"I left a message at his boardinghouse to meet me at the sheriff's office, but he never met me," she stammered. "So I left another message for him there that warned him about what was going to happen if he didn't turn himself in. Clearly, he ran the second he got the message to meet me at the sheriff's office."

"And you haven't seen hide nor hair of him?"

"Why don't you believe me?" she asked angrily. "How do you know that Heather Connor isn't hiding him? Oh, I forgot! She was born on the right side of the tracks!"

Joshua didn't know what it was about Tori's insistence that she was not to blame for Billy's disappearance that made him believe she knew more about his whereabouts than she was claiming. "I guess I don't believe you because I just don't trust you."

He was putting on his sports coat and turning around to see if she had left when he discovered that she had run across the room to take their argument to a new level. He caught her arm in midair in her attempt to slap him. Instinct gave him the jump, and he caught her other hand before her claws could injure his cheek.

"Bastard!" she wailed while struggling to break his hold on her arms.

"What's going on here?" Mary asked when she came in to find the prosecuting attorney wrestling with the defense attorney.

"Let go of me!" Tori demanded.

He released his grip and directed her to the office door. "Mary will show you out."

She gave him one last parting shot. "What goes around comes

around, Josh. Don't you forget that."

"What happened to your brilliant chief of detectives?" Joshua tried to keep the cocky tone out of his voice when he asked Sheriff Sawyer why the sheriff requested Joshua accompany him to interview Margo Connor and her lawyer instead of Seth Cavanaugh.

"Would you believe he quit?" Curt answered from the driver's seat of his cruiser. "The jerk didn't even give me two weeks' notice."

He turned off Route 8 into Margo Connor's subdivision. The former farm had been split up into two- to four-acre lots containing luxury homes for Chester's wealthiest citizens.

"He quit?" Joshua shook his head. "Must have been because he knew he was fired."

"Maybe. He came in with that stupid smirk of his and announced that he got a literary agent who got him a big advance to write a book about the Parkersburg murders. He's even got a movie deal, too! Go figure. The guy is an idiot."

Joshua laughed at the sheriff's disbelief in the turn of events before asking, "Did Seth ever tell you what he was talking to Margo about at the courthouse?"

"He claimed that he was questioning her about Heather and Billy."

"I don't believe that," Joshua said. "She never would have given him the time of day without her lawyer being there. Besides, you didn't see him. He looked scared."

"Margo Connor is a scary woman," the sheriff quipped.

"Tad swears that Seth was trying to steal that material that put Billy Unger at the scene when Grace was killed. Why was he trying to steal it? Seth wasn't going to profit from Billy getting off . . . unless he was on the take. Suppose he was trying to steal that evidence for Margo so her little girl's boyfriend would not go to jail. Then, when he failed to get it, he had to go to the courthouse to face Margo, which would have made her unhappy, and an unhappy Margo is ugly enough to scare anyone."

"I think you're right," Curt grumbled. "Hockenberry says that according to his sources, Cavanaugh was living beyond what Hancock County had been paying him. Only problem is that we can't find any definite proof, and he left town faster than a bat out of hell after your hearing in Weirton."

"He can run," Joshua said, "but he can't hide."

As expected, Margo had her lawyer lying in wait when they arrived to question her about her ex-husband's arrest and her e-mail to Sally Powell extorting her into making a false statement against Joshua.

Since Margo's name was connected to Gail's and Tricia's murders, they found it not surprising that she refused to speak to them without her lawyer being present. Her name was even a dot in Rex Rollins's murder. Joshua had not forgotten that she was Rex's former boss and that her lawyer was defending him.

Joshua had determined after speaking to Liz Yates and other witnesses who saw the scene with Gail at the restaurant that Margo Sweeney Boyd Connor did have something to hide. However, they couldn't figure out what it was since her ex-husband had reluctantly admitted to being her alibi at the time of Tricia's murder.

Christine Watson immediately went on the defensive for her client. "Why are you here harassing my client about these murders that you have been so inept at solving?"

"That is what we are working on," Joshua responded. "Interrogation is part of investigation. Your client is connected to these murders in one way or another."

"I resent that!" Margo snapped.

"The e-mail to Sally Powell threatening to reveal her affair was traced to you. I'm sure it will only be a matter of time before the five thousand dollars she received can also be traced back to you."

She scoffed, "Wanna bet?"

"My client's computer is on all day long. She is in and out of her office," Christine responded as she had to the special prosecutor. "Anyone could have sent that e-mail from her account."

Her client rolled her eyes. "Why don't you do something useful and go arrest a real criminal? Why haven't you arrested Hilda Ferguson?"

"Hilda Ferguson?" Joshua asked.

"The sticky-fingered maid my client fired," Christine explained. "She stole a ring from her over a month ago. It was a two-carat ruby ring with a carat of diamonds. I filed a report with the police on her behalf." She turned back to Curt. "Why didn't you arrest her?"

"Because Hilda says she didn't steal it and you have no proof that she did."

"Mom, what is going on here?" Heather came into the living room.

She was dressed in the latest fashion for her generation. Joshua, who was conscious of how much money his children spent on clothes, knew that a lot of expense went into Heather's ensemble, which was a duplication of something she had seen on MTV. Her skintight top had a plunging neckline that revealed her overflowing bosoms. The midriff top stopped at the waist to reveal a bulging tattooed stomach and wide hips.

The teenager greeted everyone, including her mother, with scorn. "Mom, what is he doing here?" She spat out the words in Joshua's direction.

"They'll be leaving in a few minutes," their lawyer answered with equal distaste. "They have questions about your father killing that reporter. They have the mistaken idea that your mother was involved."

"Tell him to go to hell." Heather turned to the county prosecutor. "Go to hell."

She went into the kitchen and returned with a can of beer. When she opened it to take a drink, Curt took it out of her hand with a glare before giving her mother a look of surprise that she had let her daughter do such a thing. He then looked at Joshua, who was equally astounded by the action and lack of reaction from her mother.

"It's okay, Baby. They'll be gone soon." Margo turned to Joshua. "Can't you see that you're upsetting my daughter? It is all over the TV about her idiot father getting himself arrested for murder and all her friends know. Isn't that humiliating enough?"

"Aw, forget it," Heather went to the door. "I'm going to meet Nicki."

"When will you be home?" Margo tried to take her hand to fake a picture of closeness.

"Whenever I feel like it." When she sneered at her mother on her way out the door, Joshua noted the family resemblance.

"You get what you put out," he quoted his grandmother to Curt, who was still surprised by what he saw in some of the juveniles he encountered.

Under the watchful eyes of Margo and her lawyer, the two men had paused to talk inside the cruiser before turning on the engine and leaving.

"Ever since I first knew her, Margo was self-centered," Joshua recalled. "Her mother used to be the vice-president at the bank and the power of that went to her head. It should not be surprising that Heather inherited their attitude. She doesn't care one lick that her father is in jail, as long as it doesn't put a kink in her social schedule. She would probably act the same way if

Margo was in the cell next to him."

"She doesn't seem too concerned about Billy skipping town, either," Curt observed. "Maybe because he's not really gone. I'd bet money she knows where Billy is hiding."

"Maybe. But I can't see Heather getting attached to anyone enough to cry more than ten minutes after they were gone."

Curt pointed out, "We haven't really looked at Margo as a suspect in Gail's murder. Seth immediately focused on you, and then Karl surfaced."

"I don't think Karl did it. As much as I hate to admit it, I believe him that he found her dead when he went in after I left."

"But then that would leave you as our prime suspect."

"Jan found the front door unlocked and open when she went there three days later. I made a point of locking the door and Karl said that that was why he went around the house and came in the back door. It was dark. He was unfamiliar with the house. Imagine him stumbling around outside looking for a way in. That can take time."

Curt saw where he was leading. "Enough time for someone already in the house to smother a drunken woman."

"Then the killer simply hid in the dark and waited for Karl to go out the back door before escaping out the front." Joshua concluded, "Knowing that Randy had a lot to lose and money to pay to keep up appearances, Karl lied about killing her, threatened to implicate him if he was caught, and requested cash for his silence."

The prosecutor turned his head to where the women were studying them through the living-room window. He thought they should leave, but knew that it bothered them more the longer they hung around. "Can you see that woman, already being a suspect for killing Tricia, plus having a scene in public threatening Gail, taking the chance to go into her house and killing her herself?" Aware of being watched, Joshua shook his head slightly. "She's too smart and loves money too much to take a chance like that. She's more likely to sic her lawyer on her."

"Unless Gail had something so bad on her that she couldn't take the chance of losing a lawsuit and having Gail reveal it anyway," Curt said with a shake of his own head. "Don't give Margo more credit than she's due. She may be smart, but she's not that smart. I heard through the grapevine that she paid Herb Duncan twenty-five thousand dollars for his dump. Had you seen his place? He and Blanche lived in a secondhand trailer on a one-acre lot in Birch Hollow. I wouldn't have given him twenty-five cents for it, but Margo paid him twenty-five thousand dollars. I heard that they are moving into a brand-new three-bedroom, two-and-a-half bath in Connor Estates."

"Herb Duncan?" Joshua recalled seeing him drive past his house. "Didn't he just buy a new truck?"

"Yeah, he did. He's real young, about twenty-two or so. When I was his age, I was living in a Marine barrack."

Joshua's mind was churning with possibilities.

Seeing the wheels spinning in his head, Curt leaned toward him. "What are you thinking?"

Joshua muttered more to himself than the sheriff, "She could know something that the rest of us don't know. Like that a big highway development is interested in the property, or maybe even a mall or professional development is looking at the place. Even so, it would be more prudent to offer to buy the property for its worth or even less."

Curt nodded his head in agreement.

Joshua was studying the women peering out at them while he recalled Tad's question upon seeing Herb's new truck, "What has Herb Duncan gotten himself into?"

"He got himself a job working for Margo's construction

company. She hired him as foreman."

"Foreman? Wasn't Rex Rollins a foreman?"

"Until he got fired."

"Exactly when did she hire Herb?"

"A few weeks ago." Curt grinned as it occurred to him, "It was the same week I heard about her offering him all that for his trailer and lot. A lot of people were surprised because there were at least two other guys, with seniority, who were certain they were going to get the job." He started the engine. "Are you thinking what I'm thinking?"

"I'm thinking I'm going to have to get me a warrant," Joshua's accent slipped from that of the sophisticated lawyer, "for Margo's financial records."

Saturday morning was Paula's regular day for cleaning lawyer Tori Brody's condo. She would arrive at nine in the morning and finish before noon. It did not take a lot of time for her to clean the loft apartment.

Her first clue that something might be wrong was bloody handprints in the elevator. She shuddered while imagining what had caused so much blood. She would ask Miss Brody if she knew what happened.

Miss Brody was unable to answer the question.

When the door was unlocked, Paula assumed that her employer was home. She had only to take a few steps through the door when she saw that her morning was not going to be taken up with cleaning.

She found her boss, dressed in a black negligee, seated in the chair inside the door with a bullet hole in her chest.

CHAPTER SEVENTEEN

"Tori was killed between eleven and midnight last night," Tad reported to Joshua. He was in the process of the cursory on-scene exam before having her body removed to the morgue for the autopsy.

"J.J. and I were playing chess about that time."

"You don't have to tell me you didn't do this," the sheriff assured him. "Everyone knows that she was chasing you and you didn't give her a tumble." With a grin, he asked, "Why are all these women running after you anyway?"

"I have no idea. If I were a woman, a single father with five kids would be the last thing I would want." Joshua gestured towards the hallway outside the condo where he saw crime-scene investigators scraping blood from the wall. "I saw blood in the elevator and hall. Was she shot here?"

Tad showed him the hole in her chest. "Judging from this wound, I doubt if she could have made it anywhere after being shot. I can't say for certain until I open her up, but I think she was killed instantly. It looks like the bullet hit her square in the heart." He shone his penlight on the black negligee.

Joshua knelt next to the chair to look at her. Even in death, sprawled on the chair, Tori seemed strangely sensuous.

Tad peeled the negligee from the wound. In doing so, he revealed her breasts.

"It wasn't a contact wound," the prosecutor noticed about the bullet wound. It was a hole, pure and simple, with no blackened speckling that came from the barrel of the gun. "She was shot from a distance, at least a few feet."

"But look at all the blood on the negligee." Tad made a circular motion with his latex-gloved hands.

Joshua saw the blood pattern on the front of the lacy material. It was almost not noticeable on the black garment.

While he examined the hole in her breast, the medical examiner concluded, "I don't think that's her blood."

"Must belong to whoever spread it all over the hallway and elevator."

Curt Sawyer completed his search of the condo. "No murder weapon on the scene. Whoever splattered their blood on Brody, the hall, and the elevator must have taken the gun with them."

"Here's another question." Joshua asked. "With all that blood, are we looking for the killer, or another victim . . . or both?"

"Hello, Jan."

Jan slammed her front door in Ernie Gaston's face.

He knocked again. "Jan, please, can we talk?"

This was what she had been waiting for her whole life. Someone was begging her for forgiveness after trampling on her.

"No."

She waited and hoped that he would knock again.

He did.

Then came the words she was waiting for. "I'm sorry. I need you. You are the only journalist Josh Thornton will talk to. Our whole newspaper is stonewalled when it comes to Hancock County news at the courthouse. I never realized how many political connections he has. None of them will talk to anyone from our paper."

She called through the door between them, "What about that

article about Josh, making him look like a womanizing psychopath?"

"That was Seth Cavanaugh's fault. He misled me."

She threw open the door. "And you didn't check and double-check the information he gave you?"

"Well—"

Jan grew angry with her realization, "You wanted it to be true! You wanted Josh to get railroaded into jail!" Involuntarily, her finger came up to point at the man who had been her boss. "You're jealous of Josh!"

"No!"

"Yes! Back in school, you were the school editor. Gail was your protégé because—"

"I saw that she had talent."

"Is that what you call it? Only, as it turns out, she had the hots for Josh." Her question came as an accusation, "What happened? Did you tell her how you felt about her and she told you to take a hike—after all the help you gave her to become editor—and then get my scholarship! Where were you the night Gail was killed? Were you sharing a bottle of wine with her?"

Ernie puffed out his chest. "Do you know who you are talking to?"

Jan was smug. "Yes, I know who you are, and I know who I am. I'm the news editor at *The Review* and the only journalist Josh Thornton will talk to."

"Here's a piece of information that will interest you," the sheriff slung a leg across the corner of Joshua's desk in his study and crossed his arms. "The slug they took out of Tori Brody came from the same gun that killed Grace Henderson and Matthew Landers." He held the case file for Tori Brody's murder in his hand.

"No kidding," Joshua gasped at the news. "Billy Unger. She

was his lawyer."

"And his fingerprints are all over her condo. We also found articles of his clothing there. She's been hiding him."

"Then why did he kill her?"

"Maybe she came to her senses and wanted him to turn himself in. I don't know." The sheriff shrugged. "It was Unger's bloody handprints in the elevator. There were also partial fingerprints on the call button in the hallway and the button for the ground floor in the elevator. Those weren't his. No ID on whose, though. Tad was right about the blood splatters on the front of her negligee. That blood wasn't hers. And the slug he took out of her heart, it had two blood types on it. One was hers, the other wasn't. It matches the blood in the hall and elevator."

"Then, the bullet went through someone else before it hit her," Joshua concluded.

"And it went in at a downward angle," Tad announced from where he leaned in the doorway. He had stolen yet another apple from the Thornton refrigerator.

"A downward angle? Do you mean to say that she was sitting in the chair and the killer was standing over her?" The sheriff twisted his body to confer with Tad who plopped down on the sofa and put his feet up on the coffee table.

"The bullet went in at a twenty-five-degree angle and hit her aorta." He illustrated with his hand the angle at which the shot was fired. "She also had sex with a man whose blood type was B positive—real recently, like right before she was killed."

The sheriff said, "The same blood type found in the elevator and on the front of her nightgown."

Joshua asked Tad, "What was Billy Unger's blood type?"

"B positive. You don't think she was sleeping with her client, do you?" Tad reflected on the possibility of Tori making such a foolish decision.

Joshua answered, "Evidence suggests she was hiding him from the police."

Tad admitted, "Unger was one good-looking young man . . . to young girls. I guess Tori fell for his charm."

"Until we determine who killed her, there will be people, based on Ernie's article, who will assume I did it and covered it up." Joshua grabbed the case file from Curt's hand and leafed through the reports. "Now, Billy Unger was at the crime scene. Walt Manners says he gave the gun he used to kill the Landers boy to Billy to get rid of. I don't think Billy did what he was told to do. That gun was used to kill Tori and Grace. Unger is the common denominator in both murders. Find him."

"What's wrong with this picture?" Sheriff Sawyer observed the inside of Billy Unger's car, which had been found behind some bushes on the banks of the Ohio River, downstream from New Cumberland. The car and Unger's body had been discovered by two fishermen looking for a secluded place to fish.

From the driver's side, Tad examined Billy Unger's body while the sheriff and Joshua observed the dried puddle of blood in the passenger seat. "Entrance and exit wound," he told them. "The bullet went clean through. I'm betting that it is the same one I dug out of Tori."

"He was sitting here." Joshua pointed to the blood in the seat and the streaks that went from the pool to his final resting place on the other side of the car. "He was dragged over to the driver's side."

"How long has he been dead, Doc?" the sheriff asked.

"Decomposition has already started," the medical examiner said. "If you want my guess for now, . . . I'd say three days."

"Tori was killed three days ago," Joshua reminded them.

"I'd say he was there when she was shot. The wound looks like it's at a downward angle."

"Tori got it in the chest," the sheriff said. "She was sitting in the chair when she was hit."

"If Billy was standing in front of where she was sitting—" Joshua worked out the scene in his mind. "Suppose the killer was standing over Tori and he stepped in front of the gun and took the bullet."

Tad said, "The bullet went through him and got her in the chest."

"That seat seems kind of tight." Joshua observed that the driver's seat was close to the steering wheel. "Looks like the way my car does when I've been giving Tracy driving lessons."

"No, Billy didn't drive this car last," the medical examiner agreed. "Someone was probably trying to get him to the hospital, but he died before they could get him there, so they left him here. On this road, on Friday night with the resort up the river, they wouldn't have had any trouble hitching out of here."

"The killer had his gun," the sheriff reminded them.

Joshua said, "Billy got that gun four years ago. It was hot. He was savvy enough to know that if he was found with it, then he himself would be implicated in Landers's murder."

"Wait a minute," Curt held up his hands. "We have been working on the theory that Unger kept the gun and used it to kill Grace Henderson. That's why you first suspected him of killing her. Are you now saying that he got rid of it?"

"With all the heat I put on him, you'd think he'd cough up who he gave it to, but he didn't."

"Loyalty," Tad suggested. "There are a lot of people sitting in prison right now because they refused to give up a friend to the cops to save themselves."

Curt argued, "If Unger didn't kill Henderson, then why didn't he give up whoever it was that was wearing his trench coat?"

Joshua breathed and shook his head. "Like Tad says, maybe loyalty, or fear. He ran with a rough crowd." He gestured towards Billy's dead body. "Look at what they do to each other."

The sheriff disagreed. "He didn't mind giving up Manners when it served his purpose."

"Maybe he didn't know," Tad said. "Maybe the gun was stolen by someone who didn't know it was hot."

"In which case he wouldn't know who had it." Joshua cringed. "But Billy is the only common denominator in these murders. The only other common denominator is Heather, but she doesn't fit the description of the killer leaving the scene after shooting Grace."

"There is another!" Tad exclaimed. "Didn't you say that Karl said the last time he saw Heather was at the mall with a redhead?"

"Actually he said she had orange hair," Joshua said. "What about her?"

"The orange-haired girl in the picture. Nicki Samuels. She introduced Grace to Billy. Suppose she knew Heather, too?"

Curt snapped his fingers. "Josh, didn't Heather Connor say that she was going to meet a Nicki when we were interviewing Margo at her house?"

Joshua said, "I think you need to have another talk with this Nicki."

Joshua went home, took two aspirin, chased Admiral off the sofa in his study, and lay down. He was overwhelmed and needed to clear his head.

"Oh, God," he prayed, "give me a break." When he heard the door slam, he covered his face with a pillow and tried to pretend he wasn't there.

"Dad!" he heard his youngest son yell.

"I'm in here!" he yelled back, rolled over, and covered his

ears with the pillow.

"Dad!" Donny called again.

"I'm in the study!" He muttered, "Kids? What was I thinking?" He answered his own question, "I wasn't thinking. I always get into trouble when I'm not thinking."

Donny ran into the room and looked down at his father's reclining form. "Dad, are you sick?"

"No, I was taking a nap." Joshua said. "What do you need?"

"Money."

"Of course. How much and why?"

"I got a date."

Joshua's head spun around and he looked at his ten-year-old son who stood proudly before him. "You're only ten."

"You were ten when you had your first date."

"Who told you that?"

"You."

"Who is she?" Thus began the interrogation. It ended with Joshua permitting his son to take a girl to a school dance and giving him money for dinner at a fast-food restaurant.

After his interrogation of Donny, Tracy and Murphy came home arguing over Madison. Murphy had asked Connie for a date, and she accepted. For some odd reason that only Tracy understood, Madison blamed her, and Tracy blamed Murphy for putting a kink in her social life. The slamming of doors and harsh words told Joshua that a nap was out of the question. He got up, groaned, rubbed his face with his hands, and went to the kitchen to make a cup of coffee. Caffeine might make him feel better.

Maybe Billy Unger didn't kill Grace. If he hadn't, why didn't he give up whoever he gave the gun to? Was it loyalty, as Tad suggested?

When he poured a handful of coffee beans into the grinder, he was reminded of Gail's addiction to coffee. His mind swirled to her murder. Stan considered that case closed. The special prosecutor was already on his way to Charleston to put his case together against Karl Connor. He had no interest in any more phone calls from Joshua saying it was not that pat.

He stared at the beans swirling around in the grinder while they were sliced repeatedly until they were nothing more than dust, and re-enacted in his mind the scene in the dark in Gail's living room.

He had groped for the things he had knocked off the table.

The wine bottle. The glass. The album.

Footsteps in the hall.

Fear that it was Gail coming out to make another pass at him.

He'd rushed out the door, pausing to turn the button in order to lock it.

The footsteps.

She was passed out on her bed. She hadn't even had time to take off her coat before she was smothered to death.

The killer was already in the house.

"Dad, are you making espresso?"

Startled by Tracy's voice, he clicked off the grinder.

Realizing that her father had drifted off into his thoughts, Tracy giggled and opened the refrigerator to take out hamburger to make a meatloaf for dinner.

The coffee beans had been ground to powder.

"Too bad I don't like espresso." He unscrewed the bowl from the machine and took off the lid. When the finely ground coffee splattered onto his hand, he wiped it off on the backside of his hip.

"Now you got your pants dirty," she chastised him.

"That's not dirt, it's coffee."

It was like déjà vu. Where had he heard those words spoken in that tone before?

Tad had said them after Lou Alcott tried to run him down. Joshua thought it was dirt on the front of Tad's shirt and Tad said it was coffee grounds from the broken bag he had bought at Rollins Corner Café.

Struck with the thought of what the coffee grounds would look like against the khaki material, Joshua twisted his body to look down at the back of his pants.

Coffee.

Where else—? He saw a dark powder that he'd mistaken for dirt on the case of the pillow used to smother Gail. The forensics report said that the substance was finely ground coffee beans.

The killer had coffee grounds on his hands when he pressed the pillow against Gail's face. Coffee ground to dust.

Tad was run down after leaving Rollins Corner Café where he bought a bag of coffee.

Rollins. Phyllis Barlow. Tricia's neighbor.

Rollins Corner Café.

Dorothy Wheeler had met Gail there for dinner the night she was killed.

Joshua went to call Tad.

Dr. Tad MacMillan wasn't in his lab. He was in Steubenville at the same bar where he had tracked down Nicki Samuels earlier during his investigation. He found her on the same bar stool, once again drinking a vodka and orange juice.

She barely acknowledged him when he took a seat on the stool next to her.

"Hello, Nicki."

She eyed him over her glass while she drained it. Once more, Tad took in the size of the ruby on her finger and the stones that surrounded it. Before, he'd assumed they were rhinestones and the red stone was glass. Now, he was certain they were real.

"So we meet again." Nicki grinned. "Since this isn't your first time, that means you're not a virgin anymore."

"No, I've been becoming much more worldly." He slapped a picture down on the bar between them. It was a snapshot of a group of jewels that Sheriff Sawyer had given him from the case file he had made when Margo Connor's lawyer reported the theft of her client's ring. The photograph was taken by Margo's insurance agent when she had her jewels insured.

"Recognize anything in this picture?" Tad pointed to the ruby ring that she was wearing on her finger.

She gestured to the bartender for another drink. "It looks like mine. What about it?"

"I think they are the same ring."

"Prove it."

"Okay." He grabbed her hand. "You come down to my cousin's office and we'll call Margo Connor, and she'll tell us if they are the same ring."

She wrested her hand out of his grasp.

If he wanted to hold on to her he could have, but he didn't need to hold her. He had achieved his objective of shaking her up.

"Okay! It was Mrs. Connor's ring, but I didn't steal it. Heather gave it to me."

"Why would Heather give you a ten-thousand-dollar ring?"

"Because her old lady doesn't let her have that much cash."

"I assume it wasn't a gift."

"No, it wasn't a gift."

"It was a payoff. For what?"

"Hush money. She gave me the ring to keep my mouth shut."

"About what?"

"Guess."

"You tell me."

"About her and Billy not being together when Grace was killed."

"Were you with her when Grace was killed?"

Nicki shook her head with a cocky attitude. "No, I was with Billy . . . in his room . . . alone. I was there when she called him to tell him that Grace was dead and told him that the police were going to be looking for him once they found out about him knocking her up. So she volunteered to be his alibi."

"You were sleeping with Billy, too?"

"We've been friends since we were kids." She licked her lips before she added, "Really good friends."

"Didn't it make you jealous that he was also sleeping with Heather and Grace?"

"No more than it made him jealous that I was fucking his friends."

Tad told himself that he wasn't as old and prudish as he felt. He was okay. It was the rest of the world that had gone mad. "Why would Billy agree to use Heather for an alibi if he had you?"

She shrugged. "Because Heather needed him. I mean, Grace and her were like a couple of wildcats when they got into a room together lately. If he had an alibi, wouldn't you assume she did it?"

"Did she do it?"

Nicki went on to her next drink in silence.

He fired off his next question. "Walt Manners gave Billy a thirty-eight Colt revolver. What happened to it?"

She had returned her attention to her vodka and orange juice.

"Billy is dead. So is his lawyer, whom he was sleeping with. He got Grace pregnant, and she ends up being shot with this gun. Now you just admitted that you were sleeping with him. That makes you either a suspect or a potential victim."

"Heather took it."

"Do you know that for a fact?"

Nicki turned to him. "She showed it to me when she gave me

the ring. She told me that was it. If I asked for anything else, then the next thing she would be giving me was a bullet."

That was all Tad needed to give Curt to get a warrant for Heather Connor's arrest.

Joshua Thornton and Sheriff Curt Sawyer lost no time in jumping into action when Tad told him that Nicki Samuels admitted that Heather had the murder weapon and that she, not Heather, was with Billy when Grace Henderson was killed.

Since Grace told Nicki, who told Heather, that Billy said he was going to marry her, Heather had motive for killing Grace. Heather also lost her alibi when Nicki confessed that she was with Billy at the time of the murder.

Even though Joshua was still nagged by doubt over the problem of Heather not fitting the description of the shooter, they had enough for an arrest warrant. Her arrest might be catalyst enough to get things sorted out.

It was like a relay race.

Joshua had run down the stairs from the third-floor judge's chambers with the warrant to hand to Sheriff Sawyer through the passenger window of his cruiser in which he had waited with the engine running, ready to speed to the Connor home to pick up Heather as soon as she got home from school, only to find her not there.

Upon learning that her daughter had not been in school that day, Margo turned on the sheriff. "My baby is missing! Aren't you going to do something?"

"Three people are dead," the sheriff told the angry mother. "We have a witness who saw her with the murder weapon. The witness says Heather threatened her with it."

The realization that her daughter was going to be arrested for murder hit her. "Joshua Thornton is using his job as prosecutor against me. He arrested my ex-husband. He's been insinuating that I killed Tricia Wheeler. Now he's trying to railroad my daughter into jail."

"Heather has been missing for ten hours and she is armed," Curt reminded her. "Do you know where she was Friday night?"

"She was out at a concert with her friends."

"When did she come home?"

"Sunday night."

The sheriff was doubtful. "She went out Friday night and you didn't see her again until Sunday night?"

"She went to a party," she replied as if that were enough of an explanation.

"When was the last time she saw Billy?"

"I have no idea. He called here Saturday morning."

Margo did not notice his head snap up at her claim that Billy called on Saturday morning when he had died Friday night. "Are you sure of that?"

"Of course, I am," she said. "He woke me up at I don't know what time. He told me to tell Heather that Plan A was in effect and to come over as soon as possible."

"What is Plan A?"

"I have no idea."

"Did you ask Heather?"

"I don't interfere in her business. I gave her the message last night after she woke up. She had had a long weekend and she bitched at me for not giving her the message when she got home. Anything else?" She dared him to ask another question.

He took the dare. "Do you know where she could have gone?"

"Even if I knew, I wouldn't tell you. I'm calling my lawyer now. Get out."

Margo left it up to the maid to show him out of her home while she called her lawyer to start spinning the defense that the county prosecutor had framed Heather for murder.

Curt was in his patrol car making a note that Margo neglected to ask the names of the murder victims when he got the call on his cell phone that Joshua Thornton had another warrant.

This one was to pick up Phyllis Barlow Rollins for Gail Reynolds's murder.

CHAPTER EIGHTEEN

Phyllis Barlow Rollins didn't resist when the deputies swooped into Rollins Corner Café to take the grinder and samples of her coffee stock in for evidence and her into custody. Her only display of emotion was for her brother, who watched the arrest with confusion and anxiety.

Well aware of Doug's fragile condition, Tad was waiting at the sheriff's office to take care of him during their interrogation.

She was only being taken in for questioning.

Until the lab analyzed the samples of her coffee to determine that the dust found on Gail's pillowcase came from Rollins Corner Café, they had no proof that she killed her. Even if the coffee was found to come from there, her lawyer could argue that anyone who bought coffee from the café could have committed the murder—even Tad, who was a regular customer.

The circumstance of the evidence was damning. Lou Alcott attempted to kill Tad after he had lunch at the diner. Gail had dinner there shortly before she was killed. If the coffee grounds from the handprint found on the pillow came from the café, a jury would want to know how it got there—if Joshua could get the case in front of a jury.

The county prosecutor didn't have any viable motive for Phyllis Rollins to kill Gail Reynolds. The only motive he had come up with in his investigation was that she was angry with Tricia Wheeler for rejecting her brother six months before she was killed.

Could Phyllis have killed Tricia for that reason and then killed Gail so she would not discover her crime? There was no evidence that the writer even suspected Phyllis.

So far, he didn't have a case. Ideally, she would make it easy for him and confess.

The courier had delivered the accounting autopsy of Margo Connor's business dealings from the forensics expert to his office when Joshua was leaving to cross the back parking lot to the police department. He tossed the report into his briefcase and rushed out the door and arrived in time to see Phyllis climb out of the back of the cruiser. Two deputies escorted her inside.

"She waived her rights for a lawyer," Curt told him. "Tori Brody was her lawyer."

"I don't care. Don't let anyone talk to her until the public defender gets here," Joshua said. "The way the courts are going, anything she says won't be worth the paper it's written on unless she has a lawyer present."

As lost as a lamb in a wolf's den, Doug Barlow, his ball cap pulled down over his head, wandered into the sheriff's department. The deputies had ushered his sister into the interrogation room. One deputy pushed him back and closed the door when he tried to follow them inside.

Doug took off his cap like his mother would order him to do when he was inside, and sat in the straight-back chair outside the room where Phyllis waited for the public defender.

"Doug?" Tad feigned surprise when he came out of Curt's office and crossed to where Doug sat. He pulled up a chair and sat next to him. "How are you doing?"

Nervously, Doug nodded and grinned for his answer. Tad was always nice to him. He looked beyond the doctor to the closed door.

"I haven't seen you in a while." Tad shifted to distract Doug from what was happening inside the room. He grabbed his hands in which he twisted the ball cap. "You got a new hat?" He noticed the lettering on the front.

Doug grinned.

"Let me see."

He put the cap on his head. It was dark blue with gold lettering that read "Dell Appliance." Doug said proudly, "Lou gave it to me."

"Lou who?"

"Phyllis's boyfriend. Lou Alcott. They gave him this from work, and he gave it to me."

Tad grinned broadly. "Lou Alcott was Phyllis's boyfriend?"

Doug's smile faded. "Yeah, but he died. Phyllis said these things happen, but I still feel sad. I liked him. He was real nice, like you. He said he loved Phyllis just like I loved Trish."

Tad was about to ask how much Lou loved her when there was a commotion at the door leading into the hallway.

Joshua came in with a white-haired woman dressed in an overcoat over a suit the color of which was faded with age.

A chain smoker, Ruth Majors dared anyone to tell her that she wasn't allowed to smoke in the courthouse. No one did. She had been the public defender in Hancock County for over forty years.

Joshua hated to admit he was afraid of her. Ruth was a good eight inches shorter than he was, but her inner strength made her appear to be as big as he was.

Even before the defender had spoken to her client, they were arguing the case while they crossed the sheriff's reception area to the interrogation room.

"Bullshit!" Ruth waved her cigarette. "So she sold coffee to the victim right before she died. Unless you found poison in that coffee, you have nothing!"

"Coffee grounds were on the killer's hand. We also picked up epidermal samples and sweat on the pillowcase. If that matches with your client—"

Tad stood up next to him to await a break in the argument.

"*If* is a big word, Counselor!"

"Josh?" Tad interjected.

"You have nothing," Ruth said, ignoring the doctor's presence. "My client sold the victim a bag of coffee and that is all that I'm going to tell her to say." She stuck the end of her cigarette between her lips, which were lined with wrinkles and void of lipstick, went into the room, and slammed the door in their faces.

Exhausted from the battle with the diminutive defender, the prosecutor sighed and turned to his cousin. "Do you want something?"

Tad indicated Doug, who was still sitting in the chair with the cap on his head. "Look at Doug's new cap."

Annoyed to be bothered with something so trivial, Joshua looked at his suspect's brother, who, proud to be wearing a cap the doctor considered to be special, grinned up at him. The prosecutor forced himself to be kind in the midst of the disintegrating murder case. After all, Doug was a victim in it all. "That's a nice cap."

"Isn't it?" Seeing that he did not get it, Tad added, "Phyllis's boyfriend, Lou Alcott, gave it to him."

Joshua's forced smile faded, and then reappeared with sincerity when he realized the significance of the relationship. "Really?" He looked at Tad to confirm he heard him correctly.

Tad nodded.

Joshua's smile broadened.

Ruth didn't confer with her client, she *argued*—for almost an hour. Sometimes their loud voices seeped through the thin walls of the interrogation room in the building packed with the county's offices, courtrooms, and jail cells on the third floor. In wealthier counties the offices would have been spread over three buildings.

Joshua and Curt used the hour to the best of their advantage. The case came together in their minds. Now, they needed proof to back it up. They had no doubt that Ruth would not let her client confess, so they had to prove Phyllis killed Gail.

Playing friend and confidante, Tad continued to talk to Doug while Curt and Joshua rushed to get their evidence.

Curt called his witnesses at the State Line Lounge to see if Lou was there the night Rex was killed. Phyllis never went into bars. She would have been noticed if she was anywhere near the scene of the murder.

Recalling that both Gail's and Rex's murders happened at approximately the same time, they theorized that Phyllis was smothering Gail while her lover was shooting her estranged husband.

Lou could have killed Rex for one or both of two reasons. Rex was abusing the woman Lou loved and/or to keep his lover's soon-to-be ex-husband from exposing that Phyllis had killed Tricia.

Perhaps Lou tried to kill Tad because he was afraid the medical examiner would prove Phyllis killed the author who was writing a book about Tricia's murder. Tad had announced at the café that he was going to find the killer to clear Joshua of the murder allegations.

It was all theory and had yet to be proven.

Within the hour, Curt hung up the phone with a sigh. He had spoken to the last witness he was able to reach. "Lou Alcott was not at the State Line the night Rex was killed."

"Maybe he didn't go in," Joshua said, half paying attention while he scanned the forensics report on Margo Connor's finances, more out of curiosity than anything else. If their theory proved to be correct, he would not need the report. All the murders would be tied to Phyllis trying to cover up her murder of Tricia.

He did not see Curt shaking his head. "Nope. Alcott drove a ninety-two black Ford pickup. No one saw it in the parking lot. They saw a red and green ninety-two Ford truck, but not a black one. That belonged to Herb Duncan, one of the regulars at the State Line."

"Who just got a new truck, sold his broken-down trailer for a nice bundle, and is now Margo Connor's foreman." Joshua jumped out of his seat when he read an interesting point on the report. The connection was made in stereo.

Before everything could register, Ruth opened Sheriff Sawyer's office door without knocking. She was not smiling, but that didn't mean anything when it came to her.

"All right, guys. Start your camcorders."

"Is Ms. Rollins ready to make a statement?" Joshua asked.

"Not a statement. A confession."

Joshua and Curt exchanged double takes before looking back at the defender, who stood in the doorway without any sign of amusement.

"You're kidding." The prosecutor had to stop himself from revealing that they didn't have any real evidence yet. The forensics report had not come back from the lab.

Ruth's response was, "Merry Christmas."

"That's right. I killed Gail Reynolds," Phyllis Rollins announced in the interrogation room with her lawyer at her elbow.

Still stunned by how easy the suspect was making things, Curt and Joshua sat across the table from her.

During her confession, Phyllis would stop and look at the video camera in the corner of the cramped room, along with the tape recorder in the middle of the table, and the stenographer at Joshua's elbow making every word she said part of the record.

"Why?" the prosecutor asked her.

"You know."

"You need to say it for the record."

"Because she was writing that book about Tricia Wheeler's murder, and I was afraid she'd find out that I killed Tricia."

Joshua paused.

Ruth shook her head. It was a gesture of disgust at her client rather than an order for him not to go on with his next question.

"Mrs. Wheeler called me," Phyllis continued. "She wanted to know if I could remember anything that could help her with the book. She and Gail came into the diner that night and Gail started asking me questions about Tricia again."

She took a sip of her soft drink before she went on. "Everyone was saying how she had rented that big place out by the state line and so after we closed the diner that night I went out there. I parked in the trees down the road and went to her house through the woods. She didn't lock her doors, so it was a cinch for me to get in. I saw you and her come in. After you left and she was asleep, I smothered her with the pillow."

"How did you leave the house?" Joshua asked.

"Through the back door so that you wouldn't see me in case you weren't gone yet."

"Where were you hiding?"

"Her bedroom closet."

He repeated his question about how she left.

For the first time during the confession, Phyllis betrayed a sense of being perturbed. "I already told you. I went out the back patio doors."

Joshua moved on to the book and Tricia's murder. "Did you even think of talking to Gail about the book? Maybe you could have convinced her not to write it."

Her response was a snicker. "Like she would do me a favor. She was Gail Reynolds, big-time journalist, and I was Ratched Barlow."

In school, Joshua recalled, Phyllis's no-nonsense manner and lack of humor had won her the nickname Ratched, after the cruelly humorless nurse in *One Flew Over the Cuckoo's Nest.*

He swallowed and went on with his interview. "Tell me about Tricia Wheeler."

She began with a shrug. She glanced at the video recorder before she started. "She treated us like dirt, so I killed her."

The silence in the room forced her to continue.

"She didn't used to. She used to be our friend. Then she became cheerleader and made all these big important friends, and she was too good for us."

"What happened on the day of the murder?"

"Tricia blew Doug off again. She blew him off for the prom. She told him in November that she'd go with him. Then, two weeks before the prom she said she'd go with Randy Fine, just because he was on the football team. I heard Randy bragging in study hall to his buddies about taking her."

Phyllis squinted at the prosecutor. "You should have seen Doug when I told him. He wouldn't believe me. So, he went running over to Tricia's and told her to tell me that it was a lie, and she said it wasn't."

Her face contorted with anger. "She said that it wasn't her fault. They didn't really have a date because he never told her for certain they were going."

Joshua prodded her to go on while she paused to take a sip of her soda. "Did he?"

"She said if he could go, she'd go with him. It wasn't his fault Mom wouldn't tell him yes or no about going. Only the night before Mom said he could, but Trish didn't give him a chance to tell her. She went ahead and accepted Randy's invitation." She scoffed, "Like she ever intended to go with him."

He asked her again, "What happened six months later? On the day you killed her?"

"I didn't know it was possible for any one man to cry so much. When Tricia went to the prom with Randy, Doug cried for a week solid, without stopping. Then she started going steady with Randy. He couldn't stand to see the two of them together."

Joshua leaned across the table at her. "And you?"

"What about me?"

"You say you killed her." .

She sighed and sat up straight. "I love my brother. I hated what she did to him."

"What happened on the day you killed Tricia?"

"After she broke up with Randy, Doug didn't let any grass grow under his feet. The little dummy thought he stood a chance with her. But that bitch blew him off again. She let Randy punch him, and then she took Randy back."

Phyllis sighed again and took another sip of her soda. "I knew she was going to do it. I followed Doug to pick up the pieces but there were so many—he ran away from me. He was so hysterical, I didn't know if he was going to make it home okay. I kept calling the house, but he wasn't there. I was crazy with worry.

"When school let out, I went looking for Tricia to talk to her about it. She wouldn't even talk to me. She completely blew me off. That made me even madder. So I went home and got my father's old army pistol, and when she got home, I was waiting for her. She tried to blow me off again, so I shot her. I barely remember doing it."

"Was Doug there when you shot her?"

"No," she answered firmly. "To this day he doesn't know." Her tone held a note of warning.

Joshua recalled something he read in Dorothy's statement in the former sheriff's case file. "Trish's mother says both you and Doug were out in the front yard when she got home."

"He was in his room."

"He didn't hear the shot?"

She responded with certainty. "No."

"What did you do after you shot Trish?"

"I left."

"When you shot her, did she fall on the sofa or did you lay her down on it?"

Phyllis looked at her lawyer. "I don't remember everything. It was so long ago and I was really mad."

Ruth spoke for the first time. "My client did say she was distraught at the time she killed her." There was her defense.

"She wasn't distraught at the time she killed Gail Reynolds," Joshua pointed out. "She admits that she planned and executed it." He turned back to Phyllis. "Tell us about Lou Alcott."

"What about him?"

"He was your boyfriend. He tried to kill Dr. MacMillan. Did he know about the murders?"

"Doc MacMillan said that he was going to find out who killed Gail. Lou thought that if he killed him, then he wouldn't find out it was me. I didn't ask him to do it."

Phyllis swallowed. Her face twisted before she took a deep breath and continued in a surprisingly strong voice, "Lou was a good man. He really loved me."

After Phyllis was taken to the holding cell, Ruth Majors followed the county prosecutor into the sheriff's office to barter for a deal for her client in exchange for a guilty plea. It was an exercise in futility, considering that Phyllis Rollins had confessed to killing two people. She was destined to spend the rest of her life in jail.

Curt waited until Ruth left to ask why the prosecutor stopped short of getting a confession from Phyllis for the murders of Rex Rollins and his landlady. "Why did you stop? Why didn't you question her about Rex's murder? I thought we agreed that Lou killed Rex for her."

"Because she had nothing to do with their murders," Joshua answered, before Tad knocked on the door and stepped inside without waiting for an invitation. "Plus, my gut is telling me that she didn't kill Gail or Trish."

"Your gut is having an off day," the sheriff said. "She admitted to it."

"She says she went out the back door."

"What was that all about anyway? So she went out the back door?"

"I locked the front door. Karl said that he couldn't get in the front door because I locked it, but it was unlocked and opened when Jan went there three days later. Plus—Phyllis didn't make any mention of seeing Karl, who admits he was there!"

Tad interjected, "I'm sorry to interrupt this celebration at the closing of this case, but there's a matter of a man out here in need of a guardian."

"What are you talking about, Doc?" Sheriff Sawyer said with a hint of annoyance.

"Social services can't find a halfway house for Doug to stay at."

"Isn't he over eighteen?" Curt asked Joshua in a rhetorical manner.

It was Tad's turn to respond with irritation, "Doug's parents had him declared incompetent after his second stay in the mental hospital. When they were killed in that accident, Phyllis became his guardian." He pointed to Joshua. "It is your responsibility to have the family court appoint Doug Barlow a new guardian. In the meantime, Jan and I are taking him back to his house. I'll stay with him tonight. I would appreciate it if you would address this matter first thing tomorrow morning."

"Jan?" Curt looked out the door to see her sitting with Doug and making notes on her notepad. She appeared to be interviewing their latest defendant's brother.

"*The Review* has hired her as their news editor." Tad turned back to Joshua, "I guess you didn't read the retraction in today's *Vindicator* that has reinstated you as the valley's golden boy."

"I stopped reading that paper weeks ago." Joshua assured him, "I will find a guardian for Doug."

"Can you pick up Dog on your way home?"

Joshua groaned. He held his easygoing cousin's untrained pet responsible for teaching his own dog bad habits, like sneaking up on the sofa.

Curt chuckled after Tad left. "He certainly goes out of his way for his patients."

"That's what makes him a good doctor."

Curt returned to the matter of Rex Rollins's murder. "You don't think Alcott killed Rex because he was going to blow the whistle on Phyllis?"

Joshua shook his head. "Nah, Rex's book wasn't about Phyllis."

"Don't you think he knew about her killing Wheeler?"

"By all reports I've heard, she didn't ever love Rex. He worked out at her parents' farm. I think he knew about the murder. Then, he blackmailed her into marrying him."

"So she killed Tricia." Curt said. "Then, after she divorced Rex, he wrote his book about her killing the cheerleader who broke her brother's heart."

"That falls into the category of who cares."

"I care," the sheriff stated in his most authoritative tone.

"Curt," Joshua said, "you knew Rex. I knew Rex. We are also men of the world and have been around. Do you really think any publisher is going to care about a village drunk's little book about a farm girl who blows away the local cheerleader for breaking her brother's heart?"

"Now you are saying that his book was not the motive for his murder, which, I might add, blows the wind out of our sails about it being the motive for his landlady's murder."

"Oh, it's the motive for his murder," Joshua mused. "It is also the motive for Bella Polk's murder. It just wasn't about Tricia Wheeler's murder. Her murder was small potatoes compared to the murder he was writing about."

"Whose murder would that be?"

"I'm thinking that Rex knew something about Margo. Herb Duncan has had a string of good luck ever since Rex's murder, and I think his fairy godmother is Margo Connor."

Joshua retired to his study where Doc Wilson's folder containing his report on Tricia Wheeler's murder lay in the center of the desk. He tossed it into his IN box.

Time to concentrate on Margo Sweeney Boyd Connor's dirty dealings.

He concluded that it was best to start at the beginning . . . with the murder of her first husband, which put her on the road to prosperity.

That night, after his children had gone to their separate corners to do their homework, he built a fire in the fireplace. Admiral and Dog wandered in to take up what had become their customary spots on the carpet in front of the flames. The domesticated beasts lay like a couple of lion statues at the gate of a grand city to stare into the blaze and imagine themselves as creatures in the wilderness bringing down their food in the glory of bloodlust.

A frosted beer mug at his elbow, Joshua sat back in his recliner with his feet up to read Dr. Dan Boyd's case file, which he had borrowed from the Columbiana County Sheriff's Department in Ohio.

According to the copy of the notes in the folder, the case had not been looked at in years, despite letters sent annually from Gregory Boyd, the victim's son, to request that the murder not be forgotten.

He noted the return address on the envelope of the last letter. It was Ohio State University. Dan Boyd's son was now a first-year law student. His father had been dead for eighteen years. He was four years old when his father died and he still had not given up hope for justice.

Dr. Dan Boyd was thirty-eight when his throat was slashed while working late in his dental office on a Thursday night. Meanwhile, his wife was giving a dinner party in their home.

The murder was estimated to have happened shortly after seven o'clock. The dentist had sent his receptionist home at six o'clock. He was the only one at the office because he had a seven o'clock appointment with a new patient.

The appointment book had "canceled" written across the last appointment for the day. The receptionist said the patient had not canceled when she left. The name of the patient was Harry Smith. The phone number proved to be a phony.

Joshua studied the crime-scene photos. Dan had put up a fight. He had defense wounds on his hands and arms.

Blood squirted everywhere from his severed jugular vein: in his examination room where the struggle seemed to have started, in his office, and in the reception area where the cleaning crew found his body under the receptionist's desk the next morning.

When he studied the pictures with his magnifying glass, Joshua could see the bloody fingerprints all over Margo's wedding picture on his desk in his office. It appeared as if he had grabbed it.

Immersed in studying the crime-scene pictures, Joshua leapt in his seat when the phone rang. Even the dogs were startled out of their fantasies. He pried himself out of the chair to go pick up the phone on the desk.

"Hey, sailor," Hank greeted him.

Guilt washed over him. "Hey. I take it that your flight back to Hawaii was uneventful?" He sat down in his chair.

She assured him that it was.

Silence.

He tried to recall if ever he and Hank had suffered from awkward silence between them before.

She finally asked, "I wanted to know how things were going on finding out who killed that cheerleader friend of yours?"

"We got a confession, but my gut isn't buying it." He opened the medical examiner's folder for Tricia Wheeler and flipped through the pages.

"Your gut is a perfectionist."

"But it is usually right."

"Who confessed?"

"Phyllis Barlow, the girl next door."

"The sister of the guy Tricia had ditched for a dance?"

"Yeah." He picked up the crime-scene picture of Tricia laid out on the sofa.

Phyllis said she did not remember if she laid her out on the sofa or not. The position suggested whoever did it was someone who cared about her. That contradicted his assessment of the relationship between the two girls. He would describe their relationship as one of bitterness.

The next picture was a close-up of the gun on the floor at the end of the sofa.

Phyllis said the gun was her father's old army pistol.

"What is bothering you about her confession?" Hank was asking.

"So far I have come up with nothing but questions."

The next picture was a full-length picture of Tricia on the medical examiner's table, before the examiner had cut through her flesh with his scalpel. She was naked in order to capture any injuries or evidence on film.

Joshua tried not to stare at how beautiful she was—even in death.

"I think we should talk about us," Hank said.

There was a thin gold strand around Tricia's neck. It looked like a necklace. There was a design at the well of her throat.

Knowing that there would be a close-up of her face, he flipped to the next picture. He was right.

"Josh?"

He gazed at the image of Tricia's face. It was a head and shoulder shot. His eyes fell to the gold band around her neck.

"Josh? Are you still there?"

What is that at the end of her necklace?

He held the picture under his desk lamp to make sure he saw what he thought he saw.

She begged, "Josh, please say something."

It was a chain from which hung two gold hearts held together by a diamond in the center. He stared at the necklace like a subject trying to hypnotize himself.

Where—what—who was it that said something about someone giving Tricia a necklace with two hearts?

"Excuse me, Hank," Joshua said. "But I have to make a phone call. Can I call you back?"

While he worked out in his mind the only scenario that fit, he sank back into his chair to study the hearts in the picture.

He dug through his notebook until he found Cindy's number and punched it into the phone while praying she'd be home. When she answered, he took a minimal amount of time for pleasantries before he asked her, "Is there any chance that Tricia took back Doug's necklace?"

". . . and so then the Sunday school teacher told Grandmamma Frieda to take Josh home and never to bring him back to church again."

Doug laughed.

In spite of the circumstances, the evening had turned out to be comfortable. Jan prepared dinner out of what she found in the fridge: burgers and a salad, milk, and a block of cheddar cheese while Doug showed off his rock collection to Tad. The genius was fascinated with geology and the acre and a half that they lived on along a hillside had quite an assortment of interesting rocks.

Jan concluded that he would make a good feature for the paper: the life of a certified genius suffering from mental illness.

After their meal, they sat back in their chairs at the table in the great room and sliced off bites of the cheese with a butcher knife Jan had found in the kitchen drawer.

"Did they ever let Josh go back to Sunday school?" Doug wondered.

"Oh, yes, but the Cunninghams never let him play with any of their kids again." Jan added with a giggle, "Nowadays, they could have sued Josh for punching out their son over that slingshot."

Doug failed to see her humor. He looked at the doctor with wide eyes. "Is he a good lawyer?"

Tad said, "One of the best."

"Is he going to send Phyllis to jail?"

Jan took their empty plates to the sink. She felt sorry for him.

Like an adult explaining a grown-up situation to a child, Tad told him, "That's up to a jury to decide. All Josh will do is present the people's case against her." Tad wondered if he knew that Phyllis had confessed.

"I was going to be a scientist."

Referring to his rock collection, Tad said, "And I'm sure you could have been a good one."

"But I got sick." Doug stated it like a scientific fact.

Tad and Jan exchanged sympathetic expressions when she came back to the table for an armload of condiments to return to the refrigerator.

"Well, you know, Doug," she said, "you don't have to let your illness prevent you from achieving any dreams you might have."

"I can't have my dream until after I die."

Frightened by his reference to death, she stepped back behind Tad's chair.

The doctor squinted at him. "Why is that?"

"Trish and I couldn't be together here in life because they wouldn't let us. So, we're going to have to get together on the other side."

Fear formed a lump in Jan's throat that made it difficult for her to swallow. She grasped Tad's shoulder for courage. Doug cut off another slice of cheese with the butcher knife and nibbled at it like a rat savoring a tasty find while the cat was away at the vet's office.

Tad's voice was steady. "Don't you have any dreams for here in your lifetime?"

"No." Doug continued to gnaw at the cheese and gazed at him with eyes that looked as innocent as a child talking about Santa Claus. "That's why I keep trying to kill myself, so that I can go be with her. But they keep stopping me because they don't want us to be together."

"Who are *they*, Doug?" Jan choked out.

"Them." He indicated with a nod of his head the unseen enemy that consisted of the populace who had victimized him during the course of his lifetime. "All those people who kept telling Tricia that I wasn't good enough for her, and that we were hicks, and that she could do better. She only pretended to be stuck-up and not like me. She really did love me, and it hurt that we couldn't be together. It hurt so much that she finally had to kill herself."

Tad swallowed and phrased his next question carefully. "Doug, were you there when Trish died?"

"That was when we decided that the only way we could be together was to go to the other side where they couldn't hurt us anymore."

"Was that when she told you that she loved you?"

"Yeah, that was when she gave me this." Doug reached down inside his shirt and pulled out a gold chain at the end of which hung a woman's class ring with a sapphire stone in it.

Jan gasped at the sight of the ring. She recalled Tricia grabbing it from Randy's neck hours before she was killed. She imagined how Doug had come to possess it.

Their host leaned across the table to let his guests examine the ring he wore around his neck.

While he fingered the jewel, Tad read the engraving inside. It read "TRW." Tricia Rose Wheeler. He glanced up at Jan and silently answered her unspoken query with a nod of his head. Yes, it was the ring Tricia had taken from Randy, the same one that her mother assumed had been stolen from her dead body by a morgue attendant.

"Trish gave it to me because she loved me," Doug leaned back in his seat. "And she's waiting for me on the other side where we will be together forever."

In the midst of devising a plan to call Joshua, Jan leapt for the phone when it rang.

Enthralled with his fantasy about the love he shared with Tricia, Doug continued to eat his cheese.

Tad kept a watchful eye on him.

"Tad—" Joshua blurted out when Jan picked up the phone.

"Hey, am I glad you called!" Jan said with exaggerated brightness. "We were just talking about you."

"You found out that Doug killed Tricia," Joshua told her.

"Yep!"

"Are you okay?"

"I think so." Her voice squeaked. She watched Doug slice through the cheese and offer the slice to Tad from off the point of the butcher knife.

"You stay on the phone with Donny, and I'll go have Curt run out there to take him into custody."

Tad accepted the slice of cheese.

"Well, I don't know if I can remember that far back," she said into the phone. "You know my memory is not as good as it used to be."

Laughing, she offered Doug an excuse to stay on the phone. "Josh's son has to write a paper. They want me to remember when his great-grandmother started a family feud by having the outhouse hauled out to the dump without her mother-in-law's permission."

Doug nodded his consent for her to continue the conversation and stabbed the block of cheese with the knife. His face was emotionless when he got up from the table and went down the hallway to the bathroom.

Tad followed.

Doug closed the door in his face.

At the Thornton house, on his cell phone, Joshua ordered the sheriff to get out to the Barlow house.

"Why?"

"Doug killed Tricia and now Tad and Jan are out there alone with him in that holler."

"But Phyllis confessed to killing Wheeler."

"My gut said there was something wrong with that confession!" Joshua yelled. "I should have listened to it! She confessed to protect her brother. She's been doing that her whole life!" Furious with his own stupidity, he slammed his fist onto the top of his desk. "Damn it! I knew she confessed too easily!"

"Did she kill Gail?"

"No! Doug killed Gail. He was afraid that she was going to defame Tricia in some way in her book—or maybe he was sane enough to think that she was going to find out that he killed Trish! We assumed the grounds on the scene had been on Phyllis's hands. Damn! I was sitting right there in their house when Doug told me to my face that he ground the coffee." He pounded his forehead with the palm of his hand. "Now, get a deputy out there, and we'll sort this all out later. Right now that lunatic is out there alone with Tad and Jan, and there is no telling what he'll do!"

"Okay! I've got a deputy out in that area now. He should be there in three minutes."

Curt observed the name on the roster of who was patrolling Birch Hollow and rubbed his face. It was Andrew Jones, a rookie of two weeks.

Jan kept an eye on the bathroom door while she talked fast into the phone. "—so then your great-great-grandmother sees the outhouse is missing and goes ballistic!"

Tad knocked on the bathroom door. "Doug? Are you okay?"

The doorknob turned and the door opened.

Tad stepped back.

Jan held her breath.

Doug came out of the bathroom. He seemed to be in a dazed state of consciousness.

Jan rattled on, "You see, Agnes Thornton had this thing about change. She never bought a dress that was made after 1926." Her mind raced while she tried to think of a smooth way of conveying to Donny the object Doug held down at his side when he strolled into the center of the living room.

311

Tad shielded her.

"Donny," her voice cracked in her vain effort to sound calm. "I need to speak to your father. Now."

Donny tapped Joshua on the arm and handed him the phone while he held the cell phone to his other ear. "Jan needs you."

Joshua put the other phone to his ear. "Yeah, Jan?"

"Doug has a gun," Jan said.

"What's he doing with it?"

She whispered to Tad, "What's he going to do with that?"

Tad shot his host a nervous smile. "Doug, what are you doing with that gun?"

The gun still at his side, Doug looked at Tad with a face filled with anticipation. "It's time."

"Time for what?"

"I'm going to go be with Trish."

Jan hissed into the phone, "I think he intends to kill himself."

Tad asked him, "Why now?"

"Because you're going to try to stop me. You don't want us to be together, either."

"What makes you think that?"

"Because you're one of them. Phyllis said so, but I didn't believe her. But I saw she was right when I showed you this." Doug held up the ring to show him. "I should have known. You're going to steal this and say that Trish didn't give it to me, and that she didn't love me, and that I killed her, and that I stole this."

"Is that what happened?" Tad took a step towards him.

In a flash, the gun was no longer at Doug's side. He aimed it at Tad. In the other hand, he clutched the ring like a lifeline.

Jan dropped down to crouch on the floor. "Josh! Hurry! Please! I think he's going to shoot Tad!"

CHAPTER NINETEEN

Holding up his hands, Tad stepped back from Doug and the gun. "Take it easy, man! I came here to help you."

Jan had crawled back behind the china closet.

All was still. No one moved.

Joshua held his breath and prayed.

"Doug," Tad spoke in a calm tone. "Give me the gun."

The man with the gun wavered.

"I'm your friend. Have I ever hurt you?" Tad asked.

"Phyllis says that I'm not a good judge of people. I'm smart when it comes to things in books, but not when it comes to people."

"I think you are a good judge of people, Doug. You were right about Trish, weren't you?"

"I don't know."

"She gave you that ring. A girl doesn't give a guy her class ring if she doesn't love him, does she?"

Doug wavered more. He gazed at the ring he clutched in his hand. "Yeah, Phyllis said she didn't love me, but she gave me this ring."

While Doug gazed at the ring in his hand, Tad inched towards him. "You were right there, Doug, and you're right about me being your friend. You don't want to hurt me. Give me the gun." Tad's hand was on the gun.

The doorbell rang. "Dr. MacMillan! Deputy Jones with the Hancock County Sheriff Department. Are you okay in there?"

Jones's question was answered with a gunshot.

When he heard the shot come across the phone line, Joshua yelled and dropped into his chair.

Donny took in a sharp breath and tried to think of what to do to help the situation. He decided to call for help from his sisters and brothers.

Miles away in Birch Hollow, Deputy Jones kicked in the door and ran inside the house with his gun drawn.

The scene that greeted him was that of one man on his knees clutching a bloody hand while the other man stood over him with a gun.

A screaming woman was crawling towards the man with the bleeding hand.

"Drop the gun now!" Deputy Jones took aim on Doug, who looked at him.

"He said drop it!" Deputy Pete Hockenberry appeared in the doorway behind Deputy Jones with his gun drawn. He made it just in time to back up the rookie.

Seeing both guns pointed in his direction, Tad threw himself across the room to tackle Jan. Together they rolled across the floor until they landed with his body on top of her under the dining-room table. It was too late now for him to do anything to help Doug.

Doug smiled broadly.

Tad observed that it was the happiest he had ever seen his patient in all the years that he had known him.

"I'm coming, my love!" Then, Doug Barlow took aim on the deputies and fired a shot that missed them both by a mile.

The law officers did not have time to check out his aim. They only had and took the time to experience the jolting fear of having a shot fired at them. They had no choice but to fire their weapons in self-defense.

Hancock County Medical Examiner Dr. Tad MacMillan

ruled Doug Barlow's death as suicide by cop.

The woman known in the valley as an ice queen dissolved into tears. She was rousted out of bed in her cell and brought back down to the conference room to be told that her brother was dead after confessing to Dr. Tad MacMillan and Jan Martin that he killed Tricia Wheeler.

Phyllis broke down at the news.

Jan had driven Tad to the emergency room to get his hand bandaged up. It had been grazed by the bullet when the gun went off while he was attempting to take it from Doug.

Joshua and Curt sat across from Phyllis while Ruth comforted her client the best she could. Even the seasoned professional hadn't realized that her confession to Tricia's murder was a lie. If she had, she would never have let her do it.

While Phyllis sobbed, Joshua did his best to piece together what had happened for the sheriff and the public defender.

"When you got home on the bus after school that day, you could not find Doug. While you were looking for him, Cindy brought Tricia home and she went inside her house, which was just across the yard from yours."

Joshua waited for her to confirm he was right with a nod before he proceeded. "That was when Doug shot Trish."

Phyllis broke into loud sobs and dropped her head onto the table. Ruth patted her shoulder. Having anticipated the emotional scene, Joshua handed her a handkerchief he had brought along. He waited for her to wipe her face and regain enough control to choke out, "It was an accident!"

"I have no doubt that it was."

Phyllis gave a hint of a smile of relief.

Joshua continued, "Doug had decided to kill himself because he came to realize that he could never have the woman he loved, but he could not do it without telling Tricia good-bye. So, he went home to get your father's pistol. He had a key to the Wheeler house because it was rented from your family. Tricia found him waiting for her when she got home."

He held up the picture of Tricia with the diamond necklace around her neck. "He brought this along to give to her as a good-bye present. When she saw that he intended to kill himself, she took the necklace to placate him while she tried to talk him out of doing it. The chain was too short to fit around the turtleneck of her cheerleading uniform, so she had to put it on under the sweater. Otherwise, her mother would have seen it and guessed what happened."

Phyllis's exhausted sobs were the only noise in the room.

Joshua resumed, "She must have still had her purse because her things spilled onto the floor, probably while trying to get the gun from him."

Unable to speak, Phyllis nodded.

"After Tricia was killed, you cleaned up any evidence that Doug had been there and made her comfortable on the sofa. What you didn't notice in your cleaning up was that Doug had found her class ring and taken it."

"I didn't know he had her ring until days after he killed her." Even with the tears in her eyes, Phyllis had found strength to go on. "One day I walked into his room, and there he was with the ring. It became his most prized possession. I asked him where he got it, and he said that Tricia gave it to him. He totally forgot that he killed her! He had this whole story of how she loved him and killed herself because they could not be together, and she was waiting for him on the other side!"

She sucked in a shuddering breath. "I was so afraid that they would find out and he'd go to jail or some insane asylum. That nut has been wearing that ring all along under his shirt. So, I told him that he had to make sure no one ever saw it or they would take it from him, which is the truth."

The sheriff asked her, "What about those times he was committed? How is it that no one in the hospital discovered it?"

"I'd keep it for him. When I went to visit, he would always ask to see it. So I'd have to bring it along with me to show him and let him hold it."

"Did your parents ever know?" Joshua inquired.

She scoffed, "My father never even noticed the gun was missing. Sheriff Delaney never asked him if the gun was his. Delaney didn't ask us anything. He said it was a suicide and left it at that."

"But Rex knew."

Phyllis was startled by his statement.

The prosecutor speculated, "Rex was working on the farm that day. He knew Doug killed her and he knew you covered up for him. So, he threatened to turn Doug in unless you married him."

She sniffed. "Is that what he wrote in his book?"

Ruth interrupted him, "Now that you got her off the hook for killing Tricia Wheeler, are you going to try to hang her husband's murder on my client?"

"No," Joshua answered. "As a matter of fact, if you give me a chance, I can get her off the hook for Gail Reynolds's murder, also."

The public defender was surprised.

"Are you sure that you didn't see anyone at Gail's house that night?" Joshua warned her, "Think carefully before you answer."

The media had said that Karl Connor was arrested for killing Gail but had given no details to the murder.

"I wasn't there," she confessed. "After I closed up the café I couldn't find Doug. He'd never disappeared before. He was really upset about Gail and Mrs. Wheeler being there that night talking about Tricia. I went out looking for him."

"Was he afraid that they were going to find out about him

killing her?" Curt asked.

Phyllis shook her head. "He didn't really care about that. He was afraid that Gail was going to make Tricia out to be a slut or a stuck-up bitch or something. You know how reporters are. Everyone is always looking for a skeleton in everyone's closet."

Joshua had to agree. "When and where did you find him?"

"I found him walking along Route 30 after two o'clock in the morning. I had no idea what he had done until Tuesday when the news said that Gail was killed. I asked him and he flat out said that he went to her place and waited in her closet and then smothered her with a pillow." She looked from him to the sheriff. "If anyone had asked him, he would have said that he did it. He had no idea that he did anything wrong."

"What about Rex?" Joshua suspected the answer.

"Neither of us killed Rex."

"My client is now off the hook for both murders," Ruth stated with the first sense of confidence she'd had since she was called for the middle-of-the-night meeting. "As of now, you have nothing against her."

"Accessory after the fact," Joshua responded.

"She was protecting her brother."

"The law does not draw the line at family members when it comes to accessory."

"Tell that to a jury."

"Cool it, Ruth. I don't think your client killed Rex." He looked at Phyllis. "Rex blackmailed you. That's why you dropped out of school to marry a man who didn't have a steady job and beat you when he was drunk. You're too strong a woman to stay married to an abusive husband. What you have accomplished against all odds proves that."

She sat up straight and regarded him with surprise. "What have I accomplished?"

"You built a successful business while taking care of an ill brother, even though you were in an abusive relationship. You had the strength to stand up to Rex and throw him out. And then you sat here and faced a lifetime locked up in jail for two murders that you didn't commit in order to protect your brother." He touched her hand. "Phyllis, you've made sacrifices for others your whole life. Not everybody is that unselfish. You are awesome."

"So she's free to go?" Ruth snapped and rubbed out her cigarette in the ashtray she carried in her purse. "I assume in your admiration that you are dropping the accessory charges."

"While I admit the evidence we have against your client as far as accessory is circumstantial, it is indeed damaging, and I think a jury, even without a confession, would know what she did."

He sat back and directed his comments to Phyllis even though he was speaking to her lawyer. "I am in a position to not file any charges. I'll be the first to admit that it would be a loser case. The jury will refuse to convict out of sympathy. This whole thing has been a horrible tragedy all the way around. I would like to put an end to it and let us all move on as best we can. I'm asking for her help. I'm not going to play hardball. We are all too tired for that. I'm asking her to help me out simply because she can."

"How can I possibly help you?" Phyllis asked suspiciously.

"I think you have information and can offer testimony in catching your husband's killer."

Ruth shook her head. "Why would she care to catch his killer?"

"He cared enough for Doug to not turn him in to the police after she kicked him out."

"I don't know who killed Rex," Phyllis insisted.

"You know more than you think you know. That information can help us to bring justice in more than one murder." He ignored her lawyer's scoffing. "I'm going to get this killer with or without your help. It will be easier with it."

"How are you doing?"

Joshua stepped into Tad's apartment without knocking when he saw him sitting at the kitchen table with his bandaged hand and wrist stretched out before him. Only his fingers were left exposed. The doctor had spent the night in the emergency room as a patient.

"I've been better," Tad said before rising from his chair and going to the counter to make a pot of coffee.

"Hey, Tad, you would never believe what Ziggy just told me." Clutching her cell phone, Jan rushed in from the bedroom. She stopped when she saw Joshua. It was eight o'clock in the morning, and she was dressed in the same clothes she had worn the day before.

Despite the frigid cold, Tad was shirtless and dressed in a pair of blue jeans that had seen better days.

"Hello, Jan," Joshua said.

"Hi, Josh." Her eyes wide with embarrassment, she stammered out the reason for her outburst. "I was talking to Ziggy at *The Review*—dictating my story about last night—and he said that the AP has just released a report that Seth Cavanaugh was arrested in Los Angeles."

Tad stopped spooning coffee into the filter with his hand in midair. "Are you talking about our Seth Cavanaugh?"

Joshua said to Jan, "You're kidding."

She was shaking her head. "No, it's true. Yesterday, the Quincy brothers were released from prison. Their lawyer's private detective proved that they did not kill their parents. It was their uncle."

Tad said, "Sounds like Cavanaugh was a screw up even before he came to Chester."

"More than a screw up," Jan announced. "He was arrested for accepting a bribe and tampering with evidence."

"Then I was right about him," Joshua said. "He *did* take a bribe from Margo to steal the evidence placing Billy on the scene when Grace was killed."

"I guess it wasn't his first time," Jan continued. "The PI found evidence that Seth found out about the uncle committing the murders and accepted a payoff to keep quiet about it. Not only did he accept a bribe, but he tampered with evidence to ensure that the Quincy brothers were convicted, which made them ineligible to inherit their folks' estate. Once they went to jail, the uncle got it all. But now Uncle Quincy is going to jail . . . and so is Seth Cavanaugh, as soon as they get him back to West Virginia."

Joshua surmised, "Seth didn't give Curt two weeks' notice before taking off for California. I wonder if one of his friends in Parkersburg gave him a heads up about what was going down."

"Since he's in jail now awaiting extradition to West Virginia, I guess he didn't get enough of a heads up," Tad said with a wicked grin.

"Jan, you just made my day," Joshua said.

She was equally happy. "Tad, do you have anything for us to drink in a toast to justice?"

"The orange juice is in the fridge." Having lost count of how many spoonfuls of coffee he had put into the coffeemaker, Tad emptied the filter and started over.

"How's your hand?" Joshua sat on top of the kitchen table.

Tad completed his count before he answered, "It's just a flesh wound." He added, "I'm certainly in better shape than Doug Barlow."

Dog strolled into the kitchen. He yawned and stretched. When he completed his morning stretching exercises, he dropped onto the floor and gazed up at his master. After handing both Joshua and Tad glasses of orange juice, Jan reached up into the cabinet to get a treat for the dog.

Joshua was not surprised by his cousin's foul mood. "I should have known that Phyllis was covering up for him. I'm sorry."

"It's not your fault." Tad hit the button to start the coffee brewing. He turned back to him. "I can't stand losing a patient."

Joshua did not miss Jan placing her hand on Tad's arm when she told him, "The deputies had to shoot back. Doug took a shot at them. There was nothing we could have done."

"If they had given me a chance I would have taken the gun from him," Tad argued.

Jan pleaded, "Tad, don't do this to yourself."

"Doug let me get close enough to grab the gun."

Joshua jumped down from the table and grabbed him by the shoulders. "If you keep replaying it in your mind, you're going to convince yourself that you could have saved Doug the same way he convinced himself that Tricia killed herself because they couldn't be together. It's a defense mechanism. The truth is that Doug killed Tricia, whether it was accidentally or on purpose, and you could not save him. He was not going to be satisfied until he was dead."

"I know."

Joshua said, "Eventually, he was going to succeed. Last night, he did, and we can thank God he didn't take you two with him." His voice fell when he added, "I'm sorry you had to be there."

The coffee was made and Tad turned around to fill their cups. To prevent them from seeing the sadness in his face, he stared out the window over his sink while he sipped the hot coffee with his back to them.

Jan whispered to Joshua, "He's really blaming himself." She glanced at the time. "I have to go to work. I'd hate to be late for my new job, especially when I'm scooping the competition with a first-hand account of the day's biggest story."

Joshua suppressed a gasp when he saw her kiss Tad full on the mouth before rushing back to the bedroom. With her jacket in hand, she returned and kissed Joshua on the cheek before kissing Tad once again on the lips and running out the door and down the steps.

"I guess your relationship with Jan has taken a turn."

"We're not sleeping together." Tad sighed. "I don't really want to talk about it. I'll just say that the feelings Jan and I have had for each other have changed. I'm not going to hurt her." He turned back to the window to watch his neighbors emerging to start their day.

"What if—"

"I'm second fiddle to you? She's moved on." Tad looked at him. "There comes a time when we all have to either move on, or stagnate until our lives turn into a parasitic swamp."

Preoccupied with their own thoughts, Joshua and Tad stood side-by-side at the counter and stared out at the dead leaves in the yard next door.

It was early in the morning. The neighbors letting their dogs out while retrieving their newspapers from the front stoops evidenced the first stirrings of the day. Some were climbing into their cars to get on Route 30 to head out to the Pittsburgh Airport Corridor, a stretch of land between the airport and the city where high rises provided jobs for many of Chester's residents.

The populace had changed since the days when Joshua and Tad were children. Then, most of the residents had worked in the steel mill during the week and were farmers on the weekend.

"Are you angry about Jan and me?" Tad asked about the source of Joshua's silence.

"No," Joshua lied.

★　★　★　★　★

Greg Boyd and his mother, Eve, were waiting for Joshua in his living room when he stomped home after seeing his cousin with Jan, the woman who had confessed weeks before that she loved him. He didn't want her, but he was certain that he didn't want Tad to have her. In spite of his anger, he found it hard to be mad at Tad. For Joshua, that feeling directed at Tad was impossible. He wished it wasn't.

In his night of sorting out Gail's and Tricia's murders and playing mental poker with Ruth Majors, he had forgotten that he had tracked down Dan Boyd's son to Lawrenceville, where he had come home for a visit. Overjoyed that the case was renewed, Greg and Eve Boyd said they would be at his house the first thing in the morning to be interviewed.

In contrast to his glasses, strawberry-colored hair, and freckles, Greg Boyd was tall and muscular. According to the photographs taken of the scene of the murder, the only difference between the father and son was that Dan was rail thin. Greg was a devoted son. He comforted his mother by placing his hand on hers while they rehashed the past in an effort to find the killer of the only man she had ever loved.

Eve Boyd was at least ten years older than the woman who had seduced her husband away from her family. She was a petite woman, wore little makeup, and didn't take any pains to style her short salt-and-pepper hair. She never remarried. Joshua's instinct told him that she didn't even date.

Greg was introducing his mother while pumping Joshua's hand in the front foyer when Sarah and Donny, dressed for football in the front yard, came down the stairs.

"Hey, Dad." Sarah tossed the ball into the air and caught it. "We're getting together a game outside. Care to join us?" Joshua could still see the sleep in her eyes. The visitors had awakened her.

"I'm working."

"You're always working." She led her brother out the door.

Through the open doorway, Joshua saw a group of kids gathered in the yard. He pushed aside his desire to join them and ushered Dan Boyd's son and ex-wife into his office where they could talk in quiet. The scent of Tracy's coffee and fresh cinnamon rolls drifted in from the kitchen.

When they went into the office, Joshua found Admiral sprawled out across the full length of the sofa he intended to offer as a seat to his visitors. The dog rested his head on a throw pillow.

"Admiral!" the dog's master shouted with his hands on his hips. "Get off!" He ordered him out of the room.

Admiral snorted and lifted his head to take in the people who had the nerve to interrupt his morning nap. He hesitated to size up each one of the humans standing over him. After concluding that he had better do what he was told, the mongrel inched down from the sofa until he was off and, with a sigh, slunk out of the study.

Joshua sat in the recliner with a notepad in his lap. Poised to ask and answer all the questions they needed in hopes of catching Boyd's killer, Greg and Eve sat on the sofa across from him.

"Margo did it, didn't she?" Eve peered at him with dark, round eyes in her equally round face.

"She has an alibi for the time of the murder," Joshua said. "We do suspect that she arranged for his murder, but we would have to prove it. That's one of the reasons I asked you to come."

"He was going to leave Margo," she said. "We were talking about it the month before she killed him. Dan was having a mid-life crisis. Greg was little. We had been married for quite a while, and he was feeling old and she made him feel young again. But then, after they got married, he came to his senses. He asked me if he could come back. He just hadn't gotten around to telling her yet."

"Or maybe he did and she killed him." Greg sat forward on the sofa with his elbows on his knees.

"She married him for his money." Eve asked, "Did you know that she took out a hundred-thousand-dollar life insurance policy on him just four months before he was killed? And he had already made her the beneficiary of a quarter-million-dollar life insurance policy. We only got a hundred and fifty thousand dollars."

"So she made three hundred and fifty thousand dollars in life insurance." Joshua made a note.

Greg added, "Plus the house and the dental practice, which she sold for a good deal of money, and his savings."

"All she gave up for us was Dan's Agatha Christies," Eve said.

"Agatha Christies?" Joshua squinted.

"My father was a frustrated Hercule Poirot," Greg said. "He had a full hardback collection of every one of Agatha Christie's books."

Eve told Joshua, "If Margo knew how much that collection was worth, she'd be furious. I had them appraised several years ago, and they are collectors' items. Dan bought them because he loved Agatha Christie, not as an investment. After he died, Margo wouldn't let us have anything without a fight, except his books, which I got for Greg. He still has them."

Joshua's mind was working: the blood-covered picture of Margo in his office, the picture that was upright. "Did he read them all?"

"Every single last one," she answered, "and he saw every movie made from her books. He also read Perry Mason and Sherlock Holmes, and watched all those cop and detective shows."

"How about crime documentaries? Would he be up on

modern detection techniques and forensics?"

Eve sighed, "He died before they got cable. But, he did watch, I would imagine, what he could get."

Greg had been watching the two of them talk like a spectator watching a tennis match, his head turning back and forth with each question and answer.

Joshua asked her, "Did your late husband say why he wanted to leave Margo?"

"Dan was established in his career when she went to work for him," she explained. "Then she didn't want to work. Then she got bored and took a course in real estate. After she got her license, she wanted him to take all his money out of his savings and invest it in real estate. You see, back then, a lot of families were moving out of the area because the mills closed down. She wanted to buy their old houses and fix them up."

Joshua noted, "That's how she got rich."

Eve shook her head sadly. "Dan was not a gambler. He didn't invest in the stock market. To invest in those houses was a risk. He wasn't going to do that with his money. They hadn't spoken for months before he finally decided he was going to get out."

"Which would have left her with nothing," Greg observed. "Notice that she made out like a bandit. She wouldn't be where she is today if Dad hadn't been killed. She got all she needed to invest." He pointed a finger at Joshua. "That was her motive."

The ringing phone startled Joshua out of a dozing state that he had slipped into while drinking a cup of coffee and snacking on one of Tracy's cinnamon rolls.

"Are you sure you're not mad at me?"

"I'm not mad at you, Tad," he yawned. "As a matter of fact, I pray that you and Jan do work it out as a couple. It would be great if the two people I love the most get together." *Maybe the feeling will fall into place if I say it enough.*

"Good. I hope so, too." Tad resumed with the reason for his call, "Thought you might be interested in knowing that I finished the autopsy on Billy Unger and found carbon on his hands and speckling around the entrance wound where he was shot."

"Which means he had his hand on the gun when it went off," Joshua said. "That supports our theory that he had a gallant bone in his body and took the bullet for Tori."

"But the bullet went through him and still killed her," Tad concluded. "That will explain the downward angle of the wound. My guess is that Tori Brody, who was sitting, was the intended victim. Well, I'll e-mail this report to you. What are you doing for lunch?"

Joshua suggested that they meet at Tom's, a family restaurant next to the Chester Bridge. He liked their breakfast club sandwich. Before hanging up, he asked his cousin to do him a favor.

"What kind of favor?" Tad joked, "Is it legal?"

"Last I checked it was. I want you to start a rumor."

"A rumor? Why do you want me to start a rumor? What kind?"

"To plant the fear of God into a suspect. Since you know everyone, you'll know exactly what fertile ground in which to plant this seed."

The Steubenville police had the license plate number for Heather's sports car. Since there was a warrant out for her arrest, they looked for her at Billy Unger's rooming house and found the car parked in the alley next door.

They found Heather's body lying across the same bed in which she had claimed they made love while Grace Henderson was being killed. The gun that had killed her rival was by her side.

Propped up on his dresser was a Sylvia Plath poem ripped

out of a book. The morbid tone of the poem suggested that she had left it there in an effort to confess to killing Grace Henderson, Tori Brody, and, accidentally, the only man she loved.

CHAPTER TWENTY

Sheriff Sawyer was consulting with his Steubenville counterpart when Joshua arrived to see the ending of Margo's daughter. He never did like Margo, but he didn't dislike anyone enough to wish the loss of her child upon her. The medical examiner from Steubenville had completed her on-scene examination of Heather's body when he got there.

"How long has she been dead?" Joshua asked Sheriff Sawyer.

"Twenty-four hours." The medical examiner snapped her medical bag shut. "Single gunshot wound to the temple."

"Yesterday morning," Curt clarified. "The gun is a thirty-eight Colt revolver; exactly like the one Manners says he gave to Unger to get rid of. We checked out this place right after finding his body, and neither her nor that gun were here then."

Joshua checked out the dingy room. Heather looked out of place. The clothes she wore alone were worth more than all the furnishings, which consisted of a bed, dresser, and chair.

"I thought you said that it looked like he was staying at Tori's condo."

Curt nodded. "Evidence suggests that. Men's stuff in the bath that forensics proved belonged to him. Clothes. Underwear. His semen in her body—"

"I wonder if Heather knew about that?" Joshua muttered.

"Which points to motive for this," Curt concluded.

"Do you believe that Heather was deep enough to kill herself over a failed relationship? Murder maybe, but not suicide."

Curt was reporting his findings while Joshua stepped up to the bed and observed her body before the attendants had a chance to place it in the body bag.

"She's been a busy girl. Since I talked to her mother, I called everyone who has any connection to her. She went to a concert in Pittsburgh on Friday night with three girlfriends and met up with a group of kids that maybe, maybe not, she knew. From the concert, they went to a party. The host's parents were out of town, and they wrecked the house. The party went on until midday Sunday, and then she went home where she slept almost twenty-four hours, according to the maid."

"So she didn't kill Brody and Unger." Joshua gestured towards her face. "What's that?"

Curt looked down at where he was pointing. There was a purple mark in the form of a triangle on Heather's cheekbone with a red slash across the center of it. "That looks like a welt."

Joshua peered at the hole at her temple. He saw what appeared to be a piece of foam.

The sheriff took up where he left off. "Her mother swears that Billy called for her on Saturday morning and said that Plan A was in effect. Heather went ballistic when she waited until Monday night to give her the message."

Joshua looked around the room. "And then she skips school on Tuesday to come over here to meet him, we assume." He kicked at the carpet in which he could see the vacuum marks and took a swipe at the dresser that had been polished. "This room was cleaned—recently."

Curt agreed. "The forensics people had a go at it, but they don't usually clean up after themselves."

"I want to see her car."

Joshua encountered an older woman who smelled of scotch in the hallway. She refused to let the most authoritative-looking man on the scene, since he was dressed in a suit, pass until she

331

got an answer to her question. "When are you going to be through here? You're disturbing my tenants. First, you people were tearing the place apart the day before yesterday, and now you're back and doing it again."

Joshua answered, "We're investigating a suspicious death."

"Too bad." The landlady glanced in the direction of the late Billy Unger's room. "I thought he was a deadbeat like the rest of them, but he surprised me."

"How did he do that?"

"He paid me. I hadn't seen him around for like a week. Then suddenly, he came out of the woodwork and paid me all his back rent, plus a month in advance."

"Why would he do that if he was hiding out at Brody's place?" Joshua asked in Curt Sawyer's direction. The sheriff appeared as surprised as the prosecutor.

The old woman said, "He was paying for his girlfriend. I guess he felt guilty for ditching her for a rich bitch."

"What rich bitch?" Joshua glanced at Curt Sawyer who mouthed Tori Brody's name.

"I didn't get her name," she answered. "I saw her waiting for him outside in her car when he came to pay up and get his stuff. She looked like any other tramp, except she was dressed up all fine." She craned her neck to look past him into the room. "He went through ladies like my ex went through beer. So she's dead, huh? I'm not surprised."

Curt asked, "Did you see or hear anything yesterday morning?"

"Just saw her sneaking in like she always does, like a thief in the night. I heard her running a vacuum she must have borrowed from one of the tenants. I figured lucky me. Most of my renters don't clean up. Then, I saw her sneaking down the fire exit, like I was stupid or something and didn't know that she was there."

"Why was she sneaking if he'd paid her rent?" Curt asked.

"I guess she didn't know that he had paid for her room for her." The landlady squinted when she got a glimpse of Heather's body on the bed. "Who is that?"

"That's one of Billy Unger's girlfriends," Joshua told her. "Who were you talking about?"

"The other girl. The little one with the orange hair."

Sheriff Sawyer paused to ask one of the deputies to get a statement from her while Joshua hurried down the stairs to see Heather's car. In the alley, he took no time in opening up the driver's side door and getting in. The seat was further back than the front seat had been in Billy Unger's car. "How tall is Heather?"

Sheriff Sawyer prided himself in sizing up people. "Five feet, eight inches."

Joshua picked up a purple square piece of cardboard that rested on the dashboard in the window. "Pass for a parking garage in Pittsburgh." He checked the date. "Dated for Friday night." He looked at the passenger seat, and then stepped out of the car to observe where he had been seated. "No blood. Whoever helped Billy into his car, and then pulled him over to the driver's seat, had to have gotten blood all over when they left. These seats have no blood and they haven't recently been cleaned." He observed a knapsack in the backseat. "Overnight bag."

"Heather probably never had the time to unpack from her weekend party."

Joshua pulled the trunk release, went to the back of the car, and lifted the lid to reveal a suitcase. They exchanged smirks as Curt unzipped the case to reveal that it was packed with Heather's clothes.

"Plan A," the sheriff concluded. "Let's run away together."

"If you were going to kill yourself, would you bother packing a suitcase?"

The next morning, while Oak Glen High School mourned the loss of yet another classmate, and while her mother accepted calls of condolence, Joshua went to the Fifth Street Café in East Liverpool to meet with Detective Diana Windsor, the Columbiana County Sheriff Department's counterpart to Seth Cavanaugh. He had never realized the soup and sandwich shop was there until he found it where she suggested they meet.

Joshua searched the faces of the patrons for the detective while he made his way through the diner. He had created the image of a woman not unlike the female officers with whom he served in the Navy. Efficient, perfectly groomed, handsome, maybe even pretty. He was not prepared for the woman who stopped him as he passed her. "Mr. Thornton, I presume?"

He had mistaken her for a teenage boy. Slightly built and wholesome looking, Diana looked like a boy with ultra-short, black hair and enormous hazel eyes. Her skin was olive color. She had to have Italian in her genetic background. She was dressed in a V-neck sweater and slacks under a brown leather bomber jacket.

"Detective Windsor?" he stopped and asked.

"That's me." She shot him a toothy grin.

He slid into the booth in the seat across from her. "You don't look old enough to be a detective. You probably get that all the time."

"I'm thirty-four and I have two kids. Last year, my husband traded me for a younger model with a no-kids package."

He shook his head with a laugh. "Some men don't know a classic when they see it."

"And they say lawyers are stupid."

They laughed together before the detective gestured to the envelope he was carrying. "Why would Hancock County's

Golden Boy want to meet me for lunch?"

He slid the envelope containing the case file across the table to her. "The Dr. Dan Boyd case. His widow lives in my jurisdiction, and I heard that you work Columbiana County's cold cases, of which this is one."

The waitress appeared at the end of the table with a notepad. "What can I get you kids?"

Diana told Joshua, "They have great chili here," before turning her attention to the waitress. "I'll have a bowl of the chili, and cornbread, and a cheese sandwich, and the house salad, and a chocolate milkshake, and for dessert I'll have the hot apple pie a la mode."

The waitress turned to Joshua, who was amazed at how much the wisp of a woman sitting across from him had ordered. "Sir?"

"I'll have the same."

"Well, let's see what we are looking at." The detective spread the crime-scene pictures from the 1988 murder across the table while he reported the circumstances of the case.

"Dan Boyd left blood all over the place. He died at the receptionist's desk." Joshua showed her the picture of the desk that was clear except for her computer and her keyboard.

Diana pointed out the door that was in view in the picture of the body. "Why didn't he go out into the street for help?"

"Because his larynx was cut, and he couldn't talk. He had to leave a message giving the name of his killer."

"Any normal person would have gone running for help."

"Suppose he wasn't any normal person."

"Do you think his wife did this?"

"Margo Connor."

"The real estate lady whose daughter was just killed? You're cold." She went back to the pictures. "What makes you think he left a message?"

"Boyd loved whodunits. According to his receptionist, she

bought a new computer that month to automate the office. He was killed before he had the chance to learn how to use it." Joshua leaned across the table to point to the picture of the keyboard. "Look at this. There's blood all over it."

Diana leaned across to look at the picture. A lock of her slicked-back hair tickled his nose. "The computer is not on." She showed him the monitor.

The couple parted when the waitress arrived with a tray loaded with food. With a look of amusement at their feast, she unloaded the tray, plate after plate, while they gathered up the pictures of the bloody murder to make room on the table.

Once the waitress was out of earshot, Joshua told the detective, who was slathering butter on her cornbread, "I was wondering if, being a whodunit fan, he might have left some sort of clue telling us who killed him."

"I doubt it, but I'll check out the evidence room when I get back." She then asked, "Are you going to eat your cornbread?"

Joshua passed her his plate.

Mitch, the bartender, warned Nicki with a single nod of his head when Tad MacMillan, Joshua Thornton, two Ohio State Troopers, and two West Virginia State Troopers came into the bar. They were accompanied by a man and a woman in business suits. They looked out of place in the bar that catered to the generation that devoted itself to going to the extreme in the party scene.

Nicki remained in her seat at the bar. Even with the law enforcement audience in the empty bar in the middle of the day, the underaged girl took a drink of her vodka and orange juice. "What's up, Doc?" she greeted the only one in the crowd with whom she was familiar.

Tad responded, "I guess you heard that your good friend Heather Connor is dead."

"Yep," she took another sip of her drink. "I heard she offed herself in Billy's room."

"We don't think so. It's kind of hard to run a sweeper and dust the furniture after putting a bullet through your head."

"What makes you think she did that?"

He gestured towards his cousin. "I'll let Joshua Thornton, Hancock County's prosecuting attorney, explain it to you."

Nicki rolled her eyes in response to the introduction. "He has no authority here."

"He doesn't," the man in the business suit said, "but we do." He went on to introduce himself as Frank Burger, the county prosecutor for Columbiana County, in which Steubenville was located.

The woman, Judith Morgan, was his assistant. "You should listen to what Mr. Thornton has to say," she advised the girl.

"Whatever." Nicki sighed and gave another roll of her eyes.

Joshua told her, "The medical examiner found bits of foam in the hole you put in Heather's head. After knocking her senseless with the gun you had taken from Billy, or been given, you used a pillow to muffle the shot when you killed her. Then, you swept the floor and dusted the furniture to get rid of the foam and your fingerprints. Forensics found evidence of carbon and gunshot residue on the pillow foam that you had vacuumed up, which proves that the room was cleaned after the shot was fired. The neighbor that you had borrowed the vacuum cleaner from turned it over to the police. She has seen you in the rooming house several times and will have no problem identifying you. Right before you left the room after cleaning it up, you planted a poem you had torn out of a book to make it look like a suicide. For all the work you did, you made too many mistakes."

She shrugged and turned away from them to sip her drink.

Joshua stepped up close to her. "We found a suitcase with Heather's clothes in the trunk of her car. Why would she have packed if she was going to shoot herself?"

"That suitcase was from another trip she had taken."

"Like a weekend party that she had just been at? The one after the concert she was at while you were killing Billy and his lawyer? You wanted us to believe that Heather killed them, but she had an alibi that is as tight as it comes."

"Then I guess someone else killed them." She grinned wickedly at Mitch.

The bartender responded with a weak smile.

"It was you, Nicki," Tad told her.

"Prove it," she challenged them.

"A picture is worth a thousand words." Joshua gestured to Tad, who stepped behind the bar and slipped a videotape into the VCR.

Hancock County's prosecutor whirled her stool around to force her to watch it. "There was an ATM with a security camera across the street from Tori Brody's condo, where Billy has been hiding out ever since we issued a warrant for his arrest. I don't know if he told you that was where he was staying, or maybe you hunted him down. I assume you borrowed that car we see on the tape since you don't have a car or a driver's license." Joshua looked at Mitch, who put up his hands and shook his head in a gesture of innocence.

"Can we take a look at your car or do we need to get a warrant?" Prosecutor Burger asked the bartender.

"You can't get a warrant," he objected. "I did nothing wrong. I know my rights."

"We can get a warrant if we can prove probable cause." Joshua gestured toward the television. An old Camaro pulled into the parking lot next to the condo. "Is that your car?" he asked him. "It looks just like the one out back, and according to the license plate, which is readable in the picture we had blown up from this tape, it is registered to you."

Tad continued, "A man identifying himself as Billy called the Connor home on Saturday and left a message for Heather. Billy was killed Friday night. So it couldn't have been him. The phone company says the call came from this bar."

"Are we looking at two accessory charges? One after the fact and one before?" Joshua told him. "If you lured Heather to Billy's room to be killed—"

"She told me it was a joke!" Mitch shouted.

Nicki giggled into her drink.

Joshua took the opportunity to ask Mitch, "Was that the first time Nicki borrowed your car?"

The bartender's face turned white. "Why do you ask?"

"It matches the description of a vehicle seen in the vicinity when Grace Henderson was murdered."

"What did you get me into, bitch?" The bartender turned to the doctor. "Look at my car. There was blood all over it after she took it Friday night. She didn't even try to clean it out. She said that it was a dead dog she picked up after hitting it."

"He was a dog!" Nicki snickered.

"And so you shot him like one." Joshua pointed to the television.

She glanced up to see herself going through the door leading to the condo. "You can't prove I went up to see Billy."

"Oh, no?" Joshua slapped a picture onto the bar showing her helping a doubled over Billy out the door. "It's a blowup of the security picture, even has the date and time recorded."

He surmised, "Billy took up with his lawyer and moved out of the room at the boardinghouse where you had been living with him. You went up to Tori Brody's condo to confront one or the both of them. I think you took the gun to scare her. He grabbed it, and it went off. The bullet went through him and killed her. He was still alive, and you helped him into his car. You left your bloody fingerprints in the elevator. He died before you could get him to the hospital. So you hid the car, moved him into the driver's seat so no one would know you were there, and then hitchhiked back to the car you borrowed, getting his blood in it, and came back."

Nicki scoffed when Joshua paused. "You think you're so smart."

"I think the idea of framing Heather for the two murders came to you the next day. Since you hid Billy, you had some time, but you were racing against the clock. You got your friend here—" Joshua indicated Mitch. "—to call and leave Heather a cryptic message, which told her that they would run off together. She raced to his room, where you killed her with the gun you knew everyone was looking for, and you tried to make it look like a suicide." He asked, "Did Grace and Heather even know about you and Billy?"

She answered with a shake of her head. "I was the one who crawled in through his window after they went home to their families in their big houses."

Tad recalled, "You told me that Billy had no intention of leaving with Grace."

"Heather thought he did. She was so upset that her mom paid me to get rid of her."

Joshua could barely contain his shock. "Margo Connor paid you to get rid of Grace?"

She said mockingly, "We can't have little Heather upset. She wanted Billy. So, her mom told her that if she could find someone to get rid of Grace, then she would pay for it. Heather asked me and, I had the gun, so I said okay."

Joshua further explained, "And since you lived with Billy, you had access to his trench coat, bandanna, and sunglasses to disguise yourself in." He went on to ask, "Did you intend to frame Billy, or was that by accident?"

"I guess I wanted to send him a message, but the bastard was too stupid to get it."

"How much did Margo Connor pay you to kill Grace to clear the way for her daughter?" Joshua asked.

Nicki held up her hand with the ruby ring on it.

"Did she personally give that to you?"

"Heather took me to her mother's office, and Mrs. Connor showed me this jewelry box with all these rocks in it. She told me I could have my pick and she would mail it to me after Grace was dead. I had to do it on that day after school so Heather could go over to Billy's to get an alibi for the both of them. A couple of days after I blew Grace away, I got the ring here at the bar in the mail."

"Why did Margo pay you with a ring?" Tad wanted to know.

"Because she could blame her maid for stealing it and get reimbursed for it by the insurance company." Joshua admired Margo's savvy maneuver. "She got her insurance company to pay for a hit."

Tad asked Nicki, "You knew about both Heather and Grace. What was so different about Tori Brody that you felt compelled to confront her?"

"Billy knew that I had no place to go, but he didn't give a shit. He had this big bitch lawyer to live off of. He didn't need me anymore."

Joshua told her, "But he paid for an extra thirty days for the room in order to give you time to make other arrangements."

For the first time, tears came to Nicki's eyes. "What other arrangements? I had no one. Billy and I have been together since forever! It was always him and me! Even when Grace and Heather were scratching each other's eyes out, it was Billy and me. But then this rich bitch comes along and—" Tears streamed down her face. She caught her breath. "I asked him, 'What am I supposed to do?' He said, 'Do whatever you have to do.' So I did."

CHAPTER TWENTY-ONE

At the State Line Lounge, Herb Duncan sat on a stool at the end of the bar and drank his beer. He and his wife were moving into their middle-class home this weekend. When he got home, they were going to throw out all their old stuff to buy new.

"Hey, Herb," Willie Semple called from where he leaned against the bar a couple of stools away.

Willie hung around construction sites. He had been on permanent work disability since he fell onto a foundation and hurt his back. Unable to work, he lived in a double-wide trailer in a mobile home park out on the racetrack road and drank as much of his earnings from the state as he could.

"Hey, Willie," Herb greeted him. "I haven't seen you for a while. Have a beer."

"If you're buying, I'm drinking." Willie perched himself up on the bar stool and ordered a draft. While shooting Herb a rotten-toothed grin, he punched him in the arm. "Hey! Have you heard the latest?"

"About what?"

Their beers arrived. The two men gulped down a couple of swallows before Willie wiped his mouth on his sleeve. "About what really happened to Rex. I heard that it was a professional hit."

Herb chuckled.

"From a guy out of town," Willie said. "I got it all figured out who killed Rex Rollins. This guy I know at this place out in

Pittsburgh that is run by the mob, he knows these people, and they got a call today from Mrs. Connor."

"A call about what?"

"She said she needed someone to do a little cleanup. You know what I think? I think Connor has been laundering money for the mob in her businesses and that Rex found out about it. So she had this pro come in to take him out, but he told someone before they got him and that someone has been blackmailing her. That's why she called her friends at the mob again to come in and get rid of the friend Rex blabbed to."

Willie paused before taking another gulp of his beer. "You remember what a big mouth Rex had. There's no telling who he told what. And, hell, the police can't find out who killed him. They haven't got a clue. It worked with a pro once. Why not do it again?"

"So my client's truck was in the State Line parking lot?" Ben Stiller, a hard-working man who was pretty good at getting his clients out of trouble, argued with the county prosecutor after Sheriff Sawyer arrested Herb Duncan two days later. "He's a regular. Everyone saw him drinking at the bar. That's what people do there."

"He was the only one to leave right after Rollins did," Joshua countered.

"He was sitting in his truck smoking a cigarette when I left." Herb said. "I told the police that."

"I know. You told both the detective and the sheriff that a couple of times. It is noted in your statement," the prosecutor said. "Funny, there weren't any cigarette butts in the truck."

Herb appeared shaken.

"There were no butts in the truck or in the ashtray. Rex did not smoke in his truck. It was a habit after years of his wife forbidding him from smoking in the house or the truck because she doesn't like the smell of cigarettes." Joshua pointed to Herb while he told his lawyer, "That proves your client is lying. His truck with its temporary tags was seen in front of the motel the night of Bella Polk's murder. He beat an old woman to death. That's two murders."

"He hardly knew that old lady. Why would he want to kill her?"

"Margo Connor paid him to kill her."

The defense attorney challenged him, "Can you prove that?"

"The week after Rex was killed, your client was hired as foreman over two men with more experience. Everyone has noticed that. Margo Connor also paid him twenty-five thousand dollars for his trailer and property that the state assessed at being worth nothing more than five thousand."

"I guess Connor isn't as good a businesswoman as we thought," Ben said. "My client simply took advantage of a good offer. Who wouldn't? If I was offered five times the value of my house, I'd take it, too. No questions asked. That doesn't mean I committed murder." He asked, "To get back to the Polk murder, why would Connor care to have an old lady killed?"

"Because the old lady tried to blackmail her," Joshua said.

"With what?"

"Ask your client."

Herb said nothing.

The defense attorney turned back to his adversary. "You have yet to show us any proof."

Joshua responded with the question, "What was Bella Polk's saliva doing on your client's hand?"

"What?" Ben asked.

Herb was openmouthed at the revelation.

"Your client went to his doctor two days after the murder of Rex Rollins's landlady," Joshua said. "He had what the doctor states looked like a bite mark on his hand that had become infected. The medical examiner reported that Bella Polk's teeth were chipped in the assault that killed her. Your client's doctor took a sample of the infection for analysis to find the source so he would know how best to treat it. The infection was determined to be one that is commonly found in the human mouth. After we went to him with a warrant, the sample he took was sent to our labs, and we found that there is a match between the germs found in your client's wound and Bella Polk's mouth, which puts his fist in her mouth."

Pleased with Herb's stunned expression, Joshua added, "We can get a court order to have an impression of that bite mark taken from his hand to match with her mouth."

"I'll get that evidence suppressed," Ben predicted.

The prosecutor added, "We also have his fingerprints on the bullets in the gun that killed Rollins." He grinned at Herb. "You wore gloves when you shot him. Then you left the gun, which you knew would not be traced back to you because you picked it up from a thief. But you weren't wearing gloves when you loaded it. We got some beautiful partials on the bullets and cartridges inside the gun."

Herb's dismayed expression told his lawyer that the prosecutor was on target. "We have to talk."

Without a word, Joshua stepped out into the hall. Curt was waiting for him. He had been watching the match through the two-way mirror.

"Do you think he's going to turn on Margo?" the sheriff asked.

"He will if he believed Willie Semple and saw that trooper wearing a black trench coat parked in the unmarked black sedan outside the construction site."

Curt chuckled. "You can be evil sometimes."

Ben Stiller opened the door and gestured for Joshua to come inside. Herb was sitting at the table with a cocky grin. He had something the prosecutor wanted.

"You give us complete immunity and protection from Margo Connor, and we'll give her to you."

"No deal." Joshua stepped to the door. "See you in court."

"You can't get her without my client. You have to prove motive for her wanting to hire my client to kill Rollins. We can give that to you in black and white."

Herb puffed out his chest. "I have Rollins's book."

With surprise, they watched as Joshua opened the door. The sheriff stepped inside.

"Book him for two counts of first-degree murder," the prosecutor ordered.

Curt directed Herb to stand up and turn around so he could handcuff him. Herb looked for help from his lawyer.

"He's bluffing," Ben assured him. "He needs you and that book in order to get Connor."

After two days of waiting in the cell with no protection from the professional assassin he heard rumors that Margo had hired, Herb told his lawyer to take whatever deal Thornton had to offer. He turned over the manuscript and made a full confession in exchange for protection.

Rex Rollins had dropped out of school as soon as he got his driver's license. Knowing this, Joshua did not expect the manuscript to be a masterpiece. However, while reading the tome in front of his fireplace after his children had gone to bed with dreams of the Thanksgiving turkey dancing through their heads, he was surprised to discover that the author did know how to weave a story.

Rex did not know the first thing about grammar. The sentences were either run-ons or fragments. He spelled phonetically. Also, if he had succeeded in getting it published, the lawsuits for libel would have been monstrous. He said what he thought about everyone and didn't change anything to protect anyone's identity.

Once Joshua got past those flaws, Rex took him into the life of a reluctant, paid assassin who did it all in an attempt to win the love of his wife.

Rex loved Phyllis.

Unfortunately, she would have nothing to do with him.

Then, Rex wrote, one day he was fixing the Wheelers' leaky toilet when Tricia came home from school. She didn't notice him under the toilet when she walked past the bathroom to go into her bedroom.

When he heard her shriek, he looked out into the hallway and saw Tricia, her purse still on her shoulder, backing out of the bedroom into the living room and Doug Barlow, with wild-looking eyes, coming out. He held a gun in one hand and was holding out a necklace to her with the other.

Doug had been hiding in the bedroom the whole time Rex was there, and he never knew it.

Rex froze.

While he watched in horror from the bathroom, Doug ordered Tricia to take the necklace as a last gift from him. Telling him all the while that she did love him, she did what he asked and put the necklace on.

Doug did not believe her. He turned the gun on himself. Tricia grabbed the revolver.

Too shocked to move, Rex watched while the boy and girl struggled for the weapon.

The gun went off.

For a moment, Rex was unsure who the bullet struck.

Then, he saw Tricia fall onto the sofa.

Doug lost what little sanity he had left.

Rex ran to the Barlow house to get Phyllis. Together, they cleaned up the Wheeler home. He also cleaned up any evidence that he had been there so that no one would know he was a witness. Not wanting Dorothy Wheeler to find her daughter sprawled out on the sofa with her skirt askew, Rex laid her out with her head on a pillow.

It wasn't until a couple of days later that it occurred to Rex to use what he knew to get Phyllis to marry him. He believed that over time, he could make her love him.

He was not a good provider and she had to quit school to get a full-time job to support them both.

Her resentment made Rex depressed, and he drank more. When he drank, he got mean and, more than once, he was arrested. If it wasn't for a bar fight, it was for beating Phyllis.

Then, when her parents were killed in a car accident, and she and her brother were left with the farm, Phyllis announced that she wanted a divorce. She was taking Doug and moving out of the area.

Rex risked losing her forever.

That was when the devil knocked on his door.

One night, he backed into a parked sports car at the convenience store and cracked its fender.

It was Margo Boyd's car. At that time, she was a dentist's wife who dabbled in real estate. His car insurance had been canceled because of his accidents and DUIs long ago. He offered to have her car fixed.

The next day, she offered him a job. When he asked her what kind of job, she asked him to meet her at a vacant house. Rex hoped that if he got a good job, Phyllis would be convinced to stay. So he met with Margo.

Here, the plot turned sinister.

Margo needed to have something done and if he did not go along she would turn him in for a hit and run. She had a doctor lined up to say she was injured, even though she was inside the store buying cigarettes at the time of the accident. He could do this job for her, and she would hire him to renovate the houses she wanted to buy and make it possible for him to buy a house for his wife.

Her offer, simply put, was a job, a house, and his wife, or jail. Rex felt he had no choice. He had to kill Dan Boyd.

According to the book, Margo had found out through a real estate friend that her husband was going back to his first wife. If he left her, she would have nothing to invest in her business. If her husband was killed, then the savings accounts would be hers, plus she would have his life insurance.

She told Rex when and how she wanted the deed accomplished. It was to be done on the same night in which she was throwing a dinner party. That way she would have an alibi.

On the night of the murder, Rex drank heavily while he waited inside his truck for the receptionist to leave. There was no way he could kill a man sober. He bought a pair of work gloves so he would not leave fingerprints. He would get rid of them after the murder. He would use the dentist's scalpel so the murder would have no connection to him.

His plan was to go in, do it, mess up the place, take whatever pills he could find, and get out as fast as he could. Then, the police would think it was a drug fiend's crime.

Speed, he concluded, was essential.

Rex called Dan from the pay phone right after the receptionist left to cancel his appointment, which he had made to insure the dentist would be in his office that night. Then, working to stay steady on his feet, Rex went up to Dr. Boyd's office to kill him.

He described it all as happening in a drunken fog. He went into the office to which he had never been before, and the man he had never seen before appeared in the doorway of his examination room to greet the unexpected visitor.

Dan Boyd smiled at his killer when he asked if he could help him. Rex said nothing when he stepped up to his victim, grabbed him by the throat, and pushed him back into the examination room.

The dentist put up a fight, but Rex had at least fifty pounds on him and was about ten years younger. Once he pinned Dan down onto the dental chair, Rex went after him with the razor-sharp scalpel.

"Why are you doing this?" Dan cried out. "At least tell me why you are doing this?" He begged when he saw that there was no saving himself.

Rex owed the man an explanation. He had a right to know. It was the only thing he said during the murder and the words echoed in his drunkenness.

"Because your wife told me I had to."

"Margo!"

Rex nodded before plunging the scalpel into his throat and cutting it open with one slice. He heard a gurgle and his victim slumped down onto the chair.

Wasting no time, Rex grabbed any pills he could find, rushed from the office, and never looked back.

To show her thanks, Margo Boyd offered Phyllis and Doug seventy-five thousand dollars for their farm and offered to sell them a house on two acres in Birch Hollow for eighty thousand dollars. Phyllis, who never knew about her husband's deed, didn't question why Margo would offer seventy-five thousand for a seven-acre farm the tax assessor said was worth fifty thousand and sell them a house for eighty thousand, which the original owner sold the real estate agent for a hundred thousand. It was too good a deal to pass up. At least that was what the bank vice-president, who happened to be Margo's mother, said when she approved their application for a five-thousand dollar mortgage. Margo gave him a construction job renovating the houses she bought with her late husband's insurance money.

Thinking that her husband had grown up, Phyllis chose to stay.

Rex got what he'd always wanted.

Here, his book could have ended, but it didn't. He went on to tell the price he paid for killing Dan Boyd.

Rex did not have the heart of a killer.

Not a day went by that Dan Boyd's killer did not think about his victim. He tried to drown with alcohol the image of his victim gazing up at him from his dental chair, asking him why he was doing this to him, and the sound of him drowning in his own blood.

His guilt over the murder he committed to save his marriage ruined it. In the end, Rex Rollins lost his family and his soul—he lost it all.

The fire in the fireplace was out when Joshua finished reading the last fragmented sentence of Rex's masterpiece. He turned the page and rested his head back on the headrest of his wing-backed chair. He observed the time on the mantel clock. The next day was Thanksgiving, and the courthouse would be closed. He would have to wait another thirty hours to get the warrant for Margo Sweeney Boyd Connor's arrest.

CHAPTER TWENTY-TWO

Joshua Thornton waited until he had all his ducks lined up before sending Sheriff Curt Sawyer and his deputies out to Margo Connor's real estate office to arrest her for three counts of murder and conspiracy to commit murder in the deaths of Grace Henderson, Rex Rollins, and Bella Polk.

As he expected, Christine Watson had her client playing the mother in mourning to the hilt to the media in front of the courthouse after she was arraigned. She was dressed all in black with her bosom concealed behind a high collar. A wide-brimmed black hat adorned her head.

Joshua was cast in the role of the heartless politician.

She continued to play the victim when they met in the conference room in his office for what is called a discovery meeting, in which he told the defense attorney, as ordered by law, what he had against her client.

Christine scoffed at the two witnesses who were going to testify that Margo paid them, one with real estate and the other with jewelry, to eliminate the victims. It was their word against hers. "My client is a pillar of the community. She herself has supplied employment for hundreds of people. She is a generous contributor to local charities. Who is going to believe that my client is capable of, or would have any reason to arrange, the murder of three people?"

"Including her daughter's teenaged rival," Joshua said with distaste.

"If anyone arranged for that girl to kill that cheerleader it was Heather, and she is dead."

Margo didn't flinch while her lawyer tossed up her dead daughter as a murder suspect to save Margo's skin.

"We checked with your client's secretary," he told Christine. "Nicki Samuels did show up one afternoon with Heather. When your client came in that same morning, she was carrying a jewelry box. One day after Grace was killed; your client filed a report with the police and insurance company that her ruby ring was stolen."

"Heather stole the ring and gave it to Nicki for killing Grace."

"Why did your client show her the ring?"

"Because they asked to see it. She didn't know what Heather was thinking," Christine countered. "Face it, Josh, you can't prove that a word of what Nicki says is true. They were fighting over this boy. Margo hardly knew him. Why would she get involved?"

"Because her daughter wanted something, and Grace stood in her way. Your client taught her that if something gets in your way, you get rid of it, even if that something is your husband."

"Do you mean Rollins's novel? Let me remind you of the difference between fiction and non-fiction," Christine said with a smug smile. "By the time we are through in court, if you can even get that pack of vengeful lies admitted into evidence, the jury will surely know the difference."

"Oh, I intend to prove that every word of it is true. Phyllis Rollins is ready to testify that she accepted your client's extremely generous offer for her parents' farm."

Christine countered, "And years later my client made back that investment with a housing development she built on that land."

Joshua said, "Your client also sold Rex Rollins a house for twenty thousand less than your client paid for it. Rex claims in his book that it was payment for killing Margo's first husband." He gestured toward Margo. "That is the motive for your client hiring Herb Duncan to kill Rex. If the book is a lie, why would Margo hire Herb to kill Rollins in exchange for the same deal: buying his property for well over its worth and selling him a new house in her latest development for a fraction of its value?"

He slapped the forensics accountant's report onto the center of the conference table. "Our accounting people went back twenty years, before the time of Boyd's murder. The only times your client ever lost money on a deal was when her husband died and when Rollins was murdered."

Christine was unfazed. "Two mistakes, in all her years of doing business, are pretty damn good. Donald Trump has made more mistakes than that in his career."

"I knew you were going to say that."

Christine stood up. "Then I will be awaiting your dismissal of the charges."

"That's why I checked out every word of Rollins's book . . . and I found his mistake."

"His mistake? That proves the whole book is a lie." She slung her purse over her shoulder.

"Pros make sure their victim is dead before they leave the scene." Joshua turned to Margo. "Your husband was not dead when Rex left. That gave him the opportunity to tell us exactly who had him killed."

Christine stopped and looked at him.

Margo's expression of grief gave way to one of curiosity.

Her attorney lowered herself back into her chair. After regaining her composure at the announcement, Christine objected, "If Boyd left a dying message, why are you telling us this now? Why wasn't Margo arrested when her first husband was killed?"

"Because no one bothered checking to see if he left a message."

Joshua took the case file for Dan Boyd's murder out of his briefcase. He laid out the crime-scene pictures on the conference table. The top picture was of Dan Boyd's body lying behind the receptionist's desk. The corner of the keyboard on the desk was in plain sight. There were also photographs of Margo's wedding picture sitting on his desk. It was bloodstained. There were other pictures of blood splatters on the walls and a trail of blood on the floor and carpet.

"This murder happened in 1988. Forensics has come a long way since that time. The detective in charge of the case thought that your husband was trying to go for help when he died behind the receptionist's desk. Rex said in his book that he was so anxious to get out of there that he didn't think that your husband might be alive, let alone be able to say who did it."

"Did he write a note?" Christine wanted to know.

"No," Joshua answered. "Rex said in his book that he called to cancel his appointment, which was the last one of the day. Boyd was getting ready to leave. He had locked up his desk in which he kept prescription pads, thus, locking up his pens and pencils."

Joshua paused to see how what he was telling them was affecting them. Silent, Margo stared at him.

"Your husband," he said, "had a very short time to live and he was not going to waste it getting to the hospital to die without saying who was responsible for his murder."

"Rollins killed him," Christine argued. "He said so in his book. Why would he say my client did it if she was giving a dinner party at home?"

"Because Rex told him. He said so right in his book. It was the only conversation they had. Boyd asked him why he was killing him, and Rex said 'your wife told me I had to do it.' "

Christine stated what they knew was not true, but salable to a jury. "Rollins was lying when he told Boyd that."

Joshua shrugged and laughed. "Why would he? Rex was not a drug user. Drugs were stolen. He was never arrested for dealing. He was not known in the drug circles. He was a drinker. He had no beef with the victim, nor had he ever met Boyd."

He pointed to Christine's client while he told the lawyer, "Margo had a beef with the victim. Rex says in his book that she told him her motive for wanting her husband dead. He was going back to his wife and taking his money with him. Eve Boyd is available to testify that that was true. So—" He held up a finger to stop her before she could say it. "—when you try to make a case for Rex meaning Boyd's first wife, she had no motive. We have witnesses to testify that Boyd had told them that he was leaving Margo."

Putting on a face of determination, Christine gestured for him to continue. "Humor me! How did Boyd leave this dying message when he could not talk and had no pen or paper?"

Joshua gestured to the pictures of the crime scene. "Well, at first, I thought, like the original detective investigating his murder, that the blood splatters in the dental office were from the struggle. But then, using today's knowledge and technology, we had an expert look at these pictures and got a different story, which Rex's book confirmed."

Joshua said, "The blood-splatter expert took up the story from when Rex left the scene after slicing through your husband's throat in the examination room."

While Joshua told the story, he pointed to each picture in the series. "Boyd got up from the chair and went into his office. If you look at the pictures, you see that the blood is shooting out, but not splashed against the walls, as it would be if there was a struggle going on at the time. He was alone and moving. In the office, he went to his desk."

The prosecutor held up the picture of his desk. "Notice on the desk he has two pictures. One is of his son. There is no blood on that. The other is a wedding picture of his bride. Notice all the bloody fingerprints on that."

"He picked up the picture of his wife while he was dying." Christine shrugged. "How many soldiers on the battlefield clutch the picture of their wives to their chests as they die?"

"He knew you were going to say that!" Joshua smiled at Margo. "I realized what was going through your husband's mind when I found out that he was an Agatha Christie fan. I had seen the pictures and couldn't make any sense of it. Then Eve told me that he had all of Christie's books. So I asked myself, 'What would an Agatha Christie fan do in that circumstance?' Boyd thought, 'Get his bloody fingerprints all over her picture.' But then, you have to remember that this case would go before today's courts." He gestured to the defense attorney. "You'd say his putting his fingerprints on her picture was an act of love. So he had to make his message crystal clear."

More in an attempt to intimidate him than out of disgust, Christine rolled her eyes while Joshua, amused by her annoyance, reached down under the table and held up a bloodstained keyboard wrapped in a plastic bag.

Her face fell. "He sent an e-mail?"

"This was before the Internet," Joshua said.

"He typed it out on the computer?" she scoffed. "If he did that then they would have arrested my client before now."

"The computer wasn't on." He fingered the keyboard. "Luckily for us, every fingerprint he left on this keyboard, and each one was blood covered, was recorded at the time. However, it was not recorded the way he meant for it to read. Now—"

For the first time since the interview began, Margo spoke, "Dan didn't know anything about computers."

"But he could type." In response to their looks of confusion, Joshua continued, "He typed out the name of his killer on the keyboard."

Christine appeared to become curious. "How would it be read if the computer was not on?"

"Bloody fingerprints." He explained, "Each one of his fingerprints, as the forensics report says, was blood covered, which means he touched the keyboard after Rex sliced his throat open and before his death."

Joshua presented the report. "There was blood on the edges of the keyboard and some drops. What we are interested in are the keys upon which there are actual fingerprints and, since the report listed those keys alphabetically, then his message was not interpreted until I read this report knowing that he was a fan of whodunits."

He laid a yellow legal pad on the table and flipped the top page to reveal a row of letters printed across the top of the page. The two women sat at attention to see what he had discovered.

"According to the report there were two partial thumbprints on the space bar." He placed two upward pointing arrows in the middle of the page below the row of letters.

"There was also a right-hand fingerprint from the little finger and a left-hand fingerprint on the one key. Now the upper case one is the exclamation point. So, let's say that he ended his sentence with the exclamation point." He placed the punctuation at the end of the blank sentence.

"That leaves us with the letters he typed out." He indicated the row of letters at the top of the page: A, D, G, I, M, O, R, T.

Joshua indicated each letter while he spoke. "Now, we know that he typed out three words because of the two space bars. We can't say he was talking about his first wife because there is no E or V. He didn't say Rex did it because there is no E or X. However, we have every letter we need for Margo." He spelled out Margo's name before the upward facing arrow. "That leaves us with D, I, and T. There are two fingerprints right on top of each other on the D and the I keys. That means he used them twice. There are two D's in *did* and the I is used the second time and then we have the T."

Joshua held up the legal pad for the two women to read Dan Boyd's dying message: "Margo did it!"

Christine looked at her client who gave her a silent order in the form of a glare to fix the situation.

"You still have an uphill battle, Josh," the defense attorney told her adversary. "My client is a pillar of the community, and Herb Duncan has been in and out of trouble since he was born."

Joshua said, "He's willing to testify against your client. The book will be entered into evidence because that is what he committed the murders for."

"He committed two murders."

"On your client's orders."

"Conspiracy. No jail time." Christine snickered, "As for the cheerleader murder, drop that. My client will play the grieving mother to the hilt, and I'll make sure the jury knows that your witness killed her daughter. The jury, even if they believe her story, will refuse to convict. Don't waste your time."

Joshua gave her a nod to acknowledge that she was right. "Okay, I'll give you that."

"Immunity?"

He said, "On Grace's murder, if your client cooperates fully in prosecuting Nicki Samuels."

"And for her role in Rollins's and the old lady's murders?"

Joshua chuckled. "Not total immunity."

"Immunity from murder. My client is the only one who can tie this whole thing together. Face it. Between her public image as a successful businesswoman and the appearance that she is a grieving mother, and also the fact that she has never so much as laid a hand on any of these people, no jury will ever believe that she is capable of killing anyone." Christine threw him what she painted as a gift. "Conspiracy and a sentence recommendation for parole. No jail time."

"She'll have to plead guilty to the conspiracy charges and tell the court everything," he ordered.

"Only if you give her immunity from murder," Christine threw in.

Joshua sat back and gave Margo a glare. "Your client will not be charged for murder in Hancock County."

The women smiled triumphantly at each other.

At her sentencing hearing, Margo told the judge how, in her youth, when she was too young to know any better, she hired Rex Rollins to kill her husband. Then, years later, when he was going to use her mistake against her, she hired Herb Duncan to kill Rex and then his landlady.

Pleased with the deal that kept her client out of jail for the three murders she arranged, Christine Watson stood at her side at the defense table.

There were no smiles in the rows of seats behind the defense attorney. Eve Boyd sobbed while she watched her husband's second wife tell about having her husband killed. Greg Boyd held her hand while trying to control his outrage that after years of seeking justice, finally, his father's murder was solved, only for the killer to walk away.

Equally unhappy to see injustice done in the form of a deal, Dr. Tad MacMillan, *The Review* news editor Jan Martin, and Joshua's children watched the county prosecutor pay for what some members of the media called the deal of the century.

The Vindicator's editorial declared that Hancock County's prosecutor had blown it. How can any elected official with an ounce of moral fiber make such deals?

"It was a mistake," Margo finished her statement for the judge with the remorse of a woman who bought the wrong shade of nail polish.

With her statement completed, it was time for the judge to hand down his sentence. Instead, he had a few questions for the defendant. "Could you please tell the Court again why you conspired to have Rex Rollins killed so many years after he killed your husband for you?"

"Rex told me that he saw Gail Reynolds on television talking about a book she was writing about Tricia Wheeler's murder," Margo said. "He thought that if he wrote about killing Dan, he would get rich and famous."

Joshua showed the copy of the manuscript to Christine and Margo before taking it up to the judge's bench and handing it to him.

The judge flipped through a few of the pages. "Is this the book?"

"Yes, that's the book," Margo answered.

"Did Rex Rollins let you read it?"

"No, but he told me what was in it."

The judge then asked her, "Mrs. Connor, have you had a chance to read this manuscript since Rex Rollins's murder?"

"Yes," Margo responded.

"Is everything Mr. Rollins had written, about you extorting him into murdering your first husband so that you could inherit the capital to start your business and you paying him off in real estate, true?"

"Yes."

"And when Rollins told you that he was writing this book," the judge continued, "did you hire Herb Duncan for a similar deal? Payment in the form of real estate, a truck, and a job, to kill Rollins and steal this book, and the computer on which he wrote it, in order to conceal your role in your first husband's murder?"

"I already said I did," Margo answered with growing impatience.

Christine gestured for her client to control her rising frustration. She glanced over at Joshua. The defense lawyer's smug expression was replaced with one of worry. The prosecutor had made a deal for a sentence recommendation. It was within the judge's power to decline the recommendation.

"Did Herb Duncan do the job you hired him to do?" the judge was asking Margo.

"Yes."

"When this book landed in the hands of Bella Polk, did you then order him to kill her and retrieve the manuscript for you?"

"Yes."

While Christine and Margo held their breaths, the judge then stated that he needed to review the case more closely before handing down his final judgment.

Margo beamed for the cameras when she and her defense lawyer stepped out of the courtroom.

Led by her son, Eve Boyd collapsed with grief on the first bench she came to in the corridor.

When Joshua came out with Jan, Tad, and his children, he turned away to avoid seeing the anger in Greg's eyes. He led his family down the hall.

While Margo gave her statement to the media with her legal guard at her side, Tad said, "I think you better start looking for another job, Cuz. Even if the judge rejects your recommendation and throws her butt behind bars, a lot of people are going to remember this come time for re-election."

Jan asked Joshua, "How could you let her get away with this?"

"I cannot win a conviction for her killing Rex Rollins and Bella Polk without proving that she had her husband killed back in 1988." No one noticed the smile on the corner of Joshua's lips.

"This proves it," Sarah said. "He who has the biggest lawyer wins."

Down the corridor, they saw Eve drop her head while her son squeezed her shoulders.

Joshua swallowed the lump in his throat.

Jan told them, "I should get a statement from her for the paper, but I don't have the heart."

Margo was laughing at a comment from a journalist when a woman with ultra-short black hair and big hazel eyes made her way through the crowd. Most of the journalists dismissed her as a teenage kid in her jeans and leather bomber jacket until they noticed two sheriff's deputies dressed in Columbiana County uniforms at her side.

"Ms. Margo Connor?" the woman asked.

"Yes." Margo giggled when she responded.

Diana flashed her badge for everyone, including the news cameras, to see. "I'm Detective Diana Windsor of the Columbiana County sheriff's department in the State of Ohio. We have a warrant for your arrest for the murder of Dr. Dan Boyd." There was a stunned silence while she recited her rights to Margo. One of the deputies handcuffed the prisoner.

Christine whirled around and shouted down the corridor to Joshua. "We had a deal!"

The Hancock County prosecuting attorney replied, "And I kept my deal. She's not being charged in Hancock County for murder. Dan Boyd was murdered in Columbiana County in the state of Ohio. I have no authority over there. However, I don't think, in light of all the evidence, including your client's statement before the judge about her arranging her first husband's murder and the accuracy of Rex Rollins's book, that they will be so willing to make a deal . . . over there."

Christine gasped at the realization of her error.

Eve Boyd shrieked with joy and hugged her son. Greg mouthed a thank you to Joshua.

Joshua acknowledged the gratitude with a bow of his head.

Diana stepped down the hall to Joshua and said for the defense lawyer to hear, "I'll be waiting for a copy of the transcript from this hearing."

"I'll hand deliver it."

"I was hoping you'd say that," Diana replied. "Call me sometime." She winked at him.

Stunned by Joshua's cleverness, his children, Jan, and Tad watched Diana stroll down the hall after her handcuffed prisoner.

Joshua whispered into Tad's ear, "You're right about one thing. A lot of people will still remember this come re-election."

The media chased Margo down the stairs to capture shots of her being put in the backseat of the Columbiana County sheriff's cruiser.

Joshua's children forgave him enough to take him up on his offer to take them to dinner. "Care to join us?" he invited Tad and Jan. He tried to ignore his cousin's arm across Jan's shoulders.

Tad declined his invitation. "We're going to dinner at the Ponderosa."

"Again?" she responded.

"I guess it's becoming 'our place.'" Tad steered her towards the elevator.

"Did you hear that?" Jan told the group, "We have our own place."

Joshua fought to tear his eyes away from the two of them in the elevator while the doors closed between him and them. "But I'm the one who caught the killers. Why did you get the girl?" His last sight of them was Tad waving at him.

"Are they dating or what?" Sarah asked.

"Of course they are," Tracy said. "Can't you see that they are in love?"

"I vote we go to Tom's for dinner," Murphy yelled.

The rest of the children agreed.

EPILOGUE

Common sense told Joshua that Tad and Jan would not call him that night. While he lay in his bed trying to concentrate on yet another deep book, he wished they would.

What is wrong? Joshua cursed himself. He had always wished that Jan would find someone else, and then when she did, he was upset about it.

Time to move on.

He forced himself to recall the comparison Tad made in explaining the benefit of Jan and him seeking a relationship together. *"There comes a time when we all have to either move on, or stagnate until our lives turn into a parasitic swamp."* If you don't move on, Joshua analyzed the statement, then you stagnate.

That was what happened to Doug Barlow. For two decades, he treaded stagnant water in his insane fantasy of a suicide pact with Tricia Wheeler until his mind became so polluted that he killed Gail Reynolds in order to protect his love's memory.

Then there was Gail. For years, she followed Joshua under the guise of her journalism career. Her obsession made her vulnerable to gang rape and murder. She refused to consider another relationship. She died alone.

They both refused to face the reality of relationships that were over and wallowed in their own loneliness until they reached tragic ends.

Joshua heard his children shrieking in the family room two

floors below his bedroom. They had rented a DVD of the latest action film.

His children's mother was dead. It had been more than a year, and life moved on. Donny was taking a girl to the Christmas dance for his first date. J.J. stood a good chance for an academic scholarship. Murphy was a candidate for the Naval Academy. Tracy had a boyfriend. Joshua saw Sarah wearing green nail polish at breakfast that morning. She was growing out of her tomboyish ways. All of his children had made lives for themselves in their ancestral home.

Even Jan had moved on. She was glowing when she left the courthouse with her hand in Tad's. Joshua's relationship with her had shifted. They were friends and would remain friends.

Time to move on like a river flowing with fresh clean water, or turn into a parasitic swamp.

Joshua picked up the phone and dialed the number he had come to memorize.

"Commander O'Henry here."

"Commander Thornton here." He plunged on, "I'm sorry for what happened while you were here."

"What happened while I was there?"

"I wasn't ready, but now I am."

"Are you sure?"

He braced the phone against his ear and slipped the gold band from his finger. "I took off my wedding ring."

"Did you really?"

Joshua sensed a glimmer of hope when he picked up a note of enthusiasm in her tone. "Do you want pictures? Official statements from witnesses?"

"I'll see for myself. I got re-assigned to the Pentagon. I'll be there this coming spring."

"In time for the cherry blossoms?"

"I'm planning on it."

"I'm serving my reserve duty at the Pentagon this summer."

"Then I'll see you in Washington, my love."

ABOUT THE AUTHOR

Lauren Carr fell in love with mysteries when her mother read Perry Mason to her at bedtime. From reading murderous bedtime tales, she grew up to write mysteries for television and the stage. She wrote her first book after giving up her writing career to be a stay-at-home mom. The first installment in the Joshua Thornton mysteries, *A Small Case of Murder,* was nominated for the Independent Publisher Book Award 2005. *A Reunion to Die For* is her second full length book. Lauren lives with her husband and son on a mountaintop in West Virginia. She is working on her third and fourth installments in the Joshua Thornton series and a new mystery series set in Deep Creek Lake, Maryland. Lauren Carr is available for speaking engagements and personal appearances at libraries, bookstores, writing/book clubs, and other organizations. You can visit her Web site at http://laurencarr.com.

Sutherland.